COMING HOME

Jackson Falls Book 1

by Laurie Breton

c. 2012 by Laurie Breton

Best wishes! Hope you enjoy!
Laurie Breton

This one is for Terry Plunkett,
who believed in me long before
I dared to believe in myself,
and who is undoubtedly looking down on me
from somewhere in the Great Beyond
and saying, "I told you so."

Again, I have to thank my soul sister, Judy Lineberger, for suffering with me through the endless rewrites, and for cracking the whip over my head whenever she caught me slacking. If not for you, this book might never have been finished.

www.lauriebreton.com

lauriebreton@gmail.com

OTHER BOOKS BY LAURIE BRETON:

Sleeping With the Enemy
Black Widow
Final Exit
Mortal Sin
Lethal Lies
Criminal Intent
Point of Departure
Die Before I Wake

AND COMING SOON:

Days Like This

BOOK ONE

CHAPTER ONE

Summer, 1974
Jackson Falls, Maine

A cloud of dust billowed behind the pickup truck, and Casey yanked the wheel hard to the right to avoid a pothole. Just over five feet tall, she could barely see past the hood, but she drove with an expertise acquired at the age of twelve at the wheel of her father's ancient John Deere. On the radio, Martha Reeves and the Vandellas were entreating Jimmie Mack to come on back, and she drummed her fingers on the steering wheel in time to the music.

At the end of the driveway, she pulled onto the shoulder to get the mail. There was a strange car parked beside Dad's rusted hay baler, a blue Chevy with Massachusetts plates. Casey parked next to it and shut off the engine, cutting off the Vandellas mid-note. She was juggling grocery bags when a voice just beyond her shoulder drawled, "Need any help with those, brat?"

Casey spun around in surprise. "Travis Bradley!" she said. "What are you doing here?"

As a kid, she'd suffered from a massive case of hero worship, dogging the footsteps of this older brother who'd made his escape from the family farm five minutes after the ink dried on his high school diploma. Trav had traded Maine's rural back roads for the congested streets of Boston, and it had been a long six months since his last visit.

Her brother took both grocery bags from her. "I came to see you."

Snaking her way around paper bags, she embraced him with all the strength her hundred pounds could muster. "You look like you've been living on beer and pizza," she scolded. "Does Dad know you're here?"

"Nope. He's out somewhere on the tractor. We've been drinking coffee with Colleen."

She wondered who *we* meant. Had he brought home some woman? Was the family vagabond finally settling down? Wrinkling her nose, she said, "You've been drinking Colleen's coffee?" Her sixteen-year-old sister's kitchen misadventures were the stuff of family legend. "You do realize there's a fine line between bravery and lunacy?"

He grinned. "And I think I just crossed it. Listen, Casey, I really did come home to talk to you. That tape you sent was outstanding. Where'd you learn to write songs like that?"

Her heart began a funny little dance inside her chest. "You liked it? Really?"

"Are you kidding? It was so good I let Danny drag me up here to Outer Mongolia because he wanted to hear more."

She hoisted the remaining grocery bag and closed the tailgate. "Who's Danny?"

"Just the best damn singer on the East Coast. He's dying to meet you."

Inside her, pleasure warred with embarrassment. Nobody had ever taken her songwriting seriously. She wrote them simply because they were there inside her, and she couldn't prevent them from pouring out. She'd sent the demo tape to Travis in a fleeting moment of insanity, an act she'd regretted the instant the package was in the hands of the United States Postal Service.

It was the embarrassment that won. "I didn't know you'd let anybody else hear it," she said.

"You've got talent. Don't bury it under a rock." He followed her up the steps and across the porch. "Are you working?" he asked as he held the screen door open for her.

"Just keeping house for Dad. Jesse and I will be married in a few weeks anyway." Her mouth thinned. "He doesn't want me to work." The door slapped shut behind them and they set the grocery bags on the sideboard. "Why do you ask?"

"I'll let Danny explain."

Until now, she hadn't noticed the man who leaned casually against the living room door frame, but at first sight, she couldn't imagine how she could have missed him. He seemed to go on forever, effortlessly dwarfing her six-foot brother, and she gawked at his height before gradually becoming aware of the rest of him: the broad shoulders, the narrow hips encased in worn denim, the light brown hair, shot through with golden highlights, that fell in a clean line to his shoulders. But it was his eyes that caught and held her, those wild and turbulent eyes, eyes the color of a summer sky. "Well," he said. "Hello."

Her tongue glued to the roof of her mouth, Casey stared at him like an idiot. She wet her lips and found her voice. "Hi."

Trav's hands on her shoulders nudged her forward. "This is my sister Casey," he said. "Sis, this pain in the ass is Danny Fiore." He gave her shoulders a squeeze, then released them. "She's all yours, Dan. Good luck."

Danny Fiore crossed the room, hand extended, and she finally remembered her manners. She took the proffered hand, and his grip was warm and firm. "Six-four," he said.

She wasn't sure she'd heard him correctly. "I beg your pardon?"

"I'm six-foot-four. I could see you wondering." His smile warmed the blue eyes and carved a deep cleft in his cheek. She realized that he was still holding her hand, and she quickly withdrew it. "You're a talented songwriter," he said. "I'd like to talk to you about using some of your material."

It took a moment for the meaning of his words to sink in. When it did, she gripped the edge of the countertop to steady herself. "You want to perform my music?" she said, incredulous. "In public?"

"We've been playing the same stale Top 40 stuff for two years, and I've spent ages looking for something new. When I heard your tape, I knew I'd found it." He brushed the long hair back from his face with the fingers of one hand. "I'll be straight with you," he said. "I'm looking to make a name for myself. But I need original material. Judging by what I've heard so far, I think you can give me what I want."

Casey's palms began to sweat, and she had to hunt for her voice. "I don't know what to say."

He had a smile that could melt marble. "You could start," he said, "with yes."

***

Four weeks and counting.

Clad in the wedding gown her mother had worn twenty-five years ago, Casey stood in front of her sister-in-law Trish's full-length mirror, scrutinizing her reflection. The dress was pretty and feminine, with yards of frothy white lace and hundreds of tiny seed pearls hand-sewn to the bodice. While Trish fussed and tucked and smoothed, Casey stared in disbelief at the woman in the mirror. Could this exquisite, green-eyed creature in satin and lace be the same Casey who'd grown up in jeans and Trav's cast-off shirts? She'd never thought of herself as pretty, but the antique white satin of Mama's gown complemented her olive complexion and her dark hair, and the mandarin collar lent elegance to the neck she'd always considered too long. Spellbound, she stared into the mirror. "Is that really me?" she said.

"It's really you, sweetie. And your mother would be so proud."

In the mirror, a vertical line appeared between her eyes. "Would she?"

"Of course she would! You and my brother grew up together. She thought the world of Jesse. She'd be thrilled to know that you're marrying him."

Maybe, although Casey wasn't totally convinced. Some days, she thought that the only person, aside from the groom, who was thrilled about the pending nuptials was Trish herself. Casey had been twelve when her oldest brother, Bill, had married Trish Lindstrom, and Trish had become the best friend and big sister she'd always wanted. It had been Trish who helped her through those bleak months following Mama's death when, at fifteen, Casey had stepped into her mother's shoes, taking responsibility for raising her younger sister and running a ten-room farmhouse. When Casey and Jess had set their wedding date, a jubilant Trish had badgered her into unearthing Mama's wedding gown from the attic, then had spent weeks laboriously altering it to fit Casey's slender frame.

Casey frowned at her reflection. "Trish?" she said. "Can I ask you a question?"

On bended knee, fussing with the voluminous folds of the gown's hem, her sister-in-law looked up. Around the half-dozen straight pins she held precariously in her mouth, she said a muffled, "What?"

"With Bill…how did you know? That he was the one?"

Trish spat the pins out onto her palm. "Honey," she said, "I knew Bill was the one from the time we were in third grade." She rocked back on her heels and studied Casey through narrowed eyes. "Why? Don't tell me you're having second thoughts?"

"Nothing like that. It's just that…sometimes I wonder. Jesse's the only guy I've ever kissed. I've never even dated anyone else."

"Cold feet," Trish said briskly. "Nothing more than that. Don't let it bother you. It's normal. Everything will work out fine in the end."

"But what if—"

"What if what?"

"What if it doesn't? What if he's not…you know…the one?"

Trish looked at her long and hard. Then she got up, walked to the bedroom door, and closed it. "Okay," she said. "It's just you and me now. Where is this coming from?"

"I don't know." When Trish simply stood there, arms crossed, waiting, Casey waved her hand to indicate the entire household and said, "What you have here with Bill? It's what I want. A husband. Kids. The white picket fence, the station wagon, the dog. But what if I'm missing out on something? What if I realize later that I made some terrible mistake that it's too late to fix?"

"Has something happened?" Trish studied her closely. "Is there someone else?"

She felt herself flushing. "Be serious."

"I am being serious. Do you love my brother?"

"Of course I love him! What kind of question is that?"

"A very important one. Because if you don't love him, you need to think long and hard before you go through with this marriage."

"I am absolutely going through with this marriage. That's not even negotiable. I'm just feeling a little restless, that's all."

"Honey, it's normal to feel that way. Marriage is a big step."

"Did you feel this way? With Bill?"

"I was a basket case. Major bridal jitters. Right up until the moment I walked down that aisle and saw him standing at the altar, waiting for me. And then all my doubts just fell away, and I couldn't wait to start our life together."

Biting her lower lip, Casey turned back to her reflection. "Did you and Bill plan to have kids right away, or did it just happen that way?"

Trish's mirrored reflection, standing behind her, rolled her eyes. Making a minor adjustment to the collar of the wedding dress, she said, "Let's just say that Billy was a bit of a surprise. As a matter of fact, there's a very good chance that I got pregnant on my honeymoon. There's nothing more fun than starting out a marriage with morning sickness. Why? Are you worried that Jesse will want to start a family right off?"

"Actually, just the opposite. We've talked about it. I'm ready now, but he wants to wait until he finishes college."

"That makes sense."

"I know it's the sensible thing to do. The logical thing. But every time I hold one of your babies, scrubbed and rosy and sweet-smelling from the bath, logic and sensibility just fly right out the window."

"Sweetie, you're only eighteen. I realize you're not like most eighteen-year-olds. You had to grow up fast when your mom died. But there's plenty of time for babies. Why rush it? Believe me, once those kids start coming, you'll look back at the days you and Jesse had alone together and wish there'd been more of them."

"You're right. I know you're right."

"Listen to me, and listen good: If you have even the slightest doubt about this marriage, now's the time to say so. It gets a lot harder to disengage once you've taken those vows. I love you both. I don't want to see anybody get hurt."

"It's not like that. Really. This is all just idle speculation. I'm sure you're right, and I'm just experiencing cold feet. Please forget I even brought it up."

Her sister-in-law didn't look convinced. "If you need to talk—about anything—you know where to find me."

Trish went back to hemming the skirt, and Casey stared

into the eyes of the woman in the mirror. A stranger, ripe with promise and possibility. Inexplicably, her thoughts drifted to Danny Fiore, and she wondered if he had found her attractive. Her breasts were small, but her derriere was okay, and she had great legs. What had Danny thought when he looked at her? Had he seen her as a woman, or merely as a means to an end, someone who had written some songs he desperately wanted to get his hands on?

She was mildly appalled by her thoughts. This was dangerous ground she was treading. In four weeks, she intended to become Jesse's wife. Flesh of his flesh, joined to him, in the eyes of God and the world, until death. How could she even look at another man?

The question troubled her all the way home. In the glow of the dashboard lights, she studied Jesse's profile, the taut line of his jaw, the high cheekbones and the hollows beneath. Jesse Lindstrom was a strikingly handsome man, with his Swedish father's silver-blond hair and the high cheekbones and dark eyes he'd inherited from his mother, a full-blooded Passamaquoddy Indian. To his credit, Jesse accepted his looks matter-of-factly, without a trace of vanity. Oblivious to all the attention, he went his quiet way, with eyes for only one woman. She'd known since she was twelve years old that someday she would marry him. So why couldn't she summon more enthusiasm for their impending marriage?

He dimmed his headlights for an approaching car. "You're quiet tonight," he said.

"I just have a lot on my mind."

He didn't question her further. That wasn't his style. He turned into her driveway and cut the lights and the engine. The pickup rolled to a stop, and he leaned toward her, cupped her chin in his palm and drew her mouth to his. For a time, there was only the two of them, only the sound of their breathing and the distant call of a whippoorwill. "Four weeks," he said in a ragged whisper, his breath moist and hot upon her ear. "I might not make it."

In the distance, a cricket chirped. Casey pressed her face against Jesse's shirt and felt the erratic racing of his heart and wondered why she felt nothing when he took her in his arms. It was not a desire to remain pure until her wedding night that had kept her a virgin. Nor was it fear of pregnancy, for Dr. Grimes had put her on the pill weeks ago. It was her own indifference. When Jesse touched her, she felt none of the fireworks she'd heard about.

But she couldn't tell him that. She wouldn't hurt him that way. A marriage was based on more than sex. She and Jesse would build a life together, they would have a home and children. Those were the things that mattered. Sexual attraction faded with youth. What she and Jesse had was much more lasting. She would do her best to nurture it and keep it thriving throughout the years, so that Jesse would never regret marrying her.

She tried not to think about the possibility that she might regret marrying him.

CHAPTER TWO

The hunger began early in him.

Danny Fiore couldn't remember a time when he hadn't thrummed inside with music. His earliest memories were of his mother, barely more than a child herself, singing him to sleep in a sweet, clear soprano. By the time he was two years old, he was singing with her. By the time he was four, at an age when other kids could hardly carry a tune, he'd already begun harmonizing with the pop songs he heard on the radio. His ear was flawless, his pitch true, his understanding of music elemental, its concepts vividly clear to him long before he ever learned the words for them. At the age of six, he began picking out simple tunes by ear on his grandmother's old Baldwin, and she hired a piano teacher for him.

Loretta Lucchesi's tastes ran to classical German composers, heavily interspersed with Italian opera. He reluctantly learned to play Bach, Beethoven, Vivaldi. But he hungered for something else, something to make his blood run and his toes tap. He found it when the Beatles crossed the Atlantic and changed the face of popular music forever. The piano ceased to be an instrument of torture the instant he realized he didn't have to play the classics. Danny began working his way feverishly through rock and jazz, rhythm & blues, old standards. Because the piano wasn't portable, he bought a secondhand Fender guitar and taught himself to play that. But it was his voice, had always been his voice, that was Danny Fiore's true instrument.

Thirteen months in Vietnam cured him of his youthful naiveté. When he came back, Danny had changed. His world had changed. He moved out of his grandmother's apartment over the butcher shop on Salem Street and into a room in the heart of Boston's Combat Zone, where junkies slept in doorways, triple-X-rated movies played day and night, and pimps and hookers plied their trade. He claimed an empty street corner near Filene's, sat down on a milk crate with his Fender, and began singing for the tourists.

Danny never looked back. The music hummed and throbbed inside him, and he came alive in front of an audience. His music was his mistress, a siren far more seductive than any mortal woman. And unlike mortal women, this lady wouldn't disappoint him. She was going to take him straight to the top. With a little help from Casey Bradley. Danny was a singer, not a songwriter, but he possessed an artist's appreciation for a good song, and Casey wrote songs that sent an icy blue finger down the center of Danny Fiore's cynical spine.

He plumped the pillow behind his head, took a drag on his cigarette, and watched the smoke rise toward the water-stained ceiling of the attic bedroom where his buddy Travis had spent his adolescence. Drawing the ashtray across the night stand, he said, "Tell me about Casey."

Sprawled across the other bunk, Travis looked up from a tattered *Star Trek* paperback. "What about her?"

"For starters," he said, "how come you forgot to tell me she's a knockout?"

Travis blinked. "A knockout? My sister?"

He drew deeply on the cigarette. Exhaled. "Christ, Trav, are you blind or just retarded?"

Travis returned to his book. "She's not your type. My sister's too level-headed to look twice at a bozo like you."

Dryly, he said, "I didn't say I wanted to marry the girl."

"Don't go getting any ideas, Fiore. Casey is off limits."

Obviously. The rock she wore on the third finger of her left hand clearly advertised her status. But it didn't diminish his curiosity. He knew instinctively that here was a woman who would never play games, a woman who would meet a man halfway, a woman who would demand as much as she gave. With Casey, a man would never wonder where he stood.

She scared the hell out of him.

And what the devil was she thinking of, marrying that Lindstrom character? Danny thought of her eyes, the color of jade: cool, but with a hint of fire buried somewhere in those smoky depths. He'd be willing to bet that Lindstrom hadn't tasted any of that fire.

He wondered why the thought gave him so much satisfaction.

When he crushed out his cigarette in the ashtray and sat up, Travis eyed him warily. "Where are you going?" he asked.

Danny pulled on his shoes and began lacing them up. "To buy your sister a cup of coffee," he said.

***

The Jackson Diner was deserted at this time of night, except for a lone trucker who sat at the end of the bar, sipping coffee and reading the newspaper. Elsie Cameron was washing out the pie case with a wet rag, and from the kitchen came the scratchy buzz of Todd Whitley's radio, tuned, as always, to a country station out of Portland. Their coffee sat forgotten before them as Danny Fiore traced a pattern on the chipped Formica with his spoon. "I tried to fit in at B.U.," he said, "but I wasn't like the other kids. Most of them came from money. I came from Salem Street. Little Italy. I was there on an academic scholarship, and I had a chip on my shoulder the size of the Tobin Bridge." His smile was rueful. "I didn't even dress like the rest of them. The other guys had ripped jeans, scraggly beards, hair down to their asses. I was the only one wearing chinos and a DA."

"So," Casey said softly, "what happened?"

"I lasted one semester. I had a straight 4.0 average, and I dropped out of school." Playing with a packet of sugar, he said, "It wasn't more than a couple of months before Uncle Sam caught up with me." His voice grew tight. "I was one of the lucky ones chosen to fight for truth, justice, and the American way." He shoved the sugar packet aside.

"Vietnam?"

"I wasn't exactly what you'd call politically astute. Up to that point, Vietnam wasn't much more to me than a name on a map. I never did figure out what we were doing there. Fighting Communism, they told us. I spent thirteen months in that hellhole." He stared into the depths of his coffee cup. "When you come back from there," he said, "everything's out of sync. The whole world has moved forward, but you've stayed in one place." He looked at her with those blue eyes. "You know what I mean?"

Frowning, she nodded. He ran the fingers of both hands through his long hair. "And the worst thing is, it's still with you. It's with you when you close your eyes at night and when you open them in the morning and all the time in between." He stopped abruptly and looked at her in surprise. "I'm sorry," he said. "You don't want to hear all this."

"Yes," she said. "Yes, I do."

"I didn't mean to spill my guts. I never do this. You have a strange effect on me." He studied her quizzically and cleared his throat. "So," he said, "how long have you been writing music?"

His abrupt change of subject startled her. "Oh," she said, "since about forever. I come by it naturally. Mama was a concert pianist. A very good one. By the time she was sixteen, she'd already toured Europe. When she was eighteen, she came down with pneumonia, and her parents sent her to recuperate at her Aunt Elizabeth's house. She met Dad when he came over one day to complain that Aunt Elizabeth's sheep dog had gotten loose again and was chasing his heifers around the pasture. Trying to herd them."

Danny grinned, and she responded in kind. "Six weeks later," she said, "they were married."

"And she gave it all up for love?"

Casey smiled ruefully. "When I was twelve, I thought it was the most romantic story I'd ever heard."

"And now?"

"Now," she said, resting both elbows on the table, "I wonder how she could have given up that much of herself. Even for somebody she loved."

"I'm dead serious about this," he said, leaning forward intently over the table. "I'm going all the way to the top. I'm going to be a star, and I don't want just anybody's songs, I want yours. I don't intend to give up until you say yes."

I'm going to be a star. He spoke the words as casually as though he'd said he was going to be a doctor, or a plumber. If anybody else had uttered them, she would have laughed. But there was an intensity about Danny Fiore that refused to be denied. A shiver skittered down her spine. "I'm flattered," she said. "Really, I am, but—"

"You're tremendously talented. Are you going to just throw it away? Give it all up for love, like your mother did?"

The man was a steamroller. She should have been angry, but she wasn't, maybe because in some hidden part of her, she knew he was right. She studied those blue eyes, so straightforward and determined. "I've written more," she said.

The gleam in his eyes intensified. "Can I see them?"

"You could, if there was anything to see. But there's nothing on paper that would mean anything to you." She shrugged in apology. "I don't read music."

He raised both eyebrows. "Your mother was a concert pianist, and you never learned to read music?"

"I had a natural ear and perfect pitch," she said. "I took the easy way out."

He tapped his fingertips against the tabletop as he considered the situation. "It doesn't have to be a problem," he said. "Rob's brilliant at transcription."

"Who's Rob?"

"Rob MacKenzie. He's a bloody genius, that's who he is. He composes, he arranges, and he plays guitar like he was born with it in his hands. Here's what I'm thinking. We can sit you down at a piano with MacKenzie and a stack of manuscript paper. You play, he transcribes it onto paper. The end result would be the same."

"I'm flattered," she said. "Really. But I'm getting married in four weeks."

"Come to Boston with us. Just for a few days. I'll introduce you to Rob, see if the two of you can work together." He smiled, and something happened deep inside her, something sudden and unexpected and startlingly beautiful. Her heart began a slow thudding as she thought about Jesse. About missed chances. About her wedding, just four weeks away.

And about her father, who would heartily disapprove of her taking off for parts unknown with this blue-eyed stranger. In all her eighteen years, she'd never done anything Dad would disapprove of.

But Danny Fiore believed in her, believed in her talent, when nobody else had ever given it a second thought. She was eighteen years old. Old enough to decide for herself what she wanted to do with her life, instead of what Dad or Jesse wanted her to do. And what she wanted was to follow this ride as far as it would take her.

"Mr. Fiore," she said, "you've got yourself a deal."

CHAPTER THREE

Ziggy's was a dark, dank cellar hole near Boston's Kenmore Square, marked by a chartreuse neon sign and a heavy wooden door that belched waves of music onto the sidewalk every time it opened. Danny Fiore whisked her past the bouncer and into the turmoil within. She'd never seen so many people crammed into so little space. Squeezing between bodies, she put her trust in Danny's navigational skills and followed those broad shoulders toward an unseen destination.

"The place is packed," he said over the steady boom-boom of a Doobie Brothers recording. "Do you mind standing?"

Casey looked out over a sea of occupied tables. "I guess I don't have a choice," she said. "Is it always this crowded?"

"It is," he said, raising one corner of his mouth in a wry grin, "when we play here."

He left her leaning against a splintered wooden support beam carved with graffiti. *Lizzie loves Jeff. TE & PF 4-ever. Impeach Nixon.* She flagged down a waitress and ordered a Coke, then studied the people around her. They were for the most part college kids, dressed in jeans and an abundance of hair, and they congregated in noisy groups whose boundaries were continually shifting.

The Doobies wailed their finale. Into the ensuing silence rushed the clink of glasses and the steady buzz of conversation. The lights went out abruptly, plunging the room into a blackness so palpable she could taste it. Conversation skidded to a halt. A smattering of applause rippled through the expectant hush, and Casey's fingers tightened on her glass.

Sound and light erupted simultaneously, and Danny Fiore stood in a pool of amber, all long silky hair and skintight jeans, one booted foot tapping accompaniment to the familiar driving rhythm of a rock anthem immortalized by the McCoys. The gold chain around his neck sparked and caught fire, and he tossed back all that tawny hair and jumped in headfirst.

And the bottom dropped out of the world.

As he wove the story of a girl named Sloopy, that dark,

velvet voice caressed the lyrics, slow and deliberate and naughty, infusing them with meanings never before intended. She should have been prepared for the power of that vibrant tenor. But she wasn't. She should have expected to be swept up and torn into pieces. But she hadn't. She should have run from that blatant, smoldering sexuality. But she didn't. Casey's heart ricocheted off her ribs like a ping pong ball out of control as those blue eyes captured and held hers for a single instant. And even though she knew it was an illusion, part of the act, for that instant she truly believed he was singing just to her.

With a deliberate toss of his head he sent all that silky hair flying to surround him in a golden halo before it fell, in slow motion, to his shoulders. Casey tried to swallow, but all the moisture was gone from her mouth, and her hands were trembling so hard she couldn't raise her drink to her lips. With the last shreds of her rapidly disintegrating sanity, she realized that she was seeing the first budding shoots of greatness, the beginning of a legend, a phenomenon.

His words came back then to haunt her: *I'm going to be a star.*

Oh, yes.

She joined enthusiastically in the thunderous applause. Danny paused to catch his breath. "Thanks," he said, trying to be heard above the commotion. "Thank you." He gave up then, scooped the long hair back from his face with one hand and waited for the noise to subside. "I really want to thank you all for coming here tonight," he said. "We haven't played here for a while, and we thought it would be fun to let you get into the act. So give us your requests, and if the boys here can play 'em, I'll try to sing 'em."

A blonde near the stage yelled, "Your phone number!"

"My *what*?" He flashed that billion-dollar smile. "Come on, lady, give me a break."

There were titters from the audience, then a voice from the back of the room shouted, "Sing something dirty!" There was a burst of laughter from the area surrounding the woman who had spoken, and Danny shaded his eyes with his hand, trying to see past the lights and the crowd.

"Sing something dirty?" he said in mock disbelief. More

titters from the audience. "I must be in the wrong town," he said. "Somebody told me this was Boston!"

He turned to the lanky blond lead guitarist. "Hey, Rob, do we know any dirty songs that won't bring the cops in?"

Rob grinned and mumbled something, and Danny turned back to the audience. "How about *Brown Sugar*?" There was immediate cheering and foot-stomping. "And if that's not dirty enough for you, honey," he said, "you haven't listened to the words!"

Forty-five minutes later, amid boisterous applause, he left the stage and made his way through the crowd to where she'd finally snagged a seat. He grabbed an empty chair from the next table, pulled it up beside hers, and straddled it, arms dangling over the back. His hair was damp from the intense heat of the spotlight he'd been under, and he swept it back from his face with one hand. Rattling the ice cubes in his glass, he watched them swirl around. "So," he said, still examining the contents of his glass, "what do you think?"

"You don't need me to tell you how good you are."

"I know what I think." His level blue gaze met hers, and Casey felt a shock run clear through her. "I want to know what you think."

She looked into those incredible blue eyes and wondered just what she was getting herself into. "I think," she said, choosing her words carefully, "that you're too good to waste your time singing in places like this."

He raised his glass and took a sip. "It's called paying your dues. It's a necessary evil, like death and taxes."

"And how long do you have to pay before you start getting something in return?"

He crunched an ice cube between perfect white teeth. "You work your ass off and hope and pray for a lucky break."

She frowned. "I believe in making your own breaks."

"That's a lovely theory, he said, "but it doesn't work well in practice."

"Do you have a manager?"

He snorted. "So I can pay him ten percent of nothing?"

"Maybe all you need is someone who can focus you in the right direction."

"My focus isn't flawed. It's more a matter of being in the right place at the right time."

"Where do you get all your confidence?" she asked him.

His grin was devastating. "It's all a front," he said. "Inside, I'm a quivering mass of Jell-O."

"You terrify me," she said. "You make me hungry for things I'm not sure I have a right to want."

Bluntly, he said, "Nobody has the right to tell you what to want."

Why did she have the feeling they were no longer talking about his singing, her songwriting? He stood up, and she realized that the band was already back on stage, tuning their instruments and sending pointed looks in his direction. He held out his hand. "Deal?"

For a moment, she lost herself in those blue eyes. Then she gripped his hand firmly. "Deal." Already, she knew it wasn't enough. But she had no right to ask for more. She would have to settle for what she could get.

She felt as though she'd spent her entire life settling for second best.

***

With one hand buried in the tangle of golden curls and a lit cigarette dangling from the corner of his mouth, Rob MacKenzie studied the penciled notations on the paper in front of him with total absorption. He was silent for so long that at last, unable to bear the suspense any longer, Casey spoke. "Well? What do you think?"

He looked surprised, as though he'd forgotten she was in the room. And then he flashed a grin. "You've got a winner here, kiddo," he said.

Her pulse quickened. "You really think so?"

He flicked an ash from his cigarette. "I know so."

She liked Rob MacKenzie, liked the strong Irish jaw and the sunshine smile and the devil-may-care attitude. Tall and gaunt and bony, he reminded her of a young golden retriever that hadn't yet grown into its feet, and she had felt an instantaneous rapport with him.

Danny clattered down the cellar stairs. "Careful," he said, handing her a mug of coffee. "It's hot." He passed one to Rob. "This should jack you right back up." He perched on the arm of Casey's chair. "What do you say, Wiz?"

Rob stretched out lanky legs and took a sip of coffee. "If all her stuff is this good, Dan," he said, "we've hit the motherlode."

"Let's try one more before we crash."

Casey tried to stifle a yawn, but wasn't quite successful. Rob dropped his cigarette into a nearby ashtray. "Give the girl a break, Fiore. It's five-thirty in the morning."

Danny looked surprised. "No wonder I'm starved," he said. "I've been running on adrenaline for the past twelve hours." He leaned toward Casey. "I have this friend," he said in a conspiratorial tone, "who just happens to make the best pizza in Boston. And there's even better news. His place is open all night."

Her smile lingered and warmed. "Don't say pizza, Mr. Fiore, unless you mean it."

"Wiz? Want to come with us?"

Rob shook his head. "This boy's headed for bed. You would be, too, if you had any brains."

"I'm too high. I'll come down eventually."

"After you've driven the rest of us nuts." But there was affection in Rob's voice. "Stand up to him," he told Casey. "If you don't, he'll walk all over you."

***

He was right about the pizza.

Casey crumpled her napkin and let out a sigh of contentment. "How did you ever find this place?" she said.

"I'm a third-generation North End wop," Danny said. "This is my home turf."

"You don't look Italian," she said, studying his face. "Where on earth did you get those blue eyes?"

"From my old man." Danny toyed absently with a tomato-stained sheet of wax paper. "He hung around just long enough to get my mother knocked up, and then he split."

"I'm sorry," she said, taken aback.

He shrugged. "It's hard to miss something you never had in the first place."

"No stepfathers?"

"My mother died when I was five. My grandmother raised me."

She tried to picture him as a child and could not. He seemed so much larger than life. Watching him fold and refold the sheet of wax paper, she was struck by the lean elegance of his hands. "I've never had pizza for breakfast before," she said.

"You've led a sheltered existence."

"I did," she said, "until you came into my life."

His grin was infectious, and she returned it. "Tell me," she said. "Do you get teased often about those dimples?"

He looked embarrassed. "I've cursed my parents more than once," he said, "for giving me this damn baby face."

"Why? It's a very nice face."

"Yeah?" he said gruffly. "You think so?"

"Yeah," she said softly. "I think so."

They studied each other intently, and then he cleared his throat and glanced at his watch. "How about some dessert?"

"I can hardly wait to find out where we're going for dessert after having pizza for breakfast."

It was called Haymarket, and even so early in the morning, people were crammed into the narrow walkways between carts piled high with every imaginable variety of produce. She was walled in by shoppers jabbering in a dozen different languages, while the street vendors, in their flat Boston accents, tried to outdo each other, vying for her attention, beseeching her to note the outstanding qualities of their respective merchandise.

"Lady, look at this tomato. You ain't gonna see nothing like this in no supermarket. I sell 'em ten for a buck. For you, I throw in a couple extra."

She looked helplessly at Danny. "What do I do?"

"You're supposed to dicker. Will you look at these kiwi! Have you ever had kiwi fruit?"

She shrugged an apology to the vendor and scurried to catch up with Danny. Looking at the fuzzy brown fruit he held in his hand, she wasn't sure she wanted to try it. It looked like a cross between a potato and a hamster. "What does it taste like?"

"I'll surprise you. We'll buy a couple to take with us."

They sat on a wooden bench and he watched her face as she bit tentatively into the fruit. She looked at him in astonished delight. "It tastes like bananas," she said, "sort of." She closed her eyes to better concentrate on the delicate flavor. "Or maybe like blueberries."

"I guess your old man doesn't grow these on his farm."

"It's a dairy farm, city boy. The only things we grow are calves and corn."

"And on hot summer nights, you sit around and listen to the corn growing."

"Oh, we're somewhat civilized. I hear rumors that they'll be putting in electricity any year now." She drew her knees up to her chest and studied him. A dimple lingered at the corner of his mouth as he boldly returned her perusal. She was acutely conscious of the most minute things: the warmth of the morning sun on her shoulders, the odor of overripe fruit, the way the fine hairs grew on the back of his hand. She was drunk, intoxicated by the nearness of this charismatic man who had made her feel more in two days than she'd felt in eighteen years of living. In spite of her valiant efforts to remain neutral, her traitorous body had betrayed her. Parts that should have been wet had gone dry, and parts that were normally dry were inexcusably damp. And his voice, that black velvet voice, made her stomach quiver and set the soft hairs on the back of her neck to standing up straight.

It was exquisite.

It was terrifying.

And disgraceful, and wholly inappropriate for a woman promised to another man. She had obligations, responsibilities, promises to keep. She had expectations to live up to, people she couldn't let down. A wedding in four weeks that she couldn't miss.

He took her hand in his. With the pad of his thumb, he traced a line along her palm, his touch bringing to life every nerve ending in her body. "This," he said near her ear, "is your life line. You're going to live a long and healthy life. And this—" He paused, continuing the stroking that had her heart hammering double-time, "is your love line."

She had difficulty getting the words out. "And what does it say?"

"You're going to meet a tall, handsome stranger." He pressed his lips to her palm. "You're trembling," he said.

She wanted to deny it, but she couldn't. "I'm afraid this was a very bad idea," she said.

"Having pizza for breakfast?"

She withdrew her hand from his. "Coming to Boston," she said. "I tried to tell myself it was strictly business, but it's turning into something else, and I can't let that happen. I come from conservative people, Danny. I've had that conservatism spoon-fed to me since birth. I don't believe in casual sex."

His smile faded. "Are you trying to tell me," he demanded, "that you believe anything between us could ever be casual?"

She took a deep breath and looked at him directly. "No," she said.

"You don't have to marry him."

For a fleeting instant, something resembling hope sprang to life in her. "Maybe," she said, "you'd like to make me a better offer."

Behind those blue eyes, something stilled. He stood up, shoved his hands in his pockets, and was suddenly very busy examining the brickwork in the building behind them. "I can't," he said.

A muscle clenched in her jaw as her faint hope sputtered and extinguished itself. She got up from the bench, swung her purse strap over her shoulder, and strode away, not caring where she ended up as long as it was as far as possible from Danny Fiore.

He caught up with her before she'd gone a dozen steps. "Damn it, Casey," he said, "it has nothing to do with you!"

When she refused to stop, he caught her by the elbow. "Listen to me," he pleaded. "Just listen!"

"I'm tired, Danny. I'm going to bed." Yanking free of him, she stepped off the curb and held up an arm, the way she'd seen it done on television. A yellow taxi pulled up, and deliberately ignoring him, she opened the door.

"You don't understand!" he shouted. "It's not you, it's me!"

"Don't worry," she told him. "You'll get your damn songs." And she climbed into the taxi and slammed the door.

As the car pulled away from the curb, she knotted her hands in her lap. She would not look back. The man was an arrogant, conceited fool. She wouldn't look back at him if he were the last man on earth.

When she did, he was still standing there with his mouth hanging open.

CHAPTER FOUR

She slept restlessly, her dreams haunted by a broad-shouldered, long-limbed god with probing blue eyes that looked directly into her soul. She awoke to late afternoon sunlight filtering through the window. She had lied quite creatively to herself about why she'd come to Boston. But the truth was that she had come because she wanted Danny Fiore. She wanted to kiss the long, slender fingers with their blunt tips, wanted to taste the pulse that beat in his wrist. Wanted to explore with her fingertips all that silky hair, wanted to rest her head against his chest and feel the rhythm of his heart.

But a personal relationship between them was out of the question. He had his career, and she had Jesse. Their futures were planned, their fates sealed. There was no place in her life or his for an extracurricular love affair. In twenty-six days she would marry Jess. She would go on with her life as planned, and Danny would go on with his, and if they were very fortunate, their paths wouldn't cross again.

It was the bleakest proposition she'd ever faced.

If she had any common sense she'd get on the next bus home and forget she'd ever met Danny Fiore. She would grab Jesse and rush him to the altar so quickly his head would spin. And then she'd throw away Dr. Grimes' damned pills and see to it that Jesse planted a baby in her right away.

Except that, somewhere along the way, her traitorous common sense had deserted her, leaving her ready to toss away her entire future for a man who would almost certainly break her heart.

She flung aside the bedcovers and snatched up her robe, tied the belt and yanked free her cascade of dark hair. If Danny wanted songs, then by God, she'd give him songs. But she would draw the line at that. She wasn't about to let any man destroy her life.

She found Travis in the kitchen, eating Froot Loops from a chipped bowl. Casey ruffled his hair as she walked by, and he dropped his spoon into the bowl with a clatter. "Where the hell were you all night?" he said.

"At Rob's house. Got any coffee?" She touched the side of the percolator to see if it was hot, then began opening cupboard doors in search of a cup.

"Left side, over the sink." He watched her pour the coffee. "You sat up all night with those bozos?"

She took a sip of coffee, then smiled ruefully at him over the rim of the cup. "Danny's very persuasive."

"Yeah. Like a loaded .357."

"Don't shatter my illusions, Trav. I happen to like him."

"That's fine, as long as you don't like him too much."

She busied herself at the refrigerator. "Jesse and I are getting married in a month, remember?" She checked the date on a container of yogurt. "I'm immune to the charms of other men."

"Danny's not like other guys," he said. "The Virgin Mary would have a hard time resisting him."

She searched the jumbled mess in the drawer for a clean spoon. "Speaking purely hypothetically," she said, "is that necessarily a bad thing?"

"Hypothetically or otherwise, you're my sister, and you're damn right it's bad."

She raised an eyebrow. "Do I detect a trace of Neanderthal peeking out from beneath that mild-mannered exterior?"

"Maybe I should be a little more explicit. Danny's idea of a long-term relationship is about two hours."

She ate a spoonful of yogurt. "What makes you so sure I'm not looking for a last mad fling before I get married?"

"I know you too well. You're not the type."

For some reason, his comment irritated her. "You know what, Trav? One of these days, I might just surprise you."

Her brother ran a hand through his dark hair and sighed. "Look, you're my sister. I care about you."

"In case you hadn't noticed, I'm a big girl now. I don't need a guardian." And she patted his arm on the way to the telephone.

Rob MacKenzie's younger sister answered the phone, then dropped it with a clunk and yelled, "Robbie, it's for you! It's a *girl.*"

"Hey, kiddo," he greeted her, and yawned. "What's up?"

"We seemed to be on a roll last night. I thought we might work together again tonight. That is, if you're not busy."

"Yeah, sure. Swing by around seven."

Without the overwhelming distraction of Danny's presence, she and Rob worked together like a piece of well-oiled machinery. She absorbed herself in the work as he magically transformed the music she played into written notation. His praise was direct and unembellished, his criticism specific and constructive, his suggestions for improvement unfailingly on the mark.

They broke for coffee around eleven. "I have a confession to make," she told him. "The real reason I came here tonight was to avoid Danny."

Rob took a sip of coffee. "I know."

"But I owe you an apology. I'm afraid I sold you short. You're very talented. I'm glad I got the chance to work with you."

He studied the toes of his sneakers. "Are you looking for advice?"

Cupping her coffee mug in both hands, she got up and crossed the room to look at the photographs that adorned the wall above the fireplace. "Your brothers and sisters?" she asked.

"All nine of us."

She studied the pictures. "I'm getting married in a month," she said.

"Forgive me for saying this, but I've seen happier brides."

"I thought it was what I wanted."

"Until you met Danny."

"Until I met Danny." She squared her shoulders and turned. "So tell me, Doctor MacKenzie, what's your prescription?"

He set down his coffee cup, leaned forward, and tugged at his shoelace. "Tell the world to go to hell," he said, "and follow your heart."

***

Danny circled the block for the fifth time, slowing as he

passed the lighted window. It was nearly midnight. How the hell would he explain his presence? *I just happened to be in the neighborhood and thought I'd drop in.* Rob would never buy it.

He tightened his fingers on the steering wheel. How could it be possible that in just three days, his life had fallen apart? He had his music, he had his friends, and he had his freedom, and if he wanted to go out and get laid, he did. When he came home, he didn't have to answer to anybody. And that was the way he liked it. He didn't need some skinny little starry-eyed eighteen-year-old kid ruining it for him.

A girl like that would want things he couldn't give her. A home, kids, some kind of stability. He was married to his career. If that made him a selfish bastard, he didn't give a damn. His music came first.

Besides, the girl wasn't even free. She was already spoken for, her wedding just a month away. The thought left a sick taste in his mouth. She was going to throw herself away on that bloodless Jesse Lindstrom, and there wasn't a thing he could do about it.

He left the Chevy at the curb and strode purposefully up the front walk and rang the bell. The drone of the television floated through the open window, and a moth thumped at the light fixture over his head. Rob's father came to the door and peered out at him through the screen. "Danny," he said, holding the door open. "Come on in. The kids are downstairs."

The murmur of voices floated up the cellar stairwell. Casey was sitting beside Rob on the couch with the faded chintz cover, one leg folded beneath her, all that lustrous black hair falling loose to her waist. When she saw him, her eyes widened. "Danny," she said. "What are you doing here?"

He wondered if she could hear the hammering of his heart. "I came for you," he said.

He'd come armed with a half-dozen arguments in case she turned him down, but she just nodded mutely and stood, running a hand through her hair, her slender fingers gleaming white against its darkness. "Good night, Rob," she said, "and thanks."

She sat primly in the car, hands folded in her lap, hugging the passenger door as though he were about to take a bite out of her. Tightening his grip on the wheel, he said, "I'd like to apologize."

"For what?" she said.

"For being an asshole."

She could have politely demurred. Most women would have. But Casey Bradley was not most women. "Apology accepted," she said.

"I'm not very experienced at this. I don't know what I'm supposed to say."

"I don't believe there are any rules of etiquette," she said, "that apply to this situation."

"Lindstrom's insane." He stopped for a red light and stretched his cramped fingers. "If you belonged to me, I'd never let you out of my sight. You can't imagine how I felt when I saw you sitting there with Rob tonight."

"It's not Rob I'm interested in."

Her words, so simple and direct, hit him like a blow to the gut. "Can't we start all over again?" he said. "Just for tonight? Forget Jesse. Forget the damn songs. Forget everything but the two of us."

"How on earth are we supposed to do that?"

The light changed. He wheeled the car into an empty lot and slammed it into park and took her hand in his. "Hello," he said. "My name's Daniel Fiore, and you're the most beautiful woman I've ever seen, and I want to hold you in my arms and dance with you all night."

For a moment, her hand remained limp. Then she curled icy fingers around his. "Hello," she said. She smiled, and all the air left his lungs. "My name's Casey Bradley, and I've been waiting eighteen years for you to come walking into my life."

***

The bar was small and dark and smelled of beer and stale tobacco. Danny pumped quarters into the jukebox and together they selected a dozen slow songs, and while the ice melted in his bourbon and her Coke, they danced in the dark beneath a blue Schlitz sign with half its letters burnt out. As Joe Cocker wailed his own peculiar version of the blues, she felt each tiny nuance of Danny's body, felt its damp heat through the fabric of his shirt.

She closed her eyes and filled her lungs with the scent of him, with that combination of bourbon and cologne and perspiration that was uniquely Danny.

He spoke near her ear. "I bet you thought dancing was done with the feet."

Amazed at the control she heard in her own voice, she said, "I suppose you're going to tell me it isn't."

"It's done," he said, pressing close enough to leave her breathless, "with the body. Like this."

Trying to keep the conversation light, she said, "Travis warned me to stay away from you."

"He's worried about your virtue. That's what brothers are for."

"And is my virtue in danger of being compromised?"

He caught her hand in his and turned it to kiss the underside of her wrist, sending a shiver through her body. "It's in grave danger," he said.

He was much too close. She could see each pore in his face, could see the tiny white scar near his left eyebrow. His hands on her were liquid fire and his eyes were telling her things better left unsaid. They drank each other in, feasting upon each other like ravenous beasts, while in the background Bette Midler crooned, *Oh, baby, do you want to dance?*

There'll be nothing beyond tonight, she told herself. *Can you live with that?* She harbored no illusions about him. There would be no forever. One night with him was all she would be allowed, a single night with no promises and no commitments, one that would have to suffice for the rest of her life. He would surely break her heart, but tomorrow, no matter how much it hurt, she would walk away without a single regret.

"Take me home," she said. "Take me home and make love to me."

* * *

Danny knelt to spin the tuner knob, and Bob Dylan sprang to life, *knock knock knocking on heaven's door.* The muted glow from the dial cast deep shadows into the corners of the room and formed an indistinct halo around his head. In the dim light, she explored his bedroom.

It was neater than she'd expected, the bed made, clutter minimal. A battered Fender acoustic stood in one corner. Casey picked up the silver-handled hairbrush that lay atop the dresser and stroked its smooth handle. In a jumble beside it were several dollar bills and change, a single subway token, and a broken guitar pick, and she inventoried them like an archeologist who had discovered lost treasure.

He spoke somewhere behind her. "What the devil are you looking for?"

She moved to the open closet door, touched the sleeve of a blue silk shirt, held the soft material to her cheek. If tonight were to be both beginning and end, she would have to squeeze a lifetime into a few short hours. Turning, she studied his shadowy face. "You," she said.

In the shadows, he seemed ten feet tall. She flattened her back against the wall, grateful for its support. Something was terribly wrong, for she was having difficulty breathing, and the shortage of oxygen sent a searing pain through her chest. It took him a year to cross the room to her. He rested both palms on the wall above her shoulders and leaned close, enveloping her in the heat from his body.

And he kissed her.

Nothing in eighteen years of living had prepared her for that first taste of him, for those hot, wet kisses flavored with Kentucky bourbon and Coca-Cola. The world was shattering into tiny pieces, melting into all the colors of the spectrum, and all of them were one, and that one color was Danny. And she was lost, and didn't want to ever be found.

She curled fingers in his tawny hair, and it was like silk, and she'd known it would feel that way from the first moment she saw him. With her fingertips, she explored the back of his neck, learning the feel of his heated skin and the way the fine hairs grew. He gathered the hem of her sweater in both hands, peeled it up and off over her head. Cool air rushed in to raise goose bumps on her exposed flesh. She shivered, and he ran warm hands up and down her back. "Cold?" he whispered.

"A little."

"Let's get under the covers."

Beneath the handmade quilt, their bodies fit like interlocking pieces of a jigsaw puzzle. Hard and soft, convex and concave, man and woman. He tasted of heaven, this beautiful, blue-eyed stranger who had walked into her life and redefined the parameters of her universe. He teased her with warm, wet kisses from ear to navel as she shuddered in delight. Mouth to her belly, his breath warm on her skin, he whispered, "Touch me."

Uncertainty made her hesitate. "Where?"

"Anywhere. Everywhere."

She started with his hands. One by one, she kissed those long, slender fingers. She unbuttoned first one cuff and then the other, learning the shape of the bones in his wrist and the smooth, muscled flesh of his forearms. His chest was hard and muscular and silken smooth, and she stroked and explored, admiring the sleek, hard planes of his body, memorizing it for a future time when she would take out that memory, like a precious jewel, and savor it. He caught his breath as she traced with a fingertip the fine line of hair that ran from his breastbone to his navel. She paused there, and he drew her hand down to the front of his Levi's and taught her the shape and feel of what was inside. His breath came out in a sudden heated rush. "Come here," he said hoarsely.

They devoured each other with feverish intensity, touching and tasting, exploring forbidden places as they impatiently discarded clothing which had become an impediment to closeness. His skin against hers was hot and sleek and damp, and she shuddered at the exquisiteness of his touch, at his hand on her breast, and then his mouth. He cradled her head in his hands and tasted the hollow at the base of her throat. Against her heated flesh, he whispered hoarse words of love in Italian. Understanding none, understanding all, she answered in English.

He buried his face in her hair. "I don't want to hurt you," he said. "I'm not in the habit of deflowering virgins."

She raised her chin and met those blue eyes head-on. "What makes you so sure I'm a virgin?"

"The way you looked at Lindstrom," he said. "And the way you look at me."

"I'm not afraid," she said.

"No," he said. "You wouldn't be."

Even though he was gentle with her, the pain took her by surprise. She uttered an involuntary gasp, and her fingertips dug into his shoulders, but when he would have pulled away, she held him fast, biting her lip hard as the pain momentarily took her breath away.

He stilled against her. Cradled her head in his hands and began moving slowly, carefully, his eyes searching hers for evidence of the pain she hadn't been able to disguise. But it was gone, replaced by a faint, delicate pleasure that was spreading throughout her body. She uttered a soft whimper and he kissed her, a tender butterfly kiss that deepened when she opened her mouth and his tongue found hers.

And she tumbled off the edge of the world. She moaned aloud, and his cool control vanished. He was no longer gentle, and she no longer wanted him to be. Hot and wet and gulping for oxygen, she followed his lead in a pagan dance, seeking, soaring, until without warning the universe exploded around her, sending her spinning off into space in a violent, shuddering burst of rapture.

Dazed, they lay face to face, restless hands stroking, touch more eloquent than words. "Daniel," she breathed, loving the sound, the feel of his name on her tongue.

He kissed her throat. "What?"

"Is it always like this?"

He studied her somberly with those blue eyes. "No," he said.

Dreading the answer, she still had to ask the question. "Have there been a lot of women in your life?"

"Yes," he said.

She felt an insane rush of jealousy. "I hate them. I hate every single one."

"Don't," he said. "There's no need. Nobody's ever mattered until now."

***

"You learn fast on the streets. You learn fast, and you learn early, and that's how you survive." He picked up a slice of toast, buttered it, and cut it in half.

"Oh, Danny," she said softly. "What an awful way to grow up."

He shrugged. "My grandmother tried to control me. But I liked my freedom."

She toyed with the handle to her coffee cup. "It sounds to me like a good way to get into trouble."

"Some kids do," he admitted. "I didn't. There was always something to do."

She rested her chin on her palm and gave him a bemused look. "Like what?"

"Hang out. Play a little pool. Stand in doorways with the guys to watch the pretty girls go by and see who could be the most vulgar. Smoke a few cigarettes. Talk about getting laid, lie about the details, and hope to Christ the other guys wouldn't see through my sophisticated facade to the scared kid underneath with his woeful ignorance of all matters sexual."

She smiled. Softly, she said, "Tough guy."

"You have to understand," he said. "The sisters have control of your life until that final bell rings at three. And then, no one's in charge but you, and you're out on the street, and it's yours."

He fed her the last bite of scrambled egg. "If you're lucky," he said, "you go to work for your Uncle Vito, unloading crates of vegetables off a truck. If you're not so lucky, ten years goes by and you're still hanging out."

She helped herself to half his toast. "You're not still hanging out."

"I was one of the lucky ones."

She paused, butter knife in hand. "You have an Uncle Vito you forgot to tell me about?"

"I had something better. One hell of a singing voice. I always knew it would be my ticket out of the North End."

"It's what you were meant to do," she said. "It's in your blood, like a virus."

"How is it you understand me so well?" Those blue eyes were puzzled. "You know things about me that I don't know myself."

"It's easy to see other people objectively. It's harder to see yourself that way."

"I don't know," he said. "I'm having a devil of a time trying to see you objectively." The intensity of his assessment brought a hot flush to her face. "Do you have any idea how sexy you look in my shirt?"

She looked down at her slender legs beneath his white cotton shirt. "No," she said, raising her eyes to meet his boldly. "But I know exactly how sexy you look out of it."

"Christ," he said, just before he kissed her, "I think I've created a monster."

***

Hands tucked in the pockets of his Levi's, Danny Fiore stood at the window, watching the first light of dawn touch the eastern sky and wondering when he'd stopped wanting to run away.

He'd tried to run. When running hadn't worked, he'd decided there was no reason they couldn't discuss the situation like two rational adults. But he'd been wrong again; he'd forgotten that the moment she walked into the room, one of them regressed to a fifteen-year-old, all knees and elbows and quavering uncertainty. So he'd done the only thing left to do: he'd given in to the tumult inside him.

And when he touched her, he knew he was lost.

He had nothing to offer her. Eighty-seven bucks and change, a rusted ten-year-old Chevy, and three years' back issues of *Rolling Stone*. It was no life for a woman, at least not for the kind of woman Casey was. But if he did nothing, she would go home, back to Jesse, and half his insides would go with her.

Danny rested his forehead against the window pane and closed his eyes. What he knew about love you could put in a thimble. He was no good at intimacy. Christ, that was a lie; he didn't know if he was any good at it. He'd never had a chance to find out. All he understood was singing, and the way the music made him feel. Until now, it had been enough.

She was sleeping in a tangle of dark hair and slender limbs and rumpled sheets. Danny sat on the edge of the bed and tried to think of the right words to say. She deserved champagne and roses, candlelight and soft music. Not a marriage proposal from some crazy wop bastard at five in the morning on sheets that hadn't been changed in a week.

He touched her cheek to awaken her. She stretched like a cat before opening sleep-studded eyes to his. When she smiled, his heart rolled over in his chest. "Look," he said, the words suddenly tumbling out of him so fast he was tripping over them. "I'm not in a position to offer you anything even faintly resembling an orthodox life. My life's chaotic, and I don't see it getting any better in the foreseeable future. Right now, I don't have the proverbial pot to piss in or the window to throw it out of. But it won't always be that way." He paused for breath. "By God," he said, "I mean to have it all. But there may be hard times along the way. And you have to know up front that I won't change, not even for you—" He stopped, suddenly aware that he was rambling. "I'm not making any sense, am I?"

Softly, she said, "You're doing just fine."

He ran a hand through his hair. "I had all these flowery things I wanted to say, and I'm saying this all wrong—"

"Yes," she said.

He blinked. "Yes, what?"

"Yes, I'll marry you."

He was grinning, grinning like a fool, and he couldn't help it. "I haven't asked you yet."

"If I waited for you to get to the point," she said, " we'd have to spend our honeymoon at the Sleepytime Old Age Home."

He took her hand in his and somberly studied her slender fingers. "There's something you have to know," he said. "Up front. I want to make sure you understand what you're getting into."

She closed her fingers around his. "Yes?" she said.

He cleared his throat. "The kind of life I lead," he said, "is not conducive to rearing children."

Her steady gaze didn't waver, nor did her grip loosen. But he could hear it in her voice, the faint hint of a tremor. "Ever?" she said.

He felt himself weakening. God help him if she ever figured out that he was incapable of saying no to her. "It's not an easy life," he said. "I'd have to be damn settled before I'd ever consider bringing a kid into it."

"But later," she said, "someday—"

He brought her hand to his mouth, kissed those pale, trembling fingers. "Someday," he said, "when things are more settled, we'll talk about it again."

Her eyes never left his as she removed the diamond engagement ring from the third finger of her left hand and placed it on the table beside the bed. "Are you sure?" he said hoarsely.

She smiled. "I've never been more sure of anything in my life."

***

At 4:47 on a Tuesday afternoon, in the clerk's office at the city hall in Hayesville, Maryland, while static crackled from the police radio in the lobby and pigeons cooed from their roost along the eaves above the open window, Danny held her trembling hand in his and promised to cherish her until death. With the mayor's secretary and an off-duty cop as witnesses, they exchanged the rings they'd bought a half-hour earlier at K-mart, and the city clerk, doubling as a notary public, pronounced them man and wife.

She signed the marriage certificate with a flourish. *Casey Lynn Bradley Fiore.* Danny's handwriting was small and neat as he signed his name next to hers. The secretary returned to her typewriter and the cop went home to dinner, and Danny slipped the clerk a twenty before taking Casey's arm and walking her out into late afternoon sunshine. There, on the sidewalk in front of God and half the homebound population of Hayesville, he swept her into his arms and kissed her until her insides turned to butter. The secretary came out the door and gave them a benevolent smile, and Casey returned the smile just from the sheer joy of it.

Danny cupped her face in his hands and kissed her again. "So, Mrs. Fiore," he said, "where would you like to eat dinner?"

She straightened his collar. She couldn't seem to keep herself from touching him. "Some place wonderfully elegant, Mr. Fiore. Like the Ritz."

"I'm afraid you'll have to settle for something a little less elegant," he said wryly. "Like McDonald's."

She kissed his chin. "I can't think of a more elegant place."

They spent their wedding night in a motel off the Jersey Pike, somewhere outside of Philly. In a paneled room that smelled of mildew, they drank supermarket champagne from disposable plastic goblets and explored together the mysteries of love. He shared with her his fire, she shared with him her tenderness, and they drew strength from the knowledge that nobody could tear them apart now.

And in the morning, they went home to face the lions.

CHAPTER FIVE

When the knock came on her apartment door, Casey had one foot on the kitchen counter, the other braced on the back of a straight chair that she'd weighted down with books, and she was attempting to unscrew an uncooperative light fixture. Catching hold of the glass shade to balance herself, she shouted, "Come in. The door's open."

"Casey?"

"Rob? I'm in the kitchen."

"How many times do I have to tell you to keep the door locked? This is Boston, not the sticks. And don't ever say 'come in' until you know who's on the other—" He broke the corner, took one look at her, and did a double-take. "Holy shit. Are you trying to kill yourself?"

"I'm trying to get this blasted thing down. I don't think it's been washed in forty years."

"Woman, you are an accident waiting to happen. Get down from there before you break your neck."

She caught hold of the hand he held out to her and said, "You try going through life only five feet tall."

He had the fixture unscrewed within seconds. Handing it down to her, he scowled and said, "What if you fell and nobody was here to pick up the pieces?"

Casey waved away his concern and immersed the glass in hot, sudsy water. "I'm as agile as a mountain goat." She rinsed the shade and held it up. "Look at this. I knew there was something beautiful underneath all that grime." She smiled up at him. "Have you had lunch? I make a mean tuna fish sandwich."

"You're on, kiddo. Where does Danny keep his guitar?"

"In the bedroom closet." She held out the light fixture. "You put this back up for me, and I might even let you play me a song."

He sat on the edge of the kitchen table with Danny's guitar and watched her prepare lunch. "I've seen a big difference in Danny," he said, "since he married you."

She licked mayonnaise from a butter knife and dropped it

in the sink. "Good or bad?"

"He's mellowed. You've somehow managed to smooth out all his jagged edges."

Casey opened a loaf of bread, pulled out four slices, arranged them on the counter and began spreading tuna salad. "Maybe," she said philosophically, "there's a reason why opposites attract. Maybe it's because we complement each other. Fill in the chinks in each other's armor."

He plucked absently at the guitar strings. "That's one way of looking at it."

She arranged the sandwiches on a couple of plates and handed one to him. "There's something I've been meaning to ask you."

"Ask away."

"Why does Danny call you Wiz?"

He took a bite of the sandwich, chewed and swallowed. "The first time Danny heard me play, he called me a guitar wizard." Rob shrugged his bony shoulders. "The name just stuck."

"I see. And are you a wizard?"

"Hell, no. I'm just an ordinary guy who sleeps with his guitar."

After lunch, while she cleared up, he picked away at a dank, bluesy melody. "That's pretty," she said. "I've never heard it before. What is it?"

"You've never heard it before because I just wrote it this morning."

Eagerly, she said, "Does it have words?"

"Not yet. I thought you might like to take a shot at it."

"Me?" she asked, inordinately pleased. "You want me to write the lyrics?"

"Yeah, you," he said. "Why not?"

Hours later, Danny found them huddled over his old upright piano. He turned on the overhead light and Casey blinked, trying to focus. "Hello, darling," she said. "What are you doing home so early?"

Danny eyed the papers scattered about the room, the overflowing ashtray beside Rob, the empty Coke bottles. "I'm not early," he said. "You were sitting here in the dark." He dropped his jacket on a chair and stood behind her, his hands creating a pleasant warmth on her shoulders. "What the devil are you two doing?"

Rob's long, bony fingers ran a quick riff on the keyboard. "I asked Casey to add some lyrics to a tune I wrote," he said. "We ended up rewriting the whole thing."

"Let's hear it."

Casey played it, singing harmony with Rob. When they finished, there was a moment of silence. "Christ," Danny said, "that's good." He leaned forward, hands still on her shoulders, studying the music. "Let me hear it again."

Before the song was half-through, he was singing with them. She exchanged a glance with Rob, and he shot her a quick wink.

Danny squeezed onto the piano bench between them and wrapped an arm around her waist. "How soon can we work it into the act?"

Rob flexed long, slender fingers. "We could run it by Jake and Travis at rehearsal on Sunday."

Danny's eyebrows drew together. "Not soon enough," he said. "I want them to hear it tonight."

"It's not going anywhere, Dan. Sunday's only two days away."

"Tonight," he repeated, and Rob shrugged amiably. Satisfied, Danny turned her in his arms and kissed her. "Since we have company," he said, "and I can't have my way with you, how about some dinner? We have to be at Martucci's in a couple of hours."

She brushed her knuckles briefly across his cheek. "You're working too hard," she said. "You'll kill yourself, working two jobs."

"You mean I haven't told you my philosophy?"

She eyed him skeptically. "What philosophy?"

"Live hard and fast," he said, "and die young enough to leave a good-looking corpse."

A cold draft trickled down her spine and spread into her extremities. "Stop it," she said. "Don't talk that way. It gives me the willies."

He grinned. "You're too touchy. And I'm unstoppable.

Give me a hot shower and a home-cooked meal, and I always get my second wind."

They had agreed when they got married that they wouldn't allow their marriage to interfere with Danny's career, and Casey knew she should be grateful that the band had steady work. Not for anything would she admit to him that she was lonely and restless. Not for anything would she admit that it was Trish's letters, her sister Colleen's occasional phone calls, that saved her from succumbing to the isolation. He would think she was unhappy with their marriage, and nothing could have been farther from the truth.

She lived for those early breakfasts and quiet dinners when they faced each other across the table. She lived for Sundays, for those languid hours of lovemaking when he would drive her to the brink of insanity and let her hover there in exquisite agony before plunging with her over the edge. She lived to wake up beside him each morning and to fall asleep in his arms each night. The hours they spent together were perfection. It was the time they spent apart that was the problem.

But she didn't tell him that. Instead, she smiled and said, "You get your shower, and I'll get dinner."

The next morning, while Danny slept late, she breakfasted on black coffee and a croissant, then set out down the back side of the Hill to Haymarket, where she spent an inordinate amount of time choosing from the vast assortment of produce. After trading good-natured insults with the merchants who now recognized her as a regular, she skipped over to the North End and bought from the butchers there, doing her best to ignore the bloody rabbit pelts that hung in their shop windows.

Since she was already in the neighborhood, she ended her excursion with a visit to Danny's grandmother. While Mrs. Fiore brewed tea, Casey sat on an overstuffed armchair in the gloomy parlor. The bulky furniture was upholstered in a drab maroon that time had faded to a dull brown. Yellowed lace curtains kept the sun at bay, and a small Philco television rested atop a mahogany table.

On a matching table beside her, nestled in amongst a thriving community of African violets, was a framed photo of a young woman. Casey picked it up and was studying it when

Mrs. Fiore returned with the tea. The girl in the picture was pretty, with lively, dark eyes and the devil himself in her smile. "Danny's mother?" she said.

The old woman's face darkened. "My Annamaria Teresa. He don't tell you nothing about his mama?"

Casey set the photo back down. "Only that she died when he was five years old. I got the impression he doesn't remember much."

"He remember. He just don' want to."

Surprised, she asked, "Why wouldn't he want to remember?"

Mrs. Fiore pursed her lips and expelled a long breath. "Danny never let nobody get close until you come along," she said. "Oh, he has women, plenty of women, from the time he's fourteen or fifteen. He come home smelling of them. What girl gonna resist that face? But he never bring no girl home to Nonna until you, *carissima*. You good for him. You take care of him, make him feel a little less alone. He don't tell you this stuff, so I tell you, because I think maybe this help you understand your man a little better, no?"

"Yes," she said, and picked up her cup of tea. "Of course."

"My Anna is a beautiful girl. A face like the Madonna. But she is wild. Smoking, drinking, swearing. Wearing too much makeup and running with a bad crowd. She come home at thirteen, hair all messed up, lipstick smeared, tell me she been at the movies. Hah! When she's fifteen, some sailor give her more than she bargain for, and she end up with Danny."

"Good God," Casey said, appalled. "She was only fifteen when he was born?"

"Jus' a little girl. And she try, but like I say, she is just a little girl. She run around with men, leave Danny here with me. Sometimes two, three days before she come back for the baby. And she love him to pieces, but she love the men more. Every time she meet a new man, he don' want no little baby, some other man's bastard. So Danny come home to Nonna. Before he is four years old, Anna, she move that boy six or seven times. Is no life for a baby, and I tell her so. But she get mad and stop speaking to me. She take Danny away, and for six months I don' even see him."

Mrs. Fiore sipped her tea, her dark eyes watery. "Then she come home," the old woman continued, "all smiling. She got a new man, and I never see her like this before. She tells me, 'Mama, he is not like the others. This one love me. He gonna take me to California'. She promise Danny she be back for him real soon, and she get in this man's car and they drive away. And that little boy, five years old, he sit right here in front of this window, day after day, waiting for his mama to come back for him. And he never cry, just sit here, waiting. Only his mama never come back. After a while, he stops waiting. He tells everybody his mama dead, and he never speaks of her again."

Casey's teacup rattled in its saucer. "Are you telling me," she said, "that Anna isn't dead?"

The old woman shrugged. "She jus' never come back. For a long time, I worry about Danny, because he is so much like his mama. When he go to the Army, I pray every night to the Blessed Virgin that he don't come home to me in a box. And the Blessed Virgin is kind. But when he come home, he is different. He pace the floor and smoke cigarettes instead of sleeping. He drink whiskey instead of beer. And he don' talk to me. Just like that little boy five years old, he is holding all the bad inside, where nobody can see it. And then, like a miracle, he finds you, *carissima*. A good girl, like a fresh wind blowing in his life. And he love you, like he love nobody since his mama went away. I think maybe all these years, he is still waiting. Only now, he is waiting for you."

Casey stared at her in disbelief. Wet her lips. "He lied to me," she said.

"Yes. He lie to you. But you must understand that underneath the man is still that little boy five years old, waiting for his mama to come home. This trust, it is not easy for Danny. It takes time. I tell you all this not to hurt you, but to help you understand why he do what he do." Mrs. Fiore leaned forward, reached out a wrinkled hand and clasped Casey's. "A wise woman, *carissima*, would see the truth behind the lie and understand." She patted Casey's hand. "Now be a good girl and drink your tea before it is cold."

As soon as etiquette allowed, Casey escaped. Trudging home up the backside of Beacon Hill, she weighed her options.

She loved Danny Fiore with a depth of emotion that had been beyond her comprehension until he walked into her life. A part of her was devastated by the knowledge that he'd lied to her. Another, conflicting part of her ached for that five-year-old boy who had sat by the window, day after day, waiting in vain for his mother to return.

She remembered what he'd said to her shortly after they met. *It's all a front. Inside, I'm a quivering mass of Jell-O.* At the time, she'd thought he was joking, but she realized now that he was telling the truth. He might not have realized it at the time, but she could see it clearly. And she understood instantly what old Mrs. Fiore had been trying to tell her. For all Danny's flash and bravado, beneath the facade, that vulnerable little boy still dwelt. Of the two of them, she was the strong one.

What was it she'd said to Rob just yesterday? That she and Danny fit because their opposing strengths and weaknesses complemented each other. Like Adam with his missing rib, neither of them was complete without the other. If that was really true, then she had one very special gift she could share with Danny: her strength. She could wrap it around him, absorb the shocks perpetrated by the outside world, insulate that vulnerable little boy from further pain.

That night, they made love with a tenderness that brought tears to her eyes. Each time Danny loved her, there was a sweet communion between them that exceeded anything in her previous experience. She lost herself in him, lost track of the boundaries between them, lost all worlds except the private one they created together.

Afterward, she cradled his head to her breast and closed her eyes as her fingers drew formless patterns in the baby-fine hair at his temples.

"I'd give it all up for you," he said. "I'd put on a tie and sit at a desk all day if it was what you wanted."

Horrified, she said, "I'd never ask you to do that. It would crush your spirit."

"I love you that much," he said. "I'll never let anything come between us. Nothing and nobody."

She rocked him slowly, the way she would have rocked a newborn babe. "Of course not," she whispered. "We're charmed. Nothing can ever hurt us."

And they fell asleep wrapped in each other's arms.

***

They were camped for the night.

After three days of hacking their way through impenetrable jungle, waiting for the VC to come out of hiding and blow their heads off, his nerves were stretched so tight he could have sliced the thick, muddy night with them. The stench of fear hung ripe on the air. Nights were always the worst, because you couldn't tell what was out there. Death could be a hundred yards away, behind a tangled thicket, or watching from the trees. The little bastards were like cats; they hid in the trees, watching. Waiting.

Beside him, Bailey blew on his fingers. "Man, I hate this mud. I thought the jungle was supposed to be hot."

"It's the rainy season."

"Always got all the answers, don't you, Fiore?"

He took a quick, mocking bow and cradled his rifle closer. When Chuck spoke behind him, he jumped. "Dan, do you believe in God?"

"Sure, kid," he said. "He's running around out there in the rain, disguised as a gook."

Bailey smothered a laugh. There was a moment of silence. Then Chuck whispered, "They're out there tonight. Can't you feel it?"

Danny sucked in his breath. Chuck, the skinny Jewish kid from Brooklyn, at nineteen, light-years younger than Danny's cynical twenty, had put it into words, words they had been sidestepping. Danny fondled his M-16. Friend, mistress, protector, its existence was so much a part of him now that his action was automatic and unconscious.

Bailey said, "The kid's right. It's too damn quiet."

"They're waiting," Chuck said.

"For Chrissakes, Silverstein, will you shut up?"

"Scared, Fiore?" Bailey taunted.

"Of course not. I can't think of any place I'd rather be than up to my ass in mud, waiting for some slant-eyed bastard to turn me into hamburger."

At the first staccato rifle report, he reacted on instinct. As he dove for the ground, Chuck Silverstein was jerked off his feet and tumbled like a rag doll onto the grass. Beside him, Bailey, too, dove for cover. "Christ," Bailey said, "it's a fucking sniper."

"Stay with me!" Danny barked, and began crawling on his belly, seeking cover in the thick undergrowth. But the night was as black as he imagined hell must be, and he was hopelessly lost. He knew with a sudden clarity that he was going to die. He was twenty goddamn years old and he was going to die here in this rotten jungle in a rich man's war that he'd wanted no part of.

There was more fire, and then, behind him, a sharp grunt followed by a slow sighing, like a snake slithering through the grass. "Bailey!" he whispered. "Are you still with me?"

Bailey didn't answer. The rifle fire began again, and he couldn't figure out where it was coming from. The night sounds of the jungle confused him. Where the hell was Bailey? Why hadn't he answered? Suddenly, it became imperative that he go back and find him.

Belly dragging in the mud, he began inching his way backward. He'd gone just a few feet when he bumped up against an immovable object. He reached out a hand to touch it, and his hand came back sticky. "Shit," he said. "Oh, shit."

He was quietly sick, there in the mud. Behind him, all was stillness. He didn't have time to mourn. That would come later. Right now, the only thing that mattered was getting out alive. He began inching forward again, through a pool of Bailey's blood and his own puke. After an eternity, he reached the shelter of the trees. Panting, his heart hammering, he hauled himself to his feet.

And came face to face with Charlie.

The enemy. Four feet tall. Beardless. His face devoid of expression, that damned Oriental inscrutability. He was about twelve years old.

His rifle in his hand, his finger on the trigger, Danny froze. He couldn't do it.

The kid raised his rifle in slow motion. With a strange detachment, Danny saw that it was American-made. The home of the free and the brave, amen.

He pulled the trigger.

***

"Danny, wake up!" She shook him with brute force. His side of the bed was saturated with sweat, and he was still making those godawful choked sobbing sounds deep in his throat.

He awoke with a jolt, stiffened, dropped back weakly onto the bed. Covering his eyes with a forearm, he turned away from her and curled into a fetal position, trembling violently.

She touched his shoulder. When he didn't resist, she drew him into her arms and comforted him the only way she knew. His heart was slamming against his chest with such force that she feared it would explode. "Danny?" she whispered in terror.

In a ragged voice, he said, "It'll run its course."

She held him in silent desperation for what seemed hours, until his trembling subsided and his heart rate returned to normal. He pulled away from her then and sat on the edge of the bed with his face in his hands. "So," he said, "now you know my dirty little secret."

She squeezed his shoulder. "How long have you been having these nightmares?"

Elbows braced on his knees, he ran his fingers through his hair. "Ever since I came back from Nam. I should have warned you, but I'm gutless. I didn't know how you'd react."

Softly, she said, "It must have been terrible."

His bark of laughter was brittle. "A real picnic."

"Have you talked to anyone about this?"

Suspiciously, he asked, "Like who?"

"Like a doctor."

"Forget it! I don't need any asshole in a white coat telling me I'm psychotic!"

"For God's sake, Danny, you're not psychotic. You went through hell over there—"

"Hell," he said bitterly, "would have been a vacation."

"Sweetheart, you wouldn't be normal if it didn't affect you somehow."

He got up from the bed, padded barefoot to the dresser, and lit a cigarette. "When I first came back," he said softly, "I'd be walking down the street and hear a car backfire, and I'd hit the ground. Every time I heard leaves rustling or a twig snapping, I'd freak. I was a wreck."

"And now," she said gently, "you're all better."

"I've learned to live with it. If you can't—" He left the sentence unfinished.

"We're in this together, remember? For better or for worse."

"In sickness and in health," he said dryly, and blew out a cloud of smoke. "Yeah. I remember."

"Danny, you're not sick."

"It's not something I'm proud of," he said. "I don't know too many guys who wake up crying and shaking in the middle of the night. I'm also not proud of what I did there."

"What you did there was survive."

"And by what fucked-up cosmic plan did I end up surviving? I think the lucky ones were the guys who didn't make it back."

"Don't you dare talk like that!" she snapped. "Whatever happened there, it's over. You have to let go of it!"

"You don't understand. You can't begin to imagine the things I saw, the things I did. Christ, Casey, I have to live with the monster that's inside me."

"Then talk to me about it. Hold me in your arms and tell me."

"I can't. You wouldn't understand. You'd hate me."

Furious, she said, "How can you believe it would make one iota of difference in the way I feel about you?"

"I'm a killer," he said bitterly, "a goddamn trained killer. That's who you're sleeping beside at night. And the worst thing—" He rubbed his forehead slowly. "The worst thing," he said quietly, "is that there was a part of me that liked it."

CHAPTER SIX

She learned early that musicians have difficulty putting down their instruments when the gig is over. And Danny had a way of drawing people to him, so their apartment became a sort of after-hours club, a continuous jam session that must have given the neighbors apoplexy. As a songwriter, she found the company intellectually stimulating and the music exciting. As the lady of the house, it drove her crazy. More than one Saturday morning, she stumbled out of bed to find someone she'd never laid eyes on before, some bewhiskered and bedraggled guitar player, asleep on the couch. Or eating a bowl of Cheerios at her kitchen table. They left behind empty beer bottles and full ashtrays, water rings on her tabletops and chair arms, discarded pizza boxes and bare cupboards.

Since Danny seemed to thrive on the chaos, she bit her tongue, cleaned up the mess, and kept her misgivings to herself. Since she was the one in charge of the checkbook, he remained blissfully unaware of the havoc this lifestyle wrought on their finances. It was Rob MacKenzie who brought up the subject, one Friday evening as she was standing before an empty refrigerator, balefully surveying its contents. Peering over her shoulder, he said, "Hey, kiddo, it looks like Mother Hubbard's cupboard is bare."

"Yes," she said grimly. "And don't spread the word too far, but Mother Hubbard's checkbook is looking pretty bare, too."

"I'm not surprised. Half the time you're feeding six people on a budget designed for two."

"Milk," she said in disbelief. "You have to love the irony. I grew up on a dairy farm, and now I don't have enough money to buy a gallon of milk."

He squared his jaw. "Get your jacket," he said. "We're going to the store."

"Rob," she said in horror, "I can't take money from you!"

"Maybe you'd rather starve?"

"We won't starve. We'll get by."

"Oh?" he said. "You have a cow tied up in the back yard?"

"Don't tease me, MacKenzie."

"Jesus, Casey, it's only a few bucks. Don't make a federal case out of it. You can pay me back next week."

Casey looked at him, then back at her empty refrigerator. Silently counted the days until payday. And wilted. "All right," she said reluctantly. "You can loan me a few dollars. On one condition."

"What's that?"

"That we don't tell Danny."

Although she was careful to buy only the barest essentials, they still filled two grocery bags. She and Rob distributed the contents in her kitchen cupboards, then gazed ruefully at her pathetic collection of canned pasta and tuna fish. "My mom has a great recipe for tuna noodle casserole," he said.

They shared a grin. "Hey," she said softly. "Thanks."

"Hey, yourself. Next time you need something, ask."

The whole affair left a sour taste in her mouth, even though she paid him back the minute Danny's check was cashed on Friday. So she was horrified when, a couple of weeks later, she found a crisp new twenty-dollar bill tucked into her jewelry box. She knew Danny hadn't put it there. The last time she'd checked, he'd had four dollars to his name. And she'd be willing to bet the entire twenty that in all the time they'd been married, Danny had never even lifted the cover of that jewelry box. It was somebody else who had put it there, and she knew precisely who that somebody was.

That evening, she dragged Rob off to the bathroom, shut and locked the door, and then leaned against it. She pulled the twenty from her pocket, unfolded it, and held it up for him to see. "What is this?" she said.

He wrinkled his forehead. "I could be wrong," he said, "but it looks to me like a twenty-dollar bill." And he flashed his most ingenuous smile, the one that always brought out the recessive mommy gene in even the hardest of women.

She folded her arms across her chest, determined not to be sucked in by that boyish charm. "Is there anything you'd like to tell me about it?"

"Well," he said thoughtfully, "it won't buy as much as it

would five years ago."

She bit her lip. "Anything you'd like to tell me," she clarified, "about how it ended up in my jewelry box."

He sighed. "Look," he said, crossing his arms in unconscious imitation of her. "I'm living at home, paying my mom fifteen bucks a week for board. I don't have any other expenses. You guys are having a hard time making ends meet. You're paying too much for rent—"

"How do you know that?" she demanded.

"You live on Beacon Hill," he said. "The whole damn neighborhood's overpriced. People raid your refrigerator day and night. Hell, I eat more meals here than I do at home. I should be paying board to you instead of my mom."

She ran a hand through her hair. "Rob," she said, "I know you mean well, but you can't do this."

He squared that stubborn jaw. "Why?"

"Because! Because it's—"

They were interrupted by a knock on the bathroom door. "Just a minute!" she snapped. And whispered, "Because it's not the way things are done!"

"Says who?" he whispered back.

"I don't know!" she said. "Whoever made up the rules."

"So you plan to spend the rest of your life being a sheep? I'm really disappointed in you, Fiore. I thought you knew how to think for yourself."

His words stung, at least in part because they struck a nerve. She had always followed the rules. It was what she'd been taught from infancy. The rules were there to keep life orderly, to prevent chaos and anarchy. It had never occurred to her to question their validity. But now, here stood Rob MacKenzie, daring to suggest that maybe, if she bent one of those rules a bit, the sky wouldn't tumble down on her head.

"Look," she told him, "I come from a long line of staid Baptists. We don't know how to break the rules. That ability was bred out of us generations ago." She smiled ruefully. "Along with our sense of humor."

"So I should just stand by and watch you starve?"

"It's not your responsibility to subsidize us."

"It's not a subsidy," he said, "it's a gift."

In exasperation, she said, "You are the most impossible man I've ever met."

He grinned. "I'm Irish," he said. "So sue me."

Giving up, she tucked the twenty back into her pocket. "We will not discuss this issue again. Is that understood?"

He saluted. "Loud and clear."

And they never did. But after that, whenever starvation loomed, she would find money tucked into secret places. Sometimes just a few crumpled bills stuffed into her purse; sometimes a twenty in her bureau drawer, or two fives in her jewelry box. She never caught him at it, and after a time, she stopped trying. But she kept a running tally, because somehow, someday, she would pay back every penny.

As summer moved into fall, she and Rob spent several afternoons a week writing songs together. As he jokingly told her, "We make beautiful music together," and he wasn't far from the truth. But her woeful ignorance of the technical aspects of music kept getting in her way. Finally one day, she threw down her pencil in frustration. "I can hear it in my head," she said. "Why can't I put it on paper?"

"Because you don't have the skills you need to make the transition."

"How can I get them?"

He looked pensive. "I could teach you."

"I couldn't ask you to give me that much of your time."

"We could call it an investment." He leaned back in his chair and crossed his bony ankles. "I'll get my payback when we win our first Grammy."

Her laughter was rueful. "That'll be the day."

But in the end, she recognized that if they were to continue to work together, she needed to know what she was doing on a more technical level. She couldn't continue indefinitely to let Rob carry her.

Rob MacKenzie was a patient teacher with a vast wealth of knowledge upon which to draw and the willingness to share with her everything he had ever learned about music. What started as a crash course in music theory grew into months of intensive tutelage. They studied chord progressions and intervalic relationships, structure and tempo and style. They stripped other people's songs down to the bare bones and then reassembled them to see what made them work. Over the months, he transfused knowledge to her as if by an invisible bloodline. Along the way, he taught her a healthy respect for the great blues musicians of the past and present, from Robert Johnson to Billie Holiday to B.B. King. He played their music for her, traced for her the genealogy of the music she heard on the radio every day.

In the process, she learned a great deal about Rob himself. He had picked up his first guitar at the age of nine. After that, he'd had but one love in his life. At seventeen, he'd been admitted to Berklee on a full scholarship, and during his tenure there, he'd soaked up knowledge like a sponge. At nineteen, he and Berklee had parted amicably when he'd left to pursue a career as a working musician. He was tired of waiting, eager to jump in headfirst.

Rob became her mentor, her best friend. It was a euphoric experience, seeing something she'd worked hard to create come alive in the hands of a group of talented musicians. The music germinated somewhere deep inside her, but she tailored it to Danny. She knew his possibilities, knew his limitations, knew his strengths and weaknesses as a vocalist, and she worked with Rob to write the songs which would best showcase his talents. Those afternoons became her lifeline, for during those few hours each week she lived and breathed music.

***

Boston Common was blanketed with snow. On Tremont Street, bumper-to-bumper traffic crept from traffic light to traffic light, spraying slush on those pedestrians brave enough to attempt crossing. Every few blocks, a tired-looking Santa stood next to a black pot, ringing a brass bell. It was the season of love, the season of giving, the season when short-tempered shoppers gave new meaning to the word rudeness as they mowed each other down in a mad race to reach the bargain table.

Casey forged her way through the crowds clotting the sidewalk, carrying the chopsticks and the paper parasol she'd picked up in a dusty little shop in Chinatown. She'd spent an exhausting half-hour worming through the crush of shoppers in

Filene's Basement, only to find that they'd just sold the last of the watches that Danny had been dropping hints about for weeks. She'd been disappointed, but even the sour temper of the salesgirl hadn't dampened her spirits. She loved Christmas, loved the crass commercialism, the hokey carols that permeated the air, the colored glass and the bright lights and the tinsel.

The lights strung in the leafless branches of the trees on the Common winked on as she climbed the incline from Park Street Church to Beacon Street. She stopped at the bakery on the corner and bought a loaf of French bread. Tonight was one of Danny's rare evenings at home, and she had planned a special dinner that would also be a celebration, for she had news she couldn't wait to share with him.

The apartment was freezing. Casey stashed her purchases in her bedroom closet and tried to remember where Danny had left the hammer. After a brief search, she found it in the kitchen drawer. She carried it to the bedroom, gave the radiator valve a couple of good raps. The resultant hiss was reassuring. Rubbing her hands together for warmth, Casey returned the hammer to its rightful place in the closet beneath the stairs, stopping to plug in the Christmas tree before starting supper.

She sang along with Eric Clapton while she peeled potatoes. After she put them on to boil, she marched into the bathroom and dumped the hamper upside down on the floor and began sorting laundry. Danny found her there, standing in a pile of towels and underwear, attempting to sweet-talk the reluctant Maytag into beginning its spin cycle. "Hi, beautiful," he said, bending for a kiss.

"Lord, this thing is temperamental. Hi," she added distractedly, her ears attuned to that tiny click of the dial that meant the cycle was about to kick in. The washer clicked, then lumbered into painful life, creaking and groaning as the tub began to spin. "By George," she said, "I think I've got it." She stood on tiptoe then to kiss him. "The radiator was off again."

"I'll look at it tonight. What's for dinner?"

"It's a surprise."

He raised his eyebrows. "What if I don't like it?"

"You'll like it. Besides," she added saucily, "you get me for dessert." Arms wound around his neck, she lay her head against his chest and closed her eyes. "Danny," she said, "something wonderful happened today."

He kissed the top of her head. "What?"

"I got a job."

He went stiff in her arms. "A job?" he said. "I didn't know you were looking for a job."

"We need the money. And I can only kill so much time washing dishes and scrubbing the toilet."

"What kind of job?"

"Working as a nurse's aide in the children's wing at St. Peter's Hospital. About half the children there are terminally ill. They're so brave, they just break your heart."

When he didn't respond, she continued blithely. "I'll be working second shift, so I won't always be here for supper, but it's only three days a week. That's all they could give me right now."

"St. Peter's," he said. "That's in Roxbury. Have you lost your mind?"

The tone of his voice finally registered, and she glanced up in surprise. "What's wrong?" she said.

"I don't suppose it occurred to you that you might have consulted with me first?"

She raised an eyebrow. "As a matter of fact," she said, "it didn't. Since when do I have to consult with you before I make a decision?"

"For Christ's sake, Casey, use your brain. Are you trying to get your throat slit?"

"I know Roxbury's a tough neighborhood, but—"

He slammed a fist down on the washer. "You don't know shit! I grew up here, and I wouldn't venture onto the streets of Roxbury after dark unless I was carrying a loaded AK-47!"

She gaped at him in astonishment, unable to reconcile this stranger with the soft-spoken man she'd married. He looked like Danny, his voice was Danny's, but the words he was speaking were the words of a stranger. "I can't believe you're carrying on like this," she said. "Over something so small."

"I want you to go to the phone right now and call that place and tell them you've changed your mind."

White-hot fury shot through her. "Over my dead body!"

"Damn it, Casey, that's what I'm trying to prevent!"

"I think we'd better get one thing straight," she said. "This is the twentieth century. I may be your wife, but I am not, nor will I ever be, your property. I'll work where I want, with or without your permission."

"That's odd," he said, "because I seem to remember something in the marriage vows about obeying."

"Words put there hundreds of years ago by male supremacists who regarded women as chattel!"

"I will not allow you to work after dark in Roxbury. Period."

"You can just go to hell, then, because you can't stop me. As a matter of fact—" She kicked at the pile of laundry. "—you can start washing your own underwear!"

"I can do better than that. If this is what marriage is going to be like, I don't want any part of it!"

She tried to breathe around the sudden obstruction in her throat. "Just what are you saying?"

"I'm saying that we might as well call it quits right now and get it over with!" He untangled one of her brassieres from his shoe, threw it at her, and stalked from the room.

She dropped the brassiere and followed him, catching him by the arm and yanking him around. "Where do you think you're going?"

He jerked free from her grasp. "Out."

She narrowed her eyes. "You're walking out in the middle of a fight?"

"The fight," he said, "is over. And so is the marriage."

"Fine with me, then. Get out, and don't bother coming back!"

"Don't worry! I don't plan to!"

He slammed the door so hard the picture on the wall shuddered. Casey walked to it woodenly and steadied it, and then she went to the kitchen stove and turned off the burners, methodically, one by one.

She tried to pinpoint the exact moment when Danny had stopped loving her, but she was too numb to think clearly. She should have known it wouldn't last. She should have realized that marrying Danny would be like caging a wild bird. Now she was paying for her stupidity. The love of her life had just walked out the door, and her marriage was over almost before it had begun.

***

His anger lasted for exactly twenty-three minutes. That was how long it took him to realize that she didn't love him any more.

If she loved him, she would have understood that he was only trying to protect her. If she loved him, she would have realized that all other women had ceased to exist from the instant he first lay eyes on her, and he was terrified of losing her. Goddamn stupid woman.

He stared morosely into his empty beer bottle and wondered what to do now. Scowling at the miniature Christmas tree that sat at one end of the bar, he signaled the barkeep for a refill. That was another thing. He hated the goddamn Christmas lights she strung all over the house like she was building a landing pad for UFO's. He hated Christmas carols and he hated tinsel and he hated goddamn reindeer.

He took his bottle with him to the pay phone. Fishing in his pocket, he came up with a dime and dropped it into the slot. Travis deserved what he was about to get. After all, Trav was at least partially responsible for the collapse of his life; he was the one who'd introduced them.

Travis answered on the second ring, and Danny set down his beer. Without preamble, he said, "I've lost her."

There was a moment of silence. Then, "Dan? Is that you?"

Bleakly, he said, "I've lost her, Trav."

"Lost who?"

"My wife. Your sister." He took a swig of beer and stared mournfully at the blinking lights on the Christmas tree. "It's over."

"Are you drunk, Fiore?"

"Not yet," he said, "but I have high hopes."

"You and Casey had a fight?"

"She doesn't love me any more."

Trav's snort could be heard clearly over the telephone

wires. "Fiore, you're full of shit."

He set down his bottle of beer. "She threw me out and told me not to come back."

Travis sighed. "I ought to knock both your heads together. Where the hell are you?"

He picked up a pretzel from the bowl on the end of the bar and bit into it. "The Blue Goose."

"Stay where you are, bonehead. I'll be there in a few minutes." Trav's voice softened. "We'll talk about it."

It was 11:43 p.m. when he finally let himself into the apartment. He took off his shoes and tiptoed into the kitchen. The potatoes sat on the stove untouched, a starchy, congealed mess. He scraped the ruined dinner into the rubbish and put the pans in the sink to soak, then tried to find something else to do, something else to keep him from facing her, but there was nothing left. The woman he'd married was a compulsive housekeeper.

He tiptoed into the bedroom. She was stretched out face-down on the bed, but the rigid lines of her body told him she wasn't asleep. He undressed in the dark and crawled beneath the covers, lying stiffly on his side of the bed, taking care not to let any part of his body touch hers. The radiator valve was stuck open, and the bedroom felt like a sauna. He rolled onto his left side, then his right, flipped his pillow and pressed his face to the cool side, shoved aside the bedcovers with one leg.

In the darkness, she said, "I'll have my things packed in the morning."

He swallowed hard. When he spoke, his voice sounded like it had at thirteen, uncertain of where it would finally end up. "I'll leave," he said.

Softly, she said, "Whatever you want."

He thought her voice sounded suspiciously shaky, but she'd turned her back to him, so he couldn't see her face. He reached out a tentative fingertip. When it made contact with the bare flesh of her shoulder, she flinched as though she'd been burned.

"No," he said, his heart thudding. "It's not what I want."

Silence. Then, softly, "What do you want?"

"I want you to forgive me for being an asshole."

"Fool," she said, turning to him. "There's nothing to

forgive."

Then they were in each other's arms and he was kissing her cheek, her eyelids, the tip of her nose. "You're my lifeline," he said. "If anything happened to you, I wouldn't want to go on living."

"Danny," she said, "you can't protect me by locking me up in the house. You have to trust me. You have to accept that I have a life of my own, and it doesn't always revolve around you."

"I'm an idiot."

"You're not an idiot. I have better taste than to fall in love with an idiot."

His heart rate had slowed nearly to normal. "If you ever leave me," he vowed, "I'll come after you and drag you back."

"Are you kidding? You'd have to change the locks to keep me out. I'm afraid you're stuck with me for the duration."

He kissed her bare shoulder, her collarbone, the swell of one breast. She walked her fingertips up his chest, past his Adam's apple, pausing at the sensitive spot just behind his ear. "Daniel Fiore," she whispered fiercely, "I love you."

With a tenderness that still astonished him, a tenderness he'd never known until Casey entered his life, he said, "And I love you, Mrs. Fiore."

"But I'm not quitting the job."

He stiffened. "You know how I feel about it."

"I know," she said, and touched his face tenderly. "But I'm not quitting." She sat up, pulled the bedding snugly around her shoulders, and studied him somberly. "You have to understand, Danny. There's a whole world out there, a world I never saw until you introduced me to it. I need to find out where I fit into that world."

"You fit right here," he said, wondering why he sounded so defensive. "By my side."

"Yes," she said. "And you fit right here by my side. But it would never occur to me to demand that you curtail your activities to suit me. You told me once that nobody had a right to tell me what to think or do. Yet here you are, trying to do that very thing."

Danny opened his mouth to argue, then clamped it abruptly

shut. "Shit," he said.

She was right, of course. Casey was always right. It was one of the things he loved most about her, that unshakable, infallible judgment. He let out a hard breath and lay there staring at the ceiling, torn between his innate sense of fairness and the roiling terror that clutched him low in the belly at the thought that anything might ever happen to her. While he understood intellectually that she was right, that still didn't mean he had to like it.

A subtle shift in the balance of their relationship was happening right in front of his eyes. The backbone of steel that he'd always suspected his wife of possessing had just been displayed in living, breathing Technicolor. The woman he'd married had asserted her independence, and if he wanted to hold onto her, he would have to swallow his pride—and his fears— and let her have her way.

Even if it killed him.

***

In the end, they compromised. Danny agreed to keep his fears to himself, and Casey agreed to keep him continually apprised of her comings and goings. It wasn't a flawless arrangement, and not the one Danny would have chosen, but it was better than nothing.

But they missed having dinner together every night. One Thursday evening, he showed up at the hospital with two corned beef sandwiches in a paper bag. After that, they became a fixture in the hospital cafeteria three nights a week. They would find a table in a quiet corner, and each night he would bring her something different to eat while they filled each other in on the day's events.

The job at St. Peter's opened new horizons for her. She had so much love to give, and the children there needed it so badly. She took care of their needs, read stories to them, rocked them to sleep in her arms. She experienced the joys and heartbreaks of motherhood vicariously, because she couldn't experience them firsthand.

Not until their life stabilized could she and Danny even

think about having children. Not until Danny had achieved some measure of the success he was working so hard to attain. It was a given, something she'd understood from the beginning, and if at times it was a bitter pill to swallow, she reminded herself how impossible it would be to have a child, given their current lifestyle.

And she poured out all her pent-up motherlove on the children at St. Peter's.

**

It was Rob's idea to cut a record.

Danny was skeptical. "Unless you have some powerful connections," he said, "that's a good way to lose your shirt."

"It doesn't have to be that way." Rob leaned back and rested a bony ankle on his knee. "We rent studio time, press five hundred discs, and split the cost. We try to recoup our investment by selling 'em at our gigs. And we push the local stations for airplay. What could be simpler?"

Dryly, Danny said, "Robbing the Bank of Boston in broad daylight?"

"You can't think of it as a profit-making venture. We'd be doing it for exposure, not for money."

He had hit Danny's weak spot, and they both knew it. Danny considered his suggestion. "How would we push it with the radio stations?" he said. "I don't have time to do promo work."

"I do," Casey said, and both men looked at her in surprise. "Well," she argued, "why not? I'm as involved as any of you. It's my music you're playing."

"She has a point," Rob said.

Danny looked skeptical. "You don't know anything about publicity."

"How hard can it be?"

So they hired an out-of-work sax player and obtained the free services of a rhythm guitarist who owed Travis a favor, and they went into the studio and made a record. They used one of Casey and Rob's driving rockers, *Heart of Darkness*, as the A side, backing it with a cover of *Woman, Woman*, a ballad made popular a few years earlier by Gary Puckett and the Union Gap. Two inherently different songs, each showing a different facet of Danny's potent vocal talent.

Weeks later, when the boxes of white-jacketed black vinyl 45's finally arrived, Casey opened the first box and, with a reverence bordering on awe, withdrew a gleaming disc from its protective cover. She turned it over in her hands, studied each shiny groove, each minute imperfection in its surface. Heart thundering, she read the fine print beneath the title: *Fiore/MacKenzie*. In that instant, the six-inch slab of vinyl she held in her hands became more than just a demo record cut by the boys in the band. The disc held her words, her music. She had crossed some invisible border between the hopeful and the determined, the amateur and the professional.

She had become a songwriter.

CHAPTER SEVEN

Casey Bradley Fiore had found a new love.

His name was Benito Patricio Juarez, but everybody just called him Benny. Benny had a full head of shining black curls, dark eyes set deep in an angel's face, and a seductive smile that could soften the heart of the hardest woman. He also had acute lymphocytic leukemia.

He was four years old, and the light of her life.

It wasn't as though she hadn't been warned. The nurses, the other aides, the doctors had warned her not to get emotionally involved with the patients. "They'll break your heart," she'd heard more than once. But how could she not love Benny, who never complained, but always had a wide smile for everyone? She tried not to play favorites, but it was useless. Benny was special, and she was head over heels in love with him. She brought him gifts: a coloring book and crayons, a bright green stuffed aardvark, a wall poster of his personal hero, Spiderman.

Benny's prognosis wasn't good. The doctors had already attempted unsuccessful radiation treatments. The next step would be chemotherapy. Long before she'd come to work at St. Peter's, Casey had been acquainted with chemotherapy and its side effects. She had watched helplessly as her mother grew weak and wretchedly sick, unable to keep anything down, wasting away to a skeleton and losing all her lustrous black hair. Since coming to St. Peter's and seeing numerous children subjected to the ravages of chemo, Casey had begun to question how a supposedly benevolent team of doctors could put a small child through such torture. There had to be other, less caustic options.

But it wasn't her job to question. Her job was to see to the comfort and cleanliness of the children on the cancer ward. No more and no less. The doctors, those white-coated gods whose pronouncements could mean the difference between life and death, were the decision-makers. She was nothing more than a part-time aide whose only training had come from nursing her mother through terminal cancer. She had no ties to Benny, except those of one heart to another, and Benny's mother, a slatternly woman of twenty with a sixth-grade education and limited comprehension of what was happening to her son, had given the doctors *carte blanche* in his treatment.

"Stay out of it," Danny warned her. "You stick your nose in where it doesn't belong, and I guarantee that you won't be thanked."

"But his mother doesn't understand. Nobody's told her that she has alternatives."

"And she won't appreciate you telling her. Sweetheart, listen to me. If there's one thing these people have left, it's their pride. You can't just step in and take it away from them. You don't have the right."

"But, Danny, he's just a baby. How can the doctors put him through that and still sleep at night?"

"They're just doing their job. They've taken an oath to do everything in their power to cure him."

"But at what cost?"

He didn't answer. There really wasn't an answer.

***

The letter arrived on a bright and breezy morning. The mailman was filling the boxes in the entryway when Casey returned from the corner store. "Good morning, Phil!" she greeted him. "How's your wife today?"

"Feeling much better, thanks. Lousy time of year to get the flu."

"There's no good time of year to get the flu. Give her my best."

"I'll do that. Here you go." He handed her a stack of mail, topped by a lilac-colored envelope. "Got a special one for you today."

Even without a return address, there was no mistaking her sister's girly handwriting in garish purple ink. Eager for news from home, she let herself into her apartment, dropped the rest of the mail on the kitchen table, and tore open the envelope.

Dear Casey,

This isn't the kind of news I wanted to give you over the phone, so I thought I should write instead. It will probably come as a shock, but Jesse and I are getting married in three weeks. I know you're probably thinking that I'm too young, but I'm ready for this. I love Jesse, and he loves me. Once we're married, he'll be moving in here. It seemed ridiculous for us to take an apartment when Dad has this huge house sitting virtually empty. Dad is thrilled that we'll be staying with him. He's always thought of Jesse as a son. Before you ask about school, I took a double load this term so I could graduate a year early. So I'll be free to stay home and keep house for Dad and Jesse. Since you left, I've been learning to cook, and the good news is that Jesse's been eating my cooking for months, and he's still willing to marry me. So I must be doing something right.

I have a favor to ask. Would it be all right with you if I wore Mama's wedding dress? I know that by rights, as the eldest daughter, it's yours. But since you're already married, I thought that maybe you wouldn't care if I wore it instead. It would mean so much to me, to have a piece of Mama with me on my wedding day.

There is one other thing, and I'm not sure how you'll take this. But I'm hoping you'll understand, and be happy for us. You're probably wondering why we're rushing, why we didn't just get engaged and wait for a year or two. We would have done that, but circumstances made it difficult. You see, I'm sort of pregnant. The pregnancy wasn't planned, believe me. I never expected to be settling down and starting a family at seventeen, but once the initial shock wore off, I was excited. We're both excited. This baby may have been a surprise, but he (or she) will definitely be loved.

I hope and pray that you'll give us your blessing.

Colleen

Somewhere in the process of reading her sister's letter—possibly upon reaching that loaded word, *pregnant*—Casey's expanding dismay morphed into something darker, something fierce and brutal, something with sharp teeth that sank into her throat and strangled her breathing. She held the piece of lilac-scented stationery in her hands, staring at it until the words blurred in front of her eyes. She didn't realize she was crying until a fat tear landed on the paper and smudged her sister's name.

The tears took her by surprise. As a pragmatic person, she'd always taken what life handed her and dealt with it. She made decisions and followed through without regrets. Tears were not generally part of her repertoire.

Yet here they were, these damning and betraying tears, clouding her vision and coloring her perspective, even as she recognized that fierce and brutal thing holding her in its grip as jealousy. How was it possible that she could be jealous of her sister? There was nothing romantic about having a baby at seventeen. Nor did she begrudge her sister the man Colleen was about to marry. She'd had her chance with Jesse, and she'd walked away with her head held high. Even though she thought this impending marriage between two mismatched souls was a dreadful mistake that would rapidly unravel, still she wished them happiness. And if Colleen and Jesse were able to find even a fraction of the happiness she'd discovered with Danny, their union might actually survive. There was nothing to be jealous of. Her own life was fulfilling. Satisfying. She was married to a man she adored. She had her songwriting, and her job at the hospital. She had good friends, a renewed relationship with her brother, a small but charming Beacon Hill apartment she'd decorated herself. She had the city of Boston sprawled at her feet, and a future that was wide open. Her life was charmed.

Yet that thing with teeth latched onto her every time she

saw a mother walking with a baby in a stroller. It took a sharp bite out of her heart each time she noticed a pregnant woman on the crowded sidewalks of downtown Boston, or watched a child chasing squirrels on the Common. It sank even deeper into her every time she walked onto the children's ward at the hospital.

And now this. Was this some kind of test? Because if it was, she feared she had failed it dismally.

Casey glanced again at the tearstained letter in her hand and questioned what kind of mother her sister would be. Colleen was a spoiled, self-involved, boy-crazy teenager with a strong aversion to all domestic chores and less than zero interest in anything baby-related. What possible chance would this baby have, with a mother like that?

But it wasn't her place to question. The damage was already done. She had no power to change the past, and it was too soon to determine what the future might bring. Colleen would muddle through somehow, and Casey would settle for being the best aunt in the world. That was her place in this disastrous scenario. She would offer love and support, and keep her pain to herself. In the meantime, she would intensify her efforts to move Danny's career forward, for at the end of his rainbow lay her own pot of gold.

She took a ragged breath, squared her shoulders, and pulled open the kitchen drawer in search of a writing tablet and a pen. At the kitchen table, as the morning sun poured in around her, she paused to think for a moment, then began to write.

Dear Colleen,

Of course you can wear the dress. I wouldn't have it any other way. Mama would be so proud! Danny and I wish you both the very best. We are beyond thrilled about our new niece or nephew. There is no blessing more precious than a new life. If you need any help with anything, you know where to find me.

Love always,

Casey

CHAPTER EIGHT

Anxiously examining her reflection in the mirror, Casey adjusted the navy suit and tried to settle the butterflies cavorting in her midsection. With the suit, she wore a white tailored blouse and a single strand of pearls that had belonged to her mother. Her navy pumps matched the suit, and she'd pulled her hair up into a sleek bun atop her head.

The cool, professional woman who looked back at her from the mirror seemed older than her nineteen years. She wore the clothes with a flair that said she'd been born to money and elegance. Nobody looking at her would have guessed that she had bought the suit at a thrift store, or that the pumps were borrowed from Rob's sister Rose. Or that she was so nervous, she felt like throwing up.

She was well prepared. She had spent days in the library, devouring the entertainment sections of two years' back issues of the *Globe*, the *Herald*, the *Phoenix*, making photocopies of any mention of Danny Fiore and his band. She had spent more hours listening to local radio stations, tracking programming patterns and analyzing play lists, acquainting herself with on-air personalities, targeting the stations and jocks she believed would be most receptive to new local talent. She had rehearsed her spiel so many times, she could recite it in her sleep.

At a knock on the door, she gave herself a final cursory glance and went to let Rob in. He took a look at her and let out a long, low whistle.

Casey smiled ruefully. "I'll take that as a compliment."

He was wearing a red paisley shirt and an Army jacket that had passed disreputable eons ago. Rob always looked like a rag picker beside Danny, who, even in Levi's, always managed to look as though he'd stepped from the pages of *Gentlemen's Quarterly*. "The shirt has to go," she said. "And the jacket. Let's see what we can find."

She found a green silk shirt in the closet, and a charcoal tweed jacket. "Try this," she said.

Although Rob was tall, he was whippet-thin, and Danny's shirt hung off his bony shoulders as if it had given up all hope. Casey found a green striped tie to go with it, and he stood like an obedient little boy as she knotted and adjusted it for him.

"There," she said, patting it for good measure. "You'll do." She paused to study the results of her work. "You should wear green more often," she said. "It brings out the color in those nice green eyes of yours."

He flushed and quickly changed the subject. "What's our first stop?" he said.

"WBAC. Rocky Harte, boy-wonder programming director. They play primarily Top 40 and have been known to give airplay to unknowns."

The WBAC studios were located in one of downtown Boston's elegant older buildings. The elevator glided silently to the fifth floor, the doors slid open, and they found themselves in an ornate, cavernous hallway. "Hell of a dump," Rob said.

She took a deep breath to steel herself as they approached a glass door painted with WBAC's call letters. "Just back me up," she said. "No matter what outlandish thing I say, just play along and back me up."

"I'm with you all the way," he said. "Ready?"

She took one more breath, letting it out slowly, relaxing her features to erase her nervousness. "Ready," she said, and together they went through the door.

The receptionist gave Rob a cursory glance. "Hi," she said to Casey, and snapped her gum. "Can I help you?"

"Yes. My name is Casey Fiore, and I have a ten o'clock appointment with Rocky Harte."

The girl looked doubtful, but she picked up the intercom and held a brief, low-keyed conversation before covering the mouthpiece with her hand. "I'm sorry, Miss Fiore," she said, "but Mr. Harte says he doesn't have a ten o'clock appointment."

"That's impossible," Casey said. "It's written right here in my book." She opened the briefcase she'd bought on sale at Filene's and took out her leather-bound appointment book and opened it to a blank page. "It's right here. I—oh, damn." She closed her eyes. "I did it again."

Rob, who had been unhurriedly studying the Warhol print

on the wall over the couch, scowled at her. "You didn't," he said.

"Oh, Rob," she wailed, "I did." Turning to the receptionist, she said, "I have the wrong day. I'm so embarrassed."

The receptionist looked from Casey to Rob and then back. "What day were you supposed to be here?"

"You dragged me all the way down here on the wrong day?" Rob said. He ran a hand through his disheveled hair. "Jesus, woman, can't you ever keep anything straight?"

"I'm sorry!" she hissed. "Do you think you could keep it down? I'm embarrassed enough as it is!"

The receptionist, still holding the phone, gave him a nasty look that spoke volumes. "Hang on," she told Casey. "Maybe there's something I can do for you." There was another quick, whispered conversation, then she smiled. "If you'd like to sit down, Mr. Harte will be with you in a minute."

"Thank you so much," Casey said. She cast a quick glance at Rob, who had returned, scowling, to the Warhol. Leaning toward the girl, she whispered, "You saved my life. When that man gets angry, he's a beast. An absolute animal."

The receptionist sent a frosty look at Rob's back. A door opened, and a wiry, dark-haired man emerged. "Casey Fiore?" he said.

She offered her hand. "Mr. Harte," she said. "I'm Casey Fiore. And this is my business partner, Rob MacKenzie."

The two men shook hands, and Rocky Harte ushered them into his office and shut the door. He perched on the edge of a battered walnut desk and picked up a Styrofoam coffee cup. Turning it in his hand, he said, "I don't know who the hell you two are, or why you're here, but I appreciate a good bluff as well as the next guy." His gaze left the coffee cup and fell on Rob, then on Casey. "That's why instead of having you thrown out I'm giving you exactly five minutes to tell me what you want." He checked his watch. "Starting right now."

It was all the opening she needed. From the briefcase, she pulled out a white-jacketed 45 record. "This," she said, "is why we're here."

They spent nearly an hour with Rocky Harte, leaving with his promise of two weeks of airplay, more if there was enough demand. Stomach churning, Casey left Rob waiting for the elevator and dashed for the nearest washroom and threw up.

And then they hit the next station on her list.

***

Like most children, Benny Juarez was tougher than he looked. He bounced back from chemo with amazing resiliency, surprising everyone when the doctors declared that his cancer appeared to be in remission. Casey obtained special permission from Dr. Harris to take him out for an afternoon, and they spent it at the zoo, where Benny stared in open-mouthed amazement at the monkeys and the llamas and the elephants.

But his favorite animal, by far, was the peacock. When the flashy bird strutted across his pen, his brilliantly-colored tail feathers splayed for the benefit of the peahen, Benny squealed with delight. It was all Casey could do to drag him away when it was time to leave. In the gift shop, she bought him a single peacock feather that he clutched in his grubby little hand as though it might disappear if he loosened his hold.

Danny met them for dinner at McDonald's. He offered Benny his hand and said solemnly, "So this is my competition. It's nice to meet you, Benny." Benny said nothing, but his gaze never left the blue-eyed giant who bought him a Happy Meal and treated him like an adult.

After dinner, they returned Benny to the hospital, and while Danny waited in the car, Casey carried the child to the ward and undressed him. His head flopped from side to side in exhaustion as she untied his shoelaces and pulled off his shoes and socks. He fell asleep immediately, a smile on his face and the peacock feather still clamped in his fist.

Danny was double-parked outside, and she scooted for the Chevy through a light misting rain. Slamming the door behind her, she said, "It looks like he's smitten. I'm jealous."

Turning on the windshield wipers, Danny said, "He's probably just lacking a strong male role model."

"Thank you, Dr. Freud. You took one psychology course in college and now you have all the answers."

The next day, Ruth Mendez, the hospital social worker,

called Casey into her office. "Shut the door," Mendez said, "and have a seat."

Curious, she took a chair near the window. "What's up?"

"I've heard that you and Benny Juarez have a special relationship."

Defensively, she said, "He's a wonderful little boy. I can't help loving him."

Mendez nodded. "I imagine you know a little bit about his background, but let me fill in the gaps for you. Benny's mother was fifteen when he was born. Since then, she's been married and divorced twice, she's had three other children, and now she's living with a boyfriend who has a history of abusive behavior. She's decided she can't take care of Benny."

Casey's heart skipped a beat. "Meaning?"

"Meaning," Mendez said, "she's decided to turn his custody over to the Department of Child and Family Services."

"She doesn't want him?" Casey asked in disbelief.

Mendez's mouth thinned. "I'd prefer to be kind and say she's overwhelmed."

"What will happen to him?"

"He'll go into foster care. If he's very lucky, he'll find adoptive parents. But the odds aren't in his favor. He's four years old, he's Hispanic, and he has a life-threatening disease." Mendez drummed her fingers idly on the desk. "There aren't many people out there willing to adopt a child with that many strikes against him."

Casey had to hunt for her voice. "Why are you telling me this?"

Mendez smiled. "Just playing a hunch," she said.

She worked her shift that night in a daze. If she'd read Ruth Mendez correctly, what the social worker was suggesting was an impossibility. Danny would never agree to taking in a child. He would have an arsenal of arguments, reasons why it wouldn't work, and every one of them would be valid.

But her heart ached for Benny, and when her shift ended at eleven, she took the T directly to the Back Bay to talk to Danny.

***

With *Heart of Darkness* getting heavy airplay, her telephone had rung incessantly all summer. As *pro bono* booking agent for the band, she'd actually had to turn down several lucrative offers because the boys were booked solid. This weekend, like the past two, they'd packed people like sardines into a Boylston Street watering hole known as The Bull Pen. Casey could hear the throbbing of the music while still on the sidewalk, and when she opened the door, sound poured out over her in a rolling wave. She warmly greeted the black giant who stood in the foyer. "Hello, Dud. How's it going tonight?"

"Hot." He flashed her a wide, white grin. "Very hot."

She checked her coat and purse and began working her way through the crowd, murmuring vague apologies and smiling distractedly at the men who turned to give her a second glance. She could feel it tonight—something loose in the room, some magic that spread like wildfire through the tangle of bodies and bound them together. It didn't always happen. There were good nights and bad ones, receptive audiences and apathetic ones. But Dud was right. Tonight, the electricity crackled in the air.

The final notes of *Heart of Darkness* faded away, and Danny hung up his microphone and left the stage. The crowd was rowdy, and he was stopped several times by spirited Saturday-night revelers. He kept darting glances her way as he worked his way through the crowd, and the set of his shoulders told her he was upset about something. He reached her at last, his face thunderous, his eyes steely. "I need some air," he said, brushing past her without stopping.

In the alley outside, he lit a cigarette and began pacing. His voice tight, he said, "Jake's quitting the band."

It was the last thing she'd expected to hear. Jake Edwards was a talented drummer, and he'd been with Danny for years. "Oh, no," she said. "Why?"

"Brenda's pregnant."

Her mouth went suddenly dry. "And?"

"And," he said bitterly, "they're flat broke. He's going to sell his drums and go to work in her father's shoe store."

"Oh, Danny. Isn't there any other way?"

"He says they've talked the subject to death, and it's the only answer. He's throwing away his whole damn future."

The warm glow inside her had gone cold. "Maybe," she ventured, "they wanted a baby."

He snorted. "*She* wanted a baby, not they. She stopped taking her birth control pills and neglected to mention it to Jake. I'd throttle any woman who ever did that to me." He ran a hand through his hair. "Not that you ever would," he added. "You have your priorities in order."

For some reason, she was having difficulty breathing. "What happens now?" she asked.

"We run an ad. Audition people. Hope to Christ we find someone we can work with." He flung his unsmoked cigarette on the ground and crushed it with his foot. "Did you feel it tonight?"

She didn't have to ask what he meant. "I felt it the minute I walked through the door."

He leaned against the dirty bricks of the building across the alley and kicked at a clump of dead weeds. "We've never sounded better, we've got more work than we can handle, and he decides to walk. Why? Why now?"

Casey thought about Benny Juarez. About Brenda Edwards, and about her own sister, Colleen. Then, squaring her shoulders, she crossed the alley to her husband. Beneath the cool silk of his shirt, his muscles were taut, hard. "We'll figure something out," she said.

And he took her in his arms.

***

The week the band began auditioning drummers, Benny Juarez left St. Peter's for the foster home of a young black couple in Mattapan. Casey could have made the trip out to Mattapan to visit, but what was the sense? Her heart had already been broken once, and she wasn't sure it could take any more good-byes. It was better for both of them if she made a clean break.

So she buried her despair in work. The drum auditions weren't going well. Jake was getting antsy because of the heat Brenda was putting on him. Travis paced and muttered and shook his head, while Danny and Rob turned down hopeful after hopeful, both of them intent on finding a drummer of Jake's caliber.

It wasn't easy. From Lowell to Fall River, every young hotshot with a drum set wanted to be a member of Boston's hottest rock band. Hoping to weed out the amateurs from the professionals, Danny reworded his ad to say *serious musicians only*. But it seemed that all the kids thought they were serious. Everybody wanted a piece of the action. So he tried again: *working musicians only*. But that was a flop, because the working musicians weren't looking for work.

A month later, when they still hadn't found anyone suitable, Brenda Edwards issued an ultimatum: her or the band. Brenda had been raised in a devout Christian home, and she'd always hated Jake's involvement with rock music, hated the late nights and the raucous atmosphere and the trashy women who threw themselves at him. Her father had offered Jake a job that he wouldn't hold open forever, and she'd already found a buyer for his drum set. Brenda made it abundantly clear that Jake's loyalty belonged to his wife. He didn't owe anything to Danny Fiore and the rest of that bunch. If they couldn't find another drummer, that was their problem, not his. It was time for Jake to settle down and become a responsible adult.

So in the end, they had to settle for what they could get. Out of the plethora of young drummers they'd auditioned, they picked Peter Farrell, a twenty-year-old from Somerville. Pete was a personable guy, slightly intimidated by Danny but eager to please. Although he had a tendency toward flashiness that Danny planned to break him of immediately, Pete's sense of rhythm and timing weren't bad, and while Danny popped Rolaids like they were candy, the band went into intense rehearsal.

And during off-hours, Casey and Rob wrote furiously.

CHAPTER NINE

Colleen and Jesse's son was a perfect, rosy-cheeked baby with wispy blond hair and his father's eyes. Mikey was healthy and alert, content to be by himself for long stretches of time, and it quickly became apparent that he had inherited his father's even temperament. Casey made the trip home to help out for the first couple of weeks, and while Mikey's mother recuperated from the rigors of childbirth, it was his Aunt Casey who fed him his bottle and changed his diapers, rocked him and sang him to sleep. When he awoke in the middle of the night, it was Casey who got up to tend him. Colleen had been through a rough labor and delivery. She needed her rest, and so did Jesse, who was burning the candle at both ends. So Casey slept on the living room couch, next to Mikey's cradle, where she could be at his side in an instant.

One night near midnight, she was curled up on the couch with the baby asleep in her arms when the phone rang at her elbow. She snatched it up immediately, afraid it would wake the entire household. At the other end, Rob said, "I knew you'd still be up."

"MacKenzie!" she scolded in a stage whisper. "Do you have any idea how late it is?"

"Sorry, pudding, but this couldn't wait. I think I've found a solution to the problem we've been having with the new song."

Her interest was immediate and focused. "So tell me already."

"Our thinking's been too narrow. After the first eight bars, we need to take off in a completely new direction. Listen." As he played the familiar intro to the song they'd been struggling with for weeks, she pondered the fact that even over the static of a long-distance phone call, the sounds he could evoke from a simple six-string guitar were almost ethereal. "Okay," he said without breaking rhythm, "here's where it changes." And he shot for the moon with a bridge that was a brilliant counterpoint to the original melody.

She felt that familiar excitement in the pit of her stomach, the sensation she always experienced when the music grabbed her and took her to some magical place beyond her own physical boundaries. When he finished playing, she was silent for several seconds, still caught up in the spell. And then she let out the breath she'd been holding and said, "How do you do it?"

He didn't ask what she meant. He didn't have to. "I don't know," he said. "It's just there." And just as he'd understood her question, she understood his answer.

"Do you want me to work on the lyrics?" she said.

"Sure. Want to hear it again?"

"I don't need to." Any melody, once heard, was permanently imprinted upon her brain. "Hey, hot stuff," she said. Thanks."

"No prob. Listen, kiddo, want to talk to your old man?"

Her heartbeat quickened. "Danny's there?"

"And chomping at the bit. Here he is. So long, babe."

And then Danny was on the line. "Hi," he said, and that velvet voice made her go warm all over.

"Hi," she answered, and they were both silent, the vibrations radiating between them as eloquent as words.

He cleared his throat. "When are you coming home?"

"Soon. Colleen needs me right now."

"I need you right now."

"Just a few more days, darling. I promise. How are things working out with Pete?"

Danny sighed. "He's a good kid and he's trying hard, but something's missing. I don't know if the audience can feel it, but I can. We've lost the sound."

"Sweetheart, you can't let him drag you down. You've worked too long and too hard."

"I don't have the heart to tell him it's not working. He's trying so damn hard. Maybe my expectations are too high."

"I'll be home in a few days," she said, "and then we'll brainstorm."

"Brainstorming isn't exactly what I had in mind for you."

"Oh, really?" Her voice softened. "What, exactly, did you have in mind?"

"I'm not at liberty to say right now. But feel free to use your imagination."

She toyed with the telephone cord. "That could get me into trouble."

"I was hoping," he said dryly, "it would remind you of where you belong."

"You have a one-track mind," she told him.

"All men have one-track minds. Some are just better at it than others."

"He said with humility. Good-night, Daniel."

"*Ciao*, baby. Sweet dreams."

She hung up the phone, her hand still lingering on the receiver, as though she could somehow prolong their contact. Her mind was still with Danny, in Boston, when Jesse said softly, "Everything okay?"

"I'm sorry," she said. "Did the phone wake you?"

"I wasn't asleep. Want a cup of coffee?"

"I'd love one."

While her brother-in-law puttered in the kitchen, Casey studied the sleeping child in her arms, the perfect head, covered with peach fuzz, the blue veins showing beneath milky, translucent skin. For just a moment, she allowed herself to pretend he was hers, instead of her sister's. And then she felt ashamed.

Jesse returned with the coffee. "You look so natural," he said, "sitting there, holding him."

"Jess," she said, "Is it too late to say I'm sorry? Do you hate me?"

"I don't hate you. I was hurt for a while, but I never hated you."

"I never meant to hurt you."

"It was my pride that was hurt, more than anything." He toyed with his coffee cup, and the baby yawned and stretched and settled back against her breast. "We were together," he said, "because everyone expected us to be. Ever since we were kids, everybody expected us to get married. It never occurred to either one of us that it might not happen."

"Instead," she said, "you married my sister. Who would have ever thought it?"

He looked into his coffee cup. "I've just been accepted to graduate school. Colleen doesn't know it yet." His mouth tightened. "She won't like it."

Surprised, she said, "Does Dad know?"

"He's the one who pushed me to do it. Who knows how long this place will be able to support two families? I already have a teaching degree. With a Master's degree in English, I'll have something to fall back on."

Her heartbeat quickened. "Is Dad in financial trouble?" she said.

"No. Nothing like that. But you know how risky farming can be."

"Well," she said, "you certainly are full of surprises."

He set down his coffee cup. "Casey," he said, "I think you should go home. You belong with your husband."

"But Colleen needs me."

"Mikey's ten days old. Colleen's had plenty of time to recuperate. I know you're just trying to help, but he needs to know who his mother is."

Casey looked down at the bundle in her arms and felt something akin to grief. Jesse was right. She'd known it since the day Mikey came home from the hospital, but because the situation had fulfilled her own needs so well, she'd stubbornly refused to face it. Her sister had allowed her to take over the role of mother, and it might continue indefinitely unless Casey relinquished that role to its rightful owner.

"I don't want you to think I'm pushing you out," he said.

"No," she said. "You're right. Mikey needs to know who his mother is. And Danny needs me. I'll take the first bus out in the morning."

***

When she opened the door, she thought for a moment that she was in the wrong apartment. She set down her suitcase and gingerly fingered the dirty tee shirt that hung at an awkward angle over the shade of her hurricane lamp. She took a step and knocked over a half-empty beer can. Its contents spilled and ran, pooling in a yellow puddle beneath the couch. Cigarette butts overflowed from the ashtray on the coffee table beside a plate that held the fossilized remains of something that might once have been food.

Rob came in from the kitchen, carrying a bag of trash and looking comical in one of her aprons. When he saw her standing in the doorway, he stopped so abruptly that Danny, following behind him with the broom and dustpan, crashed into him. Danny looked up and met her eyes. "Shit," he said.

Rob said, "It's not Danny's fault. Really," at the same time Danny said, "Honey, it's not as bad as it looks." And then they both fell silent.

"I'm not even going to dignify this with a comment," she said. "What I am going to do is turn around and walk back out that door. And when I come back—" She closed her eyes and shuddered. "And when I come back, this unspeakable mess had better be cleaned. Got that, boys?"

She slammed the door in their faces.

Mary MacKenzie was delighted to see her. The matronly redhead folded Casey into her arms. "Come in, come in. I was just about to make tea."

While the water heated, she told Rob's mother about the condition she'd found her apartment in. Mary clucked in sympathy. "They'll clean it," she said, pouring hot water into Casey's cup. "Both of those boys worship the ground you walk on. Men! You can't live with 'em, can't live without 'em. Well, never mind them. Tell me about your sister's new baby."

Casey launched eagerly into a description of Mikey's sterling qualities. "He's gorgeous," she said. "And so strong! When he was only four days old, he pushed himself upright in my lap." She subsided into a thoughtful silence. "You know," she said, squeezing her teabag with her spoon, "I envy her. When I held that baby in my arms, the most incredible feeling came over me."

"Baby hunger," Mary said authoritatively.

"I know having a baby is out of the question for now," she said. "With our crazy lifestyle, it would be an impossibility. But it doesn't stop me from wishing."

"Does Danny know how you feel?" Mary asked.

"No. And I can't tell him. It would be selfish of me—"

"Selfish? To have a wee babe to hold in your arms?"

She tried to explain. "Danny's so needy. He wants so

much. And I want for him, so bad it aches. Until he gets what he wants, he has to come first."

"He's a lucky young man. I hope you know how extraordinary you are, my girl."

It was dusk when she entered her apartment to the soothing strains of Mantovani and the mingled odors of roast beef and Lysol. The floor had been scrubbed, the furniture polished to a high sheen. The table was set for two, with twin white tapers waiting to be lit. Danny came into the room, carrying matching wine glasses. He stopped when he saw her. "Hi," he said.

She took off her jacket slowly. "Hi."

He cleared his throat. "I started dinner."

"Where I come from, big boy, we call it supper."

He scowled. "Damn Yankees."

She dropped the jacket on the back of a chair. Softly, she said, "I missed you dreadfully."

"Maybe I can make it up to you," he said, twirling a wine glass by its stem. "Somehow."

"Somehow," she echoed.

He moved a step closer. "I slept on the same pillow cases the whole time you were gone, because I could smell your perfume on them."

"I slept in your old B.U. sweatshirt every night."

He opened his arms. "Come here," he said.

"God help me," she said as she walked into his arms. "When it comes to you, I have no shame."

***

An hour later, she said against his bare shoulder, "If I keep skipping meals like this, I'll waste away to nothing."

"There isn't much of you now." Danny shoved aside the bedding, reached out an arm and rummaged on the night stand, returning with an article he'd torn from the *Globe*. "I have something I want you to read."

She sat up in bed and read aloud. "*'Fiore manages, through skillful artistry, to combine the raw, pulsating vitality of a Jagger with the silken smoothness of a Sam Cooke.'* Wow. Who wrote this?"

"If I knew," he said dryly, "I'd kiss the guy."

She read and re-read the clipping, then folded her arms around her knees. "Danny," she said, "I've given this a great deal of thought. I think it's time to move to New York."

He got up from the bed and walked naked to the dresser and lit a cigarette. "I've thought about it," he admitted.

"There's only so far you can go here. And with things up in the air with the band, now is probably the time to make the break."

He blew out a cloud of smoke. "We have a real following here," he said. "People know who we are. In New York, that won't mean shit. I'd be starting all over again at the bottom of the ladder."

"You did it before," she said. "You can do it again."

He spent a few minutes digesting her words. "It's a big decision," he said. "It'll mean breaking up the band."

"The band's disintegrating right in front of your eyes, Danny. It's time to move on."

"Even if it means cutting somebody else's throat?"

"It's not a matter of cutting anybody's throat. It's a matter of survival. It all depends on what you want."

His words were clean and clipped, beautiful in their simplicity. "I want it all." He crushed out his cigarette. "The whole nine yards. Immortality. I've been kissing asses all my life. I want them to kiss my ass. I want to prove I'm more than just some bastard wop kid from Boston's Little Italy."

"You are more," she said. "Much, much more."

He returned to the bed, stretched out beside her. "This is no kind of life for you."

She stopped him with a hand on his mouth. "We agreed that I belong wherever you are. Remember?"

He kissed her fingers, one by one. "Some day, by God, I'll have it all. And when that happens, I'll make it up to you. I'll make it all up to you."

***

Six weeks later, Danny stood before the fireplace, leaning casually against the mantel. Dryly, he said, "I suppose you're wondering why I called you all here tonight."

"Great opening line, Fiore," Travis said. "Now let's get to the point."

Casey shot a quick glance at Rob, who was perched on the arm of a chair, cleaning his fingernails with a guitar pick. He held her glance for a few seconds, then returned to his manicure. Danny sat down beside her and took her hand. "Casey and I," he said, "have made a decision that affects us all. We're moving to New York."

Stunned silence greeted his announcement. "We'd like to keep the band intact," he said, "but we recognize that your priorities may not be the same as ours."

"With or without you," Casey added, "Danny and I are going."

The silence built. They were all looking at Danny, Travis glaring, Pete stunned, Rob impassive, his manicure forgotten. Danny lit a cigarette.

"Why?" Travis demanded. "We have a good thing going here."

"I've never made any secret of my ambitions." Danny drew deeply on his cigarette and exhaled slowly. "New York has clubs, agents, record companies. Casey and I are convinced that this is the right move to make."

"*Casey and I?*" Travis said. "You're letting my sister run your life now? Jesus Christ, man, if she told you to jump off the Tobin Bridge, would you do it?"

Danny crushed out his cigarette. "Her judgment is infallible."

"And the Titanic was unsinkable!"

"Subtle, Bradley, but I think we have an inkling of how you feel."

"Damn it, Danny, do you realize what you're up against?"

"Trav, try to understand: I didn't pick music. It picked me."

"Well, I'll be damned if I'm going along with this. It's the craziest thing I ever heard."

Danny shrugged and met Casey's eyes. "That's one county heard from. Who wants to be next?"

Rob and Pete exchanged glances. And Pete shook his head.

"I feel like a rat deserting a sinking ship—"

"You've got it wrong, Pete. I'm not the Titanic. This ship isn't going down."

"I'm getting married in a couple of months. Ginger would blow a gasket if I asked her to move to New York."

Danny buried his face in his hands and rubbed his eyes, and Casey squeezed his shoulder. He looked back up. "Wiz?" he said. "Are you in or out?"

Rob had returned to his manicure, and for the long moment in which he didn't answer, Casey held her breath. Then he slipped the guitar pick into his pocket. "I've had my bags packed for a month," he said. And grinned. "When do we leave?"

* * *

The day she quit her job, Travis raised the roof. "No sister of mine," he roared, "is going to take off in a crummy Chevy with two half-baked assholes who think they're musicians!"

Casey ignored him and continued packing.

"Damn it, Casey, do you have any idea how many unemployed musicians there are sleeping on the streets of New York?"

She picked up the framed photo of Mama that she kept prominently displayed on her bedroom dresser. Touching a finger to the glass, she traced Ellen Bradley's sweet smile. And squared her shoulders. "I won't end up sleeping on the streets."

"Oh, Jesus." Travis ran a bony hand through his wavy hair. "Are you hearing anything I'm saying?"

"Let's turn the tables. Are you hearing anything I'm saying?"

"To hell with you! Rot in the gutter! See if I give a damn!" And he slammed out of her apartment.

She fumed for days. "He'll come around," Danny told her. "He's just stubborn."

Rob wrote her a dirty limerick to cheer her up. Danny donated his piano to a storefront church on Tremont Street. Casey packed the clothes they needed and shipped the rest to the Salvation Army.

The day before they left, she answered the door to find her

brother standing in the hall. She greeted him coolly, not sure what to expect. He was gruff, not quite ready to forgive. They spoke to the air somewhere to the left of each other's heads. After a few minutes of this, he abruptly thrust an envelope into her hands. "Take care," he said, "and don't make a damn fool of yourself."

The envelope contained five hundred dollars.

Casey was stunned. Five hundred dollars might as well have been a million. Intuition told her to hide it away and tell neither of the men. If she was the only one who knew of its existence, it wouldn't be frittered away on non-essentials. When it was needed (she was somehow sure it would be when, not if), the money would be there to fall back on.

On a cloudless morning, the three of them squeezed into the Chevy amid guitars, clothes, sleeping bags, and assorted household items, and took the expressway south. Casey looked back once at the skyline dominated by the Pru and the brand-new John Hancock tower. And then she put the past behind her and concentrated on the future. With Danny at the wheel, Rob's arm across the back of the seat behind her, and "The Ballad of John and Yoko" on the radio, they cranked the volume and sang their way out of Boston.

BOOK TWO

CHAPTER TEN

New York City
Summer, 1978

The apartment was in the Village, upstairs over Wong's
Tea House, where the mingled odors of soy sauce, fried pork,
and strong Chinese tea drifted up the gloomy stairwell and
through the open windows. The rent was exorbitant, the toilet
ran steadily, and cockroaches roamed at night as though they had
a lifetime lease. There was only one bedroom, so Rob slept on
the couch that Casey picked up for twenty dollars at a
secondhand shop. He got the best of the deal, because the
bedroom window was painted shut. Casey and Danny sweated
away the summer nights, while Rob lay in semi-comfort beneath
an open window.

They pooled their money in a communal fund, with Casey
as the designated bookkeeper. New York was not a cheap place
to live. When the first of each month came around, Casey often
had to scrape to make ends meet. Some months they didn't quite
meet. At other times, when one of them had an unexpected
windfall, there was money for extras, as well as money to put
away for the next dry spell. Casey was a quick learner. Creative
financing (also known as robbing Peter to pay Paul) became her
modus operandi, and the two men, with their implicit trust in her,
never questioned her judgment. If Casey said, "We can't
afford..." they both knew the issue was closed to further
discussion.

The one luxury she allowed was a telephone, because no
working musician could survive without a point of contact. She
bought whole-wheat flour from the natural foods store down the
street and made her own bread in the antiquated oven that every
so often belched clouds of black smoke. Late into the nights,
they drank cheap Chianti and played their music, talked and

laughed and laid out elaborate career strategies, dreamed aloud their impossible dreams.

And during the days, they looked for work.

***

Even at midday, the place smelled of beer and stale cigarette smoke. Weak sunlight filtered through the filthy windows and passed between chair legs pointed ceilingward from empty tabletops. The man behind the bar was squat and compact, his face swarthy and pock-marked beneath a thick tumble of dark hair. He deftly polished a glass and hung it in the rack over his head. "I'd like to give you kids a break," he said, "but I got no money to pay a singer. I gotta tend bar myself 'cause I can't even afford a bartender."

"Will you please just listen to him?" she said. "We've been in New York for two years, and we've had nothing but doors slammed in our faces!"

"Two years? Two years is nothing, lady. This is New York. Singers here are a dime a dozen."

"Not singers like him!" Casey said.

He sighed and picked up his rag. "You two look like a coupla nice kids. Let me give you a word of advice. Get the hell out of New York and go on back where you came from. Show business ain't all it's cracked up to be."

"Screw it," Danny said, and picked up his guitar and stalked out of the bar.

"Why?" Casey demanded. "Why won't you even listen to him?"

"I already told you, lady, I got no money to pay a singer."

"He'll work for tips!"

He paused to study the determined set of her chin. "You don't intend to give up, do you?"

"Not until you hear him."

"Okay. You win. I'll listen to him. God knows why, because there's no way in hell I can hire him. But the kid must have something going for him to have a gorgeous dame like you pushing this hard for him."

"Thank you," she said. "Thank you!"

"Hey!" he yelled as she raced for the door. "Just remember, I ain't giving him a job!"

She found Danny outside, leaning against the building, smoking a cigarette. "Danny," she said, "come back in. He's agreed to listen to you."

Those blue eyes regarded her coldly. "Screw him," he said, and tossed the cigarette in the gutter.

The anger rose unexpectedly. "Is that what you want?" she said. "Is that what you really want?"

Danny glared at her for a moment, then sighed. "No," he said. "It's not."

So they went back inside and he sat on a wooden bar stool beneath a lit Budweiser sign and sang *Elevator Embrace*, a love ballad she'd written the previous summer. When he was finished, a fly buzzed in the stillness. A lone patron at the end of the bar stared into his beer. The bartender set down his rag and came around the bar. "What'd you say your name was, kid?"

Danny lay his guitar flat across his lap. "Fiore," he said. "Danny Fiore."

"Well, Fiore, I'll give you five bucks a night, plus whatever you get in tips. Three nights a week, Friday, Saturday, Sunday. You play whatever the patrons want to hear. Any funny stuff and you're out on your ass. *Capisce?*"

Danny looked at him long and hard. And nodded. "*Capisce.*"

"And you might want to thank your lady friend, here. I never woulda listened to you if it hadn't been for her."

***

Juggling. He was always juggling.

Two years in New York had turned Rob MacKenzie into a jack of all trades. His balancing act included the occasional fill-in gig, intermittent studio work, one part-time job parking cars, and another making deliveries for a Korean grocery. He filled in the cracks between jobs by giving guitar lessons for six bucks an hour, drawing his students from ads tacked up in Laundromats and coffee houses and on bulletin boards at Columbia and NYU. He squeezed in songwriting time in bits and pieces, and in what he jokingly referred to as his spare time, he and Casey wore holes in their shoes trudging from publisher to publisher, demo tapes and portfolio in hand, hawking their songs.

Everywhere they went, they heard variations on the same theme: *Nice hook, but it's too commercial/Nice hook, but it's not commercial enough.* The excuses varied, but the bottom line was always the same: thanks, but no thanks.

At least the studio work was beginning to bear fruit. He was building a reputation as an axeman who not only possessed the necessary chops but who could always be depended on to show up on time, clean and sober, and earn every penny of his pay. So even though the world wasn't exactly beating a path to his door, enough studio work came his way to pay the bills. He was doing what he loved and getting paid for it, and in Rob MacKenzie's book, that made him a rich man.

It was his love life that was dismal.

In his matter-of-fact way, Rob accepted the fact that he was no Adonis. In spite of his lanky body and his odd assortment of features, women had always found him attractive. He'd never been able to figure out what it was about him that attracted them, but he didn't waste time dwelling on it. He was too busy enjoying, for Rob MacKenzie liked women. He liked the way they walked, the way they smelled, the silken feel of their skin. Maybe that was part of his charm: Rob not only liked women, he respected them. Most guys treated females like they were nothing more than a collection of body parts. Rob didn't buy into that philosophy. He liked to make love to the entire woman, not just to some faceless body. As a result, he often remained friends with a woman long after any sexual relationship between them had ended.

But in New York, he had little opportunity to meet women, less time to spend with them, and no privacy at home. And the women had it no better. Any woman who could afford to live alone was out of his league. So Rob MacKenzie, for the first time since he'd lost his virginity at seventeen, was going without.

Then he met Nancy Chen.

It was 4:15 on a Friday afternoon, and he was one of a handful of people riding the escalator down to the first floor of Bloomingdale's. If fate hadn't intervened, he never would have noticed the woman a few steps ahead of him. But as she stepped off the escalator, the belt to her raincoat caught in the mechanism, yanking her off balance and imprisoning her.

Rob dropped his shopping bag and rushed to her rescue. He lost a brief tug-of-war with the escalator, whose jaws refused to release their prisoner, and in a desperate move, he yanked the belt free from its loops and let it go. While he and the woman watched in silence, the machine sucked it in, like a single strand of spaghetti, and swallowed it. Then, simultaneously, they turned to look at each other.

And his heart hit the soles of his sneakers.

Common sense told him she was all wrong for him. Nancy was the elder daughter of a wealthy Park Avenue cardiologist, in her junior year of pre-med at Columbia, and, as she explained to him over coffee, she didn't have time for dating. Besides, her parents disapproved of interracial marriage, and Nancy, being a dutiful daughter, had promised to date only Chinese boys. She explained regretfully that although she found him attractive, anything more than a platonic relationship between them was out of the question.

He didn't hear a word she said.

She was the most exquisite creature he'd ever seen, and he wanted to spend the next thousand years studying the graceful movements of her hands, the sway of her black hair, framing her face in a silken curtain, the trembling of her full lower lip when she gazed at him from beneath sooty lashes.

But it wasn't meant to be. She was already late for dinner, and her parents would be worried. She thanked him politely for the coffee and for rescuing her from the clutches of the Bloomingdale's monster, shook his hand, and walked out of his life.

He watched her disappear into the rush hour crowd jamming the Lexington Avenue sidewalk. And then he did what any red-blooded American male would have done.

He followed her.

***

Early morning fog swirled around Manhattan's upper east

side, and Rob tried to look inconspicuous as he leaned against a lamp post a few doors down from Nancy Chen's apartment building. But in this neighborhood, inconspicuous was impossible, and if the doorman saw him, he'd have the NYPD on his ass and some big-time explaining to do.

A blue-haired matron in a full-length fox fur appeared out of the fog with some kind of leggy dog on a leash. Like Cassius, the dog had that lean and hungry look. Translated, that meant he probably ate scrawny young guitar players for breakfast. The dog bared his teeth. The woman paused, and Rob saw a momentary flash of fear on her face. He smiled his most engaging smile, and she sniffed, averted her eyes, and hurried past.

So much for charming the local gentry.

Nancy emerged from her building, wearing a leather coat that screamed affluent and carrying a red canvas bag large enough to hold the Statue of Liberty in case she got a sudden urge to tote it around. She greeted the doorman and strode briskly in Rob's direction, and he stepped away from the lamp post and planted himself squarely in her path.

She nearly collided with him. Conflicting emotions flitted across her face. It was dismay that remained. "What are you doing here?" she asked.

"Waiting for you."

She shot a glance over her shoulder. "How did you find out where I live?"

For a smidgen of a second, he felt guilty. But it passed. "I followed you home the other night," he said.

Her eyes widened. "If we are seen together," she said, "there will be trouble. Meet me at the bus stop around the corner."

In the anonymity of the crowd waiting for the bus, nobody gave them a second glance. "Why are you following me?" she asked. "I told you I don't date white boys."

"Who's talking about dating? Can't we just be friends?"

"I can see it in your eyes," she said. "You want to be more than friends."

The bus chugged up in a cloud of exhaust fumes. The door opened, and the line of people began to crawl. "What difference does it make," he said, "what your parents think? You're over eighteen. It's your life."

Nancy dropped her fare into the slot and moved on, and the line came to a halt while Rob scrounged in his pockets for change. "Move it, bud," some guy behind him said. "You think we got all day?" The hair on the back of his neck stood up, but he ignored the gibe, dropped his money into the slot and plunked into the empty seat beside Nancy. "If you really wanted to see me," he said, "you could."

"I am Chinese," she said. "I was raised to honor my elders, for they have more wisdom than I."

"Are you telling me you're not capable of making your own decisions?"

"It isn't a matter of capability. It is a matter of honor and respect."

"Well, I happen to honor and respect you. Doesn't that count?"

"I'm afraid," she said, "that what you feel for me has little to do with honor and respect, and more to do with hormones." She stood up. "Excuse me," she said, swaying as the bus came to an abrupt halt. "This is my stop."

He chased her down the aisle of the bus. When they reached the sidewalk, she took off at a pace so brisk he had to sprint to catch up with her. "At least let me carry your bag," he said.

"I'm quite capable of carrying it myself." She paused in front of a brick building with a wide granite staircase. "My first class begins in five minutes," she said. "I'm sorry, but I must say good-bye now."

As a stream of college students flowed around them, he said, "I'm not giving up this easy. I'm Irish. I don't know when to quit."

A flicker of a smile lit her face. "Good-bye, Rob MacKenzie," she said. "It has been very nice knowing you."

And without a backward glance, she walked away.

***

Danny raced through the Hotel Montpelier's service

entrance, buttoning the shirt he'd changed on the uptown bus. Tucking it into his pants, he stopped to examine his reflection in the huge stainless steel refrigerator. Using the refrigerator as a mirror, he ran a comb through his hair and tied the black bow tie that completed his stunning ensemble.

The kitchen was in its usual chaos. Enrico, the head chef, saw him with the comb and began wailing about sanitation. In Italian, Danny told him to kiss ass, and the older man stomped off, muttering that it hadn't been this way when he was a boy in *Firenze*. Leon, the young black guy who bused tables to pay his way through law school, swung through the double doors from the dining room. "Where you been, man?" he asked in that molasses drawl. "You better watch out for Emile. He's gunning for your lily-white ass."

"Great." He grimaced at his reflection. "Will I pass muster?"

"You'll do, Fiore. But Emile's some ripped. He's looking to have your head on a silver platter."

The petite, effeminate Emile Lafonde had been blessed with the personality of a scorpion, and he was the bane of Danny's existence. Emile was a monster, and this was the third time in two weeks that Danny had been late. The odds were not stacking up in his favor. "Wish me luck," he said, and swung through the doors into the dining room.

Emile saw him instantly. The little man stiffened, drew himself up to his full five-three, and picked his way distastefully through the maze of tables. Hoping to avoid him, Danny snatched up a tablecloth and a pair of place settings and began to set up the nearest empty table. But Emile was not to be deterred. "Ah, Mr. Fiore," he said to Danny's back. "You decided to grace us with your presence."

"I put in my time." It killed him, having to kowtow to the little asshole, but he didn't relish the idea of going home and explaining to Casey why he no longer had a job.

"You are an embarrassment to this establishment." The *maitre d'* sniffed and rubbed his hands together, as if trying to rid them of the very essence of Daniel Fiore. "This is the last time, Mr. Fiore. Next time you can't be bothered to arrive on time, don't bother coming at all."

It was amazing how Emile's accent dissipated in direct proportion to his escalating anger. Rumor said that he'd been born and raised in Detroit, and had been no closer to Europe than a travel brochure or two. But because it was his ass on the line, Danny capitulated. "Yes, sir, Mr. Lafonde," he said stiffly. "It won't happen again."

Emile spun on his heel and stalked back to his station. "Prick," Danny said to his back. Across the room, Leon caught his eye and they exchanged a quick, irreverent grin. Then the dining room began to fill, and he no longer had time to think about Emile.

The Montpelier was one of the most exclusive hotels in Manhattan, catering to the rich and the super-rich, and it was not uncommon to see well-known politicians, best-selling authors, and stars of stage and screen dining there. The men wore Armani suits and the women reeked of diamonds and Chanel No. 5, and although the cynical side of him thought it was bullshit, he was still hick enough to be impressed when John Travolta or Teddy Kennedy walked in.

Tonight, there were no celebrities, just the usual upper-crust types who looked through him as though he were invisible. At least the men looked through him. The women were another story. Most of them had hungry eyes, and they watched him with a ferocity that was as frightening as it was comical. He was used to it by now and paid them little attention. Although they looked and smelled heavenly, underneath the surface most of them were middle-aged and desperate. Not a one could hold a candle to his wife. Why go out for hamburger when you had sirloin at home?

But the babe in the black dress had him intrigued. She was tall and elegant, strikingly understated in pearls and a simple black number that had probably set her back half a grand. Her sleek blond hair fell past those elegant shoulders, and her makeup was subtle and artfully applied. Probably pushing forty, she looked about twenty-seven. And she'd been watching him ever since Emile had seated her.

He refilled her water glass, and she studied him, sharp eyes missing nothing, including the gold ring on his finger. "Hello, gorgeous," she purred. "What's your name?"

"Sigmund," he said dryly. "Sigmund Freud."

Their eyes met, and he felt that tiny flash of recognition, that acknowledgment that they found each other sexually attractive. Ancient and rusty instincts creaked to life inside him. In a previous lifetime, he'd spent many an hour dallying with women such as this one. It had been one hell of a turn-on, back in those days, the way women looked at him, the way they touched him, and as often as not, he'd been the aggressor. The challenge of the pursuit, the inevitable acquiescence of the woman, had been as exciting to him as the sex itself.

And then he'd met Casey, and he'd been transformed overnight into that most foreign of creatures, the monogamous male. Not that he was dead. He still looked at women, still found them attractive. But that was as far as it ever went, because he was a married man, crazy in love with his wife, and in four years of marriage, he'd been unfailingly faithful.

The woman laid a manicured hand on his sleeve. "I'm from out of town," she said, "and I don't know anybody in New York." Those slender fingers worked their way up his arm to his bicep. "I bet you could show me a few of the local hot spots."

"I'm married," he said.

"So? Why should we let a little thing like that stop us?"

"I'm afraid that my wife would take a dim view of that philosophy."

"Yes," she said, "I imagine she would. Not that I blame her. If you belonged to me, I'd keep you locked up."

Emile was watching him with narrowed eyes. Pretending he had an urgent errand in the kitchen, Danny swung through the doors and out of Emile's sight. He set down the water pitcher and kept going, out the back door and into the alley beyond.

He lit a cigarette and leaned against the building. It was a clear, cool night, and between skyscrapers he caught a glimpse of starlight, something as rare in New York as faithful husbands. It was the first time in four years of marriage that he'd actually been tempted, and the urge took him by surprise. So did the guilt that assailed him, guilt that was totally unwarranted. No court in the land would convict him on the basis of a few moments of libidinous fantasizing.

He finished the cigarette. Tossing the butt on the ground,

he went back to the dining room and busied himself clearing dirty dishes from a table where two middle-aged couples had just finished dissecting the newest Broadway show. Picking up the tray, he swung away from the table, and nearly collided with the blonde.

Her eyes were brown, and she was just a few inches short of his six-four. In her hand, she held a folded greenback.

"This," she said, tucking it into his hip pocket, "is for you." Her hand lingered, and through black cotton he could feel her heat. She sashayed back across the dining room in that tight black dress, pausing in the doorway to look back at him, and sweat pooled beneath his arms.

He carried the tray to the kitchen and turned it over to Rory, the dishwasher. Behind Rory's back, he reached into his pocket and withdrew the bill and something else, something solid. Heart thumping, he unfolded the hundred-dollar bill and gawked at the room key she'd tucked inside.

Jesus Christ Almighty.

For four hours, that greenback burned a hole in his pocket. There was no way he could keep her money and retain a shred of pride. He thought about leaving the whole kit and caboodle in an envelope at the front desk, but could imagine the raised eyebrows if he handed the desk clerk a room key and a C note and asked him to give them to the anonymous lady in Room 508. His wife, who worked the morning shift, would hear about it before breakfast tomorrow.

There was only one thing he could do. He was going to have to return the damn money in person.

When his shift ended, he took the back elevator to the fifth floor, avoiding the lobby and any chance of being recognized. When the elevator doors whispered open, he looked right and left before stepping out. If he got caught up here, his ass would be in a sling.

It was past eleven, and his footsteps fell silently, muffled by the plush carpeting. Behind closed doors, he heard hushed conversation, an occasional burst of laughter, the drone of a television. He stopped before the door to her room, feeling like he was about to face his own execution. Knocked briskly, then waited, hands in his pockets, rehearsing what he would say. *I believe I have something that belongs to you.* Cool and sophisticated, with just the right amount of charm. He would let her down easy. He'd always been good at turning women down without making it seem like a rejection. Inside his pocket, he turned the key over and over in his hand, traced its jagged edge with his thumb.

He heard her fumbling with the lock, and he closed his fist over the key as the door swung inward. Opened his mouth to speak, and the words died in his throat. She wore a filmy, diaphanous nightgown that didn't even attempt to hide the slender hips and the firm, high breasts beneath. As the husband in him warred with the man who'd resided there longer, the key in his hand sliced through tender flesh and drew blood. "Hello, lover," she said. "I've been waiting."

And Daniel Fiore the man stepped through the door, leaving Daniel Fiore the husband outside in the hall.

***

At this time of night, he could almost think of this dump as home. Darkness went a long way toward making it tolerable. So did the fact that Freddie Wong had recently broken down and paid for an exterminator. The night sounds of the city drifted through the open window and mingled with Rob's soft snoring. Casey had left the night light on for him in the kitchen. The clock read 2:10, and he wondered if she was asleep.

Sweet, suffering Jesus. How the hell was he going to face Casey?

He hadn't meant for it to happen. There'd been nothing meaningful about the act. It had been brief and hard and violent, undiluted by emotion, the slaking of pure animal drives. When it was over, the woman lay trembling on the carpet, one slender arm thrown across her face, and he lay looking at her, chest heaving, not sure which of them he was more disgusted with. He'd gone into her bathroom and washed himself and made an attempt to straighten his clothes. When he returned, she was slumped against the foot of the bed, still naked, a lit cigarette in her hand.

"Wow," she said.

He had pulled the hundred from his pocket and held it out toward her and released it. It fluttered slowly to the carpet, and those elegant eyebrows lifted in puzzlement. "What's this?" she said.

"I may be a son of a bitch," he said, "but I'm not a whore."

He'd hit the nearest bar and pounded down Budweisers until he ran out of money and excuses. How the hell could he explain to Casey why he'd been unfaithful when he didn't understand it himself? Casey thought he'd hung the moon. If she ever found out what he'd done, she would leave him.

She would leave him.

He stumbled in the darkness to the bathroom and locked the door and vomited. The booze didn't feel much different coming up than it had going down. He flushed the toilet and turned on the shower and stripped.

There was a soft knock on the door. "Danny?"

Every muscle in his body went on alert. "I'm taking a shower," he said.

Was it something in his voice that made her hesitate? "It's late," she said through the door. "I expected you hours ago."

He wet his lips. "I stopped off for a few drinks before I came home." It was the truth. Just not all of it.

She hesitated again. "Is everything all right?"

"I'm a little hammered, that's all. Go on back to bed. I'll be along in a few minutes."

His trusting wife did what he asked, leaving him feeling like a life form lower than raw sewage. He adjusted the water temperature to scalding and scrubbed himself violently in an attempt to remove the smell, the taste, the memory of the woman from his body. When he was done, he stood wet and naked in front of the lavatory and brushed his teeth until his gums bled, wanting to hurt, to punish himself for betraying her trust. He caught sight of himself in the mirror and turned away in disgust, unable to face the accusation in his own eyes.

By the time he crawled into bed, Casey had gone back to sleep. He lay stiff as a California redwood, feeling sullied and dirty, afraid that if he touched her, some of that dirt would rub off. Still asleep, she found him, pressing soft, round breasts close against his back, her damp heat radiating outward, into and through his resistant body. The coppery taste of fear flooded his mouth, a fear not unlike that he'd known in Nam. Then, it had been fear of death. Now, it was fear that he would lose this woman, and as a result, he would cease to exist.

In the end, wasn't it the same thing?

***

It was raining outside the coffee shop, a driving rain that gushed in the gutters and flooded the storm drains. Cars passed with headlights on, their illumination bouncing off gleaming surfaces, while businessmen and secretaries scurried, huddling beneath umbrellas, sidestepping puddles.

Danny looked like hell this morning. Of course, Rob mused as he sipped his coffee, even hell was relative. In spite of the rainslicked hair, the bloodshot eyes he'd hidden behind mirrored sunglasses and the whisker stubble he hadn't bothered to hide, Danny still looked better than Rob had ever looked in his twenty-four years. He wondered what it would be like to be blessed with the face and the physique of a Greek god, but he didn't expect to ever know.

When Danny had offered to spring for coffee and bagels, he hadn't given it a second thought. They often had breakfast together when Casey was working the early shift. Their hectic schedules usually overlapped, so when they could grab a few minutes together, they did. It helped keep the lines of communication open. But this morning, there was zero communication. Danny had paid for their breakfast and then sat staring out the window, and it was his silence that told Rob something was eating at him.

He took a sip of coffee. "How'd it go?" he asked.

Danny looked at him blankly. "The studio gig?" he prompted. "Backup vocals? Ring a bell yet?"

Danny ran a hand through his wet hair. "It went fine," he said. "I appreciate you giving them my name." He broke off a portion of his bagel and concentrated on covering it with orange marmalade.

Rob rapped his knuckles on the table top. "Okay, Fiore," he said, "what's eating you? You're acting like your favorite dog just got run over by a sanitation truck."

Danny set down his knife and looked at him. "Three nights ago," he said, "I cheated on my wife."

It took a moment for the meaning of his words to sink in, and even then, Rob thought he was joking. "Right," he said. "And I'm the Prince of Wales."

Danny continued as though he hadn't heard. "I made it with some blond bimbo upstairs at the Montpelier."

He realized then that Danny wasn't kidding. "Jesus Christ," he said.

Danny looked at his bagel. "I didn't mean to do it," he said. "I'm still not sure how it happened."

Rob's stomach had gone sour. "Maybe I should draw you a picture," he said. "Listen, Dan, I really don't think I want to hear this."

"You're my goddamn best friend! Who the hell else can I tell?"

"What the hell do you want from me? Absolution?"

"I love her, Wiz. I don't know what to do."

Rob shredded a piece of bagel. "You should have thought of that a little sooner."

"If I don't tell her," Danny said, "I'll be lying, and that compounds my sin. If I do tell her, she'll throw me out."

Rob leaned over the table. "If you tell her, Fiore, I'll drag you down to the bus station and shove your head in the toilet and hold it there until you stop kicking."

"I'm glad," Danny said dryly, "that we've clarified whose side you're on."

"What do you expect? That woman worships the ground you walk on."

"She'll know anyway," Danny said. "Even if I don't tell her, she'll know."

"How the hell will she know if you don't tell her?"

"Be serious, MacKenzie. This is my wife we're talking about. Casey knows everything. She knows it by fucking osmosis!" They glared at each other, but he didn't dispute Danny's claim, because it was the truth. "She's too good for me," Danny said. "I don't deserve her."

"No, Dan," he said, "you don't."

Something irreplaceable was slipping away from him. He'd always been slightly in awe of Danny Fiore, had always seen him as larger than life. But today, in a single instant, Danny had become bloodily, maddeningly human, and his sudden transformation shattered every one of Rob MacKenzie's illusions.

He cleared his throat. "I thought you and Casey were okay." He'd never seen so much as a ripple on the surface of their relationship. If there'd been any problem, he of all people should have noticed.

"So did I. Christ, Wiz, what am I going to do?"

"What you're going to do is forget this ever happened. For some unfathomable reason, she loves you. If you tell her what you did, it'll kill her. And then I'll kill you."

Danny looked at him silently. "Are you in love with my wife?" he finally said.

"Jesus, Mary and Joseph." Rob buried his face in his hands. "No!" he snapped. "Are you?"

"You know damn well I am!"

"Then stop acting like a nineteen-year-old stud. Keep it in your pants, for Christ's sake!"

"It wasn't like that. I didn't come on to her. It was her game all the way."

"There's a word you need to learn, Fiore: *no*."

Danny looked at him in disgust. "Why did I bother to confide in you?"

"Because I'm your goddamn best friend, that's why!"

"Yeah," Danny said softly, "you are."

And there it was, the truth of it, laid out on the table between them. "Fiore," he said miserably, "you're a real shit."

Danny saluted him with his coffee cup. "I'm glad to see," he said dryly, "that we agree on something."

CHAPTER ELEVEN

Something was rotten in Denmark.

She'd lived with Danny for four years, and Casey knew his moods, knew his quicksilver lights and darks, as well as any woman could know a man. Something was troubling him. She could feel it in the unspoken messages that leaped between them when they touched, could see it in his remoteness, could sense it in the purple aura he'd surrounded himself with. Something was terribly wrong, something that manifested itself in bizarre behaviors like his sudden coolness towards Rob. And his sudden rejection of her.

Their relationship had always been intensely physical, and to be abruptly cut off with no explanation was, to put it mildly, mystifying. He went out of his way to avoid intimacy. He'd begun locking the bathroom door. Sleeping in an old pair of sweat pants. Erecting walls where there had been none. And she wondered, frantically, if he were having an affair.

But it didn't add up. His body still responded to her touch. Asleep, he still held her in his arms. The chemistry was still there between them, strong as ever. Danny hadn't fallen out of love with her. Something else was wrong, something she hadn't yet figured out.

But Rob knew.

She recognized it with the same certainty. After all, she'd known Rob for those same four years. Both men were hiding something from her, and that explained the coolness between them. Danny was in some kind of trouble, and Rob knew about it. And he wasn't happy about the knowing.

She cornered him one afternoon in the kitchen. He was bent over the sink, shirtless, spray nozzle in hand, his vertebrae standing out in stark relief beneath his skin. "Let me do that," she said, and took the sprayer from him. She poured shampoo into her hand and began working it through his hair. She'd never washed a man's hair before, and it was a surprisingly sensual experience. Rob had beautiful hair, thick and wavy and full of body, and she massaged it with gentle fingertips until she'd worked up a rich lather. "Watch your eyes," she said, adjusting the water temperature.

"Jesus, woman," he said, "be careful. You'll drown me."

"If I drowned you, who would I eat fudge ripple ice cream with at three in the morning?" She worked her way slowly through his mop of hair until the soap was rinsed out, then poured a dollop of conditioner into her palm. "Brace yourself," she said, "this is cold." She plunged her hands back into his hair and worked the conditioner, strand by strand, from the roots down to the tips. Casually, she said, "I don't suppose you'd care to tell me what's wrong with Danny?"

He hesitated for just a moment too long. "I don't know what you're talking about," he said.

"Oh, Rob," she said, disappointed. "Don't lie to me. You of all people."

His silence was eloquent.

"He's hardly spoken a civil word to you in weeks," she said. Sprayer in hand, she combed her fingers through his curls to remove the conditioner. "He's so remote," she added, "it's like he's living on another planet. And he hasn't—I mean, we haven't—" She floundered, uncertain of the propriety of discussing her sex life with him.

But he saved her. "I think I get the picture, kiddo," he said. "Gimme a towel."

She watched him dry his hair. Rob wasn't an unattractive man. He had well-developed biceps and a dark triangle of hair on his chest that some women would find quite sexy. He just needed to fill out, to get some meat on his bones. She'd spent the better part of two years trying to fatten him up, but he was still lanky as an old mule.

He tossed all that hair back over his shoulders. "Listen, babe," he said. "If you think Danny doesn't love you, you're wrong. He's crazy about you." He slung the towel over his shoulder and busied himself gathering up the shampoo and conditioner.

"Don't patronize me, MacKenzie. Tell me the truth."

His eyes, when they met hers, were clear and deep and green. And miserable. "Don't drag me into this," he said. "Don't make me take sides."

She knew then that it was more serious than she'd feared.

It was the worst summer of Casey's life. Danny was unreachable, New York was hot and stuffy and dirty, and for the first time since her marriage, she found herself longing for the cool pine forests of home. As the wealthy escaped the city for the summer, business at the Montpelier dropped off, and her hours were cut. June dragged on into July and July into August, bringing with it a heat wave that had sidewalks steaming and air conditioners working overtime.

She was bent over the old slate sink one hot afternoon, sweat trickling down her back, her knuckles scrubbed raw as she washed clothes with a bar of Ivory soap. Danny was down to twenty hours a week at the Montpelier, and it had been two months since Rob had picked up a studio job. Today's mail had brought a disconnect notice from the electric company, and she'd just used her last package of hamburger.

They'd been in New York for two years, and this was the lowest they'd sunk. She thought about the five hundred dollars that was sitting in a secret bank account. She hadn't touched a penny of it. It was there for a real emergency, and she'd never yet had justification for dipping into it. The money was her security. In a worst-case scenario, it would pay their way home. But once it was spent, there would be nothing to fall back on.

She could have pleaded her case to city welfare, and they would have provided her with food stamps, paid the light bill. But she'd learned at an early age that self-reliance led to self-respect, and she was too proud to ask for help. They'd survived other bad spells, and they would survive this one.

Soapy water gurgled down the drain as she pulled the plug and stepped away from the sink. Without warning, the room began to sway around her, and she clutched at the rim of the sink for support. The summer afternoon began to fade to black, and she struggled to hold onto consciousness. Iron determination kept her upright. She crossed the six feet to the table, drained and shaken, and slumped onto a chair.

It was the third time this week that she'd nearly fainted. The first time, she'd blamed it on the heat. But the second time, it had happened at work, in the air-conditioned luxury of the Hotel Montpelier's dining room.

And now it had happened again.

She'd never been sick in her life. But healthy women didn't have fainting spells, not since they'd given up wearing corsets. She thought about brain tumors, about incurable soap opera diseases. About her own mother, who had died of cancer at forty-two. She thought about the empty kitty in the kitchen and dropped her face to the tabletop in despair. She couldn't even afford to pay the light bill. How was she supposed to pay a doctor?

***

Rob called in a favor from a friend who worked in the Registrar's Office at Columbia. Armed with Nancy Chen's class schedule, two pastrami sandwiches, and every ounce of charm he possessed, he loitered outside the entrance to her classroom building, waiting for her Tuesday morning class to end.

At 12:15, Nancy emerged from the building, engrossed in conversation with some geek in a crew cut and horn-rimmed glasses. When she saw Rob, she dismissed the geek, who shuffled off toward the bus stop. Looking troubled, she said, "Why are you here?"

Her voice was as melodious as the tinkle of wind chimes on a summer evening. He held up a wrinkled brown bag. "I brought you lunch."

"How many times must I tell you, Rob MacKenzie? I won't go out with you."

"Who said anything about going out?" He gave her his most endearing smile, the one that always worked on his mother and his sisters. "We're just having lunch. Breaking bread. Taking sustenance."

Those dark eyes narrowed as she pondered his words. "If I have lunch with you," she said, "will you leave me alone?"

"Probably not."

He thought he saw a glint of humor in her eyes, but it was gone before he could be sure. "I could call the police," she said, "and have you arrested for harassment."

"You could," he agreed, "but you won't."

"And why not?"

In a lilting brogue, tongue of his fathers, he said, "Because you know I'm just a harmless Irish laddie who's besotted by your beauty and your charm and your—"

She held up a hand. "Enough. Please. I will have lunch with you. If I must listen to any more of this, I'll cry."

He settled them on a grassy spot in a small park near campus. On a red and white checked plastic tablecloth from Woolworth's he spread out a repast fit for a king and queen: two pastrami sandwiches and two kosher dill pickles, a bag of potato chips, and a warm bottle of Purple Passion grape soda. To the harmonious accompaniment of a jackhammer blasting at the end of the block and Otis Redding wailing through the open window of a nearby apartment, Rob lay on the grass, his chin propped on his hand, and watched Nancy eat.

Although her movements were dainty and her manners impeccable, her appetite was enormous for such a small woman. She matched him bite for bite, then leaned back against a tree trunk, eyes closed, and basked in the sun. "Thank you," she said at last. "That was wonderful."

"You're wonderful," he said.

Her eyes, when she opened them, were hazy and troubled. "This is so difficult," she said.

"Why?"

Otis Redding had been replaced by Aretha, asking anybody within hearing distance for a little R-E-S-P-E-C-T. "I cannot change who I am," Nancy said. "Any more than you can change who you are. We are distinctly different individuals, and this difference, I believe, is the source of our attraction to one another. But to think that a relationship between us could succeed would be pure folly."

"Maybe you just think I'm not good enough for you."

"You are good enough," she said softly. "What you are not is Chinese enough."

He gave her a beguiling grin. "So? I'll learn to eat with chopsticks."

"I wish it were that simple."

"It could be," he said, "if you'd only let it."

A breeze ruffled her skirt, baring smooth, shapely brown legs. "I'm sorry," she said.

He gathered up the remnants of their lunch, stuffing napkins and paper cups and cellophane into the paper bag and tossing it into a nearby trash container. Then he helped her to her feet. "I'll walk you back to school," he said.

Outside the classroom building, he borrowed a pen from her and scribbled on a scrap of paper. "My phone number," he said, pressing it into her palm and closing her fingers over it. "When you're ready, give me a call."

As they both studied the contrast between her skin color and his, he thought she was going to throw the scrap of paper away. Instead, she tucked it into her purse. "Good-bye, Rob MacKenzie," she said.

"*Sayonara*, kiddo."

For the first time, she smiled. "That is Japanese," she said.

He shrugged, unembarrassed. "The only Chinese words I know are wonton soup and pork fried rice."

With mock solemnity, she said, "Such ancient and honorable Chinese words."

"You'd be surprised," he said, "by how handy they are when you're ordering Chinese take-out."

"Thank you," she said, "for a most memorable lunch."

They stood, warm flesh clasped to warm flesh, eyes speaking the words they dared not say aloud, until Nancy withdrew her hand. "I must go," she said, "or I'll be late for my next class." Her smile was wistful. "Good-bye, Mr. MacKenzie."

He touched the velvet skin of her cheek. "See you around, kiddo."

As she walked away, Rob MacKenzie's heart turned to stone.

***

The free clinic was uptown, in Spanish Harlem. Most of the patients were either black or Hispanic, but they couldn't turn Casey away just because she was white. If she couldn't afford to go elsewhere, they were obligated to treat her.

The young doctor with the Afro examined her thoroughly, then left her alone to dress. When he returned, Casey sat on the end of the examining table, hands clasped together, knuckles white. "Mrs. Fiore," the doctor said, "when was the date of your last menstrual period?"

"Three weeks ago," she said. "Why?"

"Was it normal? Shorter or longer than usual? Was your flow heavier or lighter than usual?"

"Why?" She leaned forward. "What's wrong with me?"

"Nothing's wrong. You're ten weeks pregnant."

Casey was stunned. She hadn't even considered the possibility of pregnancy. "That's impossible," she said. "I'm on the pill."

"Even the pill isn't foolproof."

She spent that afternoon walking the streets of Manhattan in a daze. She had longed so desperately for a baby. But now that she was confronted with the prospect of motherhood, she felt a dismay bordering on despair. They were broke, Danny's career was at a standstill, and her marriage was falling apart. Half the time the refrigerator was empty, and she'd been wearing the same shoes for two years. How could she provide security to an infant under those circumstances?

The future of her marriage was looking less and less certain. She'd tried everything she knew to break through Danny's wall of silence, but he'd failed to respond. They had become two strangers sleeping in the same bed. How could she justify having a baby when her life was disintegrating before her eyes?

In Washington Square Park, she watched a little girl in a yellow sun dress playing with the pigeons. Squealing with delight, the child swooped down on the flock, and they scattered with a flutter of wings and soft coos of reproach. The girl ran back to her mother and scrambled up onto her lap, and Casey felt a pang of jealousy so acute it took her breath away. She wanted a child's sticky kisses and grubby hands. She wanted a little girl she could dress in ruffles and lace. Or overalls and a baseball cap. A laughing child with her chin and Danny's eyes. But her hope wasn't realistic. Not at this point in time. There was no way she could keep this baby.

She was going to have to terminate the pregnancy.

***

After two weeks of hell, the heat wave had finally broken. Rain was falling in a downpour, and Rob hunched his shoulders and thanked God that he was a block from home.

Last night's gig had lasted until two, and he'd been up again at five-thirty for a shift of parking cars. This morning Ramon had caught him sleeping again. He'd only dropped off for a minute, but Ramon had carried on like it was hours. He wasn't sure how much longer he was going to make it, living this fractured life. If he could crash for a couple of days he'd be okay, but this sleeping in bits and pieces was killing him.

The apartment was silent. He tossed his sodden shirt on the floor and searched the laundry basket for a towel. His stomach rumbled as he vigorously toweled his hair. He was going to eat everything in the refrigerator that wasn't green, and then he was going to take a long, hot shower and crash for the next twelve hours.

He found Casey in the dark kitchen, bent over a cup of coffee so old the milk had curdled on top. "What gives?" he said, flipping on the overhead light. "They cut off our electricity or something?"

She snatched up her coffee cup and emptied it into the sink. "Do you have to sneak up on me like that?" she snapped.

He raised both eyebrows. "Excuse me for living."

She scrubbed furiously at the empty cup with a dishcloth. Skirting her, he opened the refrigerator and scrutinized its contents. He discovered some leftover hash in a plastic margarine tub, and half a grapefruit that wasn't too shriveled. Kicking the door shut, he dropped his bounty on the table and opened the drawer to get a fork.

It was then that he noticed the quaking of her shoulders. He stopped, fork in hand, to stare at her in astonishment. Casey was not a weeper. In all the years he'd known her, he'd never seen her cry. "Hey," he said, more gently, "are you okay?"

"I'm fine." She rinsed the cup with trembling hands. "Eat your lunch."

"You're not fine." He set down the fork and caught her by the shoulders and turned her so that he could see her face. A tear rolled down her cheek, and he wiped at it clumsily with his thumb. "Hey," he said. "What is it?"

"I'm pregnant."

His hands tightened on her shoulders until he realized he must be hurting her. He released her and crossed his arms. "Have you told Danny yet?" he asked.

"I can't."

"What do you mean, you can't? After a while, kiddo, it gets pretty hard to hide."

Come on, Rob. You know I can't have a baby right now."

"Why not?"

"Think about it. What do you think Danny would do if I told him I was pregnant?"

"Before or after the screaming?"

She didn't laugh, and he wanted to kick himself for making a joke out of it. "It's not that bad," he said. "Danny will adjust to the idea."

"Look at the way we're living. Half the time we don't have enough to eat. Imagine bringing a baby into the picture. Danny would go out and get some nine-to-five job, and that would be the end of his career, his dreams, everything. Can you picture him punching a cash register at Macy's?"

He tried to, but couldn't. Like him, Danny was wedded to his music. "What are you going to do?"

"I've weighed all the options. I'm going to have an abortion."

"Jesus Christ, Casey, women die having abortions!"

Quietly, she said, "I won't die."

He drummed his fingers on the edge of the sink. "I think you should talk this over with Danny."

"Danny would never let me go through with it."

"How are you supposed to pay for it?"

She peeled back a piece of her thumbnail. "Travis gave me some money when we left Boston. I've been saving it for an emergency." Her smile was humorless. "I guess this qualifies."

"I can't believe you'd do something this stupid!"

"I've looked at it from every possible angle. It's the only answer."

"Do you think I don't know how bad you want a baby?

You're being a goddamn martyr, and I'd like to shake you!"

"I'm not the saint you think I am," she told him. "If Danny gives up his career because of me, I'll lose him. I'm not letting that happen. He's everything to me, Rob, everything! So you see," she said bitterly, "I'm really looking out for my own interests. I'm taking care of number one."

He looked at his lunch and realized he'd lost his appetite. "Where do you find a doctor who does abortions?"

"This is New York, MacKenzie. You can walk two blocks here and find anything you want."

She was right. Even as he said the words, he hated himself. "Want me to ask around?"

"You'd do that for me?" she said.

"It beats letting you go to some butcher."

"And you won't tell Danny?"

"No." He sighed in defeat. "I won't tell Danny."

"I didn't mean to lay all this on you. I wasn't going to tell anyone."

"That's great, Fiore. We could have read in the papers about how you bled to death in an alley somewhere."

CHAPTER TWELVE

The hallway was deliberately nondescript. Rob knocked on the door and it swung open immediately, as though the dour-faced woman in the white uniform had been waiting for them. She silently studied them both before ushering them inside. Not much bigger than a walk-in closet, the room held a battered wooden desk and two hard chairs. Not exactly designed for comfort.

The woman held out her hand. "The money?" she said.

Casey opened her purse and pulled out a sheaf of twenty-dollar bills. The woman counted them, nodded, and tucked them into her pocket. "There's a place across the street," she told Rob, "where you can get a cup of coffee."

"I'm staying with her," he said.

The woman's nostrils flared. He'd upset her routine, and she didn't like it. She gestured toward one of the chairs. "You can wait here, then."

He squared his jaw. "I think you missed the point," he said. "I'm staying with her."

For the first time, he saw uncertainty on her face. "You can't go in there," she said. "It's not allowed."

"Either I go in with her," he said, "or she walks back out the door, with her four hundred bucks in her hot little hand."

The woman glared at him with glittering pig eyes. "I'll have to talk to the doctor," she said, and disappeared through the inner door.

Casey was staring out the window, her spine ramrod stiff. When he touched her, he could feel her quivering. "Are you sure you want to go through with this?" he said.

She squared her shoulders. "I don't have a choice."

He tightened his grip on those slender shoulders. " Danny should be here with you."

"No," she said, turning, eyes wide with terror. "If you tell, I'll never forgive you."

The nurse returned with the doctor in tow. Gray-haired and stooped, he looked more like a kindly grandfather than a man who made his living murdering unborn children. Rob tried to squelch the thought, but it wouldn't go away. "I'm sorry," the doctor said, "but we don't allow anybody inside while we're performing the procedure."

"I'm responsible for her," Rob said. "I can't let anything happen to her."

The doctor's eyes softened. "She's in no danger, son. I'm not a butcher."

Casey squeezed his hand. "I'll be all right. Wait for me here."

The door closed, and he was alone. He looked around for a magazine, but apparently these folks didn't encourage creature comforts. God forbid he should start liking the place too much. He stared at a shapeless brown water stain on the wall, cracked his knuckles and drummed his heels on the floor while visions of death and dismemberment danced through his head. He glanced at his watch. Three minutes had passed since he'd last looked at it, a year ago. How would he ever explain to Danny that he, Rob MacKenzie, was solely responsible for the death of Danny's wife?

He looked out the dirty window. Across the street, the torn canopy above the entrance to Florian's Mortuary hung limply, untouched by any earthly breezes. Was it an omen? *Jesus, Mary and Joseph.* He shouldn't have let her come. He should have told Danny what was going on. He should have—

The door opened, and he shot to his feet and looked at his watch in bewilderment. He'd never attended an abortion before, but he was pretty sure it took more than five minutes. Casey came out alone, still looking terrified, but some of the color had returned to her face. And he knew. "You didn't do it," he said.

"I couldn't," she said. "I couldn't go through with it."

Relief washed over him in a gargantuan wave. "You did the right thing, babe," he said. "I'm so proud of you."

"Easy for you to say. Danny'll have a coronary."

He folded her into his arms. "Danny," he said, "will get over it."

***

She decided to tell him about the baby after dinner. There was no sense in procrastinating. Somehow, she would make Danny see that her pregnancy wasn't the disaster it seemed. Maybe it was even a blessing in disguise. Maybe the birth of a child would revitalize their flagging marriage.

When seven-thirty rolled around and he didn't show, she wasn't concerned. Occasionally, when the Montpelier was hit particularly hard, Emile would ask Danny to stay late. With finances as tight as they were, Danny never turned down a chance to make extra money. She ate alone, setting aside a plate in case he came in hungry. Rob came in at nine-thirty, showered, and went directly to bed. At ten-twenty, when Danny still hadn't come home, worry began to gnaw at her. She dialed the Montpelier and asked for the dining room.

To her relief, it was Leon who answered. But her relief was short-lived. "He got fired," Leon drawled. "Smack in the middle of dinner. Called Emile a flaming fag, ripped off his bow tie and stomped out. Best entertainment most of these slick dudes have seen all year."

At midnight, she went to bed, but sleep eluded her. Instead, she watched the hands of the clock turn with agonizing slowness. It wasn't until daylight that she heard Danny's key in the lock, and she began to tremble from a combination of relief and fury.

He stumbled into the bedroom, his clothes rumpled, the stench of alcohol ripe on his breath. Slumping heavily on the edge of the bed, he pressed his face into his palms. "I got fired," he said.

"I heard." She struggled with conflicting urges: to comfort him in her arms, to pummel him with her fists. Not sure which urge was stronger, she said, "Where the hell have you been all night?"

"Around."

In disbelief, she said, "I've been lying here awake for six hours, and you've been *around*? Do you have any idea how worried I've been?"

"You should know better than to worry. If I survived Nam, I can survive the streets of New York."

Her fertile imagination, as she lay awake, had pictured in

vivid detail every conceivable horror that could have befallen him: kidnapping, arrest, mugging, hit-and-run. She'd pictured him maimed in a gutter, dead at the bottom of the East River. A white-hot fury enveloped her. "How stupid of me," she snapped. "I forgot you were invincible."

Avoiding her eyes, he lit a cigarette and began pacing the bedroom. "I warned you when you married me," he said, "that I wasn't perfect." He took a long drag on the cigarette and blew out the smoke. "I don't know why you should be so surprised."

"This goes way beyond imperfection, Danny. Try irresponsible, immature, and callous, just for starters."

The smoke rose in a lazy arc above his head as he stopped in front of the dresser and busied himself lining up her perfume bottles with military precision. "I shouldn't have married you," he said. "It was a mistake."

"Why?"

"Because I'm damn poor husband material." He picked up her bottle of Charlie, uncapped it, and took a whiff. "I'm no good for you," he said, replacing the cap. "I'll just drag you down into the mud." He lined the bottle up with the others. "I've thought it all through," he said to the wall. "I think you should go home. Back where you belong."

"What's going on, Danny?" she said. "What's really happening here?"

"It's not working," he said. "I've tried. Christ knows, I've tried. But I'm not cut out for marriage."

"What are you saying? That you want a divorce?"

He walked to the window and leaned his forehead against the glass. "Yes," he said.

Fighting panic, she said, "I won't give it to you! I'll fight you every damn step of the way!"

He hunched his shoulders. "Can't you get it through your head," he said hoarsely, "what I'm trying to tell you? I can't be what you want me to be."

"I don't care," she said, close to hysteria. "I want you anyway."

He whirled from the window and shouted, "Even if I can't stay out of other women's beds?"

Her body went numb very slowly. It began in the tips of

her fingers and her toes, worked its way up her arms and her legs, settling somewhere in the region of her heart. "How many?" she whispered.

"Just one," he said miserably. "Just once."

She'd never known she could feel such hatred for another human being. "You son of a bitch," she said.

On her knees on the bathroom floor, she retched again and again while Danny pounded on the locked door. "Damn it, Casey," he said, "let me in."

She flushed the toilet and staggered to her feet, caught sight of her reflection in the mirror. She was twenty-two years old and looked thirty-five. She splashed cold water on her face, while outside the door Danny pleaded with her. "Let me in, baby. Please. I have to explain to you."

She opened the door so suddenly he nearly fell through it. For a stunned moment, they stared at each other, she and this stranger, this man she'd thought she knew. Dully, she said, "Why?"

"It didn't mean a goddamn thing. You have to believe me." He ran a hand through his hair. "It happened. It's over. It doesn't matter now."

"It matters to me!" she screamed, realizing she sounded like a fishwife, but incapable of controlling herself. Danny shot a glance over his shoulder at Rob, still asleep on the couch. "To hell with him," she said bitterly. "He knows all about it, anyway. We have no secrets, do we, darling? Did you tell him all the juicy details?"

"Damn it, Casey, it wasn't like that! I told him because I didn't know where else to turn!"

"I guess that's what friends are for, isn't it? To listen to the details of each other's little peccadilloes."

"If it's any comfort to you, he threatened to kill me if I ever told you."

Rob sat up and rubbed his eyes, and Casey glared at him. Running a hand through his hair, he said to no one in particular, "I think I'll wander out to the kitchen and stand guard over the knives."

"Good plan," she said, and stalked back to the bedroom with Danny at her heels. At the bedroom door, she wheeled on him. "Get out of my sight," she said. "You make me sick."

"Where the hell are you going?"

"To work, darling. One of us has to remain gainfully employed."

He ignored her gibe. "You can't go to work," he said. "You haven't slept all night."

She flung open the closet door. "Watch me."

"I suppose you think this has been easy on me?" he said, pacing the tiny bedroom. "Feeling like slime and not knowing how to make it better?"

She pulled a blouse from its hanger. "Spare me," she said, and yanked the blouse over her head.

"We have to talk."

"Do you really think I could talk to you right now?" she said. "Right now, I want to kill you. I want to plunge a sharp knife into your black, adulterous heart."

"Look," he said, "I know you're upset. I don't blame you. But later, after you've had time to cool off, we need to sit down and discuss this like two rational adults."

Casey pulled a skirt from the closet and stepped into it. "That would be difficult, wouldn't it, darling? Since only one of us is either rational or an adult." And she slammed the bedroom door in his face.

She swept past Rob, hunched over a cup of coffee at the kitchen counter, one hand slowly massaging his temple. He met her accusing gaze. "Hey," he said, and held out both hands, palms up. "I'm just an innocent bystander."

Casey yanked open the refrigerator door and took out a carton of milk, filled a glass and lifted it to her mouth. The milk tasted as though it was on the verge of turning, and she had difficulty swallowing. It threatened to come back up, and she had to choke it back down.

The first pain struck, low in her belly, as she was returning the milk to the refrigerator. She gasped and clutched at the door handle. Rob stopped massaging his temple. "Hey," he said. "Are you all right?"

Before she could answer, she was doubled over by a second pain, stronger than the first. Her legs wobbled beneath her as something wet began to trickle between her thighs. She looked at Rob in bewilderment. "I think I'm bleeding," she said, and slithered to the floor.

He caught her before she landed. Bellowing for Danny, he eased her into a sitting position, picked up the phone and began dialing frantically as she sat bowlegged on the floor and stupidly watched the blood seeping through her skirt and puddling on the linoleum between her knees.

Danny took one look at her and all the color left his face. "Jesus," he said. "Oh, Christ."

"—having a miscarriage," Rob said into the phone. "About ten, eleven weeks along. Jesus Christ, step on it, will you? She's losing blood like crazy."

"Miscarriage?" Danny looked as though he'd been struck between the eyes with a fence post. "What the hell are you talking about?"

Rob hung up the phone. "Idiot," he said. "She's losing your baby."

***

At the hospital, they took her away from him. When they wheeled her off down the maze of corridors, it took two orderlies and a security guard to hold him back. "Let go of me, goddamn it!" Danny roared. "That's my wife!"

"Sir," one of the orderlies said, "you can't go with her."

"You're not big enough to stop me!"

"Either you cool it," the security guard said, "or I cuff you and call the boys in blue to cart your ass out of here. That what you want? Think that'll help your old lady any?"

Danny glared at that steely stare, and then, abruptly, all the starch left him. "Shit," he said, and closed his eyes. "Oh, shit."

"You gonna behave now?"

Quietly, he said, "I'll behave."

The two orderlies released him cautiously. "Listen," one of them said, "get yourself a cuppa coffee, park your ass in the waitin' area, and wait. When there's any news, you'll hear."

The coffee tasted like battery acid. He tossed it in the trash and sat with his face in his hands. All that blood. Jesus, all that blood. He'd seen it before, in Nam, guys bleeding to death before they could get help. He tried to remember the prayers the sisters had drummed into his head, but it had been too long since he'd held a rosary. "Christ," he said aloud. "Please don't let her die."

"Mr. Fiore? We need you to sign this release."

He looked stupidly at the woman in white who was holding a clipboard and pen out to him. "It's a standard surgical release form," she said, shoving the pen into his hand. "Sign and date here."

He signed the form and she was gone before he could ask any questions. He paced the windowless room, six steps across ugly gray tile and six steps back, in a desperate attempt to ward off the terror. It didn't work. His bowels were knotted and his legs felt like overcooked spaghetti. He dropped heavily to an orange plastic chair and ran his fingers through his hair. He couldn't lose her. Not now. Not ever.

A half-hour passed with interminable slowness. An hour. He questioned someone at the nurse's station down the corridor. "No news yet," he was told. "She must still be in surgery."

He returned to the tiny waiting room to contemplate life without Casey. If she died, everything in him that was human would die with her.

"Mr. Fiore?"

His heart slammed into his throat. "Yes," he said.

The name tag on the swarthy young man's lab coat read *A. Rodriguez*. "Your wife is a strong woman," A. Rodriguez said. "She's going to be fine."

"Oh, Christ." Danny buried his face in his hands again, not bothering to try to stem the tears that squeezed past his closed eyelids.

"We performed a routine D&C," Rodriguez said, "and a cauterization to stop the bleeding." He frowned. "Mrs. Fiore lost a great deal of blood. I'm keeping her overnight, just to be safe. As long as there are no complications, she can go home in the morning."

Now that the terrible moment of fear was past, Danny's body began to tremble. "I have to see her," he said.

"She's been sedated," Rodriguez warned. "She'll be groggy."

It didn't matter. He had to see her, had to touch her, had to verify that rich, red blood was still coursing through her veins. Had to make her know how much he loved her. "I've made a damn fool of myself," he told Rodriguez. "I have to try to set it right."

She was lying with her face turned to the wall. He sat in the chair beside the bed, picked up her hand and held it to his lips. "I'm sorry," he whispered. "I'm so goddamn sorry."

She was silent for so long that he thought she was asleep. "I guess," she said at last, "that's supposed to make it all better."

He leaned over the bed. "Tell me what you want. Anything. Just say it and I'll do it."

"Oh, Danny. I'm not sure this is something that can be fixed."

"We have to try. Christ, Casey, we can't split up over something like this."

She finally looked at him, and her eyes were puffy and bloodshot. "Can you think of a better reason?"

"I can't think of any reason. I love you."

"You're the one," she reminded him bitterly, "who asked for a divorce."

"I was talking through my ass. You know better than to listen to me when I do that."

She wrapped slender fingers around the bed rail, and he watched as her knuckles, already white, went even whiter. "I think it would be better," she told him, "if you weren't there when I got home."

The silence grew heavy between them. "I see," he said at last.

"I need time," she said. "I have to figure out what to do."

This can't be happening to us, he thought. Like an automobile accident, it was supposed to happen to somebody else. He cleared his throat. "Will you be all right?"

"I'll survive." She hesitated. "What about you?"

Fighting panic, he said, "I can stay at Tony's. There's a cot in the store room behind the bar. Don't worry about me."

"Then I guess," she said, "there's nothing left to say."

"I love you," he burst out. "There's that."

"Don't do this to me, Danny," she said. "Just leave. I

don't want to hear it."

***

Harsh artificial light from the street lamp outside the window filtered through the venetian blinds and fell in narrow strips across the foot of the hospital bed. Casey lay on crisp white sheets and listened to the lusty squalling of an infant in the nursery down the hall.

Dr. Rodriguez had been kind. He'd patted her hand and said, "Sometimes these things happen, especially with a first pregnancy, and we don't know why. But you're young and strong and there's no reason to believe it should ever happen again." Because she'd lost so much blood, Rodriguez had insisted she stay the night. He'd instructed the nurse to give her a sedative, then left her to face her purgatory alone.

She dozed. When she awoke, Rob MacKenzie was sitting in the chair beside her bed. The door to her room was closed, muffling the sounds that echoed up and down the corridor. She extended a hand. "Hey," she said softly.

In the darkness, he took her hand. "Hey," he said.

"Visiting hours are over. How did you get in?"

"It's amazing," he said, "how far boyish charm will take you."

The silence between them was comfortable, the silence of two people who knew each other well enough to negate the necessity of words. After a time, he said, "You can't blame yourself."

She blinked back tears. "What makes you think I'm blaming myself?"

With the pad of his thumb, he rubbed her knuckles. "I know you," he said.

"Not very pretty, is it? My whole life, collapsing around me like this."

Rob squeezed her hand. "I know you may have trouble believing it right now, but Danny absolutely adores you."

"Then how could he do this to me? How could he even touch another woman?"

"He's human," Rob said, "just like you and me. Human

beings make mistakes."

"I'm trying to understand, but I can't. Since I met Danny, I've never even looked at another man." She closed her eyes, but the picture in her head wouldn't go away, the picture of Danny with another woman. "I want to kill him," she said. "I want to kill both of them. I want to rip her heart out."

The sense of unreality was still strong when she returned home the next day. Danny's clothes were gone, and his guitar. His door key lay in the middle of the kitchen table, a blatant reminder of everything she'd lost. Casey locked herself in the bedroom, buried her head in a pillow that smelled of Danny, and let the deluge come.

It was dusk when Rob knocked on her door. "I brought home a pizza," he said. "Come out and have some."

"Leave me alone," she said dully.

"I can't," he said. "You need to eat."

She swiped the heavy dampness of her hair away from her cheek. "I already ate."

"Bullshit. Get dressed and get out here, or I'm coming in after you. And don't think the lock will stop me, because I'll break the goddamn door down if I have to."

She resented his bullying, but it worked. The pizza smelled like heaven with pepperoni on it. Rob poured a glass of Boone's Farm Strawberry Hill and held it out to her. "You look like shit," he said. "Have a drink."

She took the glass from him. "You certainly know how to sweet-talk a woman, MacKenzie."

He tore off a slice of pizza, gooey with elastic threads of mozzarella, and put it in her hand. "Eat," he said.

She ate. And to her astonishment, felt infinitely better. "Thanks," she said, reaching for a second piece. "I guess I needed that."

He tilted the half-empty bottle of Boone's, and a thin stream of red liquid poured into his cup. He set the bottle on his thigh and fumbled with the cap. "I promised myself I'd stay out of this," he said, "but I just can't. You're miserable, he's miserable—hell, I'm miserable, and it's not even my marriage we're talking about."

She held out her glass and he obligingly refilled it. "In

some ways," he began, "I'm an old-fashioned guy. I want the
house and the kids and the wife." His voice grew wistful. "And
I'm not ashamed to admit that I'm actively searching for that
special woman."

"Why, Rob. All this time, I thought you were a free spirit."

"Ah, yes, my sweet, but underneath there beats the heart of
an Irishman who grew up in a family of nine kids."

"So what's your point?"

"I'm getting to it. When I find that special woman, she's
going to be a lot like you."

She blinked in surprise. "Like me?"

"Oh, she might not look like you or dress like you. She
doesn't even have to cook like you." He toyed with his glass.
"But I have one absolute prerequisite. She has to love me as
much as you love Danny."

She silently contemplated his words. "I'm afraid," she
said, "there aren't many women like that around."

"Exactly."

Either her head was befuddled from the wine, or he was
speaking in riddles, because she still wasn't getting the point.
"And?"

"And. I've always held up your marriage as a shining
example, a yardstick upon which to measure all other marriages,
past, present, and future. If the two of you split up, you'll be
destroying my belief in the sanctity of matrimony."

"Oh, please. Don't make me throw up."

"Shut up. I'm not finished. I know he did a dirty, rotten
thing to you."

She sipped her wine. "What he did," she said, "was
despicable."

"And you want to see that he's justly punished for it."

"Exactly."

"But you're punishing yourself right along with him."

She considered his words. "Maybe," she said grudgingly.

"Look," he said, "I won't argue that you're the injured
party here. You know it, I know it, Danny knows it. But has it
occurred to you that you're not the only one who's hurting?
Sure, you were in the right, so at least you have your self-
righteousness. Danny's the one who got stuck with the guilt."

"Good! I hope it's eating him up!"

"Shut up and listen to me. His whole goddamn life has blown up around him, and he knows it's all his fault. So don't tell me you're the only one hurting, because he's bleeding inside just as bad as you are."

"Then why did he do it?"

He leaned back against the couch. "Sex," he said, fiddling with the lace to his sneaker, "isn't the same for a man as it is for a woman."

Dryly, she said, "Would you care to clarify that?"

"Women have trouble separating sex and love. Men don't."

She narrowed her eyes. "Are you condoning what he did?"

"I'm not saying it's right. I'm just saying the difference exists."

Three days after the disintegration of her life, Casey was back at work. The hotel's part-time employees didn't enjoy luxuries like sick leave, and without Danny's income, she wasn't sure she and Rob could stay afloat. She refused to dwell on Danny's welfare or wonder how he was surviving. As her mother used to say, he'd made his bed, and now he was going to have to lie in it.

It was September, the pleasantest time of year in New York, and as business picked up at the Montpelier, Casey took on as many extra hours as she could get. She worked double shifts and came home at midnight, feet throbbing so bad she couldn't sleep until she'd soaked them in Epsom Salts and warm water. Working so hard had its benefits, though; when she fell into bed at night, she was too worn out to think about Danny, or about the baby she'd lost.

Money was scarce. As the weeks passed, she dipped more than once into her emergency fund to buy groceries. In the evenings, when Rob was out, she sat in the dark to save on the electric bill. The soles of her shoes were nearly worn through when lady luck smiled upon them, and Rob got a break.

Rick Slater and his band were well-known around the Big Apple, and when his lead guitarist left to form his own band, the drummer, who'd done some studio work with Rob, recommended him as a replacement. Rob auditioned, Slater liked what he saw, and the rest, as they say, was history.

In October, Rob talked her into a trip to Atlantic City with some musician friends of his, Steve Stern and Chico Rodriguez. Along with Chico's girlfriend, Marietta, they drove down in Steve's red '68 Malibu convertible. It was a golden Indian summer day with a touch of breeze off the Atlantic, and after a twenty-dollar win at the slot machines (beginner's luck, Chico said), Casey left the others in the casino and strolled the boardwalk alone.

She was watching two gulls fight over a discarded French fry when she saw a tall, tawny-haired man in a suede jacket, walking arm-in-arm with a redheaded girl. Casey's heart slammed into her rib cage, and the man turned to say something to the girl, and his face was nothing like Danny's. But the damage was already done. How could she possibly long for Danny with this kind of intensity when she was so repulsed by the knowledge that he'd touched another woman? Had she become so desperate that she wanted Danny no matter what the cost to herself?

If so, this was a side to her personality that she didn't much like. She didn't want to be the kind of woman who couldn't live without a man. Hadn't she proven that to be untrue? It had been six weeks since she'd last seen Danny—six weeks, three days, and seventeen hours, to be precise—and she was doing just fine. She was getting up each day and going to work. She watered her plants regularly. There was nothing growing in her refrigerator, and Con Ed hadn't yet cut off her electricity. Didn't that prove she was a fully functioning, contributing member of society? Didn't that prove she didn't need a man to survive?

So what if she hadn't told her family about the separation? So what if she'd found his old gray B.U. sweatshirt in the hamper, and now she slept in it every night? It didn't matter that every morning when she awoke, she still automatically reached out to find him. Or that she still wore her wedding ring, and refused to even consider taking any step that might legally cement the separation. None of this meant a thing, because Casey was a survivor, and not even Danny Fiore could take that away from her.

CHAPTER THIRTEEN

He awoke with a jolt, his breath coming in short, violent gasps as he fought to banish the images that still cluttered his brain. It was the dream again, in vivid Technicolor. He swung his legs over the edge of the narrow cot and reached for the pack of Marlboros he'd left on the floor, lighting one and drawing the smoke deep into his lungs in an attempt to chase away the monsters that had been his constant bedtime companions ever since Casey had thrown him out on his ass.

He hadn't yet figured out how to run fast enough or far enough to elude them, so instead of sleeping, he spent most of his nights chain smoking in this windowless little room that smelled of stale beer and mouse droppings. Tony was probably in violation of twenty-three different municipal ordinances, allowing him to take up residence here in this empty storage room at the back of the bar. But it was either this or a cheap room in some flophouse, and at least here he wasn't in danger of being knifed in his sleep.

He'd had another report yesterday from Rob. Casey was driving herself without mercy. His wife was proud and stubborn, and if she ever found out where the extra money was coming from, she would refuse it. But Rob had sworn on his life that he'd slip it into the kitty without telling her. Better she should think MacKenzie had hit the jackpot than know that the money was coming from his job as a cabbie.

It was a crummy job, carting around businessmen to three-martini lunches and suburban housewives to Macy's and Bloomingdale's, but New York was full of crummy jobs, and at least he didn't have Emile riding his ass any more. Whenever his job took him to lower Manhattan, he managed to find an excuse to drive past Wong's Tea House, slowing the yellow cab to a crawl as he craned his neck for a glimpse of his wife in the apartment window upstairs. But all he ever saw was the Swedish ivy Rob had rescued from a trash can on the street and brought home to her. Casey had pampered and nurtured the damn thing until it resembled an acre of Amazonian rain forest.

And that, in a nutshell, was the problem between them.

Casey was a nurturer, while he was little more than a glib street
hustler. He'd known it from the beginning, but with his
customary disregard for the welfare of others, he'd taken what he
wanted, ignoring the consequences. Casey belonged in a big
house in the country, with a garden outside her door and babies
playing at her feet. But he'd taken all that away from her when
he made her his wife, and now he was paying for his stupidity.

And for what? His wife wasn't speaking to him, and his
career was in the toilet. He'd spent two-and-a-half years making
the rounds, making his face and his name known to New York's
numerous talent agencies and record production companies.
He'd always believed that the best way to get a foot in the door
was to make friends with the secretarial staff. So he made a
point of pouring on the charm, and it worked: every receptionist
in the business knew him, and most of them lit up like Times
Square at New Year's the instant he walked through the door.

The problem was that he could never get past the
receptionist to the people who made the decisions. He'd left
behind a pile of resumes and demo tapes tall enough to rival the
Empire State Building, but he'd had no bites. Not even a nibble.
All that creative energy inside him was building up, with no
outlet, until he thought he'd explode. On the nights he played
guitar at Tony's, he sang what the patrons wanted to hear. When
he was alone, he sang the music that stirred his soul. He sang in
the shower at the Y, in his cab when he didn't have a fare.

But this was New York, where struggling singers sold
watches on every street corner, and nobody gave a rat's ass about
a blue-eyed white boy from Boston. In New York, Danny Fiore
was a nobody. And he wondered, for the first time, if it was time
to quit.

***

With the final notes of *Satisfaction* ringing in his head, Rob
left the stage, worming his way between bodies in the direction
of the bar and the cold Heineken that was waiting for him.
Halfway there, an immovable object planted itself in his path.
"Hey, Mac," the tattooed mountain said. "Some lady friend of
yours come in asking for you. Seemed real upset. I stashed her

away in Jimmy's office."

At just over six feet, Rob was at eye level with Rico's Adam's apple. "Lady friend?" he said. "I don't have any lady friends."

"I dunno," the bouncer said. "This one would be hard to forget."

It had to be Casey. Something must be wrong at home. "Jimmy's office," he said. "Thanks."

Rico's massive hand caught him by the shoulder. "Lemme give you a word of advice, MacKenzie. Jimmy don't like no trouble, so you might wanna keep your little domestic problems to home."

Rob freed himself, shouldering his way through the crowd. He took the last few steps at a trot and burst through the door to Jimmy's office. The woman sat on the couch, her hands clutching a tattered tissue, her face hidden behind a curtain of dark hair. She raised her head and her eyes were brimming. Dark eyes. Almond-shaped eyes.

Oriental eyes.

His anxiety turned to astonishment. "Nancy," he said.

"Hello, Rob MacKenzie," she said in that melodious voice that had haunted his dreams for months. Those luminous eyes glistened, and a single tear escaped and rolled down her cheek. With a small cry, she got up from the couch, flung her arms around his neck, and pressed her face against his shirt front.

He stood in paralyzed disbelief. Slowly, tentatively, he closed his arms around her and allowed his fingers to touch the shining silk of her hair. The scent of jasmine clung to her, making him dizzy. He swallowed hard. *Jesus*, he thought. Was this love, this pain that felt as if it would rip him apart? He wasn't sure he was ready to handle it. At the same time, terrified that she might be an apparition, he tightened his hold. "Nancy," he said. "What's wrong?"

She lifted a tearstained face. "I'm sorry," she said. "I should not have come here."

"No," he said, needing desperately to reassure her. "You can't begin to know how happy I am to see you."

She touched his cheek with a slender hand. "I tried to forget you. But it was impossible."

He kissed the palm of her hand. "What is it?" he said. "What's wrong?"

She wet her lips with the moist, pink tip of her tongue. "My parents have chosen a husband for me. His name is Kim Soon Lee, and we are to be married at the Chinese New Year."

He tried to make sense of her words. "You mean an arranged marriage?"

"Yes."

"Are they nuts? Arranged marriages went out with hoop skirts!"

Nancy shook her head. "They still occur among the Chinese. My own parents were betrothed when they were children."

"You're twenty-two years old," he said, trying to tamp down his anger. "You don't have to do their bidding."

She shook her head. "You do not understand."

"You're damn right, I don't! This is twentieth-century America. They can't do this to you!"

"I cannot stop them."

"Jesus Christ, Nancy, just say no!"

"You do not understand how I was raised. You do not know my parents. I'm not strong enough to fight them."

"Then we'll fight them together."

She pulled away from him and crossed the room, leaving an emotional gulf the size of the Pacific Ocean between them. Toying with a pen from Jimmy's desk, she said, "I cannot involve you."

"Nancy," he said in gentle exasperation, "you already have."

"It was a mistake. I shouldn't have come here."

He crossed the space between them and took her face between his hands. "But you did," he said. "And I'm glad!"

"If I involve you," she said, "it will only make things worse. They are angry already because I told them I will not marry Kim. It would be disastrous if they discovered I was involved with a white man."

He tucked her dark head beneath his chin, and they swayed like slender reeds caught in a breeze. "I love you," he said. "More than I've ever loved anybody."

"Please don't say that."

"Why? Do you think it'll be any less true if I don't say it out loud?"

"I cannot love you," she said. "Don't you understand? I cannot allow this to happen."

"Nancy," he said gently, "it's too late. It's already happened."

It was one-thirty in the morning when he dragged Casey out of bed. "Nancy," he said curtly, "this is Casey. Casey, this is Nancy. We're getting married."

Both women gaped at him in astonishment. He picked up the telephone and held it out to Nancy. "Your folks are probably worried," he said. "They deserve to know you're all right."

While she held a lengthy conversation in Chinese with her mother, he paced the apartment. Casey cornered him in the kitchen. "I don't suppose," she said, "that you'd care to enlighten me?"

"She had a big blow-out with her folks. They told her she has to marry some Chinese guy. I'm not about to let it happen."

She exhaled loudly. "Rob," she said, "how long have you known this girl?"

"Long enough," he said grimly. "Look, I know what I'm doing. Don't try to talk me out of it."

"I'm not going to. On the other hand, I'd hate to see you make a terrible mistake."

"This is my life, babe. Let me live it."

"You," she said, poking him hard in the chest, "are an insufferable ass."

He cupped her cheek and placed a kiss on the tip of her nose. "That's why you love me," he said.

***

The anteroom outside the judge's chambers reeked with the odors of stale cigar smoke and too many bodies crammed into too little space. Casey shifted on the wooden bench, trying to find some position that didn't hurt her backside. There were two couples waiting to experience nuptial bliss ahead of Rob and Nancy. The teenage Hispanic couple held hands with terrified determination, and the middle-aged woman with the blond beehive slumped in her seat with terminal boredom next to a colorless man who leafed listlessly through a year-old issue of *Time* magazine.

Footsteps echoed down the cavernous corridor, and everybody in the room looked up expectantly at the tall, perversely good-looking man who paused in the doorway. At sight of him, Casey's heart momentarily stopped, and she saw her own surprise mirrored in those blue eyes. So Rob hadn't told him she would be here, either. She turned accusing eyes on Rob, but he had scrambled to his feet and was pumping Danny's hand. "I was afraid you wouldn't make it," he said. Danny braced a shoulder against the doorjamb and rocked on the balls of his feet until Rob said, "Sit down, man. It may be a while."

With obvious reluctance, Danny took the only empty seat in the room, the one next to his wife. Not looking at her, he said, "Hi."

Casey crossed her arms and sat up straighter on the bench. "Hi."

His gray hooded sweatshirt was rain-spotted. His hood had fallen, and beads of moisture clung to his hair. He slumped, stretching those long legs out halfway across the room. He was wearing new shoes. Three months ago, he'd been wearing two-year-old Adidas with holes in both soles. It wasn't fair that he should look this good when she'd been so miserable.

The judge's door opened, and the clerk motioned the Hispanic couple inside. "One down, one to go," Rob said, and Nancy smiled nervously. Crammed together as they were, thigh to thigh, Casey could feel the heat from Danny's body, could smell that indescribable scent that was Danny. It had always clung to his clothes, his hair, his bedding.

"I think I need a cup of coffee," she said with false brightness. "Anybody else want one?"

"I'll come with you," Danny said. "I saw vending machines on my way in."

Casey tried to pretend that walking down the corridor in step with her estranged husband wasn't an earth-shattering experience. She cleared her throat. "I suppose," she said, "he's told you the whole story."

"Yes."

"This is the craziest thing he's ever done. He'll end up with a broken heart."

"Probably."

At the canteen door she reached for her purse, but Danny was quicker. He dropped a quarter into the vending machine and pushed a couple of buttons, and a paper cup dropped into place. They watched as hot coffee trickled into it. "I see you haven't forgotten how I take my coffee," she said.

"Jesus Christ, Casey, it's only been three months."

"Really? I've lost track. But I must say that bachelorhood seems to agree with you, darling. I can't remember when I've seen you looking this good."

He handed her the cup of coffee and dropped a second quarter into the machine. "If we spoil this for Rob, he'll never forgive us." Danny opened the sliding door and removed his cup. "Let's try to be civilized, for his sake. We can bicker on our own time."

Ashamed, she returned with him to the anteroom. The wait seemed interminable before the clerk motioned them into the judge's chambers. The ceremony was brief and impersonal, and Casey tried to look anywhere but at Danny as the judge read the familiar words in a lifeless monotone. But her eyes kept being drawn back to those blue eyes fixed so intently on her face. It was inevitable, the memory of another municipal building, another couple, another wedding. Heedless of the bride and groom, they gazed at each other in mute agony until Rob cleared his throat and said, "Dan? The ring?"

Danny tore his eyes away from his wife's face and dug in his pocket for the plain gold band, and Casey kept her eyes where they belonged, on the bride and groom, as Rob placed the ring on Nancy's finger.

Inexplicably, when the judge pronounced them husband and wife, Casey's eyes filled with tears. It was an unforgivable sin; she never cried at weddings. She searched blindly in her purse for a tissue, and Danny discreetly tucked a white cotton handkerchief into her hand. The intimacy of that husbandly gesture nearly did her in. As Danny congratulated the bride and groom, Casey hid behind him, struggling to regain her composure. By the time her turn came, she was smiling as she gave Rob, and then Nancy, a brisk hug. "Be happy," she said. "Take care of each other."

She had baked a cake, and Danny had bought a cheap bottle of champagne, and they celebrated back at the apartment. It was the most peculiar wedding reception she'd ever attended. The bride and groom were terrified of what would happen in the morning when they presented her parents with a *fait accompli.* The best man and matron of honor treated each other with a formal courtesy bordering on frigidity, and they were all a little relieved to call an end to the celebration.

Amid a flurry of hugs and congratulations, Casey saw the newlyweds off for their wedding night at a downtown hotel, fully expecting to usher Danny out the door directly behind them. Instead, she found him at the kitchen sink, elbow-deep in soap suds. "I'll wash," he said. "You dry." And although she knew it was a mistake, she couldn't summon the strength to ask him to leave.

So they worked together in silence, vibrations ricocheting off the walls and ceiling of the room that seemed to have shrunk to half its size. Because she couldn't stand the silence, and because in spite of herself she cared, she asked, "Are you still working at Tony's?"

He rinsed a fistful of silverware and handed it to her. "Yeah."

"Any new gigs?"

"Nothing much. I've been driving a cab to put food in my belly."

She busied herself drying the silverware. Behind her, Danny said, "What do you want to do with this leftover cake?"

"Put plastic wrap over it and refrigerate it. Second cupboard to the left of the sink."

"I know where you keep it."

Of course. For a moment, she'd forgotten. While he wrapped the cake, she washed the stove and the table, rinsed out the sink. Danny refilled their wine glasses with the last of the champagne. "We might as well drink it," he said. "I believe in getting my money's worth out of things." He tossed the bottle in the trash, then held up his glass. "Cheers."

"Since we both already know what a sham marriage is," she said, "I can't imagine why you'd want to drink to anything."

He slammed down his glass so hard the champagne sloshed over the side. "So that's it? You're planning to spend the rest of your life punishing me?"

"You hurt me, Danny. Do you have any idea how much?"

"Not enough to justify your Old Testament justice. One wrong move and I'm a pillar of salt, with no chance for redemption."

"I'm so sorry, darling, that I can't be more sympathetic to your plight."

"What do you want me to do? Get down on my knees and grovel?"

"Groveling," she said, "won't change a thing."

"Christ, no. The dirty deed is already done, isn't it? I can't take it back, so you're going to make me suffer every ounce of punishment you can conjure up."

"What about me? What about my feelings? What about the baby I lost?"

"It was my baby, too!"

"One you never wanted!"

"No! One I never even knew about! One I had to hear about from the mouth of my best friend!"

She crossed her arms. "I think," she said coldly, "that it's time for you to leave."

"You're throwing me out for speaking the truth?"

"Leave me alone. I've suffered enough."

"Bullshit. You don't know what suffering is until you see the woman you love bleeding to death on a hospital gurney, and there's not a goddamn thing you can do except sit and pray to a God you didn't think you even believed in any more!"

Tears stung her eyelids. "What do you want, Danny? A purple heart?"

"No, goddamn it!" he bellowed. "I want to come home!"

She stared at him in stupefied silence as he slumped onto a chair and buried his face in his hands. "I want to come home," he said.

In the silence, the kitchen clocked ticked. "I trusted you," she said. "I let myself be vulnerable, because I had absolute faith in you. And you let me down, Danny."

"I know I screwed up. All I'm asking for is a second chance."

"And then a third, and a fourth?"

"It's not like that. Damn it, I can't live any longer without you. Every night, in bed, in the dark, I see you."

She closed her eyes. "Don't," she whispered.

"And I remember how soft your skin feels. And how your hair smells like violets. And how you look, lying naked on rumpled sheets—"

"Stop it!"

"—and the way you tremble and cry when I'm inside you—"

"I don't want to hear any more!"

"And I can't believe we could let something this good get away." He rose abruptly and picked up his jacket. "I've had my say. You know where to find me."

And he was gone. Devastated, she slid silently to the floor, wrapped her arms around her knees, and let the pain swallow her up.

***

It was nearly midnight when she called him. In the background, she could hear the commotion of a busy bar on a Saturday night: thudding music, well-oiled laughter, the clink of glass on glass. And then his voice, liquid velvet. And a rock-hard fist tightened up in her belly. "Hi," she said.

Silence. Then, "Hold on a minute." The phone was jostled and clunked, and then the background noise receded. "I'm hiding in the john," he said. "It's quieter in here."

"I've done a lot of thinking," she said. "And I've decided I want you to come home."

At his end, there was a sharp intake of breath.

"I'm willing to try to put this behind us," she said. "I don't know how it will turn out. It's going to take me some time to get over what's happened. I'm not even sure I can." She paused. "But I'm willing to try. It's a start."

"That's all I'm asking for."

"But if anything like this ever happens again, that'll be it, Danny. There won't be any third or fourth chances. I won't put myself through this again."

"You have my word," he said.

She hesitated. Bit her lip. "How soon can you get off work?"

"I can be there in an hour."

"I'll be waiting."

It took him twenty-eight minutes. When she opened the door, they drank each other in silently. He set down his guitar and abandoned his bag of clothes, and in a mutual move they came together, clinging like drowning souls. He kicked the door shut and lifted her off her feet, and she wound her legs around him and let him carry her. He banged his shin on the coffee table and cursed, and Casey snaked fingers through his hair and planted hungry kisses on his chin, his jaw, his ear. Oblivious to everything but each other, they fell onto the couch, his weight pinning her beneath him, their kisses hot and frantic. Weightless, boneless with desire, she whispered a single, breathy word. "*Hurry.*"

He tugged off her sweatshirt and tossed it, tore frantically at her pants, managed to pull first one leg free and then the other. She unzipped his jeans and peeled them back over his buttocks, and then he was inside her, and she no longer knew her own name. Legs splayed like a trollop, she rode him, oblivious to any reality beyond the few inches of rock-hard flesh that impaled her. Fluid, liquid, boneless, she rolled beneath him in mindless rapture.

The climax slammed into her like a freight train. She cried out, and a ragged sob tore from his throat as she took him with her over the edge. Spent and gasping and shuddering, they lay together in a sweaty tangle. He was still wearing his coat. His shoes. "You're mine," she gasped. "Do you understand that? If you ever touch another woman, ever again—" She paused, frantically gulped in air. "I'll kill you. Do you hear me, Danny? I'll tear out your heart and serve it for dinner."

He didn't answer. He kicked off his shoes, wriggled out of his pants. Pulled the afghan from the back of the couch and, coat and all, rolled them both in it. "If you ever leave me," he said,

"I'll come after you."

"I wouldn't," she said. "Never—" He kissed her, hard. "Never, ever." His kiss gentled, soothed, tore at her soul. "Danny," she whispered. "Oh, Danny."

Now that the dragons of frantic longing had been appeased, they made love again, properly this time, *sans* shoes or coat and in their own bed. Afterward, lying in his arms, she asked, "With her, was it as good as it is with me?"

"Christ, Casey, it's over with. Don't stir it up."

"I have to know."

"It was just sex. Period."

"And with me...is it ever just sex?"

He lifted his head and looked at her. "I can't believe you'd ask that. You're my whole goddamn life. Haven't you figured it out by now?"

"Promise me we'll be together always."

He kissed her forehead. "We'll be together," he said, "always."

After a time, she said, "Danny?"

"Hmm?"

"If anything ever happened to me, would you marry again?"

Sleepily, he said, "Is this a trick question?"

"I'm serious." She clasped her hands together behind her head and stared up at the dark ceiling. "If I died, would you get married again?"

"If you died," he said darkly, "I'd die with you."

"I'd want you to, you know."

"Die with you?"

"No, fool. Get married again."

He rolled over and wrapped an arm around her. "What about you?" he said. "Would you get married again?"

"I don't know. I can't imagine living with someone else. Sleeping beside someone else. Sleeping *with* someone else."

"I think you would," he said. "Marriage is something you do well."

"And you?"

"I believe I've already illustrated just how well I do marriage."

"Oh, I don't know," she said, "you seem to do quite well at some aspects of it."

"Oh?" He drew her closer. "And just which aspects might those be?"

She nibbled gently at the tendon that ran from his ear to his shoulder. "You're a big boy," she said. "You figure it out."

***

Outside the door to the Chens' twentieth-floor apartment, Rob tugged self-consciously at the borrowed tie and adjusted the suit coat that was two sizes too big. "Are you sure I look okay?" he said for the tenth time.

"You look fine," Nancy said.

He raised her chin and gently kissed her lips. "Ready?" he said.

"Ready."

She left him waiting in the foyer while she rounded up her parents. The place smelled like sandalwood, and through the entryway he could see a living room that must have been forty feet long. Its furnishings were sleek, modern, elegant. At the far end, the New York City skyline rose beyond a wall of glass. The hum of a vacuum cleaner echoed from a distant room. Somehow, he doubted that it was Nancy's mother who was operating it.

She returned silently, her footsteps absorbed by thick carpeting. "I have told my parents that we wish to speak with them," she said. "They are waiting for us in my father's den."

He followed her through a maze of rooms to a small study off the kitchen. The bookshelves were lined with somber-looking tomes in Chinese and English. Nancy's parents sat side by side on a beige love seat, her mother tiny, ageless, attractive in peach silk and pearls, her father thin and graying, looking dapper in a flawless white shirt and a suit that made Rob's look like he'd picked it out of a Salvation Army bin. They sat stiffly, eyeing him with cool courtesy.

"Mother, Father," Nancy said, "this is Rob MacKenzie."

Mrs. Chen's face remained wooden as he shook her dry hand. Dr. Chen's clasp was bony and frail. "Mr. MacKenzie," he said, in heavily accented English, "I understand you are a friend of my daughter's. What is it you wish to speak to us about?"

He looked at Nancy. She bit her lip, then nodded. "Dr. Chen, Mrs. Chen," he said. "Nancy and I—" He paused, aware of the poorly hidden hostility on their faces. "We were married yesterday."

The starched politeness on their faces slowly turned to horrified comprehension. Nancy's mother began to babble hysterically in Chinese, her voice rising and falling, the words incomprehensible to him but her meaning painfully clear. "Use English, please, Mother," Nancy said. "My husband does not speak Chinese."

"Why have you done this?" her mother shrieked. "Is this how an obedient daughter pays back her parents?"

"You insisted that I marry Kim," Nancy said. "You gave me no choice."

"And you would prefer this—" Mrs. Chen looked at Rob with venom in her eyes. "—this *stranger*, to one of your own kind?"

"He is a man, I am a woman. Does that not make us the same kind?"

"What do you know about him?" her mother demanded.

"I know that he is a good man." Nancy reached out a hand to Rob and he squeezed it, hard. "I know that I love him."

"Love!" her mother spat out. "Look at him! His clothes are cheap and they fit poorly, his hair is too long, his shoes are worn out. You believe he loves you? Fool! What he loves is your money!"

"Excuse me," Rob said, "but I'd like to clear something up. I don't give a damn about your money, Mrs. Chen. I love your daughter. All that matters to me is seeing her happy."

"And you think she will be happy, living in poverty with you?"

He squared his jaw. "I know I'm probably a big disappointment as a son-in-law," he said, "but I'm hoping, for Nancy's sake, that you'll accept her decision to marry me."

"Nancy is a foolish child," her mother said, "and I will never accept you as my son-in-law." She turned on Nancy.

"Have you thought about your children? They will be neither one race nor the other. Are you prepared to deal with that? Are you prepared to deal with the way people will look at you, walking down the street together?"

"Mother, we love each other. What is so wrong about that?"

"What is so wrong? You tell me. How will I explain this to Kim? How will I explain to his parents that my daughter has chosen to marry a white man instead of their son? You have disgraced your family." She stood up abruptly, so that she was at eye level with Nancy. In a voice as unrelentingly rigid as her spine, she said, "I can no longer acknowledge you as my daughter."

Nancy gasped, and her face lost all its color. "Mother!"

"Hey," Rob said, "wait just a minute. Don't you want to think this over, before you do something you'll regret?"

"There is nothing to think about. Please leave my home, Mr. MacKenzie, and take your wife with you."

Throughout the woman's tirade, her husband had sat silent. "Dr. Chen?" Rob said. "Are you telling me you're going along with this craziness?"

All three of them turned to the doctor. "Father?" Nancy said.

Dr. Chen's face had gone pale, and he looked as though he'd aged a decade in the past ten minutes. "I have no choice," he said, "but to agree with my wife."

The silence was overwhelming. "Fine," Nancy said. "I'll pack my things."

"No," her mother said. "You will take nothing with you."

"But my clothes. My books—"

"You have a husband now. Let him buy you new ones."

Nancy stared at her mother in disbelief. And then she raised her head. "Rob," she said, "I believe we have been dismissed."

As he stumbled behind her to the door, her mother's voice followed them. "Some day," she shouted, "you will thank me!"

CHAPTER FOURTEEN

His homecoming marked the beginning of the greatest challenge Danny Fiore had ever faced: winning back the woman he loved. Both of them tottering on uncertain legs, they performed a guarded *pas de deux*, circling each other like wary beasts as alternating shades of trust and distrust shimmered in the air between them. While Casey remained cool and apprehensive, Danny served his penance.

His was not the kind of gaffe that could be smoothed over with flowers or candy. The hurt went too deep for such trivialities. For the first time in his life, Danny set aside his ambitions and put his marriage ahead of his career. He spent every spare moment with Casey, watching old movies, playing Monopoly, going through family photo albums. He cooked and vacuumed, carted clothes to the Laundromat, scrubbed the floors and the dishes and the toilet. When she came home from the Montpelier with swollen feet, he massaged them, brought her warm water to soak them in. He took her to the movies, dancing at a succession of blues clubs, to several off-off-Broadway musicals. They took long walks in Central Park, where they bought roasted chestnuts from a sidewalk vendor and fed bread crumbs to the pigeons.

And they talked. About their marriage, about the baby they'd lost, about the mutual feelings that had drawn them together in the first place. She told him what it had been like to nurse her mother through terminal cancer, and he told her what it had been like to see his mother walk out of his life and never return. They opened up to each other with an unprecedented intimacy, and gradually, like a broken limb, the pieces of their shattered marriage began to knit back together.

They went home that year for Christmas, hitching a ride with an acquaintance of Rob's, a Columbia student who took them all the way to Farmington. It had been three years since they'd last visited, and there were changes, not all of them pleasant. There was an obvious coldness between Colleen and Jesse, although both seemed to care deeply for their young son.

Casey's father had aged considerably. The hair that had remained jet black into his fifties was slowly turning a silvery gray. He had remarried in October, to a family friend named Millie Trudeau, and Danny knew how difficult it was for Casey to see another woman so comfortably ensconced in her mother's kitchen.

He had been saving money for months, and his Christmas gift to Casey was a small but tasteful diamond ring. He'd never given her an engagement ring, just the gold wedding band, and it had been eating at him for years. Casey understood the significance of the ring. Tears welled up in her eyes, and that night, the last barrier between them crumbled.

His wife's family had always done their best to make him feel like he belonged, but the truth was that he was an outsider with no understanding of these people or their way of life. The two days passed with agonizing slowness, and he was immensely relieved when the visit ended. After Christmas dinner, they caught a ride back to Boston with Travis, and spent Christmas night in Southie, tucked snugly into one of Mary MacKenzie's spare beds.

They returned home the next day to an ashen New York, groaning under a heavy burden of snow and sand and slush. They'd only been gone for four days, but already the cockroaches had mounted a territorial campaign, and Freddy Wong had shut off the radiators, turning the water in the toilet bowl into a solid chunk of ice. While Rob went downstairs to talk to Freddy, Danny took Casey by the hand and led her to the bedroom, where they huddled together beneath the covers and waited for the apartment to warm up to its normal fifty-eight degrees.

"This isn't fair to you," he said, his breath hovering in the air above his head. "You shouldn't have to live like this."

"I'm not complaining," she said. Then amended it: "Well, not much, anyway."

"It's a rotten life," he said bitterly.

She brushed a strand of hair away from his face. "I knew what I was up against when I married you."

"I'm not sure I can do it any more."

Her hand, still hovering in the vicinity of his face, froze.

"What?" she said. "What are you talking about?"

He threw aside the covers and got up out of the bed. Paced six steps across the room and picked up the framed photo of her mother. He studied it for a minute, then set it back down and turned to her. "All I'm doing," he said, "is beating my head against the wall. We've been here almost three years, and I can't get arrested. At what point do I face the fact that it isn't going to happen? At what point do I tuck my tail between my legs and go home? Do you have any idea how tired I am of hearing, 'Don't call us, we'll call you.'?"

She sat up and wrapped the quilt around her. "I had no idea you felt this way."

He leaned against the dresser and folded his arms. "It's been coming on for a while."

Still wrapped in the quilt, she slid off the bed and crossed the room to him. She opened her arms and folded the quilt around both of them. "Danny," she said, "please listen to me. There is nobody out there who can do what you do with a song. You have a God-given talent, and it would be a crime for you to waste it."

"And it's less of a crime," he said, "for me to put you through this hell?"

"I'm a grown woman, Danny. I'm with you because this is where I choose to be."

"It's not just you," he said. "I'm tired. It wasn't like this in Boston."

"Did you think it would be easy?"

"I guess I didn't really believe it would be like this."

"You have too much passion in you to settle," she said. "You'd end up regretting it. That's not what you want. It's not what I want for you."

He pulled her closer beneath the quilt. "This isn't the response I expected from you," he admitted.

"How do you know success isn't around the next corner? How would you know you hadn't quit a month too soon? Or a day? Or even an hour? You'd spend the rest of your life wondering."

"But what about the sacrifices?" he argued. "We're living like animals here."

"Everybody has to pay their dues."

"I'm tired of paying. And I'm tired of you paying."

"Then take some time away from it. Allow yourself to do something else for a while. But don't give up. The time will come when somebody recognizes your talent. Trust me."

"Why is it that you keep on believing in me when I can't even believe in myself?"

She smiled and said, "Masochistic tendencies?"

***

When Rob tiptoed into the apartment at two in the morning, he found Nancy hunched over a textbook at the kitchen table. She smiled up at him, but her smile didn't hide the dark circles beneath her eyes. "What are you doing up so late?" he said, bending to kiss her. "You should be asleep."

"I will sleep later. This is the only time I have free to study. Was your evening pleasant?"

He grimaced. "Don't ask. Rick Slater's starting to get on my nerves."

She rested her chin on her palm and studied him quizzically. "You do not like this man you work with?"

Rob opened the refrigerator and took out a can of Dr Pepper. Sitting down across from her, he popped open the top. "It's not a matter of liking him. He's a talented musician. But he has a nose problem."

She wrinkled her brow. "Nose problem?"

Rob took a drink of soda. "He's a cokehead. Among other things. When the last set was over tonight, the drummer practically had to carry him off stage."

She looked worried. "This does not bode well for your future," she said.

"Not if we can't keep him upright." He slid the textbook away from her, turned it around and riffled through a few pages. Frowned, and checked the cover of the book. At two in the morning, she was studying advanced chemistry. He slid the book back across the table. "How's the job going?"

Nancy sighed. "Terrible," she said. "I felt so stupid tonight."

"Come on, Nance, you're about as far from stupid as it gets."

"I am very good at academics," she said. "But as a waitress, I am afraid I'm a dismal failure."

"What happened?"

She tapped her pencil on her notebook. "With academics, I have always taken my time. It is difficult to be thorough if one is hurried, and a physician must be thorough above all else. But a waitress must be all things to all people, all at the same time. I believe this goes against my natural inclination. I am by nature a tranquil person."

"And you're going to make a wonderful doctor."

"Perhaps." She smiled ruefully. "But not a good waitress. Tonight I gave a pu-pu platter to a couple who had ordered Kung Pao Chicken, then served hot and sour soup to a gentleman who had asked for egg drop. I spilled a glass of water in a woman's lap, and forgot to give another couple their bill. I'm afraid that my tips tonight were a reflection of my capabilities."

"You'll get the hang of it," he said, taking her hand. "You haven't been at it very long."

"Two months," she said. "If I cannot learn something as simple as waitressing in two months, how will I ever learn anything as complex as medicine?"

He squeezed her hand. "We'll hire you a tutor."

Her smile was faint, but it was there. "You are so kind to me," she said. "Rob, I have a problem. I don't know how to solve it."

He'd known something more than a bad evening at Wong's was bothering her. "*We* have a problem," he corrected. "What is it?"

She opened another textbook and pulled a piece of paper from it. He took it from her and studied it. "This is your tuition bill," he said, and shot her a quick glance. "Your parents didn't pay it?"

"I would not have known, except that my chemistry instructor said that I was not on her class list. So I paid a visit to the registration office. It seems that my parents returned the bill to the university. In this envelope." She pushed it across the table. Stamped on the front in red were the words *Addressee*

Unknown.

"I saved some money during the semester break," she said, "but not nearly enough to pay the entire bill. I managed to give them enough money to stall them, but if the balance is not paid within three weeks, my enrollment will be canceled."

He flung the bill down on the table. "I never thought they'd go this far," he said. "How could they do this to you? Jesus Christ, Nancy, you're their daughter!"

"Hush, please, Rob. You'll wake the entire household."

He began pacing, running his hands through his tangled hair. There was no way he could scrape together the kind of money she needed, not in three weeks. "They're the most cold-blooded human beings I've ever run across," he said. "How can they call themselves parents?"

"I told you they would make it as difficult as possible for us. I shouldn't have married you. I should not have brought you into this."

He paused in his pacing. "I'll call my folks," he said. "First thing in the morning. Maybe they can give us a loan."

"I would not ask your parents for that kind of favor," she said. "This is my battle, not theirs."

"You're my wife," he said, "and their daughter-in-law, and you'd damn well better believe it's their battle. Family sticks together."

"I would not ask this of you!"

"I'm your husband," he said. "Damn it, Nancy, I won't have you dropping out of school because those two old goats are too stubborn to pay your way. You've been planning to be a doctor since you were eight years old. I won't let them take it away from you!"

She touched his hand. "Please, can we talk about this tomorrow? It's very late, and I have an early class."

He melted. He always melted when she touched him. He drew her, warm and slender and solid, into his waiting arms. "Anybody who wants to hurt you," he said, "will have to go through me first."

In bed, he pulled her close. As usual, she was stiff and unresponsive. She and Casey had turned a corner of the living room into a sleeping alcove, complete with privacy curtain, but it failed to lessen Nancy's paranoia over their lack of privacy. Unless they were alone in the apartment, she froze the instant he touched her. "Rob," she protested, "they will hear us."

"It's two o'clock in the morning, Nance."

"They could still hear."

"We're married," he told her. "It's legal."

"I could not face them across the breakfast table."

He rolled away from her and fell back against the pillow. He had never forced himself on a woman, and he wasn't about to start now. But his wife was making him crazy. How many nights could she expect him to lie beside her, awash in the scent of jasmine and warmed by the closeness of her body, before the dam burst and his emotions surged forward and shoved chivalry aside?

**

Six weeks after Danny made the decision to take a year off from music, Rick Slater suffered a near-fatal cocaine overdose.

The instant Slater's condition stabilized, his wife carted him off to an upstate rehab facility, leaving his band without a lead singer. Rob convinced the other band members to give Danny an audition, and at Casey's urging, Danny reneged on his vow and joined Slater's band.

It was a marriage made in heaven. He and Rob had played together for so many years, there was a telepathy that happened between them on stage, a psychic energy so visible it had them striking sparks off each other. Within a few days, he'd learned all of Slater's material, and by the end of two weeks, they'd squeezed several of Casey and Rob's originals into their sets. Word on the street was that the band's new lead singer was hot, and night after night, it was standing room only at Delaney's, the East Village club where Slater and company were house band.

It soon became obvious to everyone that it was Danny who was drawing the crowds. When Slater's doctors predicted a long-term stay in rehab, the band went into an intensive huddle, emerging with a new name: *Danny Fiore and the Rick Slater Band.*

And the fickle public forgot Rick Slater had ever existed.

Night after night, as Danny stood silhouetted in the spotlight, the women in the audience openly yearned for him. The more aggressive tucked their telephone numbers into his pockets, tossed their unmentionables on-stage, blatantly propositioned him between sets. Although he made sure his wedding ring was clearly visible, none of them seemed to care. Each one fancied herself the woman who would topple Danny Fiore from his matrimonial pedestal. And each one left the show in acute disappointment, because every night, as soon as the gig was over, Danny went directly home to his wife.

In April, the band was booked for two nights into a hot new club on 42nd Street. Audience response was tremendous, and on the second night, the manager asked them to return for a three-day gig on Memorial weekend. So Danny was pumped, his adrenaline running high, when they started breaking down and packing up after the last set. Taking a deep drag on his Marlboro, he unplugged his mike and began coiling the cord.

"Hey, Wiz?"

"Yo?"

"I've got five big ones that say we can have it all packed up in ten minutes flat."

On his knees beside his open guitar case, Rob grinned. "Thinking of a career as a roadie, Fiore?"

Danny flicked an ash. "A man has to make a living."

Josh Taylor, the drummer, sidled up to him. "Don't look now, man," he said, "but those chicks from NYU are still hanging around."

"Go for it, Jocko. I'm slightly married."

"Don't let him kid you, Josh," Rob said. "He's *very* married."

Danny put out his cigarette, grinned, and turned to unplug an amp. He found himself face to face with a youngish guy in khaki shorts and a Hawaiian shirt. *Tourist*, he thought automatically. *Probably got lost on his way to the john.* "Excuse me," he said, squeezing past.

"Wait a minute," the guy said. "Mr. Fiore?"

He paused. "Yes?"

The man held out his hand. "Drew Lawrence."

Lawrence's handshake was firm and brisk. He patted his

breast pocket and drew out a business card. Handing it to
Danny, he said, "I'm with Ariel Records."

Behind Lawrence's back, he met Rob's eyes. They stared
at each other for a fraction of a second, and then Danny looked at
the card in his hand. "Ariel Records," he said. "I don't believe
I've heard of you."

"We're small. And constantly on the lookout for new
talent. I think you and I might be able to do business."
Lawrence paused. "Interested?"

It took him a moment to find his voice. "I'm listening."

Lawrence grinned. "Come sit down. You look like you
could use a drink."

CHAPTER FIFTEEN

As a small, independent company, Ariel Records was willing to take chances that the larger companies wouldn't. Perhaps because they had less to lose than the larger conglomerates, they were willing to risk more. And Drew Lawrence, acting on instinct, channeled all Ariel's available resources into Danny Fiore's debut album.

Lawrence's instinct paid off in spades.

That first album, titled *Stardust*, was a mixture of straight pop and driving rock, balanced off by a sprinkling of blues ballads so funky they fairly peeled the paper off the walls. Again acting on instinct, Lawrence chose for the first single release a catchy, hot little Fiore/MacKenzie pop tune. To the amazement of everyone except Drew Lawrence, *Tell Me Lies* debuted at number twenty-three on the pop charts, jumped fifteen places the second week, hit number one its third week on the charts, and stayed there for a solid nine weeks.

Ignoring the music industry truism that says an artist who has a monster hit the first time around may never again rival that first effort, Lawrence released a second single from *Stardust*. Another Fiore/MacKenzie creation, *Whisper in My Dreams* was a smoky, sultry ballad that climbed steadily up the pop charts to number one before crossing over to peak at number three on the R&B charts. Lawrence timed its release to coincide with a grueling six-week bus tour of the rural South.

***

There was a comforting anonymity in the ethnic mix of Sunday afternoon patrons at McDonald's. At the next table there were two Indian women in saris, and behind them, a group of lanky black teenage boys was showing off for the two giggling girls across the way. Rob brushed the crumbs off the table and sat down across from Nancy, who was watching the door with an expression so wistful it wrenched at his heart. "Don't worry," he said, opening the bag of food and handing Nancy her French fries. "She'll show up."

Nancy smiled, but he'd obviously failed to allay her fear that her younger sister hadn't been able to escape the house and the eagle eye of their mother. As he unwrapped his Big Mac, she delicately nibbled at the edges of her fish sandwich, but her gaze never strayed for long from the entrance.

The instant she saw Mei Ling, her face radiated happiness. Her sister made her way to their table, and the two women embraced and began talking and gesturing rapidly in Chinese.

He'd never met Nancy's kid sister before, and he studied their animated faces. They had the same eyes, but where Nancy's face was delicate and birdlike, Mei Ling's was broad and rounded, with a high forehead. She wore her hair in a chin-length bob, shorter than Nancy's, but with the same rich color and texture.

When Nancy introduced them, Mei Ling grew tongue-tied. He imagined that at fifteen, cosseted and pampered and kept on a short leash as she was, her experience with white males was limited. Especially given her parents' value system, which placed all white males just slightly higher on the evolutionary scale than the spawn of Satan. "Would you be more comfortable," he said, "if I left you alone for a while?"

He could see the answer in Nancy's eyes, so he took his lunch outside and sat at a table near the play area, where he could still keep an eye on the two women inside the restaurant. As he ate his lunch, kids and parents alike eyed him with distrust, suspicious of any man who sat in the play yard without a child attached. When he finished eating, he lit a cigarette and watched the kids playing. One little girl slithered down the slide and landed a few feet away from him. She gave him a shy smile and he returned it, but her mother spoke sharply to her and she scurried away. The mother grabbed the girl by the wrist and dragged her out of the play area, lecturing her loudly about the dangers of strange men.

An hour passed before Nancy and Mei Ling ended their visit. As his wife forlornly watched her younger sister leave the restaurant, he wondered, not for the first time, if he'd done the right thing by marrying her.

Three days later, he opened the apartment door to insistent

knocking. The man who stood on the other side had greasy hair and a stained shirt. "I'm looking for Nancy Chen MacKenzie," he said.

Rob looked the guy up and down, and squared his jaw. "What do you want her for?" he said.

"I got something for her."

"I'm her husband. You can give it to me."

"Sorry, buddy, no can do. I have to deliver it to the lady personally."

Nancy came up beside him. He put an arm around her, and he could feel her trembling. "I am Nancy Chen MacKenzie," she said.

"Then I guess this is for you," he said, handing her an envelope. "Have a nice day, folks."

Rob slammed the door behind him and tried to read over his wife's shoulder. "Rob?" she said, her voice rising. "What is this? I do not understand."

He took it from her, skimmed through the legalese until he got to the part that was intelligible. His throat tightened as he read, and he felt color rising in his face. "It's a restraining order," he said, "forbidding you to have any contact with Mei Ling."

Her face paled, and she sank slowly onto a chair. "They cannot do this," she whispered.

"They've done it," he said. "Jesus, Nancy, I'm so sorry."

She swallowed visibly. "And what happens," she said, "if I ignore it?"

"Then you'll be found in contempt of court," he said. "You could go to jail."

For the first time since their marriage, he was unable to console her. She locked herself in the bathroom so he wouldn't hear the sobbing she tried to muffle. But he heard. He heard every sound she made. Hands crammed in his pockets, he paced, muttering under his breath, propelled by fury. When Casey came in, he said curtly, "Take care of her. There's something I have to do."

***

When the maid opened the door, he strong-armed her aside

and followed the singsong of Chinese voices to the dining room. They were sitting around the massive table, the three of them, and they looked up in amazement as he strode into the room. "What the hell kind of parents are you?" he demanded. "How could you do this to her?"

"Mr. MacKenzie," her mother said icily, "you are not welcome here, and if you do not leave immediately, I will call the police and have you removed."

"I'll stay, by God, until I've said what I came to say. Why? Why would you do something like this to her? That girl has never hurt anybody in her life. Her sister means the world to her. What kind of heartless monsters are you?"

"We are not heartless monsters," Dr. Chen said. "We are hoping that Nancy will recognize the error of her ways."

"If she wishes to see her sister again," the dragon lady said, "she has only to divorce you. It is not such a difficult choice, is it, Mr. MacKenzie? The family of her birth—" She looked around the table. "—or you."

"You bastards." He glanced at Mei Ling, her head bowed low over her soup bowl. It was probably already too late for her. They'd probably already poisoned her mind. His hands clenched into fists. "I don't know what cabbage leaf you plucked Nancy out from under," he said grimly, "but I know one thing: she sure as hell didn't spring from your loins."

And he left them to their dinner.

***

He broke the news to Nancy on the eve of the tour. "I'm going on tour with Danny," he said as he thumped his suitcase onto the bed and snapped open the locks. "We'll be away for six weeks. When I get back, I want you gone."

Her face paled. "Rob?" she said. "What are you talking about?"

He opened a dresser drawer, took out a stack of undershirts, and dropped them into the suitcase. Deliberately avoided looking at her. "You know what I'm talking about," he said. "We made a mistake. We did something stupid. It's over, Nance. We might as well face it and get on with our lives."

"This is not what I want!"

He looked at her for a moment. Squared his jaw and turned away. "It's what I want," he said.

"Take me with you. I would not get in the way."

He rolled up a pair of jeans and crammed them in beside the undershirts. "I can't. There's no room."

"But Casey is going."

Dropping in the only tie he owned, he said, "Casey's part of the team. She has to go."

"I do not understand. If I cannot go, I will wait for you. I don't mind so very much, waiting for you."

Against his will, his mind drew a picture for him, a picture of his return, of Nancy's slender limbs wrapped around him in a hero's welcome. He pushed away the picture and strengthened his resolve. Couldn't she see that he was doing this for her? "This is how it'll be from now on," he said. "I'll be gone all the time. All the time, Nance. Is that what you want? An absentee husband?"

"You do not love me?" she said.

He squared his jaw and looked at her. "Look," he said, "we had some fun times together, but I can't deal with all this shit your parents keep throwing at us. It's not worth it. I helped you out when you were in a bind. Your next move's up to you. I just know I can't be a part of it any more."

She wet her lips. "I see," she said.

His insides knotted in agony, he played his trump card. "I couldn't even promise to be faithful to you," he said. "A guy gets lonely on the road."

The silence stretched out between them. He turned away from her, closed his eyes and swallowed hard. *I'm sorry*, he thought. *So sorry.* "It's the best thing for both of us," he said.

When she didn't respond, he slammed out of the apartment and began walking blindly, block after block after block, his hands crammed in his pockets, his thunderous expression prompting oncomers to veer out of his path. Only after the pain and the fury had turned to numbness did he go home. His wife was already gone, the apartment stripped of her few possessions. Except for the lingering scent of jasmine, she might never have been there in the first place.

That night, for the first time since he was a kid, Rob MacKenzie cried himself to sleep.

CHAPTER SIXTEEN

At twenty-three, Bryan Silver already had two platinum albums and four hit singles to his credit. He'd survived two broken marriages and had auditioned two dozen or more young hopefuls for the role of wife number three. He had a reputation as a prima donna, an ego to match, and a dusky, soulful voice that could make the little girls weep when it wailed the blues. Born Bernie Silverman in the Bronx, Bryan Silver was Ariel's biggest success story. And that summer, while *Whisper in My Dreams* held steady at number one, Drew Lawrence sent Danny Fiore on tour as Silver's opening act.

Lawrence's reasoning was shrewd. Names and faces had a nasty habit of being forgotten once their brief moment of glory was over, and one hit record was barely worth the vinyl it was stamped on. Danny needed exposure, and Silver would draw the kind of audiences Lawrence wanted him exposed to.

They were scheduled for thirty-seven appearances in six weeks at county fairs across the South. They lived in an artificial environment, in the close, insulated world of a traveling band: raucous nights and monotonous days of endless interstate highways; cotton candy and fried dough, greasy hot dogs and lukewarm coffee; precious stolen hours of sleep on the bus between gigs; too much togetherness and too little privacy; bottles passed around from mouth to mouth, and the ubiquitous, sickish-sweet odor of burning marijuana.

Between stops, they played blackjack, read newspapers, held impromptu jam sessions, wrote songs, and grew to know each other at their best and their worst. And Casey, who always tried to find something likable in everyone she met, discovered that she disliked Bryan Silver intensely.

Although from a distance Silver appeared attractive, at close range his teeth were bad and his eyes set too close together. When he talked with Casey, he leaned too close, touched her too often. Worse still was his way of looking at her, a slow, suggestive perusal that left her feeling soiled. For Silver, undressing women with his eyes was probably a reflex action, but it made Casey uncomfortable. He never did it where Danny could see, and she pointedly avoided being alone with the man.

Even worse was Silver's attitude toward Danny. The plan had been for him to play second banana to Silver. But night after night, in one dry, dusty little town after another, it was Danny they were screaming for. The audiences who had come to see Silver were refusing to let his opening act leave the stage. They ate him up, called him back for encore after encore. Silver came off looking like an afterthought, and it made him furious. This was his gig. Danny Fiore was a nobody, little more than a hired hand, and Silver made sure he didn't forget it. On the surface, the two men were coolly courteous, but beneath that surface simmered an accelerating mutual dislike. By the end of the second week, everyone connected with the tour realized that it would be a miracle if Fiore and Silver managed to survive the entire six weeks without some cataclysmic confrontation.

***

The midway was alive with color and sound, and she clung to Danny's hand as they threaded their way through the massive throng of people. Smells mingled in the air: French fries and cotton candy, pizza, and the underlying odor of animal dung. Casey paused at the entrance to a garish purple tent. The sign beside the door read *Madame Zelda, Palm Reader*. "Let's go in," she said, tugging on Danny's arm.

He turned to see what had caught her attention, and his brows drew together. "That stuff is bullshit," he said.

"You're not supposed to take it seriously. It's supposed to be fun."

He followed her reluctantly into the tent. An ancient woman was seated behind a card table, her silver hoop earrings gleaming in the candlelight. "Come in, come in," she greeted them. "I am Madame Zelda. And you are?"

"Casey. And this is my husband, Danny."

"Sit down, my dear."

Her skin as dry and thin as rice paper, the gypsy took Casey's hand in her gnarled, brown one. She studied the markings, ran a bony finger along the lines that were scattered like a road map across Casey's palm. When the old woman's fathomless dark eyes met hers, a shock like an electrical current ran through Casey's body, and the hair on the back of her neck stood up. "You are a strong woman," the gypsy said.

The old lady couldn't possibly know what she was talking about. This was nothing more than a clever parlor trick, designed to dupe the gullible. "You have a long life line," the gypsy said, pointing. "Here. See? I see many years, much happiness. Children. Grandchildren." She paused, still studying the lines that criss-crossed Casey's palm. "I see a time of great turmoil," she said, "of heartbreak. But you will emerge stronger than before."

Again Casey experienced the odd sensation that the gypsy could see directly into her soul. "And I see a great love," the woman said, "one that will last into your old age."

Shaken, Casey gave up her seat to Danny. He sat gingerly in the chair and the old woman took his hand, closed her eyes and held it for a moment. She opened them, and a slight smile curved her lips. "You," she said, "are not a believer."

Danny leaned back in the chair and rested his ankle on his knee. "No," he said. "I'm not."

She smiled thinly, then turned her attention to his palm. "Such an intriguing palm," she said, tracing its lines and whorls with a fingertip. "Full of chaotic energy. I see success ahead of you. But unhappiness, too. You must learn to temper your ambition, or it will lead to your demise."

He snorted, but the gypsy merely shrugged. "See here?" She touched his hand with her fingertip. "You have a short life line. You must ground yourself, or like a shooting star, you will burn out."

"Oh, for Christ's sake." Danny yanked his hand away and rose from the chair. "This is pure bullshit," he said to Casey. He grabbed her by the arm and dragged her out of the tent and back onto the midway.

Outside, there was light and noise and confusion. Behind them, tuneless calliope music tinkled from the carousel. "What on earth is wrong with you?" she said.

"I told you, I don't believe in that bullshit. All her talk about heartbreak and suffering. She's nothing more than a money-grubbing phony."

"You're not supposed to take it seriously," she said.

He shrugged his shoulders as though to ward off some evil spirit. Pulled out a pack of cigarettes and lit one. "It's all prepackaged garbage," he said. "A man comes in, she predicts success and burnout. A woman comes in, she predicts babies and everlasting love. She throws in the turmoil and the suffering because who doesn't experience turmoil or suffering in the course of a lifetime? It's still bullshit, no matter how you package it."

They turned and began walking slowly along the midway, past the crowds and the carnival barkers. "I suppose I should be grateful," she said ruefully. "After all, she did promise children and grandchildren. Not to mention everlasting love."

"But with whom? I'm supposed to crash and burn, remember?"

"Hah! You have a bit farther to go, my darling, before you crash and burn."

***

The bus developed engine trouble in a small town in Arkansas. Amid a chorus of complaints, it was towed to a repair shop, and Bruce, the road manager, booked the crew into a roadside motel for the night. It was a rare opportunity for a hot shower and a real bed, a chance to sit in the dimly lit motel bar and lift a few while listening to a bunch of locals perform mediocre covers of C&W tunes. Although country & western scored low on Casey's list of favored music, when Danny collapsed across the bed and began snoring before it was even dark, she was bored enough to leave him there and join the rest of the noisy crew in the bar.

They made room for her at the table and somebody bought her a Bud, and she nursed it slowly, watching the animated faces and enjoying the hilarity as the group collectively shrugged off the stress created by weeks of confinement. Who else in the world but a musician would work killer hours, then spend his precious free time watching other people do the same thing? It was a busman's holiday, but Casey felt the same draw they all did: she couldn't escape from the music. It lived inside her head, night and day, and when she wasn't creating her own, she was compelled to listen to others create it for her.

During lulls in the cacophony, she tried to carry on a conversation with Kitty Callahan. Kitty was twenty years old and had a voice like an angel, and singing backup for Bryan Silver was her first professional job. Like Casey, Kitty was a farm girl, raised in Ames, Iowa, and during endless hours on the road, the two of them had struck up a friendship of sorts. But tonight, the music was too loud and the crowd too raucous, and after ten minutes of trying to talk, their throats hurt from shouting, and they gave up. Then the band began a rousing rendition of *Jambalaya*, and Rob swooped down on Kitty and carted her off onto the dance floor, leaving Casey to watch the dancers.

Across the table, Bryan Silver lifted his beer bottle and emptied it in a single long draught, his Adam's apple bobbing as he gulped. Eyes boring into hers, he wiped his mouth and added the bottle to the growing collection of empties. Casey quickly looked away, but the uncomfortable sensation of being watched remained with her. When the band slowed its tempo with a waltz, Silver got up from the table. Skirting Kitty, who was just returning, he made a beeline for Casey. "Hey, doll," he said, "let's take a spin around the floor."

He'd deliberately put her in an awkward position. Everyone at the table was watching, and she couldn't refuse him without making a scene. Swallowing her distaste, she plastered on a smile so fake it hurt and let him lead her out onto the dance floor.

She knew she'd made a mistake the moment he put his arms around her. He pulled her so tight against him that her breasts were crushed. His breath reeked of beer, and she turned her head to avoid his sour smell. "Oh, baby," he said, one hand moving in the direction of her ribcage. "You don't know how long I've been thinking about this."

She pointedly removed his hand from her left breast. "Back off, Silver," she said.

"Come on, baby. Be nice to old Uncle Bry."

She shoved hard at his chest. "My family tree," she said,

"doesn't include simians."

"What I got for you, baby, will really make your motor purr."

With the heel of her boot, she stepped down hard on his instep. He stumbled and missed a step. "Oops," she said.

Regaining his balance, he lowered his head and began to slobber all over her neck. "I've been watching you," he said. "Waiting."

She struggled to push him away. "Bryan," she said, "you've had too much to drink. I'd like you to let me go. Right now."

"Come on," he said, sliding his tongue into her ear. "A hot chick like you can't be saving it all for Fiore. Share the wealth, baby."

Casey gave him a hard elbow to the ribs. He uttered a soft explosion of sound and staggered backward. "Come near me again," she said, "and you'll regret it."

The music followed her out into the sticky Arkansas night. Fueled by anger, she stalked past the mud-spattered pickup trucks that littered the parking lot, past the tattered screen door of the motel office, past the crimson neon sign that buzzed and sputtered its *no vacancy* message. She had just reached the first ugly cinder block building when a hand caught her by the elbow and she was thrust up against the gritty concrete wall. "You didn't really think you'd get away that easy, did you?" he said, his face inches from hers.

His eyes were glassy, his breath fetid. "Bryan," she said, "you're drunk."

"Not that drunk," he said. "Not too drunk for what I have in mind."

"I'm not interested," she said. "I'm a married woman."

"Fuck me once, baby, and you'll never go back to him."

"You're revolting," she said, shoving at his shoulders. "Leave me alone."

"I don't think so," he said, pinning her wrists against the wall with a single powerful hand and crushing her against the concrete with his body. "I've been waiting too long to nail you, doll."

"Damn it, Bryan," she said, "let go of me!"

He cupped her breast with his free hand. "Don't fight, sweet thing. You're gonna love it."

Mingled with the revulsion was the first stirring of fear. His mouth was wet and slack against hers, muffling her protests. Casey choked on his beer breath. He forced his tongue into her mouth, and she gagged. She tried to knee him in the groin, but her boots kept slipping in the moist red earth, and his hips, pressed close enough against hers to make his intentions impossible to misunderstand, pinned her fast against the wall. He tore open the front of her shirt, scattering buttons, and then his palm touched bare flesh and she panicked, struggling like a wild animal. He toyed with the lacy edge to her brassiere, followed it down to the hollow between her breasts, hooked two fingers beneath it, and yanked. The fabric tore, and her struggle escalated. Undaunted, enjoying the struggle, he changed tack, insinuating a hand between their bodies, running it down her bare belly to the waistband of her jeans. While his tongue continued its drunken exploration of her mouth, his hand maintained its southbound progress and slipped between her thighs.

And she bit him.

He howled like a wounded animal. Eyes wide with disbelief, he released her and his hands went to his injured mouth. His fingers came away wet with blood. Casey kicked him hard in the shin, knocking him off balance. He grabbed at her drunkenly, catching his fist in her hair and taking her with him as he fell. They rolled in the dirt, Silver bellowing with rage, Casey kicking and gouging and cussing him out with words she hadn't realized she knew. He grabbed a fistful of her hair and yanked hard enough to bring tears to her eyes, and then she was on her back in the dirt and he was on top of her, both of them gasping for breath, his eyes hard and cold, his hand crammed against her mouth so hard she felt the imprint of her teeth on the back of her lips. "Bite me again, bitch," he said, "and I'll kill you."

Then, suddenly, he was gone, torn off her with a surprised yelp. Rob MacKenzie slammed him up against the wall with enough force to elicit a sharp crack when his skull made contact with the concrete. Pressing a bony forearm flat against Silver's windpipe, Rob held him there, a half-inch off the ground, scrambling for a foothold. "You stupid son of a bitch," he said. "You pathetic piece of shit."

Silver's eyes bulged, and he flailed his arms and legs frantically. Rob pressed harder, and Silver made a guttural choking sound. Rob leaned into his face. "Touch her again," he said, "and I'll shove my foot up your ass so far it'll come out your throat. Understand?"

Silver nodded in terror, and Rob released him. He fell to the ground and slumped there in the dirt, gasping and coughing and spitting up blood. Rob nudged him with the toe of his sneaker, as if he were something rank and dead. "Consider yourself lucky," he said, "that it wasn't Danny who caught you mauling his wife. If it was, you'd be a dead man right now."

The hard look in his eyes was unfamiliar. Rob had just displayed a side Casey had never seen, and she wasn't sure she liked it. "Cover yourself," he said curtly, and she realized that her buttonless shirt was hanging open over tattered lace for all the world to see. With sweaty hands, she held her shirt front together, and while Silver continued to gasp and retch, Rob placed a hand between her shoulder blades and escorted her to the door of his motel room.

He locked it behind them. Casey sank onto the edge of the bed, her legs suddenly weak, her body quivering now that the moment of danger had passed. Rob disappeared into the bathroom, returning a moment later with a paper cup. He knelt on the carpet in front of her, placed the cup in her hand and folded her trembling fingers around it. "Drink," he said.

She looked stupidly at the cup in her hand. What is it?" she said.

"Something to make you feel better."

Casey drained it in a single gulp. Her eyes watered as the liquor burned all the way down, but she felt its soothing effects almost immediately. She licked the bitter taste from her lips, then shuddered at the memory of Silver's mouth on hers, his hands on her body. "How did you know?" she said.

Rob's mouth thinned. "I saw him follow you."

She took a deep breath, struggling to fight off tears. Her eyes filled, and a small, strangled sob broke deep in her throat. Mortified, she covered her face with her hands, more embarrassed by her tears than by her state of undress.

Rob patted her shoulder awkwardly. "It's okay to cry," he said gruffly. "It doesn't mean you're weak."

She didn't want him to be nice to her. Right now, she couldn't handle nice. The floodgates opened, beyond her control, and the flood began in earnest. "Ah, hell," Rob said, and wrapped his arms around her and rocked her gently, rhythmically, while she bawled like a baby all over him. It might have been five minutes, might have been an hour, before the sobs subsided and she pulled away from him, reclaiming what was left of her dignity. "I'm sorry," she said. "I don't mean to be a baby."

"You don't always have to be strong, Fiore. Sometimes it's okay to lean on someone."

"If you hadn't come along," she said, "he would have raped me."

Rob squared his jaw. "I know," he said.

She got up from the bed and began pacing. "I was so afraid. I felt so vulnerable. And I hated it." She wheeled to face him. "I hated it!"

"Sweetheart," he said, "you did more damage to him than he did to you."

"But I should have been able to stop him!"

"You're a woman. And stop looking at me that way. The guy's a foot taller than you and he outweighs you by sixty pounds. Those are crummy odds."

She glared at him. "Maybe it's time I did something to even up the odds."

Rob dragged a battered brown suitcase out from under the bed and snapped it open. "Like what?" he said, pulling out a wrinkled tee shirt and tossing it to her.

Still pacing, she said, "Like carrying mace. Or taking a self-defense class."

"Or like telling your husband."

She paused, tee shirt in hand. "I'm not telling Danny." Green eyes met green eyes, searched deep, and came to an understanding. Both of them pondering the secrets that lay between them, some spoken, some merely understood.

Rob unfolded like a gazelle. "You'll feel better after you

take a shower. I'll be right outside, having a smoke."

She peeled off the ruined shirt and bra and discarded them in the bathroom wastebasket. If she could have, she would have cut them into small pieces and flushed them down the toilet. She felt dirty, used, violated. He'd had no right to touch her that way, and she wished Bryan Silver a slow and painful death. Preferably one she could watch.

Every muscle in her body ached. Even her scalp hurt where Silver had pulled her hair. Her wrists were already turning color, and her back was scraped raw in places. How the hell would she keep this from Danny? The needle-hot spray of the shower hurt her chafed skin, but she forced herself to stay under it because it made everything else feel so much better.

She dried herself off awkwardly, her aching muscles screaming in protest, then borrowed Rob's comb to work the snarls from her wet hair. She dusted off her jeans, wiped the mud from her boots, and pulled Rob's tee shirt down over her head. It clung to her damp body, revealing far too much of her unbound breasts. But Rob wouldn't notice, and it was only a short walk from his room to hers.

He was waiting outside in the hot, sticky night. There was no sign of Silver; he must have slithered back into his hole. Rob angled a glance down at her, then quickly looked away, leaving her with the uncomfortable impression that she'd been wrong, that he had noticed precisely what she wore beneath the tee shirt. They walked to her room in a silence broken only by their footsteps and the whine of a distant eighteen-wheeler.

At her door they paused, and Rob leaned a bony shoulder against the door jamb. Looking at the neon sign that loomed over the yellowed grass of the courtyard, he said softly, "Will you be okay?"

Although it was nearly ninety degrees, she shivered and folded her arms across her chest. "I'm fine."

He looked at her then. "Silver'd better leave you alone," he said, "because I'll be watching."

"I don't need a bodyguard."

"Just say thank you, Fiore, and leave it at that."

She opened her mouth to argue. Closed it. And swallowed. "Thank you," she said.

He pulled away from the door jamb. "See you in the morning, kiddo."

Danny awakened when she crawled into bed beside him. He turned over and wrapped an arm around her, drawing her close. "Hi," he said.

She settled into his warmth. "Hi."

"Your hair's wet."

"I just took a shower."

"I'm sorry I fizzled out on you so early. What time is it?"

"Almost midnight. Try to get back to sleep, sweetheart. We have to be on the road early."

Outside the window, the neon sign flashed red, then yellow, red, then yellow. Inside the motel room, Casey lay awake, watching the play of colors on Danny's face as he slept. If he ever found out what had happened tonight, he would kill Silver. She never for a moment doubted that he was capable; she'd seen how cold and hard and silent he could become. Like a snake about to strike. She couldn't let that happen. Better she should let sleeping dogs lie than allow this nightmare to be carried any further.

It was after three when she finally fell asleep. Danny woke her around six, and they made love for the first time in weeks, slow and sweet, but she was bruised and sore, and it was one of the few times that she had ever been left unfulfilled. She lay beneath him, hands tangled in his long hair, sweetly content with his drowsy weight atop her. "I'm sorry," he said.

"For what?"

"I rushed you...you weren't ready...it's been too damn long."

"I'm just tired," she said, gently kneading his shoulders. "You didn't do anything wrong."

He let out a long sigh of contentment. "Christ, that feels good."

She continued kneading. "It's supposed to."

The phone rang, and they looked at each other balefully. "We could ignore it," he said.

"Then whoever it is would just come pounding on the door."

He scowled and reached for the phone. "Yeah?" he said.

"Yes. Fine." He dropped the receiver back into its cradle. "We pull out," he said, "in forty-five minutes."

"I guess that means playtime's over."

He kissed the palm of her hand. "I guess it does." He peered at her forearm. "What's this?" he said.

Her heartbeat quickened. "What's what?"

"This bruise on your wrist. Christ, I didn't do that, did I?"

"My loving husband," she said dryly, "Daniel de Sade. Of course you didn't do it. I probably bumped into something. You know me. I bruise if you look at me the wrong way."

He looked unconvinced. She planted a kiss on the tip of his nose. "Stop worrying," she said, "and let's get dressed before the bus leaves without us."

Two days later, Silver telephoned Drew Lawrence and demanded that Danny Fiore be replaced as his opening act. When Lawrence refused to cave in to his demands, Bryan Silver packed his belongings and called a cab.

And Danny, by default, became the headlining act.

***

Twelve hours after the bus limped into the Big Apple, Danny found himself again facing Drew Lawrence across a massive oak desk. "Sit down," Lawrence said, pumping his hand with enthusiasm. "Congratulations. I hear you were a smash."

Danny rested his weight on his tailbone and extended his long legs. "It definitely went well," he said.

"It went better than well. Album sales have gone through the roof. They love you." Lawrence leaned back in his swivel chair and locked his hands together behind his head. "You've got big things ahead of you, Danny. That's why we want you back in the studio as soon as possible to start working on a second album."

"A second album," he said, surprised. "Already?"

"We want to strike while the iron's hot. How much time do you need to get ready?"

He did some quick thinking. New York was a Mecca for musicians, and he and Rob had contacts everywhere. Pulling together a band shouldn't be difficult. As for material, Casey and Rob were pros. They'd give him what he needed in whatever time frame they were given. "Six weeks," he said.

"Excellent." Lawrence punched a button on his intercom. "Lorraine, will you bring me that check for Mr. Fiore, please?" He studied Danny bemusedly. "I just want you to know," he said, "that we're impressed. Damn impressed. All of us here at Ariel believe we have a spectacular future together."

The secretary brought in the check. She shot a quick, speculative glance at Danny and discreetly disappeared again. Lawrence slid the envelope across the desk. "Remember," he said, "this is just the beginning."

"I hope you're right." Danny took the envelope, folded it, and started to pocket it.

"Ah, Danny? You might want to open it."

Danny tore open the envelope. Looked at the check, did a double-take. And all the blood left his brain. Lawrence chuckled. "Listen," he said, "I'll get the studio time set up. You'll be hearing from our publicist, who'll be setting up a photo session, some magazine interviews. In the meantime, you take care of things at your end." He stood and held out his hand. "Keep in touch."

***

Two days later, they moved uptown, into an airy, three-bedroom apartment in an old brownstone on Central Park West. Though the building wasn't as upscale as the newer high-rises, it had an elevator and a doorman, and compared to Freddy Wong's roach-infested slum, it was a palace. As Casey was trying to figure out a way to make their pathetic collection of mismatched furniture look a little less wretched, Danny walked through the door and dangled a set of car keys in her face. Parked illegally next to the curb outside was a spanking new, shiny red Mustang convertible with a V8, a five-speed transmission, and the best sound system on the market. "I've been thinking," he said, as she admired the car's luxurious interior. "Now that we have new wheels, don't you think it's time we took a honeymoon?"

They'd never spent more than a day or two of uninterrupted time together, and the idea was wildly appealing. They left Rob the task of assembling a band, and on a bright Thursday morning, she and Danny climbed into the Mustang, crossed the George Washington Bridge, and rocketed south on the Jersey Pike.

They explored the Maryland shore, shopped for antiques and trinkets, took in the breathless blue vista of the Chesapeake Bay. They danced beneath the stars in Virginia, ate barbecue at a roadside stand in North Carolina. Made love in the sand on a lonely stretch of beach on the Outer Banks. It was a halcyon time with no schedules, no deadlines, no expectations to live up to. Just the two of them, alone on the open road, free to explore and enjoy the world around them.

But as all good things must, it eventually had to come to an end. At a record store in a strip mall in Newport News, they were approached by a hesitant teenage girl carrying a copy of *Stardust.* "Mr. Fiore?" she said.

Danny was reading the liner notes on Springsteen's latest album, and he looked up distractedly. "Hmm?"

Flushing, the girl held up the record album. "Can I have your autograph?"

He looked stunned. Then he turned the full force of the infamous Fiore smile on the girl, two hundred megawatts of dimpled splendor, powerful enough to fell the hardest woman. Against that kind of ammunition, no mere teenage girl stood a chance. "What's your name, sweetheart?" he asked, looking at the girl as though she were the only female left on the planet.

Her eyes were feverish. "Heather," she said. "Heather Gladstone."

"Well, hello, Heather Gladstone," he said as he scribbled. "Pretty name. And a pretty face to go with it. Here you go." And he winked at her as he handed back the album.

The girl clutched the record to her bosom, her eyes the size of dinner plates. Her mouth worked as though she were trying to speak. Without a word, she spun on her heel and fled.

Casey met his eyes. "You," she told him, "are a wicked, wicked man."

The corner of his mouth twitched. "But nobody does it better."

"And humble as well, I see."

He turned that grin on her, and she took a step backward.

"Oh, no," she said. "I know how you operate. I'm immune to your considerable charm."

The grin widened. "Bullshit," he said, and backed her up against the wall and kissed her, right there in the record store. Face to face, they studied each other until their grins faded and they grew serious. And Danny voiced the thought that was running through both their heads. "It's time to go back," he said.

Her heart constricted with regret. She'd hoped for more time. "These have been the most wonderful six days of my life," she said.

He cupped her cheek. "There's a part of me," he said, "that wishes we never had to go back."

Then don't, she wanted to say, but she knew that was impossible. A bittersweet sadness pierced her, a fierce longing to cling to the present, to hold on with all her might. But it was too late for that. The winds of change had already begun to blow, and some profound force had taken control of their fates. She had no idea what shape those changes would take, but they would happen, as surely as tomorrow's sun would rise.

They spent a final night in Virginia Beach, but Danny was distracted, a part of him already somewhere else, some place where she couldn't follow him. He sat on the balcony outside their motel room while the breakers rolled in below, the tip of his cigarette a pinpoint of light in the darkness as he listened to music only he could hear.

Never enough time, Casey thought. Not in a lifetime would there be enough time to satisfy her hunger for him. Or to appease the hunger in him that she couldn't satisfy.

She took the lead in their lovemaking that night. Aggressive and demanding, she loved him with an unprecedented fierceness that took them both to dizzying heights before plunging them back to earth in a spent tangle of hearts and bodies and damp sheets. The next morning, immediately after breakfast, they shot back across the Chesapeake, Bob Seger blasting from the Mustang's stereo. Eight hours later, they were crawling through rush hour traffic in the Lincoln Tunnel. "Welcome home," Danny said dryly as he edged the Mustang ahead half a car length.

Casey yawned. "Some things," she said, "never change."

But others do. And neither of them had an inkling on that ordinary Wednesday afternoon that life as they had always known it was about to blow up around them with a magnitude beyond their wildest imaginings.

***

That year, they spent 300 days on the road, and Casey got to see up close and personal the glamorous life of a recording artist. As a bit player in a big boy's game, Danny didn't qualify for the luxurious accoutrements given to the big name acts. They toured in a converted Greyhound bus, fifteen people sharing one bathroom with a hand-held shower nozzle and a twenty-gallon hot water tank. Privacy was nonexistent, sleeping arrangements were abysmal, and bathroom time had to be staggered. Timing was everything, and creativity the name of the game. Casey was the only woman in the group, and at first, the men didn't know how to take her. But as time and proximity wore down the initial discomfort, she became one of the guys, treated to the same raunchy humor and off-color jokes as the men. Practicality took precedence over vanity. She wore her hair in a single thick braid that reached her waist, gave up wearing makeup, and slept in sweat pants and a ragged sweatshirt. They made bologna and tuna fish sandwiches in the tiny galley, drank endless cups of coffee laced with bourbon or rum, and sang silly songs. While Danny took advantage of his considerable poker playing skill, she and Rob spent hundreds of hours working together with his new Gibson acoustic at the tiny table in the galley.

Life on the road was an educational experience. Casey learned to drink hard liquor, to win at blackjack. She learned that a healthy twenty-three-year-old woman could go for the better part of a year without sleep. That two people could share the same narrow bunk as long as they didn't mind being close. She learned that it was imperative to check the position of the toilet seat before attempting to sit on it in the dark. And that it really was possible to make love with a six-foot-four, hundred-ninety-pound man in a shower enclosure the size of a broom closet while rolling down the highway at fifty-five.

The towns all looked the same. It was only when they

rolled into a new burg and hit the stage and this ragtag assortment of lunatics transformed instantaneously into professional musicians that she realized it was worth every ounce of the craziness. The clean, clear timbre of Danny's voice, the indescribable sweetness of Rob's guitar, could bring tears to her eyes.

The venues were relatively small: county fairs and small-town armories, old converted movie theaters that still smelled of popcorn, the occasional 4,000-seat civic auditorium. A representative cross-section of middle America. But no matter what the differences, they all had one thing in common: a sellout audience that was seventy-five percent female.

Casey wore a laminated tag hanging around her neck that identified her as a member of the crew and allowed her the run of every facility they played. As soon as the boys hit the stage, the first thing she did was sprint out front and check out the crowd. There were never more than a handful of empty seats. Night after night, she stood at the back of some darkened auditorium, arms folded across her chest, listening to the weeping, the yelling, the screaming that was so loud it drowned out the music. And night after night, she wondered just where, and how far, this merry-go-round ride would take them.

There was one place it definitely didn't take them. They came home only four times in twelve months, and during those rare visits, New York no longer felt like home. They'd been so busy working on the album that they'd never really gotten settled into the new apartment. A year after the move, boxes were still piled in corners. Rob was still sleeping on the couch, and she hadn't yet unearthed Mama's antique china. The new Mustang sat in storage, gathering dust, and during the first three-month stint on the road, all her houseplants died.

They were in a hotel room in Buffalo when they got the news. Rob nearly pounded the door down in his enthusiasm. "Wake up, children," he said. "Santa Claus has just arrived."

Grumbling, Danny crawled out of bed and went to the door. "This had better be good," he said.

Rob waltzed in, newspaper in hand, and plunked down heavily on the foot of the bed. With one hand, he shook Casey's hip. "You might want to be awake for this one," he said.

She pulled the covers over her head. "Go away."

"Fine," he said, and folded up the newspaper. "If you're not interested in hearing who's been nominated for a Grammy for Song of the Year, it's fine with me."

It took a moment for his words to register. "What?" she said, her mind fogged with sleep. "What did you say?"

Rob stood at the foot of the bed, grinning like the Cheshire cat. Casey reached for the paper. "Let me see!" she shouted.

He pulled it back out of reach. "Oh, no, Fiore. You wanted to sleep instead, remember?"

"Give me the damn paper or I'll pluck out your eyebrows, one hair at a time!"

She snatched the paper from his hands, folded it in her lap, and devoured the list of nominees. And there it was, in black and white: *Casey Fiore and Rob MacKenzie.* "Ohmigod," she said. "Ohmigod, ohmigod, ohmigod."

"Her eloquence," Danny said, "is matched only by her—"

She picked up a shoe and threw it at him. "Geez," Rob said. "I don't believe I've ever seen her quite this feisty."

"I never thought this day would come," she said.

Rob patted her knee. "I told you it would, kiddo. You just didn't believe me."

She peered at him over the top of the newspaper. "No," she said. "I didn't."

"Don't get your hopes up too high," Danny said. "A nomination is just that. It doesn't mean you'll win."

"It doesn't matter," she told him. "What matters is that we've earned the recognition of our peers."

Rob chucked her under the chin. "The bus pulls out in an hour." He pulled a pair of mirrored sunglasses from his pocket and put them on. "Meet me in the restaurant in twenty minutes," he said, shoving the glasses up the bridge of his nose, "and I'll spring for breakfast."

"If those things got any flashier," Casey said, "they'd blind me."

Behind the wire frames, he waggled his eyebrows. "Just call me Flash MacKenzie."

"Right. Then get your carcass out of here, Flash, so we can shower and get dressed."

CHAPTER SEVENTEEN

Her heart in her throat, Casey leaned forward, fingers threaded with Danny's on one side, Rob's on the other, as the presenters named the nominees in the Song of the Year category. She'd grown numb, her circulation dammed, her fingers tingling, her chest aching from the need to breathe. Danny squeezed her hand, and she squeezed back as Elly Simmons, lead singer for the band Crossroad, opened the envelope, glanced at it. Smiled, leaned toward the microphone. "The winner of this year's Song of the Year award is—" She paused dramatically, and the audience was hushed, waiting.

"—Casey Fiore and Rob MacKenzie, for *Whisper in My Dreams.*"

All Casey's bodily functions had ceased. She sat there, stunned, as the applause grew around her, and then Danny was standing to let her get by, and Rob, tugging at her arm, bent to whisper in her ear, "Jesus Christ, Fiore, don't fall apart on me now."

She plastered on a smile so wide her cheeks ached and took Rob's hand and somehow managed to place one foot in front of the other until she reached the stage without falling on her face. Elly Simmons was waiting with the coveted award. Casey clutched it to her with both hands, looked at it in utter disbelief as the applause grew and then died down. She looked out over the sea of faces in sheer terror. "I'm speechless," she said aloud. And then, in a whisper meant for Rob's ears alone, "Help me, Flash."

Rob leaned forward without a trace of nervousness. "Casey and I," he said into the microphone, "have been writing songs together for a long time. But we never thought that what started out as a way to pass a few long winter afternoons would ever end up here." He looked out over the audience, caught her hand in his and squeezed. "And we can't take full blame for this."

There were a few scattered laughs. Casey searched for Danny and found him, told him with her eyes that she loved him, and anticipated Rob's next words. "Sure, we wrote a great song," he said. "But a great song's not enough. It takes somebody with the colossal talent of Danny Fiore to make it a monster hit."

The applause was wild, and Rob waited patiently for it to die down. "So we have to share this award with Danny, because without him, there wouldn't have been any *Whisper in My Dreams*. Thank you." And he held her arm aloft in a victory sign.

***

The celebration party was in full swing when she returned from the powder room. Danny was standing half-hidden by a potted palm, smoking a cigarette and watching the dancers. "Where's Rob?" she asked.

He nodded in the direction of the buffet table, where Rob was leaning casually against a marble column, talking animatedly to a petite, blond goddess. "Isn't that Monique Lapierre?" Casey said, watching as the woman with the blond-streaked hair tossed her head and uttered a crystalline, silvery laugh.

Danny dropped his cigarette into the plant pot. "*Vive la France*," he said dryly.

Casey caught Rob's eye and motioned to him. He said something to the blond actress and then crossed the room to them. "Hey, guys," he said, "tell me your hearts won't be broken if I skip out on the celebration."

"She's out of your league, MacKenzie," Danny said. "She'll eat you up."

Rob grinned. "I can always hope."

Casey laughed. "You're totally incorrigible."

Rob kissed her cheek. "And you love me just the way I am. If I'm not back in a month or two, have me declared legally dead." He saluted smartly, then walked away without a backward glance.

"Well, darling," Casey said to Danny, "I guess it's just the two of us. Do you think we can find an appropriate way to celebrate?"

"I'm sure," he said dryly, "we can think of something."

***

"I tell you guys, this is it, this is love, this is the real thing."
Nibbling on a celery stick, Rob perched on a bar stool in the
kitchen of the Fiores' new Venice Beach apartment. Two blocks
away, the Pacific Ocean roared, and palm trees dotted the
courtyard outside the window. "This girl has the face that
launched a thousand ships," he said. "She's intelligent, witty,
talented—"

"But can she cook?" Danny said.

"Who cares? She has a house full of servants to do that
stuff."

Casey exchanged a glance with Danny. "But, lovey, isn't
this rather sudden? I mean, you've only known her for a month."

"And lusted after her image on the silver screen for many a
month."

"Rob," she said, "all we're asking is that you give it some
time. Don't rush into something you might regret later."

"Hey, I appreciate the concern. But I'm a big boy. I can
take care of myself. Listen, I thought I'd bring her around this
weekend. That is, if you don't have other plans."

"We'd love to have her," Casey said. "Come by for supper
on Saturday."

"Thanks for letting me bend your ear." He kissed Casey's
cheek and slapped Danny on the shoulder. "See you Saturday."

The apartment was uncomfortably silent after he'd gone.
Casey bent over the bar next to Danny and leaned her chin on her
palm. Picking up the celery stick Rob had discarded, she chewed
on it thoughtfully. "He's lost all sense of reason," she said.

"He's thinking with what's between his legs, instead of
what's between his ears. I know. I've been there."

"What can we do?"

"Not a damn thing. Let it run its course. Maybe she'll be
good for him. We haven't met her yet, after all."

"I know." She stared glumly into space. "I just have a bad
feeling about it. I haven't forgotten how the last one turned out."

"Neither have I. Listen, there's something I've been
meaning to talk to you about. I've been doing some thinking."

She set down the celery stick. "This sounds serious."

He tapped his fingers absently on the bar. "It looks as though we've both launched ourselves solidly, career-wise."

Wondering what he was getting at, she sat on the stool beside him and rested her chin on her palm. "And?" she said.

"It's probably the right time," he said, "to buy a house."

"A house?" Her heart began a slow hammering. "Are you serious?"

"Yes. I also thought, while we're about it—" He paused, cleared his throat. "It's probably time to start thinking about having a baby, too."

***

Monique Lapierre waltzed through Casey's door with the air of a queen in the midst of the peasantry. She eyed the new living room set with distaste, then plunked her dainty rump down on the antique love seat. Rob sat stiffly beside her, and Danny attempted conversation while Casey escaped to the kitchen to bring in the tray of *hors d'oeuvres*. Monique looked askance at the stuffed mushroom caps, cubed Monterey Jack, and cocktail shrimp, poked a lacquered fingernail at a mushroom, and delicately plucked a single shrimp from the tray. Ignoring Casey, she presented Danny with a dazzling smile. "Rob has told me so much about you," she said.

"Don't believe a word of it," Danny said dryly. "It's all a lie."

She laughed as though he'd made a splendid joke. She reached for a second piece of shrimp, peeled away the shell, and held it up in front of Rob. "*Robert*," she said, giving his name the French pronunciation.

Flushing, Rob ate the piece of seafood from her fingers. She patted his knee as though he were a particularly obedient child and said to Danny, "Tell me, Mr. Fiore, have you ever considered a career in the movies?"

"Right now," he said, "I'm concentrating on my singing career. I suppose movies might be a possibility for the future."

"*Mais oui!* Such a face as yours would certainly make the young ladies flock to see your pictures. You would be an overnight sensation. You could perhaps make musicals. With my *Robert*, of course, writing the score."

Rob cleared his throat. "Casey and I," he said, "generally write together. We've been working together for years."

"Yes, of course. Casey, *chere*, I must have your stuffed mushroom recipe to take home to Cook. She's really a horrible little woman, but her cooking is *magnifique*. Sometimes—" Those limpid blue eyes took on a faraway look. "Sometimes I wish I'd been born with some domestic talent, but unfortunately, it has bypassed me completely. How fortunate you are to be able to do your own cooking and cleaning." Those elegant shoulders heaved in a thoroughly Gallic shrug. "Good help is so difficult to find these days."

Heat rose slowly from Casey's chest, up her neck to her face, and she clamped her jaw, hard. Then Danny spilled his drink, and she ran for a wet cloth to clean up the mess. By the time she returned, the conversation had drifted to other topics. On her knees in front of Danny, she glared at him. "Sorry," he said, bending until they were at eye level. He took the cloth from her hand and dabbed clumsily at the carpet. And winked at her.

He joined her in the kitchen as she finished last-minute dinner preparations. "I can't believe him!" she fumed. "Has he lost his mind? The woman is a monster!"

Danny took the salads from the refrigerator. Balancing one on his arm, he said, "I told you before, he's not thinking with what's between his ears, he's thinking with—"

"Please," she said. "Don't make me throw up."

He flashed her the infamous Fiore grin.

"And you!" she accused. "How could you deliberately drop that drink on the carpet?"

"It worked, didn't it? I had to do something. You were about to start breathing fire."

"Oh, Danny, what can he possibly see in her? She treats him like he's her pet poodle."

"Do I really have to spell it out for you?"

Dinner was a disaster. Monique dominated the conversation with stories about her leading men, pausing only long enough to fork food into her mouth or issue orders to Rob. She spoke only to the men, pointedly ignoring Casey, as though she were a servant, to be seen but not acknowledged. It was during dessert that she delivered the *coup de grace*. "Perhaps," she said, "*Robert* would like to tell you our news."

Danny stirred sugar into his coffee cup. "Pray tell, *Robert*," he said wryly, "what news might this be?"

Rob looked slightly embarrassed, then he grinned sheepishly. He gazed at Monique with obvious adoration. And cleared his throat. "Monique and I," he said, "are getting married."

CHAPTER EIGHTEEN

Rob MacKenzie spent his wedding night drinking alone at the hotel bar.

The flight to Palm Springs was smooth, and the flight attendants fawned over Monique. As did the skycaps, the limo driver, and the hotel staff. Everything was going along fine until Rob made the mistake of opening his mouth as they crossed the hotel lobby. "The way everybody's acting," he said, "if I didn't know better, I'd think you were some visiting dignitary."

The rigid set of her chin told him the comment hadn't gone over well. Monique was what his mother had always called high-strung: brimming with nervous energy, and ready to take offense at the slightest injustice.

Sometimes, he had to admit that he saw unbecoming signs of pettiness in her. Her priorities were screwy because she'd been brought up as the pampered only child of a French diplomat. It wasn't her fault that she'd grown up spoiled and pandered to, and had come to accept it as her due. It wasn't her fault that they fought more than most couples. Or that the fights could get nasty. When she wasn't on her high horse about some imagined slight, Monique could be warm and cuddly as a kitten. And making up was heaven, for Monique was nothing like his first wife. Nancy had been a frightened child, but Monique was a woman, one who knew exactly what a man needed, and who provided it with fervent expertise.

Her sour mood dissipated once they reached the honeymoon suite. He tipped the bellboy a twenty before carrying his bride across the threshold and locking the door behind them. On a heart-shaped bed in a room that was costing him a thousand bucks a night, the kitten became a tigress as they enthusiastically proceeded to consummate the marriage. He poured them both a glass of Dom Perignon, and then, just in case for some reason the first time didn't count, they consummated the marriage a second time.

The trouble began when they went downstairs to dinner. They ordered Oysters Rockefeller, spinach salad, and prime rib *au jus*. While he sat there in abject mortification, his little love muffin complained to everyone within hearing distance that the beef was overdone, the oysters were tough, and the spinach was gritty. By the time she was done verbally shredding the place, the manager himself had come out to grovel at the feet of America's Sweetheart. He refused to allow Rob to pay for the meal, and followed them all the way to the door, red-faced and apologizing profusely.

It was in the elevator that he made mistake number two. "Monique," he said once the doors had closed behind them, "that behavior was absolutely uncalled for."

She froze in front of the mirror where she'd been primping. When she turned those huge blue eyes on him, they were glistening with tears. "Tell me the truth, *Robert*. You married me for my money, *non?* Because if you loved me, you would never, ever speak to me that way."

It wasn't the first time she had pulled this routine on him. *If you really loved me, you would.* It was her favorite tool for getting what she wanted. He'd seen her use it on her father, the ambassador, and the aging gentleman always melted the instant those huge blue eyes shed crocodile tears. But Rob had no intention of letting her manipulate him that way.

His third mistake was telling her so.

He'd forgotten the cardinal rule governing baseball and interpersonal relationships: three strikes and you're out. The fight was loud, violent, and embarrassingly public. In the corridor outside their suite, in front of a horrified maid, Monique slapped him, hard. Then, wailing like a pretty French air horn, she fled to the suite and locked him out with nothing but his American Express card and the clothes on his back.

It was not an auspicious start to the marriage.

***

The Malibu house had been built three years earlier as a love nest for film director Nikolai Vronsky and his bride, model Kelly Adams. During the course of their brief but fiery union, it had been the site of numerous battles, including one legendary occasion when Adams had thrown a $30,000 bronze statue through one of the enormous tinted plate glass windows. After a lengthy and bitter courtroom battle, the house had been put on the market as part of the divorce settlement. Vronsky was anxious to sell, and Danny got the house for a fraction of its market value.

When Casey said it was a shame that their good fortune should be bought with someone else's bad fortune, Danny told her it was a wonderful house and she was being ridiculous. And it was a wonderful house: a master bedroom half the size of Rhode Island, three smaller bedrooms, a Jacuzzi in the master bath. A sunken living room that boasted an enormous fieldstone fireplace offset by one wall of tinted glass, and carpeting thick enough, in Rob's words, "to lose a Chihuahua in." French doors off the formal dining room led to a redwood deck that looked out over the beach, and the kitchen's gleaming ebony appliances were a gourmet's dream.

They moved in the day after Christmas. Danny and Rob and a few musician friends moved furniture while Casey, in bare feet and jeans and Danny's old B.U. sweatshirt, supervised. At noon, they broke for tacos and warm beer. After lunch, the men went back to moving boxes, and Casey began the enormous task of setting up housekeeping.

Three thousand miles from home, she'd found a piece of New England to offset her homesickness: in a Rodeo Drive gallery she'd bought a framed Andrew Wyeth print that would look perfect on the south wall of the living room. She held it in both hands, admiring Wyeth's delicate brush strokes, then looked dubiously at the bare white wall that swept twelve feet upward to meet the cathedral ceiling. "Danny," she shouted, "come here a minute. I need you."

From somewhere in the house, Danny answered, his voice muffled. "It'll have to wait. I'm busy."

Rob loped down the six carpeted stairs to the living room, carrying a half-empty bottle of Heineken. "Last time I saw him," he said, "he was holding one end of your bedroom dresser over his head. Will I do?"

"You certainly will." Handing him the hammer, she said, "Men do occasionally have their uses."

"Watch your tongue and hold my beer. Where are we

hanging this thing, Fiore?"

"It's not a thing, MacKenzie, it's a Wyeth. And it's going on that wall, high enough so it doesn't look too lonely."

They spent a few minutes arguing over where to hang the print, then Rob hammered two nails into the wall. He hung the print, adjusted one corner of the frame, then stood back to admire his handiwork. "Not bad," he said, reaching for his beer. "I should have been a carpenter."

"Two nails doth not a carpenter make."

He flashed her a grin before walking to the wall of windows and looking out at the endless blue of sky and sea. "Some view," he said.

She stood beside him. "At sunset, the whole room turns sky-blue pink."

Still looking out the window, he sipped his beer. "Danny tells me you're trying to have a baby."

She folded her arms. Quietly, she said, "We decided it's time."

"You and Danny will make terrific parents." He held out a hand, and she gripped it hard with her own.

"Rob," she said softly, "do you really think he's ready?"

"He loves you, sweetheart. He'll do fine."

"I know he does. And I love him. I love him so much."

"Hang onto it. You two are lucky. Your marriage is the eighth wonder of the world."

She dropped his hand. "If I didn't know better," she said lightly, "I'd swear I detect a hint of jealousy. Don't tell me there's trouble in paradise?"

"Don't ask."

Her humor fled instantly. "You and Monique aren't getting along?"

"Out of bed? No."

She patted his arm. "The first year is always the hardest. You both have to make so many adjustments. It'll get better."

Rob shrugged and drained his beer. "We'll see," he said. "Got any more pictures you want hung?"

That first night in the house, with the waterbed still too cold to sleep on, she and Danny arranged pillows and blankets on the living room floor, where they toasted marshmallows and drank a hundred-dollar bottle of champagne bought especially for the occasion. As Robert Plant's raspy tenor rhapsodized about stairways to heaven, there beneath the eyes of God and the gulls who swooped and soared above them, they relearned the fire and the tenderness that had drawn them together so many years ago. Later, as they lay naked in the darting shadows of the firelight, Casey pressed her cheek to the damp warmth of Danny's chest and thought about how it was all coming together at last, the life they'd worked years to achieve. There was just one thing missing to complete the picture: a baby.

"Danny?" Her voice was little more than a whisper.

"Hmm?" His sounded drowsy, satisfied.

"Do you suppose it happened tonight?"

He didn't have to ask what she meant. "Honey," he said, "it may take some time. Don't be disappointed if it doesn't happen right away."

But she was impatient, ripe and ready for motherhood, and she'd waited so long. She'd already begun decorating the nursery. Now all she needed was a child to put in it. "Maybe we need to keep practicing until we get it right," she said.

"Christ, Casey, I'm dead. I moved furniture all day."

She raised an eyebrow. "What happened to that hot-blooded stud I married?"

"Old age."

"You, old? Hah! You won't be old when you're ninety."

"Shut up and go to sleep." He folded her into his arms and turned them both on their sides. "Tomorrow morning," he promised. "Tomorrow morning, baby doll, I'll give you loving until you beg for mercy."

***

Rob's relationship with Monique ran on only two speeds: fast and faster. When they weren't fighting, they occupied themselves with far more pleasurable pursuits. He'd thought himself quite knowledgeable regarding the erotic arts, but Monique did things to him in bed that he'd never even dreamed of. And then she taught him, with explicit and extensive instruction, exactly how a woman wanted to be pleased. How to move slowly, when all his instincts were rushing him toward the finish line. How to map out and pleasure a woman's erogenous zones until she became putty in his hands. When to use finesse, and when to forgo it completely.

Monique was an exhibitionist. She had mirrors on the ceiling above her bed, and she took great pleasure in making love in unusual, semi-public locations, where the risk of getting caught intensified the excitement. They made love in the swimming pool at noon, in the elevator at the Ritz on a trip to New York, on the butcher-block table in the kitchen at midnight, while the maid watched *The Tonight Show* in the next room.

She was insanely jealous if he so much as looked at another woman. If he made the mistake of actually speaking to one, she would fly into a jealous rage. Yet the arrangement was not reciprocal. When they went out in public, she teased, cajoled, flirted, and made intimate eye contact with every man between the ages of eight and eighty. And expected him to tolerate it.

For reasons he failed to understand, she detested Casey, muttering insults in French every time Casey's name came up in conversation. Rob's knowledge of the French language was limited, but he thought the words "stupid cow" might have surfaced once or twice. At times, he walked around on eggshells, because Monique's rages were so unpleasant that avoiding them became imperative.

Yet she wasn't always unpleasant. Although her rages could erupt at unexpected moments, most of the time she was attentive, affectionate, and generous. She was forever buying him little gifts: a set of onyx cufflinks, a diamond pinkie ring, a gold cigarette lighter. The diamond was ostentatious, and he hated it, but he wore it because she'd given it to him. She replaced his funky wardrobe with stylish and expensive clothes that made him feel like he was dressed up for Halloween. And she dragged him, kicking and screaming all the way, to *Monsieur Henri* and had his hair cut and styled.

When she was finished with him, he looked in the mirror and didn't recognize himself. He looked like a gigolo. But Monique was so impressed by the results that he only complained a little. She soothed his ruffled feathers by making love to him on the chaise longue- in the solarium. And on the piano bench in the library. And on the dew-sprinkled grass of the back lawn, beneath a ripe and heavy moon.

He told himself that he tolerated the jealousy and the tantrums because he was so desperately in love with her. He told himself that she showered him with gifts because she was so desperately in love with him. It was easier than admitting the truth, that something this hot was destined to eventually blow sky-high. Easier than admitting that Monique, like an unbroken filly, would eventually throw him and he'd end up on his ass in the dust.

It was easier to just hold on for dear life and try to enjoy the ride.

**

Four months after she threw out her birth control pills, Casey got up one Sunday morning, looked at the calendar, and realized her period was two days late.

Elation and terror waged war within her. She'd waited so long for this moment that she was afraid to hope, afraid to know the truth, afraid of what Danny's reaction would be. As each day passed with no sign of her period, the elation and the terror grew proportionately. Finally, on a Friday afternoon while Danny had a photo session downtown, she donned dark glasses, drove to a nearby drugstore, and purchased a home pregnancy test.

She spent the longest ten minutes of her life cleaning the kitchen stove while she waited for the results of her test. She pulled off all the burner plates and scrubbed them with Brillo, wiped down the oven that was already clean, and polished the porcelain until she could see her face in it. Suddenly reluctant to know the truth, she took her time returning to the bathroom and the tiny test tube of urine that sat on the shelf.

The code was simple: blue for pregnant, red for not pregnant. Casey took a deep breath and pushed open the bathroom door. She crossed the room on shaky legs and stared in disbelief at the blue liquid in the test tube. She sat down hard on the toilet seat, suddenly terrified of what Danny would say. He didn't really want a baby. He was doing this because he knew it was what she wanted. Would that be enough? Would it be fair to the child, to have a father who had never really wanted him? Would she be strong enough to deal with it? Strong enough to be a proper mother to the child?

This time, there was no question of whether or not she would keep her baby. Danny had always been the be-all and end-all of her existence, but a single instant of staring at a test tube of blue urine changed her loyalties forever. She rested a hand protectively on her abdomen. This unborn child needed every ounce of his mother's strength in order to survive. She'd been given a second chance, and no matter what Danny said or did, this time she wouldn't blow it.

* * *

Rob called, asking her to meet him at a seafood place near the Santa Monica pier. He was already sitting with a cup of coffee, staring out the window, when she arrived. "Hey, hot stuff," she said, sliding into the booth across from him.

"Hey," he said, but didn't smile.

They both ordered broiled scallops, and then she leaned back in the booth. "You look glum," she said. "What's wrong?"

He set down his coffee mug, drummed his fingers on the table top. "Monique's on a rampage again," he said.

She bit her bottom lip. "Oh," she said.

"She's come up with this crazy notion." He cupped his coffee mug in both palms and turned it in his hands. "She thinks that you and I—" He looked at her, squared his shoulders, and shrugged apologetically. "She thinks there's something going on between us."

It took her a moment to understand. And then her mouth fell open. She closed it with difficulty. "As in something sexual?" she said.

"You got it, sugar."

"You and me?" she said in astonishment. "But I'm married."

He gave her a look that said she was incredibly naïve. "*Happily* married," she amended.

"I know that, and you know that, but Monique doesn't get it. She doesn't believe it's possible for a man and a woman to be friends—the kind of friends we are—without sex rearing its ugly head."

She snorted. "That's the most ridiculous thing I've ever heard."

"Yeah? Well, it gets better. She's forbidden me to see you."

"How the hell can she do that? Does she think you're her lap dog?" She saw the look on his face and clamped her mouth abruptly shut. "I'm sorry," she said. "That was uncalled for."

"I tried to make her see how ridiculous she's being. I pointed out that you're not just my friend, you're my business partner. But she's not buying any of it. She's issued an ultimatum. Stop seeing you, or she walks."

A dozen thoughts vied for supremacy in her mind. But she gave voice to just one. "Oh, sweetie," she said. "I'm so sorry."

Their lunch arrived, but neither of them felt much like eating. "Rob," she said at last, toying with her food, "do you love this woman?"

He squared his jaw and busied himself rearranging the salt and pepper shakers. "She's a goddess," he said at last. "The most beautiful woman on the planet. There must be at least a couple million guys who'd cut off their right arm to have her. She could have any man she wants. And she picked me. Plain, ordinary me. Do you have any idea how remarkable that is?"

"I think it's time for a reality check." She lay both her hands atop his in the middle of the table. "I hate to tell you this, sweetie, but you don't have an ordinary bone in your body."

"Be serious, Fiore. I have a face only a mother could love."

"Damn it, Rob, not all of us can be gods and goddesses. There's not a thing wrong with your face. Women fall at your feet!"

"Not women like her," he said darkly.

"So you're going to spend the rest of your life being grateful to her for throwing a few crumbs your way? That doesn't sound like you."

"Do you have any idea," he said, "how long I've waited for the right woman to come along?"

Hands still clasped with his, she sat back against the seat

and sighed. "Look," she said, "you know how much I love you. I'd never say or do anything to hurt you. But I have to say this. I don't think you've found the right woman."

She felt him stiffen, watched his shoulders square, then slump. "I'm sorry," she said. "I should learn to keep my mouth shut."

He sighed. "You only spoke the truth," he said.

"Are you mad at me?"

"I'm mad at myself."

"I shouldn't have said what I did. Nobody knows what goes on inside somebody else's marriage."

Rob picked up his mug in both hands and took a sip of coffee. "Listen, can we talk about something a little more upbeat? This is depressing."

"I'll give you upbeat," she said. "Guess what?"

"What?"

"I'm pregnant."

For a moment, he looked stunned. And then he gave her a grin so wide, so genuine, that she couldn't help reciprocating. "Hot damn!" he said. "About time! What does the Italian stallion have to say about it?"

"I think he's still a little stunned that it happened so fast. But he's positive. Very positive."

"Ah, sweetheart, that's wonderful. Are you happy?"

"Ecstatic. And terrified."

Some of the elation left his face. "Why?" he said.

She toyed with the strap to her purse. "There's always the possibility of another miscarriage."

"Hey." He took her hand in his and squeezed it. "Stop worrying about things that won't ever happen. You're going to have a beautiful, healthy little baby who'll be spoiled rotten by his Uncle Rob."

"I get it. Spoil the kid and then leave us to deal with the monster you've created."

"Hey," he said, "isn't that what uncles are for?"

After lunch, she drove directly to Monique Lapierre's Bel Air mansion. The grounds surrounding the house would have rivaled the gardens at Versailles. Lush tropical flowers blossomed everywhere, water erupted from a myriad of fountains tucked in amongst the Greek statuary, and in the distance, a gardener cut a wide swathe through acres of green lawn on a John Deere mini-tractor. While she waited for the door to be answered, Casey tried to picture Rob living amid all this opulence. But she couldn't imagine it.

The heavy oak door swung open, and a middle-aged woman in a starched maid's uniform peered at her from beneath heavy brows. "Good afternoon," Casey said. "Please inform Miss Lapierre that Mrs. Fiore is here to see her." She brushed past the startled maid, into an entry hall dominated by the biggest crystal chandelier she'd ever seen. Catching sight of the gleaming Steinway beyond an open door, she said, "I'll just wait in here."

The maid, obviously unaccustomed to such directness from visitors, closed her mouth and disappeared into the bowels of the house. While she was gone, Casey roamed around the room, studying the spines of the leather-bound books on the shelves, books she seriously doubted that Monique had ever read. She was picking out a one-fingered tune on the piano when Monique's voice behind her said curtly, "Mrs. Fiore. To what do I owe this unexpected visit?"

Monique was dressed in a blue satin robe, belted at the waist, her hair uncombed, her eyes just a bit too bright. "I just had lunch with your husband," Casey said, getting right to the point.

Monique took her time lighting a cigarette. "Really," she said, and blew out a cloud of smoke.

"You and I," Casey said, "need to have a talk."

"*Certainement*. Can I offer you a drink? Scotch, perhaps?"

"Nothing," Casey said. "This isn't a social call."

Monique turned and gave rapid orders in French to the hovering maid. And then she turned her attention back to Casey. "You will sit down?" she said.

The maid returned with a silver tray bearing a squat glass of amber liquid. Monique took it and waved the maid away. "And what did you and my husband talk about?" she said.

"I think you already know."

Monique sipped her drink. "I see. He told you that I have

forbidden him to see you."

"You must realize how absurd this is. Rob and I are partners. We've been writing together for years. We're right in the middle of producing Danny's next album. We can't just walk away from it because of your paranoia. You're the one who'll be hurt if you persist in making these irrational accusations. I've known Rob for a long time, and I'm telling you that he won't stand for it."

Monique drew in the smoke from her cigarette, held it for a count of five, and released it. "You are threatening me?" she said.

"Oh, for the love of God." Casey closed her eyes. "Look," she said, glaring at Monique, "you don't like me, and I'm not particularly fond of you. I tolerate you because you're Rob's wife, and I happen to care about him. For months, I've been watching the way you treat him, and it's been difficult to hold my tongue. But I've held back from telling you what I really thought of you because for some inconceivable reason, he seems to love you. Or at least he thinks he does, which amounts to the same thing."

Monique's lips pressed together in a small, tight smile. "Please," she said, "feel free to express yourself."

For an instant, Casey considered just how far she wanted to go. "Rob and I," she said finally, "will not break off our professional relationship because of you. Period. And if, in spite of your infantile threats, he chooses to continue our friendship, you will not stand in our way."

Monique's eyes narrowed in sullen acknowledgment of the challenge Casey had thrown down in front of her. "Well," she said, "you are a more formidable foe than I had imagined."

"And you," Casey said, "are no more than a bitch in heat. A beautiful bitch, but no matter how you dress it up, a dog's still a dog, isn't it?"

As she swept from the room, she took immense pleasure in noting that Monique looked a good ten years older with her mouth sagging open.

CHAPTER NINETEEN

Written and produced by Rob MacKenzie and Casey Fiore, Danny's third album, *Going to the Dogs*, went platinum within weeks.

During production, Casey and Rob tried desperately to prevent their working rapport from being tainted by the awkwardness that had sprung up in their personal relationship. But it was impossible to pretend that nothing had changed, impossible to take back the words she'd spoken to Rob's wife. Impossible to ignore the fact that Rob had not set foot inside her house since her confrontation with Monique. She understood that he was trying to save his floundering marriage, but it hurt to know that he could cast aside their friendship so easily for a woman as shallow, as vain as Monique Lapierre.

As record sales went through the roof, Danny was besieged by offers from television talk show hosts and movie producers. His new manager, Rudy Stone, was pushing him to accept as many offers as possible to promote his escalating career. The end result was that now, when Casey needed him the most, he was spending great chunks of time flying between Los Angeles and New York, taping guest spots for *The Tonight Show* and *Saturday Night Live*. Every magazine from *Tiger Beat* to *Rolling Stone* to *Playgirl* wanted an interview. The scandal sheets, on the other hand, didn't bother with interviews. They had a field day, printing the lurid details of Danny's nonexistent extracurricular love life.

At first, as her pregnancy progressed, she tolerated it all. She even found some of it amusing, until love-stricken women began calling on the telephone at all hours, forcing her to have their telephone number unlisted. When one bold fan had the audacity to walk right up to their door with a copy of *Tiger Beat* in her hand, Casey threw a conniption. The next day, Danny had a security system installed. As Casey watched the closed circuit cameras being mounted on the new gate at the end of her driveway, she wrapped her arms around her growing belly and wondered how she would manage to raise a normal child, locked inside a glass house, with the rest of the world locked out.

***

"You should dress this way more often, *cher*." Monique fingered the tuxedo jacket he'd tossed carelessly on the back of the commode. "You look terribly handsome in black."

Rob scowled into the bathroom mirror. "Easy for you to say." He bent and splashed water on his face. "You're not the one wearing the monkey suit."

"But you do it for me," she said. "Because you know how important they are, these little charity functions."

Important for her image, perhaps. Monique was continually sponsoring one benefit or another. The publicity was good for her career, and that spectacular face sold tickets to these thousand-dollar-a-plate affairs. But he doubted that his little love muffin even knew what charity tonight's benefit was raising money for. Patting his rear pocket absently, he said, "Bring me my wallet, will you?"

She stepped away from him, elegant in a clingy black silk gown that revealed everything, including the fact that she wore nothing beneath it. Her heels clicked on blood-red tiles, and he watched her go, aroused by the sight, the sound, the smell of her, troubled by the knowledge that every man who saw her tonight would have the same response. "*Robert*?" she said a moment later. "What is this?"

He dried his hands on a plush, floral-scented towel and followed her. "What's what?"

"This?" She held up a mottled blue slip of paper.

"It's a check. What does it look like?"

"*Oui*. I can see that," she said. "But what is it for?"

"It's for my mother," he said, taking it from her and tucking it back into his wallet. "What is this, the Spanish Inquisition?"

"Why are you sending your *maman* a check for five thousand dollars?"

A muscle knotted in the back of his neck. "I send a little money home once in a while. Okay?"

Her mouth thinned, and two deep lines bracketed those lush lips. "We are now supporting your parents?" she said.

The anger rose in him slowly, so slowly he could measure its ascent, like the thin line of mercury rising in a thermometer. "Don't worry," he said. "I haven't touched your precious money. Every goddamn penny of it's mine."

She raised those slender shoulders in a Gallic shrug. "You are too—what is the word? Thin-skinned. You grow angry each time I mention money. Why is that?"

"I can't stand the waste I see all around me. My folks are scraping to get by, and you're terrified that I might send them a tiny fraction of your money and leave you too poor to buy the bare necessities. Like expensive Scotch and designer dresses." He eyed the revealing black gown and his mouth drew tight. "How much did that one cost you?"

"That is not your concern, *cher*. Perhaps I made a mistake when I married you. You still think like a poor man. And you wish to live like one."

"And what are you, the world's expert on poverty? You wouldn't know poor if it bit you on the ass. I'll be glad to tell you what poor is. Poor is wearing the shoes your brother wore last year, because your dad got laid off again and there isn't money to buy shoes for nine kids. Poor is digging through the box of clothes Father McMurphy brought over, looking for something that won't look too ridiculous. And then wearing it to school, wondering who'll recognize the old clothes their mother gave to the church last week. Poor is your mother coming home at night with her knees all bloody because she spent the whole fucking day on them, scrubbing floors for some rich bitch who doesn't give a goddamn about her or you or anything except her damn money. So you can build your altar and pray to your money god, but don't expect to see me kneeling there beside you!"

Her face hardened, erasing any beauty that had been there. Or perhaps her beauty had never been anything more than illusion. "I was right," she said. "You're nothing more than a peasant."

For a moment, as he studied her face, he wondered what he had ever seen in this woman. "That's right," he said. "I'm a peasant. I come from a working-class, blue-collar, meat-and-potatoes family. And you know what? I'm damn proud of it.

My people know who they are. Nobody I know is pretending to be Queen of the World."

Her face went white. "You bastard," she said.

"Right." He picked up his car keys and his wallet, crammed them into the pocket of the monkey suit, and headed for the door.

Her voice followed him. "Where are you going?" she said. "We have a dinner to attend in forty-five minutes."

Without breaking stride, he said, "I'm not going."

"How dare you walk away from me?" she said. "Nobody walks away from me!"

"I'm not fighting with you tonight, Monique. Just give me some space, before I do something we'll both regret."

"Nobody walks away from me!" she repeated. "Do you hear me? Nobody!"

He stopped abruptly next to the antique telephone table in the foyer and turned to look at her. She was standing in the archway, her fists clenched, her eyes furious. "Watch me," he said.

"If you walk out that door," she screeched, "don't expect to be allowed back in this house!"

He paused, squared his jaw, and for a full ten seconds, he just looked at her. "Fine," he said bluntly. "I've had enough of living with a lunatic anyway."

She gaped at him in astonishment, and then her blue eyes filled with tears. "Monster! *Fils de chienne!* Nobody has ever walked away from me!" She threw herself on him, clenched fists beating ineffectually at his shoulders, his chest, his face. He peeled her loose, imprisoned her wrists in his hands and held her away from him. Breathing heavily, he said, "Grow up."

Monique was not the kind of woman who was attractive when she cried. "You are not the only man in the world!" she shouted. "There are a million other men who would be thrilled to be where you are, sleeping in my bed every night!"

"That's fortunate," he bellowed, "because that position just became vacant!" He released her, bent and pulled the telephone directory from beneath the hall table and flung it at her. "You still have forty-five minutes," he said. "If you start calling now, I'm sure you can find another date for the benefit."

It took five minutes to pack what was his. He left the new clothes hanging in the closet, the diamond pinkie ring and the gold wedding band on the dresser. He loaded all his worldly possessions into a single suitcase and put the top down on the Porsche so the wind could blow through his expensively styled hair. And without looking back, he drove away from the Bel Air mansion that had been his home for the past twelve months.

***

Danny was in London taping a BBC special when she went into labor, three
weeks early. She'd been having Braxton-Hicks contractions for a week or more, but Mark Johnson, her doctor, had insisted they were nothing to worry about. Just the day before, he'd patted her hand with his huge, warm paw and said, "This baby isn't coming for another three weeks. Danny will be home long before then. Cheer up. It's almost over."

She believed him until her water broke as she was hoisting her lumpy body out of bed the next morning. She sat there in disbelief as the sheet beneath her sopped up the liquid and the overflow ran down her legs and into her slippers. Her first thought was that they'd gone through six weeks of Lamaze class for nothing. Danny wasn't going to be here for the birth of his child.

Unexpected resentment bubbled up inside her. Why was he never here when she needed him the most? Just once, it would have been nice to come ahead of his career.

She called Mark, who nearly had a coronary when she told him she would drive herself to the hospital. "There's nobody you can call?" he said. "A relative? A neighbor? A taxi, for heaven's sake. Once your water breaks, labor can set in quickly."

She thought fleetingly about calling Rob, but decided that if he could be a jackass, so could she. "I'm not about to deliver on the freeway," she told Mark. "I can do this."

"I'm sending an ambulance for you," he said.

"Over my dead body," she said, and hung up the phone.

Just for spite, she took Danny's new Ferrari. It was bright

red, had 3,000 miles on the odometer, and had cost him more than the annual budgets of several third world countries. If she didn't make it to the hospital, he would be dealing with some interesting new stains on the upholstery.

Mark was waiting at the emergency room entrance, looking not a little exasperated. She pointed a finger at him. "This is all your fault," she told him. "If you'd told the truth yesterday, I could have reached Danny in time."

He patted her shoulder and chuckled. "We'll videotape the birth if you'd like."

"Doctor J?"

"Yes?"

"Stuff it."

As most first babies do, this one took its time being born, and its mother discovered a heretofore unseen shrewish side to her nature. Casey ranted, she raved, she yelled and cried, she cussed out Danny Fiore and Dr. Mark Johnson and several hapless nurses. The pain went so far beyond her vague imaginings that she begged for medication, and when her plea was refused, she threatened to sue the entire medical establishment for keeping womankind in the dark. The doctors and nurses, saints all, just patted her hand and wiped her brow and fed her more ice chips.

Katherine Ellen Fiore was born at twilight, and when the red-faced, lumpy, squalling mass of humanity was placed in her arms, Casey burst into tears. She cooed and stroked, counted fingers and toes, and gazed into the blue eyes, so like Danny's, that solemnly gazed back at her. "Welcome to the world, Katie Fiore," she said.

She was reluctant to let go when they took the baby away. Mark chuckled. "Wouldn't you rather have her clean and sweet-smelling?" he said.

"I'll take her any way I can get her."

"How's the pain now?"

She grinned. "What pain?"

"That's my girl."

"I was horrible, wasn't I?"

"Quite. And you loved every minute of it."

"Mark, is she healthy?"

"We're performing the routine neonatal testing—Apgar scores, and so forth. But she looks fit as a fiddle to me, robust and attentive and loud."

"I feel like I could climb mountains."

"You just did. Now you need your rest."

"I can't rest. I have to call Danny."

"I already talked to Danny. The hospital finally got through to him an hour ago, but you were eight centimeters dilated, and not in any condition to chat on the phone. He's probably a basket case by now."

She wanted to walk back to her room, but Mark won that battle, and she was wheeled in on a stretcher. Moments later, Katie was brought in by one of the nurses and placed in her arms. She lay back against the pillows and watched the baby suckling at her breast, tiny fists curled in contentment, blue eyes gazing into hers with avid interest.

Beside the bed, the telephone rang. The nurse answered it and handed it to her. Danny's voice, coming from across the Atlantic, sounded tinny and insubstantial. "Casey?" he said. "Can you hear me?"

"Of course I can. Oh, Danny, you should see her, she's beautiful. She looks just like you."

"I'm so sorry, sweetheart. I wanted to be there with you."

"It's all right, darling, I understand. We didn't know she was going to come early."

"Are you all right? Christ, I've been frantic ever since they called."

"It wasn't that bad."

"Is she really beautiful?"

"She's just perfect, Danny. Absolutely perfect."

"Honey, I have to go. I'm on standby for the next empty seat at Heathrow. I'll be there as soon as I can."

"Take your time," she said. "Katie and I will be just fine."

***

Armed with a plush white teddy bear the size of Kansas, a massive bouquet of white camellias, and his most persuasive smile, Rob MacKenzie poured on the boyish charm and talked

his way into the closed maternity ward of the expensive private
hospital where Casey Fiore had just given birth.

He paused at the doorway to her room. Casey was sitting
up in bed, propped against a pile of pillows, her hair pulled back
in a thick braid and the sleeping baby cradled against her breast.
She wore a look of such radiant bliss that he was reluctant to
intrude on their intimacy. He took a step backward, but the
movement caught her attention. She looked up, and Rob crossed
his ankles and leaned against the door frame. "Hey," he said.

He saw it in her eyes, before she could conceal it, the quick
flash of pleasure at sight of him. Then the mask came down as
those eyes studied every detail of his appearance, missing
nothing. They paused when they reached the bouquet of flowers,
and her mouth thinned. "Do I know you?" she said.

"Go ahead," he said. "Rub it in. I deserve it."

"Where's the little woman? Home doing the wash?"

He cleared his throat. "We, ah—" Cleared it again.
"Monique and I aren't together any longer."

She raised a single dark eyebrow. "Threw you out, did she,
MacKenzie?"

"Actually," he said, "I walked."

"Oh, really? So you finally managed to get your brain to
function somewhere north of your belt buckle?"

He took the blow straight to the heart, wondering if the
truth always hurt this much. "I'm here," he said, holding the
furry polar bear in the air above his head, "to propose a truce."

Coolly, she said, "How touching. Is the bear for me?"

"Actually," he said, "it's for the baby. The flowers are for
you."

She eyed them suspiciously and said, "My mother always
warned me to be wary of men bearing gifts."

"Look," he said, "we both know I've been an ass. You're
my best friend, and I let Monique come between us. It was a
shitty thing to do."

"Yes," she said evenly. "It was."

"You're not going to make this easy on me, are you?"

She shifted the baby against her breast. "Does the word
grovel mean anything to you, MacKenzie?"

Without waiting for an invitation, he stepped into her room and dropped the teddy bear on the foot of the bed. Bouquet in hand, he sat on the edge of the mattress. "Take a sniff," he said, tilting the flowers in her direction. "They're spectacular."

She leaned forward to take a single, dainty whiff, and he thought he detected a softening in the hardness around her mouth. "So," he said with forced joviality. "Where's the Italian stallion?"

The lines around her mouth deepened. "London," she said.

"*London*?" he said, outraged. "You mean he wasn't here when the baby was born?"

"It wasn't his fault," she said. "Katie came three weeks early. There was no time to reach him. He's on his way home now."

It was inconceivable to him that Danny could have missed his daughter's birth. Nothing short of death or dismemberment could have kept Rob MacKenzie away from the birth of his child. "Why the hell didn't you call me, Fiore? I would have come in an instant."

"And do what? Sit by my side through twelve hours of labor?"

He squared his jaw. "If that was what you needed, yes."

"It's not your job."

"Tough. Better me than some nurse you don't even know."

As she continued to study his face, the lines around her mouth gradually dissolved. "You'd do that," she said, "wouldn't you?"

"Damn right I would!"

Softly, she said, "Damn, Flash, I've missed your ugly mug."

He reached out, picked up the end of her braid, and tugged playfully at it. "I've missed you, too, sweetcakes."

"So where are you staying?"

"I found this great apartment. Hardwood floors, French doors, stained glass windows. It's in this Gothic monstrosity of a house that looks like something out of a Stephen King novel." He grinned. "I call it the Hotel California."

"How'd you manage to find something like that in Southern California?"

"A wizard," he said, "never reveals his secrets."

"You don't have to be in such a hurry to set up housekeeping," she said. "You could stay with us for a while."

"You guys need your privacy. You have a family now. You don't need me hanging around." He laid a single finger on Katie Fiore's velvety cheek. "Of course, if my mom had anything to say about it, I'd come home to Southie and marry Mary Frances O'Reilly."

She raised a single eyebrow. "Mary Frances O'Reilly?"

"She has thick ankles and buck teeth and Coke-bottle glasses. She used to follow me around the school yard at recess." He flashed her a wicked grin and added conspiratorially, "She wanted to have my babies."

"You might be surprised. Most girls grow out of that awkward stage. When was the last time you saw her?"

He grimaced. "Last year, and believe me, if anything was about to give me nightmares, it would be the thought of marrying Mary Frances."

Her smile was rueful. "Have you told your mother about the split?"

"I called her. She wasn't impressed. Two crashed marriages in three years. Basically, she told me to get my head out of my ass and grow up."

"Not bad advice, hot stuff."

He held out a single finger and the baby grasped it. "Maybe," he said darkly, "I should think about entering the priesthood. Every good Irish Catholic family's supposed to produce at least one priest. The MacKenzies are behind on their quota."

"You'd never survive," she said dryly. "You have to take a vow of celibacy."

"Yeah," he said. "Right. Well, you can stop worrying about me, because I'm never having another serious relationship. Just lots of cheap, superficial sex with as many women as possible."

"That certainly is what I'd call a mature solution to your dilemma."

He wiggled Katie's hand. "Shut up," he said. "It's my life. I'll live it my way."

"Not for a minute do I doubt that," she said. "You're the most independent jackass I've ever known."

The baby yawned and stretched, and she adjusted her hold on the precious bundle. "Would you like to hold her?" she said. "After all, since we're still speaking, I suppose I have to ask you to be her godfather."

He let out the breath he'd been holding. "Sweetheart," he said, "I thought you'd never ask."

BOOK THREE

CHAPTER TWENTY

Los Angeles, California
April, 1986

"Why can't I go with you?" Katie Fiore crinkled her dimpled face as she watched her mother pack. "I hate it when you go away."

"I know, sweetheart. I don't like it, either. But it's only for a few days. And Daddy will be here with you. The two of you can have fun together."

"I don't want Daddy. I want to go to New York with you."

Another first for history, Casey thought, taking a black cocktail dress from the closet. Katie always preferred her father's company. At five, she was already smitten by the infamous Fiore charm. "I told you," Casey said, "this is not a vacation. Mama and Uncle Rob are going on a business trip." She opened a drawer and selected several pairs of silk undies. "You'd be very bored. Besides—" She arranged the undies in her suitcase and bent to plant a kiss on the tip of Katie's nose. "You're sick, remember?" Katie's kindergarten class had been passing around a respiratory virus all winter. This was the third time in as many months that she'd come down with a sore throat and a runny nose.

Katie glowered, those blue eyes identical to Danny's. "I hate being sick!" she said. "I hate having a red nose! Jimmy Bostwick called me Rudolph!" Katie had inherited more from her father than his looks; she'd also gotten a healthy dose of his vanity.

Casey held back a smile as she folded a blouse and neatly tucked it into the suitcase. "I know, Katydid, but guess what? Your red nose will be all gone by the time I get back."

Those blue eyes continued to accuse her. There was one other thing Katie had inherited from Danny: his intelligence. She knew when she was being pacified, and she didn't like it one bit.

Casey threw in a pair of black heels to match the dress.

She hated leaving Katie, especially when she was sick, but this was a career opportunity she couldn't afford to pass up. Gabe Rothman, the Broadway producer, had discovered a brilliant but heretofore unknown playwright with the unlikely name of Sam Adams, and he was in the process of turning Adams' newest work into a Broadway musical. Rothman had approached Casey and Rob about writing the score. It was all very tentative at this point, but if they were able to work out a satisfactory deal, and if the play was a hit, it would be a very large feather in their caps. That was a lot of ifs, so Casey was trying to rein in her enthusiasm. There would be plenty of time for that once they had a signed contract.

It was too soon to think ahead to the actual work, which would have to be done in New York instead of California. She would cross that particular bridge when she arrived at it. In the meantime, she and Rob would meet with Rothman and Adams and director Eli Walton, and test the waters. If things worked out right, they might just come home with a contract in hand.

"I'll bring you a present from New York," she told her daughter. "Something special."

Katie reached into the suitcase and touched her mother's black silk slip, rubbed her fingers against the soft material. "A doll?" she said.

"Is that what you want?"

"Yup. A new Cabbage Patch doll."

"But, honey, you already have five of them. Wouldn't you like something different?"

Katie shook her head vehemently. "A Cabbage Patch doll, Mommy. That's what I want."

Casey smiled at her daughter as she closed and locked her suitcase. "A Cabbage Patch doll it is, then, a special one for my Katydid."

***

He hated it when Katie was cranky.

She'd been running a fever ever since Casey left for New York, and he'd tried everything he knew to pacify her. Together they'd watched the Muppets take Manhattan, they'd played

Candyland until he thought he'd lose his mind, and they'd feasted on Katie's favorite food in the whole world, macaroni and cheese from a box. He'd read every Dr. Seuss book she owned, and they'd even gone a second round with *Green Eggs and Ham*. But Katie was whiny, and nothing had held her attention for long. "I hurt, Daddy," she said for the hundredth time in the past two hours.

"I know, sweetheart. Why don't we take a nap together? Maybe you'll feel better afterward."

"No! I hate naps. I want Mommy!" And she started to cry.

Danny sighed. "How about we turn on the TV and see what's on? Maybe we can find a movie."

"I don't want a movie. My throat hurts."

He gave her the antibiotic that Mark Johnson had prescribed, the one she'd been taking, off and on, for three months. The infection kept returning, bringing its own special brand of misery: a sore throat and earaches, sniffles, crankiness. Katie hated medicine, and she fought swallowing the foul-tasting stuff. He bribed her with chocolate milk, her second favorite thing in the whole world. "Why don't we cuddle together on the couch?" he said. "Later, we'll call Mom in New York."

"Okay."

They lay together on the couch in front of the television, Katie's warm little body curled up against his, her mangy Pooh bear clutched in her arms. When she was born, he and Casey had agreed to give Katie as normal an upbringing as possible. It wasn't easy. She'd spent her infancy on the road, carted around from backstage to backstage in an infant sling, cuddled close against her mother's chest. By the time she was two, she'd been to Europe several times, and was as comfortable on an airplane as she was riding in a car. By the time she was three, she knew the lyrics to all his songs, and wasn't shy about belting them out for any unsuspecting victim she could coerce into standing still to listen.

In spite of this rather unorthodox upbringing, there were no nannies or fancy private schools for their Katydid. Katie Fiore attended public school, and was a very ordinary kid whose father just happened to be one of the world's biggest rock stars. As a result of this enforced normalcy, Katie was a charming child, bright and inquisitive and open to new experiences. And she was the absolute light of his life.

They napped for a time. When he awakened, Katie was fussing, rubbing at her eyes, her nose, her neck. "Daddy," she said, "my neck hurts."

She'd grown terribly warm in the last hour, limp and sticky and listless. The glassy look in her eyes made him uneasy. He got the thermometer from the bathroom and took her temperature, and was stunned to see that it was nearly 106 degrees.

He tried to reach Casey at the hotel in New York, but she was out. He left a message, then dialed Mark Johnson's private home number. Mark and his family were eating dinner, and he apologized for the interruption. "But this isn't normal," he explained. "She's never run a fever this high."

"It's probably nothing," Mark said, "but I'd like to check her out, just to be safe. Meet me at the emergency room in a half-hour, and we'll see what's up with Miss Katie."

***

The dinner meeting with Rothman and company was a resounding success. Casey was almost certain that the producer had already made up his mind before he met them, and the deal he offered was sweet. Rothman was anxious to start work as soon as possible, perhaps even by the first of the week if they could swing it. By gentlemen's agreement, they shook hands and celebrated their partnership with a magnum of Dom Perignon.

They called it a night relatively early by New York standards. Outside the restaurant, Rob tucked his hands into his pockets and jingled a handful of change. "It's a beautiful night," he said. "Let's walk."

They fell into step together and began to amble, in no hurry on this beautiful spring evening. "So what do you think?" she said.

"About the deal? I think it's one hell of a coup."

"Big bucks," she said.

"True, but I was thinking more about the opportunity to reach a new audience. Broadway—that's serious stuff for a composer."

"It is, isn't it?" She tucked her hands into the pockets of her jacket and looked up at the sky. "What, oh what, am I going to do about Katydid? I can't leave her behind in California. Not for three months. But I don't want to pull her out of school before the year's out."

"Leave her there with Danny. He'll take good care of her. He's absolutely nuts about that kid."

"I know. She's the best thing that ever happened to him. But I'd go crazy if I had to go three whole months without seeing her."

"Then hire a nanny and bring her with you."

"What about school?"

"She's only in kindergarten, Fiore. Are you afraid she'll flunk sandbox?"

"I'm being silly, aren't I?"

"No. You're being a mother."

"Look," she said, "a toy store. I promised Katie I'd bring her a Cabbage Patch doll. She'll never forgive me if I forget."

The display window was loaded with toys of every conceivable kind. Inside, a twenty-foot sculpture constructed entirely of giant Lego blocks stood behind a makeshift fence designed to keep small fingers from toppling it. She dragged Rob past it and followed her nose to the doll department. Somewhere along the way, she lost him. Knowing he'd eventually come wandering back, she studied the endless array of dolls, trying to decide between the gypsy and the cowboy. Or maybe the ballerina.

Rob came around the corner, carrying a mammoth plastic laser gun. He pointed it at her and squeezed the trigger, and it erupted into flashing red lights and an ear-splitting electronic shrieking that probably had dogs howling in all five boroughs. "That's a big gun you have there, sailor," she said. "Sure you know how to use it?"

"Ow." He grabbed his midsection and staggered backward as though he'd been shot. "What a low blow, Fiore," he said. "You should be ashamed of yourself."

"That's what you get," she said, "when you play in the big leagues. Come on, Flash, you're Katie's godfather. Help me decide which one to get."

"Well, let's see." He stepped back and studied the shelf display with a frown of concentration. "I'm partial to the clown."

"You would be."

"But the doctor's okay, too. Why don't you just get her both?"

"Those words could only be spoken," she said dryly, "by a man who has never raised a child."

"Why?"

"Because if you don't exercise restraint, lovey, they turn into merciless tyrants. Where do you think the term *enfant terrible* came from?"

"Aw, come on, Fiore. How can you say no to a face like that?"

"Years of experience with the big kid before I got the little one."

"Tell you what. You buy one, and I'll buy the other one."

Casey rolled her eyes. "I knew it was a mistake when I asked you to be Katie's godfather."

"Too late," he said. "I'm non-returnable."

As they crossed the hotel lobby, the desk clerk discreetly flagged her down. "Mrs. Fiore," she said, "your husband has been trying to reach you all evening. He said it was urgent."

Casey felt a pang of unease. Rob squeezed her shoulder. "I'm sure it's nothing serious," he said. "We'll call him from upstairs."

But when she dialed home, all she got was her own recorded voice telling her that although the Fiores weren't home, they would be more than happy to return any messages. "Danny?" she said after the beep. "Are you there?"

There was no response. She met Rob's eyes and frowned. "I'm back at the hotel," she said into the phone. "Call me when you get in."

"See," Rob said when she hung up, "he's not even there. Probably took Katie out to McDonald's."

"Maybe." But the uneasiness refused to go away. She

hung her coat in the closet and kicked off her heels and drew her hair up off the nape of her neck. "I'm going to take a shower," she said. "Let me know if he calls."

The phone rang before she'd taken two steps. She exchanged glances with Rob, backtracked, and picked it up. "Hello?" she said.

"Jesus Christ," Danny thundered, "where the hell have you been? It's past eleven. I've called every fifteen minutes for the past three hours."

"You knew we were having dinner with Rothman. We walked back, and we—" She stopped suddenly, realizing how uncharacteristic it was for him to shout at her. Or to question her whereabouts. "Danny," she said, "what's wrong?"

"Katie's in the hospital," he said. "She has meningitis."

She could actually feel the blood draining from her face. "Meningitis," she echoed in disbelief. Across the room, Rob set down the cabbage patch doll he'd bought. It wore gaudy pantaloons with red and purple polka-dots, and ridiculously big shoes. "That's not possible," she said, her voice shaking. "Katie's never been exposed to anything like that—"

"Mark says it's a complication of that throat infection she keeps getting."

She wet her lips. Terrified to ask, more terrified to not ask, she said, "How serious is this?"

"It's bad," he said, and his voice broke. "You have to come home. I need you."

***

Those first twenty-four hours, while Katie Fiore struggled for life, were the darkest hours Casey had ever lived through. She sat in mute agony while Danny paced like a caged tiger, wrinkled and unshaven, smoking cigarette after cigarette in blatant disregard of the NO SMOKING sign on the wall above his head. While Mark Johnson and his colleagues battled the infection with antibiotics, Casey was rendered helpless, unable to do a thing except pray that God would spare her daughter's life. They were allowed to see Katie once each hour, for five minutes at a time, and then they were hustled back to the waiting room for another interminable fifty-five-minute vigil.

At some point during that endless night, Mark came in to talk to them. He looked wiped out as he took both Casey's hands in his huge, capable paws. "We're doing everything we can to fight this," he said. "We're taking the most aggressive stance that's humanly possible."

Casey's tongue felt twice its normal thickness. She licked her lips and tried to find her voice. "Is she going to die?" she said.

Mark squeezed her hand. "I don't know," he said.

Across the room, Danny leaned his forehead against the cinder block wall. "This is my fault," he said raggedly. "It's all my fault."

Mark released Casey's hand and said smoothly, "It's not your fault. You had no way of knowing how serious it was."

Danny turned on him. "I should have recognized the signs! I was in Vietnam with a guy who died of meningitis! I watched him die!"

"Even we weren't sure until we had the lab results. Stop punishing yourself and start comforting your wife. She needs you right now." With a pat to Casey's shoulder, he left them alone again.

Danny sat down heavily beside her. "If she dies—" he said brokenly.

"Stop it!" Casey snapped. "She's not going to die!"

He fumbled for her hand, took it in his. Squeezed it, and they took strength from each other. "I love you," he said. "I know I don't say it often enough. I thought I'd go crazy while I waited for you to get here."

"I know. I felt the same way."

"She'll be all right," he said. "She has to be."

Somehow, she fell asleep, right there on the waiting room couch, with her head cradled in Danny's lap. She awoke when Rob arrived with doughnuts and coffee. "How is she?" he said.

Danny ran the fingers of both hands through his hair. "No change," he said. "It's so goddamn frustrating."

Rob put a steaming cup of coffee in Casey's hand and wrapped her fingers around it. "Drink," he said.

She inhaled the coffee's rich aroma and closed her eyes.

"Thank you," she said. "How is it that you always know exactly what I need?"

"I'm a wizard. Dan?" He handed Danny a second steaming cup. "You both look like shit," he said. "Why don't you go home and get some sleep? I can watch over things here for a while."

"No," they both said at once.

"Look," Rob said, "you won't be doing Katie any good if you both get sick. Somebody has to take care of her when she comes home."

"There is one thing you can do for me," Casey told him. "Call Rothman."

Rob's mouth thinned. "And tell him what?"

"Tell him I have a family emergency. Give him my regrets. Convince him that you can do the job without me."

"Without you? Are you crazy?"

"Do it," she said. "Do it for me."

Rob didn't look pleased, but he didn't argue. Because there was little he could do at the hospital, he left again. Casey tried to eat one of the doughnuts, but after a few bites, she gave up. Still in the black cocktail dress and heels she'd worn to dinner with Rothman, she lay on the couch with Danny's arms around her and fell back into a shallow, troubled sleep.

She woke when Mark came in, carrying a clipboard and looking as though he hadn't slept in weeks. "Guys," he said, and sat down in the chair across from them.

Casey sat up and leaned forward, her heart in her throat. "Mark? Has there been a change?"

He tapped his pen on the clipboard. "It appears," he said, "as though we have the infection under control. Her fever's dropped four points."

"That's good news," Casey said hesitantly. "Isn't it?"

His face remained solemn. "It's good news," he said.

Danny leaned forward, his elbows resting on his knees. "But?" he said.

"But." Mark cleared his throat. "She doesn't seem to be responding."

"What do you mean?" Casey demanded. "What does that mean?"

"It means that—" Mark looked at them, ran a hand through his rumpled hair, and sighed. "Katie's slipped into a coma."

Casey's fingers, entwined with Danny's, tightened.

"I've called in a neurologist, and we'd like to do some tests. A CAT scan, an EEG, possibly an MRI. To check brain functioning. See what's going on."

"Brain functioning," Danny said sharply. "Why?"

Mark cleared his throat again. "There's a possibility," he said, "that the infection may have left Katie with some degree of brain damage. That would explain why she isn't responding. But we won't know until we've done more testing."

The waiting dragged on. Rob returned, toting clean clothes and toiletries. They left Danny asleep in the waiting room and walked the hospital corridor. "Did you talk to Rothman?" she said.

Rob sighed. "I talked to him."

"And?"

"Under the circumstances, he's willing to work with just me. Damn white of him." He tucked his hands into his pockets. "I'm just not sure I'm willing to do it without you."

"You don't have a choice," she said. "You can't pass this up."

"We're partners. We've been partners for twelve years. We've always worked together."

"You've written hundreds of songs without me. This isn't any different."

"Damn it, Casey, you need me here!"

"Ah," she said softly. "The truth comes out."

"I feel so helpless. I don't know what to do."

"There's nothing you can do. Danny and I have to get through this on our own. If you let it stall your career, I'll spend the rest of my life feeling responsible."

He exhaled and rubbed the bridge of his nose. "What about you? Will you be okay if I go traipsing off to New York for three months?"

"I'm a big girl. I don't need a keeper."

"Danny's not taking this well."

"Danny and I," she said, "will take care of each other. That's what marriage is all about, remember? For richer, for poorer. In sickness and in—"

"Yeah," he said. "Right."

"Listen to me, Robert, and listen good. If you let this screw up your life, I'll never forgive you. And never is a damn long time. *Capisce?*"

"I *capisce*," he said reluctantly. "Look, the minute I'm settled somewhere, I'll let you know where I am. And you'll call if you need me?"

"If I need you, I'll call. Now get your carcass out of here, go to New York, and do what you do better than anyone else on the planet."

They embraced fervently, then he patted her on the cheek and said, "I'll call."

She watched him walk away, a tall, rangy man with a distinctive, loose-jointed stride, and felt as though the foundations beneath her were crumbling. At the end of the corridor, he paused to look back at her. She lifted a hand, and he saluted smartly and turned the corner. For the first time since this nightmare began, she felt tears welling up beneath her eyelids.

But she couldn't cry. Not in front of Danny, for she suspected that it was only her strength that was holding him together. In all their years together, she'd never seen him like this. She had to hold herself together for his sake. She'd always been the strong one. It had been that way when Mama died, and it was still that way, fifteen years later. While everyone else around her crumbled, Casey invariably remained a pillar of strength, not because she was so much stronger than everyone else, but because it was expected of her. Somebody had to do it, and somehow she always ended up being elected Somebody.

She crossed her arms over her chest, squared her shoulders, and went back to her husband.

***

They'd called this impromptu conference for 10:30, but while she paced and Danny chain smoked, Mark and the neurologist with the unpronounceable Eastern European name were twenty minutes late. Mark flew in, tossing breathless apologies, and introduced them to the stranger in whose hands they had placed their daughter's life.

They sat around a rectangular table, Casey and Danny huddled together, Mark across from them, the neurologist at the head. "We've completed our tests," Mark said.

Casey gripped Danny's hand beneath the table. "And?" she said.

He steepled his fingers on the tabletop. "I'm afraid the news isn't good. The tests reveal minimal brain function."

"Minimal brain function?" she said. "Exactly what does that mean? How minimal?"

"Katie's brain," he said, "is still sending the signal to continue basic physiological functions. Heartbeat, respiration, elimination. Beyond that—" He cleared his throat. "Beyond that," he repeated, "there's little to no activity."

Danny released her hand and rested both elbows on the table. "Are you telling us," he said, "that our daughter's brain dead?"

The neurologist stepped in at that point, speaking in a Southwestern twang completely at odds with his name. "We prefer not to use that term, Mr. Fiore," he said. "Katie's breathing on her own, her heart and her kidneys are functioning. There's a possibility that this could be a temporary condition. There have been cases—"

Casey gripped the edge of the table to steady herself. "Do you mean to say that she's not going to come out of the coma?"

"That's a strong possibility."

"Jesus H. Christ!" Danny exploded. "Why the hell aren't you doing something? We're talking modern medicine here! There must be something you can do!"

"There are some things," Mark said, "that we have no control over. Unfortunately, this happens to be one of them."

"Damn unfortunately! How the hell would you feel if it was your daughter in there?"

"Just as terrible as you do," Mark said.

Casey addressed the neurologist. "You said there's a possibility it might be a temporary condition?"

"A very slim possibility, I'm afraid. There have been documented cases in which patients have awakened from a persistent vegetative state. Sometimes after weeks. Sometimes years. But those cases—"

"Years," Casey repeated. "You did say years."

"That's right. But those cases are extremely rare. Most patients never recover. I'm very sorry."

She wasn't sure she could continue breathing. Her chest ached with the effort, while every other part of her body had gone numb. She could feel her heart hammering, could hear the blood rushing in her ears.

"Why?" Danny asked, his voice unrecognizable. "How did this happen?"

"Bacterial meningitis," Mark said, "moves very quickly. It can kill in a matter of hours. Small children often run high fevers even when they're not terribly sick, so parents don't realize how sick the child is until other symptoms appear. If we catch the infection early enough, we can turn it around. If it's advanced too far when the child reaches us, the mortality rate is high. Those who survive often end up with some degree of brain damage."

"So what you're saying is that it's my fault."

"I'm not saying anything of the kind. You're not a doctor, Danny. You're not a psychic. You're a father who did everything in his power to see that his little girl got the medical help she needed."

"And failed," Danny said.

"Don't," Casey whispered. "Please don't. Not now. I can't take it."

"Why the hell didn't I just put a gun to her head and pull the trigger? It would have been just as effective."

"Danny," she shouted, "stop it!"

They looked at each other, both of them breathing hard. "I can't," he said. And his voice broke. "I can't." He got up and slammed out of the room.

She tried to follow him, but her legs wouldn't hold her up. Mark pushed her back into the chair. "Ivan," he said to the neurologist, "a cup of water for Mrs. Fiore." Taking Casey by the hand, he said, "Let him go. It's what he needs right now."

"I can't do this, Mark. I can't."

"Yes, you can. You're a remarkably strong lady. Don't

forget, I was there when Katie was born. I remember what you went through."

Ivan returned with the water, and she drank it. "I'm not strong," she said. "It's only that everybody's always expected me to be, and when Mama died there wasn't anybody else, and Danny's always needed so much, and—" She looked up at him, realized she was babbling. "What am I going to do?" she said.

Mark patted her hand. "We'll figure that out together."

***

She refused to leave her daughter's side. Mark had a cot brought in, and that was where she pretended to sleep during those bleak hours when she was alone except for Katie's labored breathing and the eerie sounds of the electronic equipment that was helping her daughter stay alive. She ate hospital food from a tray that Mark had sent up especially for her, and went home only when she needed a shower or a change of clothing. After a few days, when Danny could no longer bear it, he went home and left her there.

He called several times a day to beg her to come home, but she always refused. As long as she stayed by Katie's side, nothing could happen to her. She was Katie's guardian angel, her fairy godmother, her good luck charm. Mark, of course, disapproved. "You're not doing your daughter any good," he said, "and you're killing yourself. Go home to your husband. He needs you."

But she refused to budge. When Katie started convulsing and the electronics went haywire, the entire pediatrics team came rushing into the room. One of the nurses shoved Casey out and shut the door firmly in her face. She leaned against the wall, arms crossed over her chest, and slid limply to the floor with her head cradled in her arms.

Rob called from New York, and for the first time, she cried, loudly and inelegantly, snuffling and snorting, while at the other end of the telephone line, he spoke soothing, nonsensical syllables. "That's it," he said, when she'd finally stopped. "I'm coming home."

"No," she said, wiping her nose. "I'll be fine. I just needed to let off some steam."

"Sweetheart, you're wound tighter than a top. Where's Danny?"

"At home."

"Why the hell isn't he there with you?"

"He can't face it. Will you call him? I'm worried about him. He shouldn't be alone right now."

"I can think of a few things I'd like to call him right now."

"Don't. Please. You don't understand. You don't know all of it. Danny's not as strong as I am. He needs your support right now."

"Yeah, and you're the tough one, aren't you?"

"I'm a survivor. Danny's not so good at that."

A week passed with no change. Katie continued to undergo convulsions several times each day. Casey, who had borrowed several medical volumes from the hospital library, talked to her constantly, read to her, sang to her. Medical science knew little about what went on inside the mind of a comatose person. Seemingly hopeless cases had been known to respond to the voices of their loved ones, and Casey grasped frantically at any possibility, however remote, that her daughter would come back to her.

Danny called. "Come home," he said. "Please come home. I need you."

"I can't. I can't leave Katie. You come here."

"Jesus Christ, Casey, I can't sit around that hospital room for hours on end. Every time she makes a sound, it terrifies me."

They were at a stalemate, and they both knew it. She curled up on her cot, furious with him, furious with herself, furious most of all with a God who would allow this to happen to her daughter.

Hours later, she awakened, disoriented, to find Danny on his knees beside the cot, his head resting on her abdomen, one hand gently kneading her breast. A shaft of pure desire shot through her, followed immediately by guilt that she could even think about sex under the circumstances. "Danny?" she said thickly. "What time is it?"

"Three-thirty in the morning. Come home with me. Just for a few hours. I need you."

"I can't."

He responded by closing his mouth over her breast, hard enough to leave her gasping. Even through the fabric of her shirt, his damp heat was electrifying. Torn between duty and desire, she ran a hand around to the back of his neck. Beneath his collar, his skin was hot and moist. "All right," she said. "But just for a little while."

It seemed like years since they'd made love. They undressed each other on the way to the bedroom, and their lovemaking was hot and sweaty and erotic, a primal celebration of life, a desperate act of defiance against the specter of death. Afterward, she dozed in his arms, content and sated, his skin warm and sticky against hers.

It was daylight when the telephone woke her. She grappled for it, her body still sore from their lovemaking, and brought it to her mouth. Peeled apart her gummy lips and wet them with her tongue. "Hello?" she said.

"Casey? This is Mark Johnson. Is Danny there with you?"

She was still fuzzy-headed from lack of sleep. She sat up, groggy, and drew the long hair back from her face with one arm. "He's right here," she said. "What is it?"

"I'd rather talk to Danny," he said. "Can you put him on?"

She finally came wide awake. "Mark?" she said sharply. "What's wrong?"

At the other end of the phone, he hesitated. "I'm so sorry, honey," he said. "We lost Katie this morning."

CHAPTER TWENTY-ONE

Three weeks after she and Danny buried their daughter, Casey flew to New York to join Rob. It was for the best. She and Danny both needed space to deal with their grief, and work was the only outlet that would distance her from Katie's death. She threw herself into her work, pushing Rob mercilessly by day. By night, she dragged him around to the clubs of Manhattan, desperate for something, anything, to take the edge off her grief. Never much of a drinker, she grew glassy-eyed and nauseous with only two or three shots of liquor, but she belted them down with gusto, and Rob kept his mouth shut because he understood the demons that drove her.

For six weeks, Casey walked around in an alcoholic stupor. Each morning, her head roared and her legs quibbled about going to work, but she and Rob still managed to put out some of the best material they'd ever written. She knew that people were talking behind her back. Some admired her stoicism. Others called her cold and unfeeling. Nobody in New York saw her sorrow. Nobody saw her cry. Nobody knew that when they'd lost Katie, she and Danny had also lost each other.

Only once during the entire time she was in New York did she speak to Danny, and then the conversation was stilted and pointless. At the end of two months, she and Rob finally wrapped up the project. She stayed around until the loose ends were tied up, until Rothman had approved the material and she'd bidden him and his cronies farewell. And then she packed the lone suitcase she'd brought with her to New York, got on a plane, and went home to find out if she was still married.

At home, things weren't any better. Night after night, she lay alone in their king-size bed while Danny sat at the piano for hours, abusing the keyboard with dark, tormented music, pounding out Tchaikovsky, Beethoven, Mozart, until she wanted to scream. He'd long since given up on sleeping, for every time he tried, the nightmares woke him, and he refused her comfort, instead lying stiff and unreachable beside her. Nothing Casey could say would convince him that he wasn't responsible for

Katie's death, and his grief, compounded by guilt, was agonizing to watch.

Katie's room stayed just as she'd left it. Neither of them ventured near. The pain was still too new, and Casey was far too brittle to subject herself to that kind of torture. So the door remained closed, and they pretended it had always been that way, pretended that nothing was wrong, pretended that their marriage wasn't disintegrating right before their eyes.

But as time went by, Casey recognized the truth, could see it as clearly as if it were encased in crystal, could hear it in the music he played, night after night after night. Like two comets speeding through space, they were on a collision course with impending disaster, and she was helpless to do anything but watch, and wait, and hope their marriage survived the impact.

The play went into production, and Rothman called them back to New York to iron out a few wrinkles in the score. That took several weeks, and when Rob flew back to L.A., she stayed behind in New York alone, to walk the streets and ponder the disaster that had become her life. Her career had reached unprecedented heights, but her personal life was a shambles, and she was afraid that this time, she and Danny weren't going to make it.

She flew into LAX on a sticky summer afternoon. Smog hung low over the city, exposing the tarnished underbelly of the city of angels, glamour capital of the world. Traffic was snarled everywhere, and the trip from the airport took twice as long as it should have. When she drove through her front gate, her mouth thinned. Danny's Ferrari was missing from the garage, and she wondered just where he was, and with whom.

When she unlocked the door, the phone was ringing. She nudged the door shut behind her and set down her suitcase. The answering machine kicked in, and a perky young voice said, "Mr. Fiore, this is Marilyn from Dr. Vogel's office. The doctor's been called out of town unexpectedly, and we need to reschedule tomorrow's appointment."

Dr. Vogel? Who the hell was Dr. Vogel? Casey picked up the phone. "Hello?" she said.

"Oh, hello. Is this Mrs. Fiore?"

"Yes."

"I'm really sorry for the inconvenience, Mrs. Fiore, but Dr. Vogel had a family emergency and he won't be able to keep his appointment with your husband tomorrow. Can he come in at ten on Tuesday instead?"

"I wasn't aware that Danny had a doctor's appointment." She paused, trying to tamp down the fear that nowadays was never far from the surface. "Is everything all right?"

"Oh, sure, we always do a routine checkup six weeks after surgery. You know, to make sure everything's healing properly. And to run a sperm count."

Sperm count?

Her legs began to tremble, and she set down the purse she was still holding. "What surgery?" she said.

For the first time, the voice at the other end hesitated. "Naturally, I assumed you knew."

Tersely, she said, "Feel free to enlighten me."

And the voice said, "Your husband had a vasectomy six weeks ago."

***

Most of what was in the house belonged to Danny.

Casey spent a couple of hours packing her clothes and the few personal items that mattered to her. She loaded up her BMW, then went back inside and made herself a grilled cheese sandwich. It tasted like sawdust, but she forced it, by sheer will, to stay in her stomach. With mechanical motions, she loaded the dirty dishes in the dishwasher, and then she opened the door to Katie's room for the last time.

Katie's pink ruffled pajamas still hung over the bed post, and her beloved Pooh bear lay alone in the center of the bed. Casey picked up the scruffy yellow bear and cradled him to her breast. She took a last look around, then raised her chin and marched to the door, resolutely shutting it behind her. She stuffed the Pooh bear, all she had left of her daughter, into her overnight bag, and sat down on the couch to wait for her husband.

It was nearly ten o'clock when he came home, moving cautiously, smelling of liquor. Even half drunk, he moved with graceful, sinuous elegance. At thirty-five, he was still the handsomest man she'd ever known. When he saw her sitting in the dark, he stopped and looked at her quizzically. "What's all that stuff in the car?" he said.

She squared her jaw, her shoulders. "I'm leaving you," she said.

He blinked, wobbled a little on unsteady feet. And snorted. "What in hell are you talking about?"

A swirl of emotions roiled around inside her. Love. Hatred. Grief. Fury. Bewilderment. "After everything I've been through," she said, "I can't believe you could do this to me."

To his credit, he didn't pretend to misunderstand. He snapped on a lamp, and in the sudden brightness, his face blurred. "I'd hoped," he said, "that you wouldn't find out."

"The doctor's office called," she said curtly, "to reschedule your appointment. I don't suppose it occurred to you that I might find it a bit odd, the inability to ever conceive again?"

He sighed deeply and sat on the arm of the couch. "Before you go off half-cocked," he said, "just listen to me."

Betrayal was a hard, sharp pain in her chest. "I don't want to listen to you, Danny. I'm through listening to you."

"I've gone through hell these last few months," he said. "I've watched you go through hell. It's all but destroyed our marriage."

"No," she said bitterly. "It's you who's destroyed our marriage."

"For Christ's sake, Casey, think about it." He scooped the long hair back from his face with the fingers of both hands. "Do you want to go through something like this again? I can't even bear to think about the possibility. It would kill both of us. Think about what it would be like, having another baby. The hell we'd go through every time he bumped his head or fell off his bike. Can't you see that I did it to save us both from more pain? I did it because I love you."

In disbelief, she said, "You took away any hope I might have of ever conceiving another child. You didn't bother to consult me, just made the decision for both of us. And you expect me to believe you did it because you *love* me?" She buried her face in her hands, rubbed her tired eyes. "Lord, Danny," she said, "I believe you've gone off the deep end."

"You know damn well I love you."

How could he look so earnest when her heart was a leaden weight, lodged hard against her breastbone? "I don't care any more," she said.

"Bullshit! Look me in the face. Look me in the face and tell me you don't love me any more."

She closed her eyes and shook her head. "Oh, Danny," she said sadly. "This has nothing to do with love."

"It has everything to do with love!"

"No," she said. "It has to do with trust. And the simple truth is that I can't trust you any longer."

"So that's it?" he said in utter disbelief. "You're throwing away twelve years just like that?"

"Right now," she said, "I'm so angry, I can't even look at you. I can't stand the sight of you."

"Christ, Casey," he said, "I love you!"

She looked at him through tears. "I know," she said. "I love you, too. But it's not enough any more."

She drove aimlessly for a couple of hours, uncertain of what to do, where to go. She'd been so propelled by fury that she hadn't thought beyond getting in the car and driving as far away from Danny Fiore as she could possibly get. She passed one seedy motel after another, but eventually, inevitably, she found herself pulling into Rob's driveway.

It took him a while to answer the door. Dressed in nothing but a pair of gray sweat pants, he combed a hand through his tangled hair while his startled gaze took in her overnight bag, her slumped shoulders, her puffy eyes. "Hey," he said.

"Hey yourself." Not quite successful at hiding the tremor in her voice, she said, "I realize it's the middle of the night, but do you think an old friend could borrow your couch?" She hesitated. "And maybe your shoulder?"

He opened the door wider, and she stepped past him and into the living room. In the middle of the floor, a pair of black high heel pumps had been carelessly discarded, and her face went red-hot. "You have company," she said.

"I, uh....yeah."

"I'm sorry. I never thought. I should have called first. Just go on back to your lady friend and forget I was here. I'll go to a hotel."

"You'll do no such thing, Fiore. If you need a place to stay, you'll stay here."

"What about your date?"

"Not a problem." He switched on the lamp and she stood rocking from one foot to the other as he bent and picked up the black pumps. "Make us some tea," he said. "I'll find something a little stronger to go with it." His mouth thinned. "You look like you could use it."

Casey busied herself making tea, trying to ignore the murmur of voices from the bedroom. Rob returned, wearing a wrinkled gray sweatshirt that matched his pants. He opened a corner cupboard and took out a bottle of Jack Daniel's. "I'm sorry," Casey said, pouring hot water over a matched set of Lipton's finest. "The last thing I wanted was to interfere with your sex life."

He uncapped the bottle and poured a shot into her cup, another into his. "Stop worrying," he said. "The only thing you interfered with was my sleep."

She took a sip of tea and grimaced at the taste. "What did you tell your lady friend?"

"The truth. That I had a friend with a domestic problem."

She leaned over the kitchen counter, holding her teacup in both hands. "Pretty pathetic, isn't it?" she said, examining the intricate design of red and white roses that circled the cup. "I've lived in this burg for six years, and you're the only person I know well enough to impose on at one o'clock in the morning."

He took a bag of Chips Ahoy cookies from the cupboard. "I'd be crushed," he said, "if you imposed on anyone else." With his free hand, he picked up his teacup. "Couch?" he said.

"Couch."

They settled at opposite ends. He opened the bag and handed her a cookie. She set her teacup on the arm of the couch and snapped the cookie in two. With a calmness she was far from feeling, she said, "I've left him."

He studied the cookie in his hand. "Permanently?" he said.

"I don't know. Right now, I'm too furious to be thinking

straight. Did he tell you what he did?"

He broke off a piece of cookie and dipped it into his tea. Grimly, he said, "Surprise me."

She got up from the couch, walked to the fireplace, studied the Behrens original that hung above the mantel. Closed her eyes and swallowed. "He had a vasectomy," she said. "Six weeks ago."

Rob's mouth fell open. "You're shitting me."

She crossed her arms and began pacing. "The worst thing," she said, "is that a part of me understands why he did it. But, good grief, Rob, I'm only twenty-nine years old! He has no right to make a decision like that behind my back, without even discussing it with me! And you know what he says? 'I did it because I love you.' *Because I love you!* I think he's lost his mind."

Rob scowled. "I ought to put my foot up his ass."

"What good would it do? The deed's already done. It's a little late to take it back."

At Rob's elbow, the telephone rang, and they both froze. He raised his eyebrows, and she bit her lip and shrugged. Rob picked up the phone. Eyes still on hers, he shot her a wink.

"That's okay," he said into the phone. "I wasn't sleeping. Yeah, she's here." He paused. "I don't think so," he said, "but I'll ask." He covered the receiver with his hand. "Do you want to talk to him?"

"I've already said everything I have to say."

"Dan? She says she doesn't want to." He paused, continued nodding his head. "I know, I know. Well, Jesus, Danny, if you really want the truth, I'd say this time you blew it good. Listen, you don't have to worry about Casey, she's right here with me. Try to get some sleep. I'll call you tomorrow, okay?"

He hung up the phone, slowly massaged his temple, and exhaled. "Your husband," he said, "is on one hell of a tear."

She sat back down beside him and propped her feet on the coffee table. "I shouldn't have come here," she said. "It's not fair to put you in the middle of this."

"Wrong," he said. "How many times have you picked me up and dusted me off?"

She leaned her head back against the couch. "Too many," she said.

"Well, kiddo," he said, and patted her shoulder, "this is payback."

The lamp light softened the sharp angle of his jaw. "You're a good man," she said. "Why didn't I fall in love with you instead of Danny?"

He waggled his eyebrows. "It's never too late," he said.

"It's far too late," she said. "I love you far too much to fall in love with you."

"So what are you going to do? You're welcome to stay here, you know."

She took a deep breath. "I'm moving east. Back to Boston."

He didn't say a word, but the stubborn set of his jaw gave away his feelings on the subject. "I need to be by myself for a while," she explained. "Away from Danny. After everything that's happened, I need some time alone to heal."

He threaded fingers with hers. "I'll miss you every damn day of my life."

"You'll visit, won't you?"

"Wild horses couldn't keep me away. Do you have a place to stay when you get there?"

"I'll find something. There are plenty of hotels in Boston."

"Mom will have a kitten if you stay in a hotel. You'll stay with my folks until you get settled."

"I don't want to impose."

"Be serious. I'll call Mom first thing in the morning."

"You're an angel." She squeezed his hand. "Now be a good boy and find me a pillow, and then get your carcass back to bed before your lady friend stops speaking to you."

**

When his wife left him, Danny Fiore went on a three-day bender.

He locked the doors and closed the shades, cracked open a bottle of Jack, and threw himself a whopper of a pity party. While he drank and brooded, brooded and drank, he waited like some pathetic teenager for her call. The phone rang occasionally, but it was never Casey, and he let the answering machine take care of everybody else. He had nothing to say to any of them. Sooner or later, when Casey realized what a monumental mistake she had made, she would call, begging him to take her back, and it would be a hell of a thing if she couldn't get through because somebody else had the line tied up.

Except that for some inexplicable reason, she didn't call.

Every couple of hours, Danny picked up the phone and listened to make sure there was a dial tone, that it was still working properly. Reassured, he would hang it back up and take another swig of Jack and wait some more. Sometimes, when the waiting got too difficult, he would press the outgoing message button on the answering machine, just to hear the sound of her voice. And sometimes, deep into Tennessee whiskey and depression, he wouldn't bother to hold back the tears that were always waiting just a blink away. On the evening of the third day, after one more call that wasn't from her, he picked up the telephone, ripped the cord from the wall, and heaved it across the room. It hit the bedroom mirror, and the sound of shattering glass was immensely satisfying.

On the morning of the fourth day he emerged from his stupor, bleary-eyed and hung over, shaky, unshaven, and rank, to the growing suspicion that maybe this time, she wasn't coming back. He put an inch-long gash in his finger picking up the broken glass, and then the only Band-Aids in the house had Oscar the Grouch on them, remnants of a happier time in his life. Cursing, he wrapped two of them around his injured finger and carried the broken glass out to the trash bin. When he returned, he stripped off his clothes in the bedroom, leaving them where they landed. Avoiding the bathroom mirror, he took a long, hot shower.

The shower took away most of the *eau de Jack*, but it did nothing for the pounding in his head. Still naked, he went to the kitchen and mixed himself a concoction consisting of tomato juice, crushed aspirin, and hair of the dog. He gagged it down, then returned to the bathroom to brush his teeth.

He handled his toothbrush gingerly, because even the smallest movement sent daggers through his head. Frowning into the massive mirror over the vanity, he took a good, long look at Danny Fiore, Superstar. King of all he surveyed. A teenybopper's wet dream. If his adoring fans could see him like this, eyes swollen and bloodshot, face buried in whisker stubble, they might think twice before shelling out big bucks so they could scream and swoon at his concerts. He looked every day of his thirty-five years, and then some. "Christ," he told his reflection in disgust, "you're pathetic."

Eventually, inevitably, there was business to take care of. He went back to the bedroom and picked up the clothes he'd left on the floor and played back the messages on the answering machine. Rob had called to make sure he hadn't hung himself from a rafter; Drew Lawrence had called to talk about the new album; his manager had called to remind him that the photographer was coming on Friday to shoot the new album cover, and he needed to be there first thing in the morning. And his publicist had called twice: somehow, the tabloids had already gotten wind that Casey had left, and they were circling, sniffing for blood.

He called his manager first, assured him that he'd be there on Friday, and then he called his publicist. Jackie Steinberg was as straightforward as anyone he'd ever met. "You know how these people are," she said in her distinctive whiskey-throated voice. "If you don't give them something, they'll manufacture it. It's better for you, in the long run, if you give them what they want now."

So he reluctantly agreed to a press conference, and then he called Rob. "I want to know where my wife is," he said.

After a brief hesitation, Rob said, "I can't tell you. I gave my word."

He rubbed the side of his face. Cleared his throat. "Look," he said, "I have a press conference scheduled for two o'clock, and I have no idea what to say to them."

"You want me to call her and ask?"

He closed his eyes. "Yes. Please."

He paced while he waited for Rob's call. Picked up the phone on the first ring. "She says it's up to you," Rob said. "You're the one in the public eye. Say whatever you think is best, and she'll go along with it."

A few minutes past two, he strolled into Jackie Steinberg's reception area, wearing his suede jacket and a pair of mirrored sunglasses. Jackie's receptionist glanced up and gave him a smile that must have cost her parents a small fortune. "Conference room B, end of the hall," she said, and he nodded without speaking.

They were waiting for him inside, a dozen reporters, impatiently if the buzz meant anything. Danny stepped up to the podium and adjusted his glasses and rested his hands, palms down, on the textured oak. The buzz instantly ceased, the room growing so still he could hear Jackie's secretary in the next office, clicking away on the computer keyboard. "Mrs. Fiore and I," he said, "have separated. Obviously you've already heard, or you wouldn't be here. So let's get this over with so we can all go home."

Andy Constantine, from *People* magazine, raised his pen high in the air. "Mr. Fiore," he said, "who initiated the separation?"

"It was a mutual decision," he said.

Kimberly Downes asked, "Are you filing for divorce, Mr. Fiore?"

He rocked back on his heels. "There are no plans at this time," he said, "for a divorce."

A red-haired woman he didn't know shouted from the back of the room, "Danny, is either one of you involved with someone else?"

Jesus H. Christ. He reached into his pocket, pulled out a cigarette. Lit it. Drew deeply and exhaled a cloud of smoke. "No," he said.

"Mr. Fiore? Can you tell us why you and Mrs. Fiore are separating?"

Danny took another draw on the cigarette. His hands were shaking. He cleared his throat. "You've all heard about our daughter's death. The adjustment has been difficult for both of us. We decided that for a time, it would be in our best interests to maintain separate residences. Period."

He looked out over the sea of faces. Vultures, all of them. "One more thing," he said. "I'd appreciate it if you'd leave my wife alone. She's had a rough year, and she doesn't deserve to be plagued."

***

This was the first time Rob had been to the Malibu house since shortly after Katie died, and there was a sadness hovering on the air, an emptiness that made his skin crawl. He wasn't sure how Danny could stay here, now that his wife had left him and his little girl was buried on a rocky hillside in Maine. But then, he'd never really understood what made Danny Fiore tick. He'd come tonight because Danny had called, looking for a shoulder, and he couldn't refuse. In spite of everything, in spite of the fact that he wanted to strangle the guy for what he'd done to Casey, underneath it all, they were still brothers. Bound not by blood, but by two decades of history and an inexplicable loyalty that sometimes really pissed him off.

"Marrying Casey," Danny said, staring into his drink for inspiration, "was the smartest thing I ever did. If wasn't for her, I'd still be playing the bar scene for thirty bucks a night."

Rob leaned back against the couch cushion and crossed his legs at the ankles. Studying the toes of his Reeboks, he sipped his bourbon and water. "If it wasn't for her, Dan, you'd be washed up."

"When I met her," Danny said, "I was an arrogant, wise-ass kid from the streets who thought he had the world by the tail. But she saw something in me. I still don't know what the hell it was."

His mouth thinned. "You mean besides your pretty face?"

Danny shook his head vehemently. "It wasn't that. She looked past that. She looked at that nobody wop kid and she saw something. She made me feel good about myself."

He got up and went to the bar and mixed himself another drink. Casually, he said, "And you're going to let her just walk away?"

"She's better off without me. What the hell did I ever give her?"

He turned and leaned his lanky frame against the bar and studied the tinkling ice cubes in his glass. "Somebody to believe in?" he said.

"Hah! I've been nothing but an albatross around her neck since day one. She deserves better than that."

"And you can be sure she'll get it." He uncovered the crystal candy dish on the bar and took a fistful of peanuts, popped a few into his mouth. "Women like Casey are damn rare. Some guy will grab her up so fast your head will spin." He took another fistful of peanuts. "Who knows? It might even be me."

Danny scowled. "Screw you, MacKenzie."

"I'm just giving it to you straight, Danny. You let her get away, you're a bigger goddamn fool than I thought you were."

Danny snorted. "Thus saith the world's leading authority on women."

"We're not talking here about my track record. You and Casey are a fucking institution, for Christ's sake! How can you let her go?"

"She doesn't want me any more."

"Bullshit! What she doesn't want is the flaming asshole you've been for the last few months. She wants a guy who has something better to do than sit around feeling sorry for himself."

Danny scowled. "Are you finished? Is there anything else you'd like to add, since you've already got me down for the count?"

Rob hesitated, then shrugged his shoulders. Might as well get it over with. "There is one more thing," he said.

Danny raised his glass in a mock salute. "Go ahead. Make my day."

He took a deep breath, then looked Danny directly in the eye. "I've decided to go solo."

There was a moment of silence before the explosion. "You're walking?" Danny asked, his voice cracking, disbelief oozing from every pore.

"Ah, shit, I knew you'd take it that way. Damn it, Dan, it has nothing to do with you. I want to try it on my own for a while. It's something I have to do for myself." He paused. "I made a commitment to finish this album, and I'll honor it. But once it's done, I'm history."

"If I was sober, I'd probably throttle you, but I'm too wasted. How the devil will I ever find anybody who can replace you?"

He grinned. "Try Clapton."

"The man has no chops."

The grin broadened. "Still love me?"

"Fuck you."

That's a healthy attitude, Fiore. Hang onto it."

"You'll go far, MacKenzie. You're a better musician than I am."

"Correction: more technically proficient. You're the one with the talent."

"I'm glad to see," Danny said dryly, "that we're still each other's biggest fan."

"Yeah, well, old habits are hard to break."

The three weeks it took them to complete the album were the longest Rob had ever lived through. He was tired of it all, tired of the hype, tired of the parties and the groupies and the drugs. He and Casey talked on the phone daily. He knew the separation was difficult for her, but Casey avoided talking about her life. Instead, they talked about his, about his frustrations and about the idea that was gestating inside his head. And she gave him her blessing.

"You gave me a piece of advice once," she said, "to tell the world to go to hell and follow my heart. It was good advice, and because I love you, I'm giving it back to you now."

He clutched the phone tighter. "You don't think I'm nuts, then?"

"Rob, listen. I've known for years that you wouldn't be happy forever playing second fiddle to Danny. You're a talented musician. And if you have to go off alone in order to straighten out your head, then that's what you should do."

Three days after he heard the final playback of the new album, he rented a Jeep, packed up his clothes and his guitar and his cat, and headed north. With no particular destination in mind, he knew a freedom he'd never before experienced. He took his time, exploring the coastal villages, walking the beaches, studying the flora and fauna. When he reached San Francisco, he headed inland, through the verdant Sacramento Valley and into the mountains of northern California and Oregon.

Here, the air was clear and smog-free, the land a vast

wilderness totally foreign to a man city-born and bred. The cool mountain streams and cascading waterfalls beckoned him, as did the lakes and the trees and the abundant wildlife. If paradise truly existed, this was it.

He was several days out of L.A. when he stopped for gas at a rustic general store tucked into the shadow of a towering mountain. While the dour-faced attendant filled his tank and checked his oil, he wandered around inside. The place held an eclectic collection of goods: everything from corn flakes to ammunition; from fishing supplies to a dust-laden copy of *Hustler* tucked away on a back shelf just behind the latest issue of *Rod and Reel*.

The guy was taking his own sweet time with the gas. Rob picked up a six-pack of Heineken and a bag of Fritos. To kill time, he began idly scanning the notices tacked on the bulletin board near the cash register. He saw it almost immediately, hand-scrawled on a yellowed three-by-five index card. *Cabin for rent. See Al for details.*

The old guy came back in and rang up the sale, the stench of unleaded gasoline clinging to his yellow slicker. Rob handed him a fifty. As he was making change, Rob asked, "You wouldn't happen to be Al, would you?"

The codger slammed shut the cash drawer. "Depends on what you want," he said.

Rob handed him the fly-specked card. "This," he said.

The guy eyed him up and down, taking in the faded jeans, the army jacket, the riotous blond curls that fell past his shoulders. "The rent's two-fifty a week," he said.

Rob nodded. "That sounds reasonable."

The bushy white brows drew closer together. "That's two-hundred and fifty dollars," he clarified.

"Money's not a problem."

"No partying, no drugs—"

"All I'm looking for is a quiet place where I can rest, play my guitar, commune with nature."

The guy looked at him as though he'd just landed from another planet. And maybe he had. This place was a far cry from L.A. "How long you planning to stay?" Al asked.

He shrugged. "Until I get the urge to move on."

"I have to have the first week's money up front. Cash."

He opened his wallet again and began counting out bills as the old guy watched, bug-eyed. "There's a month's rent, in advance." He looked up and grinned. "When can I move in?"

He didn't have to stay. He kept reminding himself of that as the Jeep navigated the rutted road up the mountainside. Al had given him a door key and vague directions, and he'd bought enough supplies to get him through the first week. His last glimpse of Al had been in his rearview mirror as he pulled out onto the blacktop road. The crusty old gent had stood beside the gas pumps, cap in hand, scratching his head. *He's wondering where the money came from*, Rob thought. *He'll probably run right down to the local post office to see if they have my picture on the wall.*

The Jeep crashed over one last bump and the road ended abruptly in a clearing next to a small cabin. Ahead of him, the lake shimmered and sparkled in the afternoon sun. He stopped the Jeep and got out, and the profundity of the silence overwhelmed him. There were no horns honking, no sirens wailing, no human sounds at all. It was so quiet, he could hear the crunching of his own footsteps.

The place smelled musty and unused. There was a single room, simply furnished with a table and chairs, a built-in bunk, a small refrigerator, a wood stove. He shoved open several windows, and the pine-scented mountain air rushed in, chasing away the stuffiness.

He went back outside and let Igor out of his carrying case. The svelte Siamese slunk, belly to the ground, then dashed for the open cabin door. Igor, too, was a city boy.

It took just a few minutes to unload all his gear. He fiddled with the small generator in the lean-to behind the cabin for a while before he got it going. The refrigerator had the same musty scent as the cabin, but it was clean and it worked, and he stowed away his groceries while Igor sat ignoring him elaborately, tail wrapped around his front legs, wearing his haughtiest Siamese look.

"You're nobody," he told Igor, "until you've been ignored by a cat." Igor's ears twitched. Rob closed the refrigerator. "Come on, mouse breath. Let's go see what kind of mess we've got ourselves into."

Igor trotted along behind him like a faithful dog, down the hill to the water. The weathered dock creaked when he walked on it, but it didn't cave in. From this vantage point, he could see the entire lake, and as far as he could tell, there were no other humans within miles. He saw no cabins, no telltale plumes of smoke rising. No motor boats, no water skiers, no kids splashing around wearing orange life preservers. "Looks like it's just you and me and Mother Nature," he told Igor.

He built a fire in the wood stove and fried hot dogs in the skillet he'd found hanging on the wall. Belly full, he sat barefoot on the dock with Igor and watched the sun set.

Evening came quickly, the darkness seeming to crowd in upon him without warning. The night sounds were different from those of day, and he wondered what the hell he was doing in this godforsaken place.

A good night's sleep changed his outlook. He couldn't remember when he'd slept so soundly. He and Igor breakfasted on a MacKenzie Special, made with eggs and cheese and leftover hotdogs. Then he got out his razor and prepared to shave.

The sight that greeted him when he peered into the cracked mirror above the sink was enough to stop him in his tracks. His eyes were bloodshot, his complexion pasty and sickly. He looked like he'd either gotten drunk last night or should have. Grimacing at his reflection, he held up the disposable razor, looked at it for a moment, then tossed it into the trash. If he was going to live like a hermit, he might as well look like one.

He spent most of that first day lying on the dock, absorbing the sun's warmth. By nightfall, the hated freckles had begun to pop out in a light sprinkling across the bridge of his nose and on his shoulder blades. He'd grown to accept the inevitability of the freckles (his mother said it was just the Irish coming out in him), but he'd never, ever come to like them. He comforted himself by remembering how much luckier he was than his sisters, with their milky-white complexions that turned as red as their hair the minute the sun hit them. The hair on his head was blond, but his body hair was several shades darker, and he knew from experience that the freckles would soon give way to a rich, mahogany tan.

By his third day of solitude, he'd begun to realize that he truly was the only human around. In three days, he hadn't seen a single sign of humanity, not even a plane flying overhead. For the first time in his life, he was absolutely alone. He stripped and swam in the frigid depths of the lake, then lay naked in the sun, its gentle touch nudging him in places he'd never before exposed.

On Saturday he headed for the store, sporting a week's growth of reddish beard and feeling better than he had in years. He'd slept soundly each night and spent the days alternating between exploring the area and sunning himself on the dock.

While Al's distrustful eyes followed him around the store, he stocked up on groceries, then bought a rod and reel. He'd never been fishing in his life, and he had no idea what to buy for tackle, so he bought one of everything. He picked out a half-dozen mysteries from the paperback book rack, bought batteries for his Walkman, then carried his loot out to the Jeep.

He spent the second week reading Robert B. Parker and learning how to fish. He was as excited as a kid when he caught his first bass. It was nearly a foot long, and it lay on the wooden dock, flipping and spattering him with lake water when he tried to remove the hook from its mouth.

That night, he and Igor had fish for supper, and for the first time Igor seemed to approve of this place he'd been dragged off to. He sat contentedly next to Rob on the steps, washing his paws and his face, before curling up in a ball and purring a final benediction.

That evening, Rob sat on the crumbling dock and played his guitar. The Gibson was the first thing he'd bought when the money started rolling in. After years of picking away at third-hand, second-rate guitars, the Gibson was his reward for the virtue of patience. The sweet vibrato echoed out across the silent lake and he felt its thrum through his fingertips and all the way into his soul. He began working on the tune that had been circling around in his head for the better part of a week. Strummed a chord, picked a few notes, frowned and changed pitch slightly. Satisfied, he continued on, gaining momentum as the music began to pour forth from his fingertips, his instrument, his soul.

And there on that dock, a million miles from the bustle of Los Angeles, Rob MacKenzie slowly began his journey home.

***

Three days after Rob left L.A., Danny spent the afternoon sitting on his deck, staring out over the Pacific, smoking cigarettes and sipping bourbon. That night, in spite of the booze circulating through his system, the nightmares poked insidious fingers into his sleep. The images were blurry and confused, visions of Vietnam stirred into the pot along with images of Katie, his Katydid, lying in that tiny white coffin.

He woke up crying, spent the rest of the night battling his demons at the piano. With the first light of day, bleary-eyed and exhausted, he tossed the booze bottles—both full and empty— into the trash. And then he packed an overnight bag, locked up the house, and climbed into the car.

It was a beautiful day for a drive, and once he was on the freeway, he opened up the Ferrari and let her roll. It felt wonderful, the powerful machine beneath him, the wind threading fingers through his hair. He was doing the right thing, and he wished that Casey could see him, for she would be proud of his decision, proud of what he was about to do. He'd been battling these particular demons for too long. It was time he finally laid them to rest.

The V.A. hospital wasn't hard to find. Danny circled the block several times before he mustered the courage to drive into the lot and park. He locked the car, squared his shoulders, and walked determinedly toward the building.

He paused in the lobby to read the wall directory, then took a sharp left and strode to the end of the corridor and through the door marked MENTAL HEALTH SERVICES.

The woman at the reception desk looked up at him, then did a double-take. Her mouth fell open as he pulled his discharge papers from his pocket and slapped them down on the counter in front of her.

"Hello," he said. "My name is Danny Fiore, and I'm here to collect on an old debt."

CHAPTER TWENTY-TWO

She rented an apartment on Hanover Street, in Boston's North End, a cozy little two-bedroom with crooked wooden floors and one wall of ancient brick. From the window that looked out over the street below, she could watch Coca-Cola trucks unloading, and tourists in white shorts with Japanese cameras around their necks, and a never-ending stream of traffic, night and day. She turned the spare bedroom into a workroom, with a day bed and a rolltop desk and a small upright piano that was carted up the stairs by two grunting, muscle-bound deliverymen. She covered the floors with colorful scatter rugs and the windows with venetian blinds, filled the sunny open spaces with a jungle of green plants, stocked the refrigerator with yogurt and fruit and Diet Coke.

And she took up running.

It was a way of relieving her frustrations, a way of temporarily escaping her problems, for while she was running it was impossible to think of anything except the white-hot agony of pushing her body to the point of collapse. Running was a monster, a fire-breathing dragon, an enemy she met with obsessive fury. Gradually, as she built up her endurance, it evolved into a challenge as each day she pushed herself just a little farther. Until one day, she realized she was no longer running to escape her problems or to prove something to herself, but for the simple, sheer exhilaration of running itself. Daily, no matter what the weather, she ran up one side of the Esplanade to the Harvard Bridge and back down the other side. Afterward, she bought the morning paper and a cup of steaming coffee from the grocer downstairs and then stood beneath a scalding shower, face up to the spray as the water sluiced off tender, aching muscles.

There were times when the loneliness overwhelmed her. Nights were the hardest, because she'd been sleeping beside Danny for twelve years, and even during their most difficult times, he'd still been there beside her, a comforting warmth to curl up to. At home, his scent had lingered on the bedding. But her new pillows smelled like K-Mart, the new pillowcases like laundry soap. And she lay awake, night after night, cursing Danny to hell, and herself right along with him, because she would have traded her soul to have him lying there beside her.

Yet there was another side of her that relished the freedom of having to answer to nobody but herself. At times, she looked around her little apartment in amazement at the realization that everything in it was hers and she possessed sole responsibility for her own life. For twelve years, Danny had been the center of her universe. Now she took small, fearful steps into the unknown in an attempt to cultivate the acquaintance of the woman whose green eyes gazed back at her from the mirror each morning. For twelve years, she'd thought she knew who that woman was. Had been absolutely certain of her identity. Now, she was forced to rediscover who she really was, to relearn her own tastes, her own interests, her own dreams.

On the morning of her thirtieth birthday, she awoke engulfed in a deep blue sorrow that played a striking countermelody to the liquid brilliance of the spring morning outside her window. It was so uncharacteristic, this paralyzing sadness, that for a moment she wondered if she'd contracted some exotic flu bug. She'd never allowed melancholy feelings to control her, had always refused to take the time for them. But this was like a heavy blanket of despair, so thick she had difficulty getting out of bed.

Age had never held meaning for her before. A birthday was simply a birthday, a cause for celebration, the actual number meaningless. But thirty was loaded with meaning, ripe with recognition of her own mortality. At thirty, she'd lost some symbolic youth, had stepped over a threshold into an alien territory from which she could never return. At thirty, she should have had it all. Instead, her life was a shambles. And she was forced to face the truth that her chances for attaining that elusive happiness were growing slimmer with each year that passed.

Most of the time, she tried not to dwell on thoughts of Danny, but today she allowed herself just a few minutes to wallow in self-pity, wondering if he even remembered it was her birthday. How was he coping? How was he making it through the nights, when the nightmares woke him in the wee hours and she wasn't there to ward off the evil spirits? Was he in as much pain as she was? Did he hate sleeping alone as much as she did? Or had he even noticed she was gone?

She exorcised her demons by running, pushing her body to its limits and beyond, breaking her own records for speed and endurance. She returned home sweaty, gasping, barely coherent, but her depression had lifted. The hallway was dark, and it took her eyes a few moments to adjust to the gloomy interior. She was halfway up the stairs before she saw the shadowy figure sitting on the top step. She reached into her pocket and closed her fist around the can of Mace she carried everywhere. And then a familiar voice said, "About time you got here. Don't blame me if the Cherry Garcia's already soup."

Her entire body responded with an exultant, resounding joy. She released the Mace, let out a bloodcurdling whoop, and took the stairs two at a time. "MacKenzie, you insufferable jackass!" she said as she threw her arms around him. "What are you doing in Boston?"

He returned her bone-crunching hug. "It's your birthday, Fiore. Didn't think I'd forget, did you?"

"Let me look at you." She stepped back, held him at arm's length and studied him while he watched her with a bemused smile. "You look wonderful," she said.

He chucked her under the chin and said, "Listen, the ice cream really is melting. I've been sitting here for the better part of an hour."

She looked at the packages strewn over the landing. "You really brought ice cream?" she said.

"And cake. And gifts. A woman turns thirty but once, my sweet. It's a milestone that deserves to be commemorated."

She took out her keys and unlocked the door to her apartment. Ruefully, she said, "I'd just as soon commemorate it by drinking hemlock."

"What you need," he said, picking up the last of his packages and kicking the door shut behind him, "is an attitude adjustment. And that's just what I'm here to provide."

While she watched, he unpacked a pint of Ben & Jerry's, a homemade cake that looked like one of Mary's specialties, two bottles of sparkling wine—one red, one white—and an assortment of packages hastily done up in Sesame Street wrapping paper. "Sorry about the paper," he said. "It was all Mom could dig up on such short notice."

"You didn't have to do this," she said.

He picked up one of the bottles and perused the label. Frowning, he said, "Which do you think goes better with ice cream? Red or white?"

"You're a lunatic," she said, "but I love you. Let's go with the red."

Without asking for permission, he began opening cupboard doors until he found a pair of wine glasses. "And note," he said, "that I spared no expense." He released the cork with a loud pop. "See? No screw-on cap." With a flourish, he poured wine into one of the glasses and handed it to her.

"Duly noted," she said dryly.

He filled his own glass and held it up. "To thirty," he said, "and whatever's on the other side."

"To old age, infirmity, and senility," she echoed darkly, and drained her glass.

He leaned those lanky hips against the counter and rolled his wine glass between both palms. "Bad day, kiddo?" he said.

"Try bad year."

Those green eyes examined her at length. At last, softly, he said, "Yeah. I know."

She picked up the bottle and refilled her glass. Digging a fingertip into his breastbone, she said, "I don't want your damn pity."

"Pity's definitely not on the agenda," he said. "But a birthday party is."

So they drank red wine and ate Mary's chocolate cake topped with a generous puddle of Ben & Jerry's Cherry Garcia. His gifts were eclectic, and typical of him: a coloring book denoting the joys of senility; an oversized white tee shirt that said *Sexy Senior Citizen*; and an exquisite pair of earrings, fashioned of jade and onyx, that must have cost him dearly. "Oh, Rob," she protested, "they're beautiful. But they're too expensive. You shouldn't have done this."

"Why not? I'm loaded. I can afford it."

"I know, but—"

"I seem to remember a certain person who bought me a leather jacket last Christmas. One I saw on Rodeo Drive and refused to shell out the bucks for."

"That was different."

He squared that stubborn jaw. "What's different about it?"

"Jewelry is so personal. A man buys jewelry for his wife, not for—" She stopped abruptly and bit her lip.

"For what?" he said. "Another man's wife? Is that what you were about to say?"

She shrugged in silent apology. "Look," he said, more gently, "if said man is stupid enough to let his wife walk out of his life, then I'll buy her anything I damn well please."

Casey raised her wine glass. "*Touché*," she said.

"Oh, I almost forgot." He picked up the aforementioned leather jacket and began rummaging through the pockets. "There's one more."

"More? MacKenzie, you'll spoil me rotten before you're through."

"This one's different." He finally found what he sought, a flat, square package done up in the same Sesame Street paper. He held it in his hand for a moment, thumb caressing it lazily, and then he slid it across the table to her. "Happy birthday, kiddo," he said, and to her surprise, got up from the table and walked to the window.

Casey picked it up, looked at it, glanced quickly at his rigid back, his squared shoulders. And knew. Instantly, she knew. She fumbled with the ribbon, tore at Big Bird and Elmo to reveal the CD inside. In the cover photo, he stood beneath a huge maple tree, his guitar balanced on one booted toe, deeply shadowed morning light filtering in through the branches and teasing golden highlights from that riotous mass of curls. *Rob MacKenzie*, the words on the spine read. *The Edge of Nowhere.*

"You did it!" she said, hands trembling with excitement. "Hot damn, Flash, you really did it!"

He turned away from the window, the color flushing his cheekbones the only indication of his true feelings. He shoved his hands into his pockets. "You might want to listen to it," he said, studying the toes of his Reeboks, "before you get too wound up."

Casey snorted, in a loud and most unladylike manner, and didn't bother to respond. Cake, ice cream and earrings forgotten, she carried the disc to the living room and popped it into her CD player. She plunked down onto the couch and folded her arms around a raised knee, and while he paced her kitchen, she listened to his first solo album all the way through.

The music was complex, cool and jazzy, with that sophisticated edge that marked all his work. He'd written and produced the album himself, backing himself up with some of the best studio musicians in the business. How many times had she heard him sing over the years? They'd been collaborating for twelve years, and they'd sung together maybe ten thousand times, yet the soft, slightly husky voice pouring from her twin Pioneer speakers still managed to surprise her. He'd always taken a back seat to Danny, but without Danny there to overshadow him, she could hear the strength in his voice. Rob MacKenzie had been born to make music, and no matter what the instrument might be, he handled it with aplomb.

"I've had this stuff rolling around in my head," he said. "A second album that's not like anything we've ever done before. I want to go off in a completely new direction. A little blues, a little rock, a little fusion. Remember Van Morrison's *Moondance*?"

"So rich you could taste it."

"Exactly. Use something like that as a starting point and take it from there. Are you game?"

His enthusiasm was irresistible. "I'm game," she said, "but how are we supposed to work together if we're on opposite coasts?"

"Elementary, my sweet. The first thing we do is go out and buy you a fax machine. Then we engineer our schedules so we can work together. Sound okay so far?"

"It sounds wonderful. I hate to have to admit it, but I've missed your ugly mug."

He patted her cheek. "Let's go check out that fax machine, kiddo. I hear there's a monster sale going on at Woolworth's."

She hadn't returned to work after her life blew up in her face. After pouring all her pent-up grief and frustration into the Rothman project, she had needed to be in a different space for a

time. Now, she took comfort from the familiar patterns of
working with Rob. They spoke on the phone constantly, sent
faxes back and forth between Boston and Los Angeles.
Whenever he could wrangle a block of free time from his hectic
schedule, he flew to Boston and they spent exhausting twenty-
hour days working together. He arrived one weekend carrying
two suitcases and a slightly cantankerous Siamese cat in a plastic
carrier. After that, he just stayed. They spent their days
enveloped in cool, jazzy rhythms, their evenings lingering over
dinner at Polcari's or the Union Oyster House. Late nights often
found them in some smoke-filled blues club, drawing in the
music with every breath, absorbing blue notes into the very
marrow of their bones.

Rob insisted that the work week should end at five o'clock
on Fridays, so on the weekends, they played. They took
advantage of Indian summer, went for long drives in the country
to admire the foliage, visited flea markets and antique dealers
and auctions. They fell into a comfortable pattern of eating
Sunday brunch in Southie with his parents, then loading Mary
and Patrick MacKenzie into the back seat of Casey's BMW and
taking them sightseeing. The four of them visited Plymouth
Rock, admired the mansions of Newport, shopped the outlet
stores in Kittery and North Conway.

The first time Rob went running with her, he made it as far
as the end of the block before he collapsed onto a bench, gasping
and wheezing and clutching his chest. "Are you crazy, Fiore?"
he said. "Are you trying to kill me?"

"Throw away the cigarettes," she told him, "and you might
just surprise yourself."

"Jesus, woman, I've been smoking since I was fifteen."

"And your point is?"

"You're cruel, Fiore. Damn cruel."

"Hey, it's your lungs, hot stuff. But don't think you'll keep
up with me if you don't quit." And she sprinted away and left
him sitting there.

The next morning, when she emerged from her bedroom,
dressed to run, he was already up and waiting for her. "I just
want to make sure you witness this," he said as he solemnly held
up his last pack of cigarettes and dropped it into the trash.

She gave him a quick round of applause. "Congratulations, MacKenzie. Welcome to the first day of the rest of your life."

"Just remember, Fiore, this was your idea. You're the one who'll have to put up with me once the nicotine withdrawal kicks in."

"Give it a break, Flash. You're all bark and no bite."

For the three weeks it took to rid his body of its nicotine addiction, he bore an amazing resemblance to Attila the Hun. He took umbrage at Casey's most innocent remarks, slammed doors and kicked drawers, and got involved in a shouting match with another driver who cut him off in downtown traffic. But Casey had to give him credit for determination. He fought nearly unbearable cravings and continued to run with her every morning until he was sweaty and gasping and unable to continue. Because he'd smoked for so many years, he built up endurance more slowly than she had. Casey slowed her speed to a crawl to accommodate him until his pace picked up. And one fine morning, he actually made it the entire six miles.

He was like a little kid, so proud of his accomplishment that he called his mother to brag. After that, there was no stopping him. He took to running with the same zeal he exhibited in every other area of his life. Within a month, he could run circles around her. And Casey wondered if there was anything that Rob MacKenzie couldn't do.

CHAPTER TWENTY-THREE

In January, Danny hired a private investigator to locate his mother.

Katie's death had been the catalyst, but it had been building for some time, the need to know who he was, the need for answers to his questions, answers that only Annamaria Fiore could give him. When his V.A. counselor urged him to seek those answers, for purposes of closure if nothing else, he found Brad Logan in the telephone book and hired him on the spot. It was easier than he'd expected. Two days after he hired Logan, he got the information he was looking for: his mother was living in East L.A., only a few miles from his Malibu home.

Only a few miles, but worlds away. As he drove the mean streets of the *barrio*, suspicious eyes followed his progress. He slowed in front of a pink stucco house surrounded by weeds and crammed tight against a chain link fence. Swallowing hard, he pulled the Ferrari to a stop and looked around. Two scrawny kids were hanging off the fence, gaping at the Ferrari with huge, dark eyes. "Keep an eye on my car for me," he said, "and I'll give you both a brand-new twenty-dollar bill."

The tallest one puffed out his chest and drew himself up to his full height. "You want us to watch your car, man, you show us the money first."

He'd forgotten that trust wasn't in a street kid's vocabulary. Danny opened his wallet and pulled out two twenties. "Take care of her for me, guys, and there'll be two more just like this when I come out. But if I find so much as a scratch, you can forget it."

There was no doorbell, so he opened the torn screen door and knocked on the glass. From inside came the canned hysteria of a television game show. He knocked harder, and after a moment, shuffling feet approached the door. The dirty blind lifted, and dark eyes peered out at him. He swallowed again, his throat clogging up with some unexpected and unrecognizable emotion. The door swung open, and with it came the moment he'd spent thirty years both dreading and anticipating.

His legs were trembling, and he tried to find his voice. But

Anna Fiore Montoya was quicker. "I figured you'd show up one of these days," she said.

***

She should never have brought Rob with her to buy a bikini.

Anything he liked, she wouldn't have worn out of the dressing room. Anything she liked, he declared suitable for his grandmother. Finally, he picked out a minuscule number made of shiny green Spandex. "This one," he said.

"You can't be serious. There's not enough material there to cover a poodle."

"Trust me, Fiore. This is the one."

Casey made sure the fitting room door was locked securely behind her before stripping down and squeezing into the few square inches of fabric. She was scandalized by how little of her it covered. The bottom dipped low at the pelvis and narrowed to tiny knots at the hips. The halter top cupped her breasts and dissolved into spaghetti straps that tied behind her neck. The shiny knit fabric left nothing to the imagination. She turned left and right. If she was going to be scandalous, she should at least look good while she was doing it. With a certain smug satisfaction, she noted that her thirty-something body was as taut as any nineteen-year-old's. The bikini fit her like a glove. She narrowed her eyes, wondering just how Rob had known that it would look spectacular on her. For the first time in her life, she felt like a temptress. What a shame that all this would be wasted because she'd come to Nassau with Rob instead of somebody who could appreciate her.

Hell's bells. She tore off the bikini and yanked her tee shirt back down over her head. Casey Fiore would never be a temptress. She was too proper. Too much of a lady. Too damn square to wear a bikini she could have fit into the change compartment of her wallet.

Only one man had ever seen her that close to naked, and Danny would be apoplectic if he saw her dressed that way in public. The image pleased her, and she mentally thumbed her nose at the specter of Daniel Fiore. She was an independent woman, and if she wanted to wear the most outrageous bikini this side of Cannes, she would wear it. And if she wanted to carry a rose between her teeth and thread ostrich feathers in her hair and dance the can-can while she wore it, she would do that, too. It was time she let loose a little. Maybe even time she went out and had an affair. There were other men in the world. She'd wasted the better part of a year waiting for Danny Fiore to come running after her. It was pretty obvious that he wasn't coming.

Well, she wasn't waiting any longer.

They spent the rest of the morning dropping their money in the tourist traps, buying baubles and trinkets to bring home to nieces and nephews and other family members. Rob bought his mother a flowing cotton skirt of such vivid colors it hurt the eyes to look at. Casey bought a carved wooden alligator for her father, and for her stepmother a cassette tape of calypso music. They ate lunch at the hotel, then returned to their rooms to drop off their loot and change into their swimsuits.

She put on the bikini and stared at her reflection in horrified fascination as her hard-won nerve dissipated, her vow to start life anew as an Outrageous Woman swirling away with it. Why not just prance on the beach naked? At least naked would have been straightforward. This was worse. This was secretive. This was exotic. This was sexy.

She'd never in her life been sexy. She slept in flannel all winter, cotton all summer, wore her skirts at a respectable length and her shirts buttoned all the way. She never showed any cleavage. She wasn't even sure she *had* cleavage. Maybe, she thought, eyeing her reflection, she'd been wrong about that. Studying herself from a different angle, she decided she'd definitely been wrong about that. It was amazing to discover, at the age of thirty, that she had a chest.

Her confidence rapidly disintegrating, Casey folded a terrycloth beach jacket around her and knotted the belt, tied a wide-brimmed straw hat on her head and stepped into her beach sandals. Gathering her nerve around her like a suit of armor, she stepped out into the corridor.

Rob was waiting outside, by the pool. They set up beach chairs on the pristine white sand. She wedged her tote bag into the sand between their chairs, left her hat on her chair, and together they walked down to the water's edge.

The ocean's warmth delighted her. It tickled her toes and lapped at her ankles. Beneath a cloudless sky, the water was a deep emerald, and the midday sun reflected off the stucco buildings that lined the beach. "This place is spectacular," she said. "I'm so glad we came."

"Told you that you'd like it." Rob moved his feet around in the swirling surf. "When I came down with Kiki last year, I swore I'd come back the first chance I got."

"Kiki," she said with interest. "I don't believe I remember Kiki."

"You never met her."

"What a shame. She sounds so intellectual."

"Shut up, Fiore." He reached down, cupped a palmful of water, and tossed it at her. She squealed, took a step backward, and splashed him back. Like two kids, they splashed and laughed until they were both thoroughly wet. Casey held up both palms in surrender and they staggered back up the beach to their chairs. While Rob liberally spread sunscreen across the bridge of his nose, Casey took a deep breath and removed the beach jacket.

And the sky didn't fall. The sun's heat explored her flesh like warm fingers. She settled herself in the chair, smoothed sunscreen on her exposed areas, and opened one of the paperback novels she'd bought in the hotel gift shop.

After a while, the heat made her drowsy. She set aside the book and adjusted her chair and lay back, eyes closed, enjoying the sun's sensual warmth. Beside her, Rob was reading. Every so often, over the ebb and flow of the surf, over the buzzing of insects flitting from tropical flower to tropical flower and the distant voices of people cavorting in the water, she heard him turn a page.

She turned her head to study him. His lanky legs were sprawled, bony knees extended, feet buried in the sand. Above baggy cotton shorts of an exotic, vivid jungle print, his stomach was flat, his chest generously covered with hair. His shoulders were bony but wide, his biceps surprisingly well developed. All in all, not a bad package. "I've decided to have an affair," she announced.

"Oh?" he said without looking up from his book. "Anyone

I know?"

"I haven't decided yet." She closed her eyes again and made a lazy mental run-through of all the men she knew. The list wasn't very long. Or very promising. Disappointed, she opened her eyes again. "I never knew you had freckles," she said.

He scowled and muttered, "The curse of the Irish."

"I think they're cute. So what do you think?"

He looked up from his book. "About what?"

"Who I should have an affair with."

His eyes made a slow perusal of her, head to feet and back, lingering briefly on her breasts. "I don't know," he said, "but if you run around looking like that, you'll have no shortage of potential victims."

She felt an all-over heat that had nothing to do with the sun. "This was your idea," she accused.

"What was?"

"This *thing* I'm hardly wearing."

"I'd say you're doing a pretty spectacular job of wearing it, Fiore."

"How would you know? You've had your nose stuck in that book ever since we got here."

"Not every single minute," he said.

"Oh, please," she said. "I'm going down to the water."

She stood up, resisting the urge to adjust her bathing suit to adequately cover her bottom. Ignoring him, she walked determinedly across the sand to the water's edge and waded into the surf. She was waist high when a bright red Frisbee hit the water directly in front of her. She picked it up and turned around to see Rob standing a few feet away. "Truce?" he said.

She grinned wickedly and sent the Frisbee sailing. "Go fetch."

Like an overgrown golden retriever, he splashed off to catch up with the Frisbee. He shot it back to her, and she jumped to catch it. They continued the game until they grew tired, returning damp and sandy to their beach chairs. "I'm starved," she said. "Let's get something to eat."

He pulled on a tee shirt and she threw her beach jacket over her shoulders and they went in search of sustenance. They found it at a beachside cafe, where they sat at a wrought-iron table beneath a pink and white striped umbrella and ordered the catch of the day. While they waited for it to arrive, Casey sipped her strawberry daiquiri and studied the couples sitting at the other tables. The island was a regular Noah's Ark. Everybody seemed to be in pairs, most of them young and tanned and in love. "I feel like a misfit," she said. "I think we're the only people on this island who aren't honeymooners."

Rob set down his bottle of Heineken and looked around. "Funny," he said, "I never noticed it the last time I was here."

"That," she said, "is because you were here with the vivacious Kiki. You probably never left your hotel room."

"Fiore," he said, "you're a prude. What the hell is so wrong with recreational sex?"

"I am not a prude. I told you I'd decided to have an affair. Does that sound prudish to you?"

"I know you too well. You'll never go through with it."

"You don't know me half as well as you think you do, MacKenzie. I'm not exactly a stranger to the delights of recreational sex. It may have been a while, but I haven't completely forgotten."

He sipped his beer. "If you're married," he said, "it doesn't count."

Her mouth fell open. "That's not the way I remember it."

"That's because you have no basis for comparison."

"Oh, really? Well, for your information, great oracle, Danny and I had sex *before* we were married." Smugly, she added, "More than once."

"Doesn't count."

She bristled. "And why not?"

"You and Danny," he said, "got married three days after you met. That's not recreational sex, it's commitment."

"And just what the hell is wrong with commitment?"

He held up both hands in a gesture of defenselessness. "I didn't say there was anything wrong with it. I just said it wasn't the same thing."

"Oy," she said. "I think I need another drink."

***

"I don't give a damn what you think," Danny told Anna Montoya, "or why you did what you did. But there's one thing I want from you. I want to know who my father is."

Her eyes narrowed, and she took a drag on her cigarette. Exhaled. "Why should I tell you?" she asked.

"Because I've lived thirty-six years as a bastard, and I have a right to know the truth. I have to know where the hell I'm coming from before I can figure out where I'm going."

She continued to smoke her cigarette. When she was done, she crushed it out in the ashtray. "His name was Eddie," she said. "Eddie Carpenter. He was a sailor, stationed at the Navy Yard over to Charlestown."

"And?"

She shrugged. "We had a thing for a while. Then he shipped out, and I never heard from him again."

He raked trembling hands through his hair. "Do you know anything else about him? Where he was from? Anything?"

"Somewhere in the Midwest. Iowa? Idaho? Something like that. Geez, I haven't thought of Eddie in years. He was one hell of a looker." Her thoughtful expression momentarily softened her face, erasing years from her age. "Must've been a strong gene pool," she said. "You're the spitting image of him."

Danny leaned forward intently. "Did he know about me?"

"Nah. He was gone before I ever figured out why I was throwing up every morning."

He left her there on the couch, half-drunk, still musing over her star-crossed romance with the dashing Eddie Carpenter. At the door, he paused to look around the kitchen, at the broken window over the sink, the empty whiskey bottle on the table, the roaches that ran among the toast crumbs. He cursed and wheeled back around. Her attention was riveted on *The Price is Right*, and he stood in the doorway with his mouth open, not sure what to call her. *Anna? Mother? Mom?*

"Mama?" he said quietly, inevitably, the only name he'd ever called her.

When she looked up, her face softened, and he saw traces of the young girl he remembered. "It's been a long time," she said, "since anybody called me that."

"This place is a hellhole," he said. "Let me move you out of here. Some place clean, in a decent neighborhood."

"I been here thirty years, Danny. This is home."

"It's a rat-infested slum."

"Yeah, but it's my slum. It's bought and paid for, and nobody can tell me what to do or how to do it. I got no landlord knocking down my door, nobody telling me how to live my life. I got my independence, Danny."

For some inexplicable reason, he understood. "Do you suppose," he said, "I could stop by and visit you once in a while?"

"You really want to?"

He thought about it. "Yes," he said. "I really want to."

"Somebody might steal the hubcaps off that fancy car you're driving."

He came close to smiling. "I'll take that chance," he said.

"Danny?" she said.

"Yeah?"

"I just wanted you to know that there ain't been a single day in the last thirty years that I didn't think about you."

***

She slept soundly that night and awoke feeling reborn. She dragged Rob out of bed at seven and pushed his grumbling form toward the shower. He emerged human, and they ran on the beach for an hour. After breakfast, they set up their beach chairs near the water and spent the morning lounging in the sun and drinking wine coolers until they both had a buzz going. "This is decadent," she said. "Not even noon, and we're both half crocked."

He lay flat on his back, knees spread, his wine cooler dangling from slack fingertips. "Gives you a whole new perspective on life, doesn't it?"

"I may never go back. I may just stay here and pick up some nineteen-year-old stud muffin and spend my sunset years in drunken squalor."

"You've got a mile or two to go," he said, studying her idly, "before you hit your sunset years."

She adjusted her shoulder strap. "Shut up," she said, "and pass me another wine cooler."

"So," he said, uncapping it and handing it to her, "you've decided on a stud muffin?"

She lifted her sunglasses and peered at him from beneath them. "Excuse me?"

"For that mythical affair you keep talking about having."

"Oh." She tugged discreetly at her bikini bottom. "I haven't decided on anyone yet. I'm still working on it."

"Maybe I can help. I know lots of people."

"Help like yours," she said, "I don't need."

He looked hurt. "Just to show you I'm a prince among men," he said, "I'm going to ignore that remark."

"Come on, Rob. You know it's not that easy. Surely you've heard of great chemistry?"

"Geez, Fiore, you and I have great chemistry, but I don't see us rushing to jump each other's bones."

This time, she didn't bother to lift her glasses. She just stared at him through them. "Be serious," she said. "You know I don't think of you that way."

He opened another wine cooler and took a long, slow swallow. "Okay," he said. "Let's look at what we have here. At one end of the spectrum, the Pope. At the other end, Attila the Hun. In between, we have one giant question mark."

"You're making fun of me."

"I am not."

"Look," she said, "celibacy is an unnatural condition. For women as well as men. Don't you think I'm entitled to the same fun you guys have been enjoying all your lives?"

"Sweetheart," he said, suddenly serious, "I think you're long overdue."

***

Danny held the scrap of paper in his hand, staring at the telephone number he'd read so many times he could have reeled it off in his sleep. This wouldn't be like confronting his mother. If Anna had told the truth, his father didn't even know he existed. What if he made a fool of himself? What if Carpenter refused to acknowledge him? What if his mother had lied?

With trembling hands, he picked up the phone and punched in the number to his father's home in Iowa. It rang several times before a man answered. Danny cleared his throat. "Hello," he said. "I'm looking for Eddie Carpenter."

"Yeah, this is Eddie."

His innards knotted until he realized the voice was far too young. Carpenter's son, perhaps? *His brother.* Danny closed his eyes and swallowed. "This would be the Eddie Carpenter who was in the Navy back around 1950."

"That would be my dad. Hold on."

The young man dropped the phone, and Danny could hear the murmur of conversation in the background. Then an older man's voice said, "This is Eddie Carpenter. Can I help you?"

Danny wet his lips. "I think so," he said. "My name is Danny Fiore, and I'm looking for a man named Eddie Carpenter who was a sailor stationed at Boston Navy Yard back in the winter of 1950."

"I was stationed in Boston for a couple of months. Who did you say you were?"

"Do you remember a girl named Anna? Anna Fiore? A pretty little dark-haired Italian girl?"

There was a pause. Then: "I remember her. Who the hell are you?"

Danny cleared his throat. "It appears," he said, "that I'm your son."

***

He flew from LAX to O'Hare, then hopped a commuter to Dubuque. From there, his final destination was a town so small that he flew in on a six-seater twin-engine turboprop. He'd never quite grasped the concept of family. Growing up, there'd been just his grandmother. No mother, no father, no aunts or uncles or cousins. As a result, he'd never completely understood Casey's attachment to her various relatives, or Rob's complex relationships with an extended family so large it made the Kennedys look like hermits.

But the moment he saw Eddie Carpenter standing in the

single room that served as a terminal, legs braced apart, hands nervously jingling the coins in his pockets, Danny understood. The man who stared back at him shared his blue eyes, his full lower lip, his dimples. Carpenter's hair had started to gray, but his shoulders were broad, his body solid and still muscular, although he was in his mid-fifties. *This*, Danny thought, *is what I'll look like in twenty years.*

They stood for a long time, just staring at each other, before Carpenter said in a shaky voice tinged with a distinctive Midwestern twang, "I'll be damned." And held out his hand.

Fully intending to shake hands and then coolly retreat back into his personal space, Danny grasped his father's hand. But as they stood there, hands clasped, blue eyes studying identical blue eyes, something amazing happened.

He discovered that he couldn't let go.

Carpenter squeezed his hand. Danny squeezed back. And then his father spoke the words that would change his life, the words that Danny had waited thirty-six years to hear: "Welcome home, son."

***

Beneath a whispering paddle fan, Rob sipped a 7-Up and checked his watch for the third time. He'd quit drinking around three, but Casey had gone to her room two hours ago still carrying a bottle of sticky pink liquid. She'd never been much of a drinker, and wine coolers were deceptive. You'd think you were drinking soda until you tried to stand up and couldn't find your feet. He was about ready to go looking for her when she walked into the restaurant, wearing high-heeled sandals and a dress that in Boston would have been grounds for arrest. It was white, backless, damn near frontless. She smiled and began crossing the room to his table. And every man in the place looked at her, then at him, every damn one of them trying to figure out what a guy like him was doing with a woman like that.

She'd put her hair up into some kind of elaborate concoction that lent her an aura of sophistication that intimidated even him. It was the craziest thing; they'd spent the better part of twelve years living inside each other's pockets, but as she approached, his throat dried up like the Sahara. He emptied his drink in one quick gulp as she slipped into the chair opposite him. "I hope I didn't keep you waiting," she said.

"Fiore," he said, "I'm at a loss for words. That is some dress."

She shifted position, looked down at herself, nervously adjusted the material in an attempt to cover more flesh. It didn't work. "You don't think it's too much, do you?"

"It's spectacular. And you look stunning in it. Or you would, if you'd stop fidgeting."

"I can't help it. I feel naked."

"You damn near are."

"I knew it," she said, scraping back her chair. "I knew it was too much. I'm going back upstairs to change."

He caught her by a slender forearm. "Stay. I'm trying to cultivate a reputation as a stud."

The waiter arrived, and she ordered a Singapore Sling. "You might want to go slow on the hard stuff, kiddo," he said. "After all those wine coolers, you'll have a big head tomorrow."

"I can hold my liquor, MacKenzie."

"Who are you trying to kid, Fiore? I've seen you get tipsy just sniffing the bottle cap."

While they waited for dinner to arrive, she sipped her Singapore Sling and he tried not to stare at her breasts. He'd been trying not to stare at them ever since he'd first seen her in that nothing little bikini. In his book, bigger was not necessarily better, and Casey Fiore had a pair of ripe little peaches sweet enough to bring tears to his eyes. Round and firm and high, they cried out to be touched, and they'd kept him awake for a good part of last night.

It was crazy, because in all the years they'd known each other, he'd never thought of her that way. Not more than once or twice. There had been that one sticky night in Arkansas when she'd come fresh from the shower, his tee shirt plastered to her damp body, and he'd nearly swallowed his tongue. But it had been a brief moment in time, easily forgotten. He trusted her with an absolute certainty he'd never known with any other woman. It had never mattered that Danny was the one she slept with, because that wasn't what he wanted from her. He could get sex anywhere. Casey gave him something better: warmth and wisdom, sass and strength, respect and laughter and unconditional love.

Somewhere in the course of that first Singapore Sling, she stopped fidgeting. By flickering candlelight, she rested her chin on her palm and studied him with a Mona Lisa smile. "What?" he said.

"You're looking particularly handsome tonight," she said.

That was when he knew the booze had gone to her head. By no stretch of the imagination could he be called handsome. The Danny Fiores of the world were handsome. The Rob MacKenzies were average. It was a simple fact of life, one that had never bothered him until now. "Sweetheart," he said, "you're drunk."

She leaned on both forearms, low over the table, giving him a brief, unobstructed view of paradise. "I've never been drunk in my life," she said.

Where the hell was their dinner? He was about ready to invade the kitchen in search of it when the waiter arrived with a laden tray and began setting dishes on the table. "I'd like another drink," Casey said.

He exchanged glances with the waiter. "Babe," he said, "don't you think you've had enough?"

"Come on, Rob. I thought we came here to have a good time."

The waiter flashed him a salacious grin, and he made a mental note to cut five percent from the guy's tip. "I just don't want you to have too much of a good time," he said.

She patted his cheek. "You take such good care of me."

"Shut up and eat your dinner. You need something in your stomach to absorb all that alcohol."

Dinner was a curiously silent affair. Casey nibbled at her food, but Rob found that his appetite had deserted him. He watched her eat, relieved when the meal was over. After he paid the check, stiffing that leering son of a bitch on the tip, he pulled out Casey's chair and helped her to her feet, afraid she'd fall off those three-inch heels. She had enough booze in her to fell a longshoreman.

Music floated out of the lounge as they passed, and like

lemmings to the sea, they were drawn in. They stood just inside the doorway watching couples move around the floor to the kind of soft, romantic music their parents had danced to a generation ago. He saw the wistfulness on her face, and he touched her bare arm. "Come on, sweet stuff," he said. "Let's dance."

It was a mistake. He knew it the instant that warm body melted into his and he forgot who he was, forgot who she was, remembered only that he was a man and she was a woman and she felt like heaven in his arms. She rested her head on his shoulder while he tried to figure out where to put his hands. It wasn't an easy decision. The dress left her bare in all but the most crucial spots, and he finally gave in and rested both hands on the small of her back. Her heat pierced his fingertips and radiated into and through his body. Her hair smelled like violets. He fixed his eyes on a single freckle on her bare shoulder. Beyond it, in the heated spot where their bodies met, the dark hollow between her breasts was visible. He swallowed. Closed his eyes. Buried his face in her hair and clung to her in agony and ecstasy.

Until he could stand it no longer. "Babe," he whispered.

She looked at him, those green eyes hazy from the alcohol. "What?"

"I need some fresh air."

He let her go with a mixture of reluctance and relief. Side by side, they walked down to the beach, both of them thinking private thoughts they didn't choose to share. The alcohol had finally taken its toll, and she was wobbly on the heels. When they reached the sand, she bent and slipped them off. Dangling a sandal from each hand, she walked beside him, every so often listing in his direction. At the water's edge, she dropped the sandals and waded into the surf. He kicked off his shoes and rolled up his pant legs and waded in after her, water washing around his ankles. He shoved his hands in his pockets. "Hey," he said to her retreating back, "where do you think you're going?"

"Swimming."

"You'll ruin your dress." Hands in his pockets, he watched her wading deeper. "Crazy broad," he said. She was in up to her knees, her dress bunched up around her thighs, a section of hem trailing in the water behind her. "Hey," he said, "that's far enough. Come on back now."

Still holding the dress, she braced her legs against the onrushing waves and turned to look at him. And smiled that Mona Lisa smile. "Come and get me," she said.

He grinned. "Oh," he said. "You're wanting to play games now, are you?"

He advanced on her and she backed away slowly, water lapping at her thighs, the white dress billowing and swirling around her. "Fiore," he said, "you're about to fall on your pretty little ass."

"Hah! If I go down, MacKenzie, you go with me."

"Too bad about the dress."

He lunged and missed. She shrieked and went over backward, came up laughing, water running off her like Niagara, that dress plastered to her body like a fresh coat of paint. He held out a hand and she took it, and he hauled her into his arms and kissed her.

She gasped and clutched his shirt front in her fists. Heart hammering like a locomotive, he took his sweet time exploring those lush lips. She tasted of salt water and grenadine and warm, willing woman, and this was an even bigger mistake than the dancing had been because she was kissing him back for all she was worth, and he wasn't sure this time he could let her go.

Oh, Jesus, he thought. And finished it: *Help me.*

They came up for air, both of them gasping, both of them drenched, both of them suddenly dead serious. That ridiculous Duchess of York hairdo had fallen and was hanging about her shoulders in sodden strings. She lifted a hand and shoved a wet strand away from her face, and he wrapped his fingers in the rat's nest at the nape of her neck and pulled her back to him.

This time she was ready for him. She uttered a soft sound of pleasure as he teased her mouth open and plunged his tongue inside, and they met in a silken duel of thrust and parry. Her hips moved restlessly against his, and he caught her and lifted her, thrusting her up hard against him.

And she moaned aloud. Her arms went around his neck and they rocked together, straining to be closer, to swallow each other, to become one. He rained a trail of kisses from the corner of her mouth, down over that pretty little pointed chin, inch by inch, kiss by kiss, along the slender white column of her throat. And then he did what he'd been waiting all night to do: he slipped a hand beneath the wet dress and cupped one of those ripe peaches.

It fit his hand perfectly. He held it until the flesh warmed in his hand, and then he found the hard little peak and began to stroke it, gently, with the tips of his fingers. She made a soft strangled sound deep in her throat and went weak against him, head thrown back, eyes closed, mouth open just enough for breath, just enough to show a glimpse of white teeth and the pink tip of her tongue. Still stroking, he watched the pained pleasure on her face and knew that she was his for the taking. He could have her right here in the surf, if that was the way he wanted it, like Burt Lancaster and Deborah Kerr in *From Here to Eternity*. He closed his eyes as an image of her naked and writhing beneath him burned itself into his brain. It would be hot and hard and hungry, and nobody would come away unsatisfied.

And then what?

The thought washed over him like ice water. He opened his eyes and looked at her rapt face. He'd never wanted a woman more in his life. He could give her what she needed tonight, but tomorrow would be a different story. No matter how bad he wanted her tonight, once the deed was done, they could never go back. Was he willing to destroy everything they had for a single night of hot sex?

Jesus, Mary and Joseph. Was this some kind of test?

With overwhelming regret, he released her breast and drew her dress back to cover it. Through the wet fabric, the nipple was still clearly visible. He cleared his throat. "Bad idea," he said hoarsely.

She opened her eyes. They were hazy and unfocused, liquid and puzzled. She wet her lips. "What?" she said.

He took a step backward. "I'm sorry," he said. "I was out of line."

She looked at him with those eyes, deep and green and unreadable. Without warning, she placed both palms flat against his chest and shoved him, hard, catching him off guard and nearly knocking him on his ass. "You son of a bitch," she said.

"Hey," he said, surprised, "cut it out."

She advanced on him, shoved him again. "You rotten, cruel, sadistic son of a bitch."

He held up both hands. "I'm sorry. I said I was sorry. I got carried away."

She punched his shoulder. Hard. The damn woman had a mean right hook. "How could you?" she shouted.

"What the hell do you mean, how could I? It takes two to tango, sweetheart."

"How could you do that to me?" She aimed the next punch at his face, but he ducked and she missed.

"Hey," he said, "you seemed to like it—"

"How could you take me that far—"

"—just as much as I did!"

"—and then just leave me hanging?"

He blinked. Stared at her. Blinked again. He couldn't believe it. The little witch was slugging him and screaming like a fishwife not because of what he'd done, but because of what he hadn't. Fury burst in him. "I won't be a stand-in for any man!" he shouted.

"What the hell is that supposed to mean?"

He advanced on her until they were nose to nose. "You tell me just one thing, sugar. If Danny Fiore was standing beside us, right here, right now, would you even remember I was here?"

She stood there in all her drunken splendor, mouth working but no sound coming out. And he bent closer. "You're trying to use me," he said. "I won't be used."

She seemed suddenly to have shrunk into herself, and he could see the sheen of tears in her eyes. "Let's get one thing clear right now, Fiore," he said. "If, by some wild stretch of the imagination, the time ever does arise when you and I take a tumble between the sheets, it'll be for one reason, and one reason only: because we're so hot for each other that we're both half crazy with it. In which case, there'll only be two of us in that bed. There won't be any room for Danny Fiore. Furthermore, we'll both be stone cold sober, because I like my women to remember me in the morning." He squared his jaw. "And believe me," he said, "you'll remember."

And he turned and slogged his way to shore, leaving her

standing there in the water.

CHAPTER TWENTY-FOUR

So this was how it felt to die.

Every time she had the audacity to move her head, a massive Chinese gong went off inside her skull. Her stomach felt like she'd swallowed a gallon of turpentine, her mouth tasted like old socks, and her teeth were sticky. Moving like a hundred-year-old woman, she followed the bellboy to the elevator that would take them to the lobby. It didn't look as though she'd be fortunate enough to die, so she would have to settle for second best, a quick, anonymous departure from this insidious hell.

But it wasn't meant to be. As the elevator doors whispered to a close, she saw Rob sprinting down the hall with his suitcase. He caught the doors with mere inches to spare. "Leaving without me?" he said.

She adjusted her dark glasses. "I don't want to talk to you."

"A little edgy this morning, are we?"

"Oh, shut up."

He reached into his pocket and pulled out a pack of Juicy Fruit. He unwrapped one and popped it into his mouth, then held out the pack to her. "Gum?" he said.

She glanced at it quickly, then returned her gaze to an invisible spot between the bellboy's shoulder blades. "No, thank you," she said.

"It might settle your stomach."

"My stomach," she said archly, "is just fine, thank you."

"Look," he said, "about last night—"

"Last night never happened."

"Funny, but that's not how I remember it."

"Too bad. That's the way it's going down in the history books."

"Well, listen, I just want to say that I'm really flattered—"

"Don't be. It wasn't anything personal. You just happened to fit my demanding criteria: you walk upright, you're breathing, and as far as I could tell, you're anatomically correct."

The bellboy cleared his throat. The elevator came to a

shuddering halt, the doors scraped open, and Casey adjusted her glasses and strode to the front desk, where she and Rob had a minor squabble over who would pay her share of the bill. Rob won, and she glared at him as they loaded their bags into a waiting cab.

The scenery on the way to the airport was breathtaking. At least she thought she remembered that it was, from their arrival two days earlier. "Sweetheart," he said, threading his fingers through hers, "you're missing the view."

"I'm missing it," she said, "because every time I open my eyes, shards of pain dance through my head."

"I told you not to drink so much."

"Go away. I hate you."

He leaned back against the seat and sighed. Touched her bare shoulder with one finger. Moved it around a little. "Do you really hate me?" he said.

She rubbed her temples with all ten fingers. Opened her eyes and winced. Closed them again. "No," she said. "I hate me. I've never felt so wretched in my life."

"Come on, Fiore, it wasn't that awful, was it?"

"Oh, yes, it was."

"Thanks for stroking my suffering ego."

"I didn't mean that part was awful." Remembering just how far from awful it had been, she flushed hot all over. "If it had been," she said, "I wouldn't have made a fool of myself."

"You had too much to drink. We all do stupid things when we're loaded. By the way," he added, "you hit pretty hard. For a girl."

She covered her face with her hands. "I can't even look you in the face, I'm so embarrassed."

"I'm not. We're two normal, healthy adults who just happened to spend a few absolutely spectacular minutes sharing some normal, healthy lust. What the hell is so awful about that?"

Silence. Then, "Do you hate me?"

"Come on, babe, this is me you're talking to. Haven't we always been honest with each other? You were straight with me last night, and I was straight with you. Now we both know where we stand. Where's the shame in that?"

"You may know where we stand," she said, "but I must

have slept through that part. Suppose you clarify it for me."

"Okay. I think the air needed a little clearing, and that's what we did."

Dryly, she said, "That certainly clarifies things."

"It might, if you'd shut up until I'm finished. Right from the start, there's always been something there between us. And don't bother to deny it, because you know as well as I do that it's true."

She rubbed her temples. "And what might we call this mystical something?"

"Damned if I know. For lack of a better word, let's call it chemistry."

She opened one eye. "Chemistry," she said.

"Right. But it's not something either of us has ever attempted to act on, because we value our relationship too much. There's a delicate balance that neither one of us wants to upset. Push a little too far, and we risk losing the most meaningful relationship either of us has ever had."

She thought it all through. It frightened her that he was making sense. "Then what happened last night?" she said.

"For some reason, the balance shifted. Neither one of us is involved with anyone right now. As you pointed out, celibacy is not a normal condition. We've been working together night and day. And we just spent two days together in a honeymooner's paradise. We're two healthy, normal, reasonably attractive adults who happen to care about each other. I'd say what happened was inevitable. It had to happen, sooner or later. We don't have to make a federal case out of it. It's not that big a thing."

"It was a very big thing to me," she said.

"Yeah, well." He looked out the window. "My mother may have trained me well, but saying no last night wasn't the easiest thing I've ever done."

"Then why'd you say no?"

"I already told you. I won't be a stand-in for Danny. And you're my closest friend, and that friendship means more to me than any night of spectacular sex could ever mean."

She zeroed in on a single word. "Spectacular?"

"You know damn well it would be spectacular."

He was right. She did know it. She'd known it for years. But because she loved Danny, and because she felt that having sexual feelings for another man was somehow inappropriate, she'd refused to acknowledge it, even to herself. But his matter-of-fact explanation had taken away that risqué element and made it seem innocuous. "You know what, MacKenzie?" she said. "You are one incredible human being. And you're going to make some lucky woman one hell of a husband."

"I don't know," he said. "I don't seem to have much luck in that department. I've struck out twice already."

"You know what they say. The third time's a charm."

"They also say that after three strikes you're out of the game."

"Hah! Those women out there don't know what they're missing."

"And I suppose you do?"

"Yes," she said softly, regretfully. "I believe I'm just beginning to understand."

Their flight to Boston was uneventful. Rob watched the in-flight movie while she nursed her hangover. There was a delay at Logan, and they were forced to circle the city for a half-hour before they could land. At the baggage claim, he said, "I'm not going back to your place."

She turned to look at him. "What are you talking about?"

He was taking an inordinate interest in the rotation of the baggage carousel. "I'm catching a flight to L.A. I have business to take care of."

"How long will you be gone?"

"Not long. Three, four days. A week, tops."

"It's because of me," she said, "isn't it?"

He still wasn't looking at her. "No," he said. "It has nothing to do with you."

"Don't lie to me, MacKenzie. I know you too well. I can see right through you."

He squared his jaw. "Look," he said, "I just need a few days away. I have to get my head clear. That's all."

She didn't like what she was feeling. "Hey," she said softly. "We are going to be all right, aren't we?"

"Babe, I have to say this. You're living in limbo. You're

not single, but you're not married, either. You have to make up your mind what you want. Divorce him and get on with your life. Or if you can't do that, then go after him and give it another shot. Either way, you have to get off the fence. I can't stand to watch any longer."

And for the second time in less than twenty-four hours, he walked away and left her standing alone.

It was 42 degrees in Boston, cloudy and dismal. She'd become so accustomed to Rob's presence that her apartment felt barren and lifeless without him. She made herself a bowl of clam chowder and sat on the couch, listening to his CD and thinking about what he'd said. Fish or cut bait, that was the gist of his advice. But was that all there was to it? She replayed his every word, seeking hidden meanings, finding none. The interlude on the beach had torn away her emotional safety net and turned her perception of the world upside down. Suddenly, she was questioning things she'd spent her entire adulthood taking for granted.

She never finished the chowder. Instead, she went to the phone and called Millie and asked if she could come home for a few days.

The family was thrilled to see her. She made the rounds, visited everyone. She took Mikey to see a re-release of *Star Wars*, went for a bumpy ride on Billy's snowmobile, and traipsed through the muddy snow with Jesse as he tapped maple trees. She spent a day with Colleen, divorced now from Jesse, remarried and living a couple of towns over. In the evenings, she sat by the fire with Dad and Millie, relaxing and indulging in quiet introspection.

On the morning of the fourth day, she drove back to Boston and called Danny. "I think we need to talk," she said. "Shall I fly out there, or do you want to come here?"

***

She vowed she wouldn't dress up for him, then changed her mind at least three times before she chose a teal silk blouse and a matching calf-length print skirt. *This is not a date*, she reminded herself as she tied her hair back with a ribbon and put on tiny diamond teardrop earrings and a matching choker. *We're only having dinner.* The irony of it wasn't lost on her. She and Danny had fallen in love, married, lived together a dozen years and had a child together. But they'd never been on a date.

He showed up twenty minutes early, resplendent in a charcoal tweed jacket over pressed jeans and a dress shirt that precisely matched the color of his eyes. In his hand, he carried a small bouquet of violets. *Oh, lord,* she thought when she saw the flowers. *It is a date. What am I doing?*

But it was too late to question her motives. Danny stepped through the door, and instantly her apartment shrank to a third of its size. "I'll put these in water," she said. "Take a look around if you'd like."

While she searched the kitchen cupboards for a vase, his slow, deliberate footsteps made a tour of the apartment. It didn't take long. He was standing in the kitchen doorway when she returned to the table with the vase of flowers. "This is how you always wanted to live, isn't it?" he said. "Simply, with no fanfare."

Her heartbeat accelerated. "Yes," she said.

"Was life with me so terrible?"

Something tightened in her throat. "Not life with you," she said. "It was the craziness that surrounded you that I found so hard to live with."

He helped her on with her jacket, and together they walked the narrow streets of the neighborhood where he'd grown up. There were few places he could walk openly without attracting attention, but on a week night in the old neighborhood, he was just another passerby, greeting in Italian the old men who hovered in doorways, pausing to pet a greyhound tied to a lamp post outside the corner grocery. In North Square, a stone's throw from the Paul Revere house, they found a quiet restaurant that served them veal piccata and red wine by candlelight.

Casey toyed with her pasta, nibbled at her veal, less interested in her dinner than in watching Danny. He ate left-handed with a grace that was too elegant to be anything but natural. He had the most beautiful hands she'd ever seen, their movements precise and exquisite, their gestures eloquent. He set down his fork. "You're not eating," he said.

She shrugged. "I guess I wasn't really hungry."

He picked up his fork, cut off a small bite of veal, and carried it to her mouth. Casey looked into those blue eyes, so intent, so solemn, and felt something turn over deep in the pit of her stomach. She opened her mouth and slowly took the veal between her lips. Chewed and swallowed, and he cut off a second piece and fed it to her.

Beneath the table, his knee touched hers, and a shock ran clear through her. Those blue eyes held hers, his intent clearly written in them. In response, she caught his wrist in her hand and guided the next bite of veal to her mouth. Without a word, he set down his fork and signaled for the check.

Moments later, they were back outside in the mild spring evening. On Hanover Street, they passed restaurant after restaurant, light spilling out through plate glass windows, loud talk and hearty laughter mixed with the clink of glass and cutlery floating out the open doors. For Casey, it was all a blur; in the three blocks to her apartment, her feet didn't touch the ground even once.

They didn't bother with the lights. Off came the tweed jacket, the silk blouse, their clothes forming a pool of expensive fabric on the floor beside her bed. It didn't matter that they had differences, or that they hadn't talked them out. It didn't matter that neither of them knew what would come after tonight. None of those things made one iota of difference. None of them ever really had.

This was what mattered, this touching of flesh against flesh, this fierce giving and taking, this exquisite merging that brought them together, again and again and again. Everything else had always been secondary. In the darkness, they found each other and melded with a fluid oneness that left them breathless. With a soft cry of gladness, she locked her legs around his hips, drawing him deeper into her.

And they took each other home.

***

"It never grows old."

His head was resting on her belly, her fingers wandering

aimlessly through the silk of his hair. "What?" she said, half asleep. "What never grows old?"

"The way I feel about you."

In the moonlight, her fingers found his face. "Oh, Danny," she said in despair. "Why are we so terrible at being married?"

"You're not terrible at it. I am."

"It would be so easy, if only I didn't love you so much."

He was silent for a long time. "I've changed," he said at last. "I went off the deep end for a while. But I got myself straightened out. I got help. And there's so much I have to tell you."

Quietly, she said, "Where do we go from here?"

"I was hoping you'd tell me."

She sat up and wrapped the blanket around her. "I don't think you have any idea," she said, "what it was like for me, living with you. You swallowed me up, Danny. You ate me alive."

"If you were so unhappy," he said, "why didn't you tell me?"

"I wasn't unhappy. That's the point. I wasn't anything. I had no identity except as your wife. I look back at that person, and I realize I don't much like her. In the last year, I've begun to discover me. And I'm not about to give up me. Not even for you."

"I see," he said.

"I'm not blaming you," she said. "You were honest with me from the start. I guess I just wasn't listening closely enough. Or maybe I was too dazzled to hear. For twelve years, we lived on your terms. We got caught up in it and it just snowballed. But I can't live life on those terms any more."

"Do you want a divorce?"

"I don't think you ever understood just how much I loved you. From the first time I saw you walk across my kitchen floor, you were the whole world to me. The only thing that mattered. No," she said, "I don't want a divorce."

"What do you want?" he said.

"I want to go back. Back to the way it was in the early days. But we can't do that."

He cleared his throat. "What if we tried living on your

terms?"

"Do you really think it would work?"

"Why don't you tell me what your terms are. Then I'll answer your question."

She studied the wall absently. "We stopped talking, Danny. That was our biggest mistake. My biggest mistake, because I let you withdraw from me. I tried to give you the space I thought you needed. It was the wrong thing to do."

"When Katie died," he said, "I went to pieces. I couldn't handle it. She was the only pure, sweet thing in my entire life, and I couldn't bear to lose her."

"I was furious with you for such a long time."

"And I was afraid I'd driven you away forever." He paused. "Is it too late to ask you to give me another chance?"

She considered it. "I'll give it another try," she said, "but only if you'll agree to marriage counseling. I don't think we'll make it without help. And I won't live in California. You'll have to move back to the East Coast."

"I'm willing to do whatever it takes."

"I won't climb back on the merry-go-round, Danny. I got too dizzy."

"We could look for a house in the country," he said, "near your father."

"There'll be no more tries," she warned him. "I can't keep letting you break my heart. I'm getting too old for it. If we blow this one, Danny, it'll be for good."

"I've grown up," he said. He looped his arms around her shoulders and pulled her tight. "I'm sorry it took me so long."

***

He used the shower first in the morning. While Casey showered, he made a cup of instant coffee, lit a cigarette, and carried them into her workroom to take a look at what she'd been doing. The rampant disorder told him she was in the middle of a major project. Meticulously neat in every other area of her life, it was only in her work that Casey allowed creative chaos to reign. Danny sat down in the middle of the mess and drew a sheet of manuscript paper across the table top. Sipping his coffee, he studied it. The handwriting was Casey's, but it didn't take him long to recognize the work as Rob's. Subtle nuances identified it as his: brief phrasings and key changes, the use of certain diminished or augmented chords. He heard her footsteps in the doorway. "You didn't tell me you and Rob were working together," he said.

"You didn't ask."

He turned to look at her, and did a double-take. His wife was wearing Nike running shoes, blue silk athletic shorts, and a matching warm-up jacket. Headphones dangled around her neck, the other end plugged into a Walkman clipped to her waist. While he stared in stupefaction, she bent at the waist and did half a dozen toe touches. "What the hell are you doing?" he said.

"Running. I'm up to six miles a day."

"*Running?*" He tried to comprehend, but it was too incredible. Imagining her threading her way through downtown Boston's rush hour traffic, he said in alarm, "Where the devil do you jog around here?"

"The Esplanade. Up one side of the river to the Harvard Bridge, then back down the other side. Want to join me?"

The very idea gave him indigestion. "Thanks," he said dryly, "but I'm afraid I'll have to pass."

"That's too bad. It's more fun with a partner. Rob runs with me whenever he's in town."

The picture of Rob MacKenzie's lanky shanks in running shorts only made his indigestion worse. Casey bent and brushed her lips across his. "I'll see you in an hour," she said, and adjusted her headphones. "I'll bring you a napoleon from Mike's." And she was gone, leaving him to wonder if he'd awakened in the twilight zone.

He was still knee-deep in her work forty-five minutes later when footsteps clattered up the stairs and a key turned in the lock. "You're back early," he said, shoving aside his cold coffee. "Did you remember my napoleon?"

Silence. Then footsteps approached the doorway and a voice that was definitely not his wife's said, "Danny?"

He spun the swivel chair in stunned amazement. "Wiz?" he said.

"Hot damn," Rob said, and they greeted each other with

grins and handshakes and a brief, eloquent hug. "You're the last person I expected to see here."

"That makes two of us," he said. "Come on out to the kitchen. I'll throw together a pot of coffee."

He put the kettle on to heat and began opening cupboard doors in search of coffee cups. "Left side," Rob said, "over the stove."

He found the cups just where Rob had said they'd be. Dryly, he said, "You've obviously spent some time here."

Rob was standing at the kitchen window, looking out. "Yeah," he said without turning. "I guess I have."

Danny studied his back. There was something odd about the set of his shoulders. But before the thought could take concrete form, Rob turned away from the window. "Does this mean you and Casey are back together?" he said.

The kettle whistled, and Danny turned off the stove. "It looks that way," he said.

Rob opened the refrigerator. From behind the door, he said, "Just don't hurt her, Dan."

"What?"

"You heard me." Rob took out a quart of milk and closed the refrigerator door. "If you hurt her again," he said, "I'll rip your throat out."

"Christ," he said, "some things never change, do they? You're still on her side."

"Wrong. I'm not taking sides." Rob uncapped the milk bottle and poured milk into his coffee. "Damn it, Danny, I love you like a brother. But it kills me to see what you do to her. The woman thinks you're God." He recapped the bottle and looked Danny square in the eye. "Do you have any idea how lucky you are? If any woman ever looked at me the way Casey looks at you, I'd die a happy man."

"I love her," he said, hating the defensiveness he heard in his own voice. "You know that."

"Yeah, Dan, I think you really do. Just be careful with her, okay? I don't want to have to pick up the pieces again. Every time it happens, the cracks get a little bigger and a little harder to glue back together."

Before he could respond, the hall door opened and Casey

breathlessly called from the foyer. "Danny? I'm home."

He cleared his throat. "In the kitchen," he said.

"Mike's was out of napoleons," she bubbled, "so I brought you a couple of creme puffs instead. I'm going in to take another shower. I'm all—" She stepped into the kitchen, saw Rob, and stopped. "Oh," she said in an odd little voice. "You're back."

Eyes averted, Rob spooned sugar into his coffee. "I flew in about six last night," he said, stirring. He licked the spoon and dropped it in the sink. "I spent the night with my folks."

Danny looked curiously from one to the other, wondering just what the hell was going on here. Casey set the bakery bag down on the table and unclipped her Walkman. To Rob she said briskly, "Did you get your business taken care of?"

Still not looking at her, Rob took a sip of coffee. "Yeah," he said.

"Then you're ready to get back to work?"

Rob turned, cup in hand, and leaned his lanky frame against the counter. "That's why I'm here," he said crisply.

The tension in the room was thicker than smoke in a pool hall. There may have been three people present, but only two of them were speaking the same language, and Danny was odd man out. He narrowed his eyes, looked at them more closely. He and Casey had been separated for nearly a year. Could it be possible that during the course of those months, she'd had something going with Rob?

The notion was absurd. Casey and Rob had a dogged and complex relationship, one he hadn't always understood, but as far as Danny could tell, there was nothing remotely sexual about it. Yet the possibility, once implanted in his brain, refused to go away. It explained so many things. Like why Rob had read him the riot act. Why he'd known exactly what was where in the kitchen cabinets. Why he'd let himself into Casey's apartment with his own key.

He felt as if he'd been kicked hard in the stomach. His lungs closed up, refused to function, and suddenly his only desire was for fresh air. "I have to go," he said abruptly. "To check out of the hotel. Pick up my clothes."

They both looked at him oddly. "You're leaving?" Casey said.

"I'll be back in an hour."

She followed him to the door. Caught him by the arm. "Danny?" she said. "Are you all right?"

He cleared his throat. "I'm fine." He bent and brushed his lips across hers. Hesitated before pulling her into his arms and kissing her with desperate intensity. "I love you," he whispered. "Christ, I love you so much." And left her standing there in the hall, gaping after him in stunned amazement.

He stewed as he drove across town and checked out of the hotel he'd never even slept in. How the hell was he going to work this out? He had to be back in Los Angeles tomorrow. He was so tired of obligations. Maybe it was time to chuck it all. Grab the money and run. Take Casey and move to Anchorage. They could live in an igloo and keep each other warm through the long, cold winter nights.

When he returned, he found Casey alone in the kitchen, elbow-deep in soapsuds. Whenever she didn't know what to do with herself, the woman washed dishes. "Where's Rob?" he said grimly.

She turned in surprise at his tone of voice. "He went back to his mother's," she said. "What's wrong?"

"Nothing's wrong. I need to talk to you, and I only have a few minutes. I have to fly back to California. I'd rather stay here with you, but I have commitments I can't back out of."

She dried her hands on a kitchen towel and circled her arms around his waist. "It's all right," she said. "I understand."

He brushed a strand of hair away from her face. "I'll be back on Friday," he said. "I thought we could drive up to Maine and go house hunting."

"I'll call Dad and tell him we're coming."

He studied her face. Cleared his throat. "Can I ask you a question without blowing the roof off the place?"

"Of course." She looked puzzled. "What is it?"

He took a deep breath. "Are you and Rob having an affair?"

"Are we *what?*" The look of astonishment on her face was genuine. "Where did you get an idea like that?"

"The way he wasn't looking at you this morning. What the two of you said. Mostly what you didn't say." He hesitated, then added grimly, "What he said to me before you got here."

She opened her mouth. Closed it. "Rob and I are not having an affair," she said. "You're the only man I've ever slept with."

It wasn't quite the answer he'd been seeking. Not *you're the only man I've ever loved,* but *you're the only man I've ever slept with.* Not all affairs involved the body. Some only involved the heart. "What on earth did he say to you?" she asked.

"He read me the riot act. Told me how lucky I was to have you and threatened to rip out my throat if I screwed up."

She smiled ruefully. "He does have a tendency to be overprotective, doesn't he?"

He scowled. "Overprotective, my ass. The man's in love with you."

She stepped away from him and returned to her sinkful of dishes. "Bullfeathers," she said. "You're having pipe dreams. Rob is my dearest friend. He and I have already covered this ground. We both know exactly where we stand, and we're both comfortable with our relationship, just the way it is. You're being paranoid."

Something hard and unpleasant settled into the pit of his stomach. "I don't suppose you'd like to clarify what *already covered this ground* means?"

She rinsed a plate and wedged it neatly into the plastic drainer on the sideboard. "That's between Rob and me," she said, "and it's none of your business."

He gaped at her in disbelief. "None of my business?" he repeated. "I'm your husband, for Christ's sake!"

"Yes, you are my husband," she said with maddening calm. "And he's my friend. He doesn't ask for intimate details of my relationship with you. I'd appreciate you according us the same respect."

CHAPTER TWENTY-FIVE

Casey wandered through the empty rooms of the deserted farmhouse, trying to get the feel of the place. There was something about it, something she couldn't put her finger on, that she found immensely appealing.

"Lathes and plaster," Helen Goldman, the real estate agent, was saying. "You don't see much of that any more."

Casey entered the kitchen. It was a bright room on the north side of the house, a room where she immediately felt at home. She could picture a jungle of green plants growing in the windows.

Mrs. Goldman's voice followed her. "The former owner closed off these fireplaces for practical reasons, but they could be reopened easily."

She could hear the low murmur of voices from the cellar, but Danny and Jesse were too far away for her to hear what they were saying. She opened a cupboard door, and the hinge squeaked.

Helen Goldman followed her into the kitchen. Briskly, she said, "You have to realize that the place has been empty for some time. Try to picture it without the cobwebs and the rodent droppings." She paused. "I can give you the name of a good exterminator."

Casey heard the heavy tread of footsteps on the cellar stairs, then Danny came into the kitchen, wiping his hands on his jeans. "The furnace is fairly new," he said, "and the foundation seems to be sound."

"You won't find anything like it at this price," Mrs. Goldman said. "With a little work and a fresh coat of paint, it can be turned into a showplace."

Casey looked dubiously at Danny, read his eyes. "My wife and I will talk it over," he told Helen Goldman. "We'll call you tomorrow." But Casey knew he'd already made up his mind.

On the ride back to her father's house, he was already talking about what he could do with the place. "Sweetheart," she said gently, "I hate to be a wet blanket, but do you realize how much work is involved? The place is a disaster."

"I'm not afraid of work."

"That wasn't what I meant. It can take a long time to restore an old house. You may get very tired of it before it's finished."

"I need something to do with my hands. And Jesse's offered to help."

She raised an eyebrow. "Then you're planning to do the work yourself?"

"Of course. What did you think?"

"I think, my love, that it's a very ambitious undertaking for a guy who doesn't know an allen wrench from a monkey wrench."

"Hey, Jess, do you think she's casting aspersions on my city upbringing?"

Jesse signaled for a left turn. "It sure does sound like it," he said.

"That's hitting below the belt, lady. I spent two years in the Army—"

"Where you learned everything you always wanted to know about plumbing, but were afraid to ask."

"What I learned," he said, "is that I've already been to hell. And after hell, anything else is a piece of cake."

Six weeks later, they closed on the property and began the gargantuan task of making the house livable. Once the exterminator had done his thing, they started cleaning. The floors, the woodwork, the kitchen counters, the bathroom fixtures, all had to be disinfected, and Casey scrubbed until her knuckles bled. The pipes were old and rusty, and until they could be replaced, she and Danny carried their drinking water from her father's place. They had insulation blown in, replaced both toilets, discovered in the upstairs bath a handsome antique claw-foot tub that some enterprising soul had boxed in with plywood.

Life that summer fell into a routine, slow and easy and comfortable. Mornings, as the sun peered over the horizon, she ran her six miles to the tune of birdsong. By the time she got back, Danny was up and Jesse had arrived and the two men were already at work, hammering and sawing, tearing at the plumbing,

rerouting ancient wiring and installing new fixtures. With the
help of her nephew Mikey and a couple of his prepubescent
friends, Casey sanded and refinished hardwood floors,
replastered walls, painted woodwork and ceilings, hung
wallpaper. To Danny's everlasting horror, when they got to the
roof, she climbed the ladder and straddled the ridgepole and
nailed shingles with unerring accuracy. And then she and Mikey
spent two backbreaking weeks scraping the clapboards in
preparation for painting.

She grew strong and wiry and tanned, amazed by her self-
efficacy, proud of the new skills she'd learned. And one rainy
afternoon, when Danny had gone with Jess to Farmington to pick
up some gadget that Mason's Hardware didn't carry, she drove
into town, to Shelley's Cut 'n Curl, and had Shelley Mainwaring
cut off the hair she'd worn hanging to her waist since seventh
grade. Shelley shortened it to just above the collar, layered in the
back, rounding to a modified ducktail, with wispy bangs in front.
The cut gave her a waiflike look, emphasizing her cheekbones
and magnifying the size of her eyes. Casey stared in stunned
amazement at the total stranger who stared back at her from
Shelley's mirror. She would probably have to pick Danny up off
the floor and revive him, but the deed was done, and she felt
twenty pounds lighter.

Danny's mouth fell open when he saw her, and he turned
slightly green. Even Jesse looked stunned, but both men knew
better than to say anything negative. She knew that for some
inexplicable reason, men had a tendency to build erotic fantasies
around long hair. But it was her body, her decision, and she was
comfortable with it. Danny would have to live with it.

And he did. She knew he wasn't happy about it, but he
respected her decision. They were different people than they'd
been before, their relationship in transition. They were feeling
their way now, step by torturous step. Slowly, painfully, she was
learning that her own needs were as important as his. And
slowly, painfully, he was learning that he couldn't always think
of himself first. They were refining themselves, smoothing
rough edges, making adjustments and improvements to the solid
core already inside each of them. The result was a contentment
that would have been perfect if not for the inescapable, gnawing

feeling inside her that something was missing from her life.

It struck her at odd times, this sensation of unmet need, and she puzzled over what could be lacking. There was an empty spot inside her that was clamoring to be filled, only she had no idea how to fill it. She toyed with the idea of going back to school. Adopting a baby. Taking up ceramics, or carpentry. Getting a job. But none of these came near to quelling the restlessness that had taken hold of her.

When she and Mikey finished scraping the house, she took him to Boston for a week as payment for his hours of hard work. They saw the sea lion show at the Aquarium, climbed Bunker Hill, gazed out at the world from the top of the Pru. Spent an entire day at the Museum of Science. Ate *dim sum* in Chinatown, attended a Red Sox game, saw a Bryan Adams concert at the Garden.

She pampered and spoiled him, sparing no expense, and with typical twelve-year-old fervor, he wore her out. She'd always adored her nephew, and she loved every exhausting minute. But the high point of her week was the afternoon she spent in Mary MacKenzie's back yard, drinking iced tea with Mary and Rose and looking at faded family photos while Mikey roller-skated out front with Rose's boy, Luke, who was also twelve, and a holy terror.

She returned to a house that was barely recognizable. While she'd been away, Danny and Jess had begun painting the old Gothic Revival the warm cream color that she had picked out. The shutters, freshly painted Wedgwood blue, leaned against the side of the barn. Danny meandered over to the car, shirtless, paint-spattered and deeply tanned, and leaned in the open window to kiss her. "So, Mrs. Fiore," he said, "what do you think?"

She toyed with a strand of his hair. "I think, Mr. Fiore, that you look good enough to eat."

He hunkered down beside the car so they were at eye level. His eyes were still the bluest she'd ever seen. Wryly, he said, "I was talking about the house."

"Oh." And she smiled. "The house." She looked past him to where Jesse was standing atop an aluminum extension ladder at one peaked gable. "It's beautiful," she said. "I can't believe how far it's come."

"If you saw the back side, you wouldn't say that. But it's coming along nicely."

She adjusted her sunglasses. "What happened to my rosebushes?"

"We had to cut them. Don't worry. Jesse promised me that they'll be back next year."

"They'd better, or you'll both die a slow and painful death."

There were further surprises inside. They'd found time to install the new countertop, and the shiny new stainless steel sink was up and running. And brim-full of dirty dishes. Some things never changed. Casey went upstairs to unpack, then came back down and tackled the pile of dirty dishes that awaited her.

The view from her kitchen window was spectacular. It faced north, down along the valley toward Dad's, overlooking pine groves and pastures and in the distance the broad, shimmering river. She was halfway through the sinkful of dishes when a bright red compact car labored up the steep driveway and stopped beside her BMW. The driver's door opened, and Rob MacKenzie unfolded his lanky body from behind the steering wheel.

And something cool and fluid went *zing* at the base of her spine.

A woman got out of the passenger door, tall and blond and athletic, dressed in L.L. Bean chic: loose khaki hiking shorts, a plaid shirt, and work boots that had never seen work. Rob grinned as Danny approached the car, and the two of them began talking animatedly. Casey could hear the rise and fall of voices, but couldn't make out what they were saying. Danny held out a hand to the woman, realized it was covered with paint, and shrugged apologetically. The woman shook his hand anyway, and then the three of them stood looking at the house while Danny talked and gestured and pointed.

Normally, she would have rushed outside to greet Rob with a hug. This time, some inexplicable something held her back. She returned to her sinkful of dishes as the trio on the lawn moved out of sight around the corner of the house. Outside her open window, a fat bumblebee buzzed, and in back where the black-eyed Susans grew, Mikey and a friend shouted back and forth. Inside the cool quiet of the house, the kitchen clock ticked, and then the door to the shed opened and footsteps approached the kitchen, footsteps she would have recognized anywhere. They stopped in the doorway. "Holy mother of God, woman," he said. "You've been scalped."

One soapy hand went to her hair. She stepped away from the sink, wondering what he thought, hoping he'd like it, wondering why it mattered. He was looking at her as though she'd just landed from another planet, and she tried to read past the disbelief in those familiar green eyes to whatever else was there. "Turn around," he said softly. "Let's see."

Like an obedient child, she made a slow, 360-degree turn. "This is scary," he said, "but I think I could pass you on the street and not recognize you."

"You hate it," she said.

"No! No, really, I love it. It does something to your face. It's like—" He paused, still looking stunned. "Remember those paintings of the puppies and the kittens with the great big eyes?"

"So what you're saying, MacKenzie, is that I look like an animal."

"Come on, Fiore, you know damn well you could put on war paint and a football helmet and you'd still be gorgeous. You just look so different. I—wow."

"So where's my hug?"

He opened his arms and she embraced him fiercely. He felt lean and wiry, his heartbeat strong and steady against her chest. "Oh, I've missed you so much," she said. He placed a hand on the back of her neck, just beneath what was left of her hair. His skin was warm against hers. Outside the window, Danny was telling the blonde about the claw-footed bathtub upstairs. "You smell so good," Casey whispered.

"Me?" he said in mock astonishment.

"Yes," she said, wondering why it was that she felt so right when she was with him. "You."

"Geez, Fiore, it must be the sexy new cologne I'm wearing."

"You're not wearing cologne." Confused by the jumble of emotions she was feeling, she realized it was time to disengage.

She took a step backward and he released her immediately.
"So," she said briskly, "who's your lady friend?"

"Her name's Christine. She's a lawyer with the L. A.
County D.A.'s office."

She raised both eyebrows. "I'm impressed, MacKenzie.
You've moved up to the big leagues."

He shrugged. "She's a good kid," he said dismissively.

"So what are you doing in this neck of the woods?"

"She has a cousin who's getting married in Camden the day
after tomorrow. I figured since we were coming to Maine
anyway...." He ran out of words, stood there staring at her.
"Jesus," he said, "I still can't believe how different you look."

She held out a hand. "Come on. I'll show you around."

She gave him the deluxe tour, cellar to attic. "The place is
a disaster right now," she said as they ascended the stairs to the
second floor. "Even worse than usual, because I just got home
from a week in Boston."

He reached out a finger and wiped plaster dust from the
banister. "I know," he said absently. "Mom said you stopped
by."

"Your mother's a sweetheart," she said.

"That's what she says about you." He looked around the
upstairs hall. "So you and the Italian stallion did all this?"

"With a little help from our friends. I sanded and
refinished all the hardwood floors." She grimaced. "What a job
that was. And I painted the ceilings and the woodwork and the
doors. Come see the bedroom. You'll love the paper."

***

After dinner, while Danny and Christine Hamilton matched
wits against each other with a rousing game of Trivial Pursuit,
Casey and Rob wandered off to the living room with a bottle of
wine and two jelly glasses. The hours flew by as they caught
each other up on the last few months of their lives. The house
grew dark and quiet, and they still hadn't run out of things to say
when Danny finally came downstairs to drag his wife off to bed.

"Casey?"

They both looked up in surprise at the sound of his voice.

He was standing in semi-darkness at the foot of the stairs, wearing nothing but his Calvins. "Hello, darling," Casey said, and smothered a yawn.

"It's almost one-thirty." Danny rubbed a hand across his bare chest. "Aren't you coming to bed tonight?"

Casey looked at the mantel clock. "So it is," she said. "I had no idea it was so late."

"It's my fault," Rob said. "We were shooting the bull and we lost track of time."

"I'll be right up. Just let me get things taken care of down here—"

"Go," Rob said. "I'll clean up and turn out the lights."

When she reached the foot of the stairs, Danny wrapped an arm around his wife's shoulders. "See you in the morning," he said to Rob.

Rob saluted with his glass. "G'night," he said, and watched them climb the stairs together.

Directly above his head, he could hear their footsteps, Casey's light, Danny's heavier, as they got ready for bed. He poured himself another glass of Chablis. The footsteps stilled, and Rob took a long, slow swallow. The house was old, the walls thin. He sat one floor below them, jelly glass in hand and a hollow, empty feeling in his gut, and listened to the unmistakable sound of them making love.

He knew he should get up, leave the room, go outdoors if that was what it took, but he was rooted to the spot, nailed in place by some masochistic need to torture himself. They were being quiet, but he could still hear every soft, breathy cry, every hushed moan. He pictured her face, transformed into blurred softness by passion, and something knotted up in his belly. Above his head, the bedsprings began to creak with a steady, unmistakable rhythm. His fingers tightened on the jelly glass as the sounds coming from upstairs grew louder, seeming to go on forever before they finally reached a crescendo, and the creaking of the bedsprings slowed. Silenced. Rob drained the rest of his Chablis in a single gulp.

He put away the bottle of wine, left the jelly glasses, hers and his, in the sink. Turned off the lights and shut the guest room door, stripped off his clothes and crawled into bed with

Chris. He pressed himself up against her backside, kissed her awake, and without speaking, rolled her onto her back.

It didn't take long. Chris fell asleep again almost immediately, but he lay awake, still unsatisfied, the world's biggest hypocrite. *Stay away from her*, he told himself. *She's Danny's wife. Get the hell out and don't come back.* There was only one sensible thing to do: pack his belongings the first thing tomorrow morning and head directly to Camden and Chris's cousin's house, putting as many miles as possible between himself and both of the Fiores.

But in the morning, he was sitting on the back steps, lacing up his Nikes, when Casey came out for her morning run. "Good morning!" she said. "What are you doing up so early?"

He gave her that little-boy grin, the one that always seemed to melt women right where they stood. "Waiting for you," he said.

She rocked from one foot to the other, wearing a beatific smile and that pixie haircut that made her look about twelve years old. "Up for a long run this morning?" she said.

"Are you kidding, Fiore? I can outdistance you any day."

"Oh, really? We'll see about that."

It was a spectacular morning, ripe with birdsong and deep shadows, dew weighing heavy on the grass. He matched his pace and his breathing to hers. *Sublimation.* Running was hard, sweaty, physical activity that made the lungs ache and the heart hammer and left the body in a state of satiation. Running was something they shared with each other and nobody else. It didn't take a Freudian scholar to figure out the connection.

He couldn't remember when he'd seen her looking this good. Strong and tanned and muscular. Exotic, her entire face changed with the new haircut. The same woman, only different. Healthier. Stronger. Better. Casey Fiore had always been a pretty woman. Now, in her thirties, she'd matured beyond pretty into a full-blown ripeness that had never been there before, and he couldn't keep his eyes off her.

They took a route that was unfamiliar to him, winding among hills and valleys and pastures, across brooks and bridges and past a primeval bog with blackened tree stumps poking out of murky water. Past cattle that stared at them with vacant brown eyes, past a covey of wild ducks who arose as one from their watery nest, wings thrashing as they honked a protest at the disturbance. He was used to running on flat land, and even at a moderate pace, he had to push himself to keep up with her in these western Maine hills.

She threw him a knowing glance. "Ready to quit?" she said.

He grinned. "Are you?"

They'd always pushed each other this way, prodded each other to excel. "Let's take a break," she said, and dropped onto the grassy shoulder of the road. He flopped down beside her, flat on his back, staring up into the cloudless blue heavens. "Woman," he said, arching his back and stretching like a cat, "you're a killer."

She broke off a long blade of grass and ran the tip of it playfully across the two inches of bare belly his stretching had revealed. "Don't," he said. "It tickles."

"That's the idea."

"You're asking for trouble," he said lazily.

"Are you kidding, Flash? I make trouble happen."

"Hey, cool it, woman! I'm ticklish there!"

She grinned. "And here?"

"Cut it out, Fiore."

The grin widened. "Why?"

"Because you'll be sorry if you don't."

"Hah! You talk so big, MacKenzie. Put your money where your mouth is."

He grabbed her wrist and yanked her, giggling and protesting, to the ground beside him. They rolled in the grass like a pair of five-year-olds as he tickled her without mercy, until she was laughing and crying and begging him to stop. "Who's in charge now?" he said.

"Stop," she said weakly, letting out a burst of laughter that ended on a groan. "Oh, stop, please, it hurts." Still laughing, she struggled in a halfhearted attempt to fight him off. "MacKenzie," she sputtered, "if you don't stop—right this minute—"

"Yeah?"

"—I'll pee my pants."

He grinned. "That wouldn't be a pretty sight, would it,

Fiore?"

"You win," she cried. "You win!"

"That's more like it," he said. "I like to see a little humility in a woman."

They lay on their sides, his hand resting on her ribcage as it rose and fell with her labored breathing. In the melee, her tee shirt had ridden up, exposing a vast amount of skin. Their eyes met, green probing deeply into green, and the playfulness melted away. He could see her pulse beating steady and strong at the base of her throat. Beneath his fingers, her skin was hot and sticky, and of their own volition, his knuckles brushed against her satin smoothness, raising goose bumps on her flesh and sending a searing pain through his chest.

Then a car passed, and the spell was broken. Casey blinked her eyes, yanked her shirt back into place, and rolled to a sitting position beside him. While he struggled to get his breathing back under control, he busied himself brushing grass and debris from his clothes and retying sneaker laces that didn't need tying. When he thought he could speak again, he cleared his throat. "If we don't get back pretty soon," he said, his voice sounding odd to his own ears, "they'll send out the bloodhounds."

"Insufferable ass," she said, but without conviction.

"That's me, kiddo," he said. "Let's roll."

They finished their run in a heavy silence. He had planned to stay for another day, but directly after breakfast, he packed his bags and headed out. All the way to Camden, Chris kept sending him speculative glances, but she didn't ask, and he wasn't about to volunteer any information.

He just got the hell out and didn't look back.

***

That fall, the air turned crisp, the leaves wore their best and brightest colors, and with the bulk of the work on the house completed, for the first time in years she and Danny had time to spend together, away from the prying eyes of the world. When they'd reconciled, he had promised to take a year off, and so far he'd held to his promise. She had expected that idleness would be difficult for him, but he found other avenues of expression.

They attended weekly counseling together, and they were slowly working through the problems in their marriage, working through their grief and their anger and a myriad of other emotional booby-traps.

Although they still weren't able to talk about Katie openly without the anger and the pain resurfacing, other topics were safer ground, and they explored their emotions with a depth that was sometimes unsettling. Even after thirteen years, she was still captivated by Danny, still drawn to his dry wit, to the vulnerability he tried so hard to hide. Their love had matured, had mellowed into something more tranquil than the obsession they'd experienced in previous years. At times she felt so close to him it brought tears to her eyes. At other times, she felt something very near to indifference.

"It's normal," her sister-in-law Trish said when she confided her misgivings. "Every marriage goes through dry spells. You've been together for thirteen years. Be grateful you're still speaking to each other."

"Is it like this for you and Bill?"

"Honey, I love the man more than life itself, but there are times when I wish he'd go away for about a year. Trust me, there's nothing wrong with your marriage. It'll pass."

But she wasn't convinced. Trish didn't know about the incident with Rob. Casey still wasn't sure precisely what had happened on the grassy roadside that August morning. She wasn't even certain that anything actually had happened. Perhaps it had been all in her mind. Perhaps she'd imagined being caught with Rob MacKenzie in a moment of sexual awareness so crystalline that she had only to close her eyes to recall every detail: the warmth of his breath on her face, the laugh lines around those green eyes, the damp patterns of perspiration on his sweatshirt, and her own inability to draw breath.

No, she hadn't imagined the incident. It had been real. But its meaning was obscured in a morass of jumbled emotions too risky to explore. They'd been on the verge of—what? She would probably never know, for their relationship could survive only if she tamped down these offensive emotions and locked them away in a safe place. All Casey knew with any certainty was that she had come very near the jagged edge of a dangerous precipice, and had somehow managed to escape without tumbling into the abyss.

She didn't understand it, for she still loved Danny. The sight of him still made her go warm all over. She still slept in his arms at night, still thrilled to his lovemaking. If their marriage was in a slump, it was for the reasons Trish had said, and was perfectly normal for a couple who'd been together as long as they had. The problem, if there was one, sprang from internal conflict, not from any outside influences. She and Danny were learning to handle these emotions, and with time, the situation was bound to improve.

It was in counseling that they first started talking about visiting the Vietnam Veterans Memorial. "You're both seeking some kind of healing," Kevin Johanson, their counselor, said. "I've been there, and I have to say that even though I never served in Vietnam, visiting the Wall was a tremendously cleansing experience."

Danny had mentioned the idea to her once or twice over the years, but until now, he hadn't been ready. He'd been too afraid it would stir up the turmoil he'd left behind in Vietnam. But Casey knew there was still a piece of his life missing, the piece of himself that he'd left behind in Southeast Asia. And Southeast Asia was clearly still inside him, shifting and swirling like the colored patterns of a kaleidoscope, distorting his every emotion, his every action. She was afraid that he would live in emotional tumult for the rest of his life if he didn't purge himself of some of that violent emotion and try to put his experience into some kind of meaningful perspective. So it was with immense relief that she agreed, that first weekend in December, to drive down to DC with him.

CHAPTER TWENTY-SIX

Early morning shadows lay long and heavy on pale winter grass whose tips were touched with frost. The sky had that whitish look that precedes full blueness, and when she exhaled, she could see the faint cloudiness of her breath. Beside her, Danny was silent, tense, and in the distance, the bare branches of the trees along Constitution Avenue reached skyward. The Wall stretched out to their right, long and low and glossy black, deserted except for a lone man who knelt near the apex, his fingers following the words etched into the stone. Together they paused to absorb the power, the magnitude of it. Danny turned to her, blue eyes guarded, and she realized that she had no business going any farther. She took his face between her hands and kissed him. "Go," she whispered.

His eyes questioned hers. "Are you sure?" he said.

"I'm sure, sweetheart. Go."

He looked relieved. Kissed her gently, squared his shoulders and turned away. Hands in his pockets, he walked slowly along the Wall's length, his form a faint reflection in its glassy surface. The kneeling man looked up at his approach and they exchanged nods as he passed. Danny turned the corner and disappeared, and Casey tucked her hands into the pockets of her jacket. Time passed. He reappeared, crossed the grassy verge and began reading the names inscribed in the stone. After a time he paused, shoulders tensed, then he lay both palms flat against the smooth stone. With one finger, he followed a line of print, knelt and continued reading, stopping every now and then when he reached a familiar name. He bowed his head at one point, resting his forehead against the stone, and Casey felt like a voyeur, driven to watch, yet repelled by the pain of watching.

The sun was high in the sky when at last he stood up and dusted off his knees and came back for her. She was still waiting where he'd left her hours before. He took her in his arms and held her shuddering form until they both warmed. "I'm sorry," he said.

"No," she said, and brushed the hair back from his face.

"Don't ever be sorry."

"You're freezing."

"So are you." She took his icy hand in hers and rubbed it until the warmth returned. "Do you want to talk about it?"

"I can't," he said. "Not yet."

"I'll wait. I'll wait as long as it takes."

He stroked her face with his thumb, gazed tenderly into her eyes. "After all these years," he said, "after everything I've put you through, you still love me. Why?"

She warmed her freezing hands in the layer of air between his coat and his body. "I don't know," she said. "I just do."

That evening, they returned, and together they walked down the path and crossed the grass to the place where the names of fifty-eight thousand men were inscribed. Together, they read the names of his fallen comrades: Kenny Bailey and Chuck Silverstein, Tico Ramirez and John Duquesne, Bill Taylor and Jack Cooke and Ramsay Brown. Beneath her fingers, the stone was hard and cold; at her back, Danny was warm and gloriously alive. Casey shivered and leaned back into his reassuring warmth, and he wrapped an arm around her. "There's nobody here I even know," she said. "Why do I feel so much like crying?"

Danny rested his cheek against hers. "They say it has that effect on everybody." He reached into his pocket and removed something and held it up to the light, and she recognized the dog tags he kept tucked away in his underwear drawer. He studied the tarnished military I.D., then kissed it lightly. "This one's for you, buddy," he said softly, and placed it on the ground beneath Kenny Bailey's name.

That night, in his arms, she rediscovered the commitment she'd doubted for so long. For better or for worse, she had bound herself to this man, had chosen him out of all the men in the world. Together, they had weathered pain and tragedy, and had not only survived, but had become stronger. Nothing could hurt them now.

In the sweet aftermath of passion, he pulled her close. He smoothed back her hair and said, "For a while there, I wasn't sure we were going to make it."

She wrapped her arms around him. He was big and solid,

sticky and warm. "Neither was I," she said.

"I suppose," he said, "I should feel honored."

It was an odd choice of words. "Honored," she said. "Why?"

"Because he's a good man."

It took her a moment to understand, and then she went stiff in his arms. "It's not like that," she said.

"Christ, Casey, give me credit for having a few brains. I didn't just fall off the turnip truck. What I'm trying to tell you is that it doesn't matter. Whatever went on between the two of you, it doesn't matter to me. What matters is that you're here, with me, and we're okay." He paused, then said, "We are okay, aren't we?"

She let out the breath she'd been holding. "Yes," she said. "We're okay."

***

"You grow up with rules," he said. "Some of them are drummed into your head. Others are implicit. Either way, you know what they are. Your boundaries are clearly defined. You understand what is and isn't acceptable. But over there, the rules didn't apply. There was only one rule, and that was survival."

He stared blindly into the darkened room. "After the first couple of times I caught the clap," he said, "I learned to stay away from the brothels and the Saigon street whores. The teenage peasant girls were usually clean, at least if you got there ahead of everybody else. There we were, a hundred thousand horny twenty-year-olds, raping and pillaging our way across the country, all in the name of democracy. We took whatever we wanted. We thought we were entitled. We took turns gang-banging thirteen-year-old girls. We set old men on fire, just to watch them dance. We'd march into a village, and they'd be hiding from us, because they knew why we were there. To steal their food, to kill their animals, to burn their crops." His face hardened. "To rape their daughters."

"Oh, Danny."

"None of it bothered us, because we dehumanized them. They weren't people, they were gooks, and everybody knew that the only good gook was a dead one. You couldn't trust any of them, because even in the South, the Cong had infiltrated everywhere, and if you turned your back you'd end up with your throat slit. All the fear, all the frustration, all the anger, we had to convert into something, so we turned it into rage. Do you know that Dylan Thomas poem, the one about not going gentle into that good night?"

She took his hand. "Yes," she said.

"That's what we were doing. We were raging against the dying of the light. On the outside, we were killing machines, doing what we'd been trained to do. On the inside, we were a bunch of scared kids who didn't want to die, and we needed a way to handle the fear. There weren't many options. You could stay stoned all the time. Some guys did that. Everything from grass to smack. It was their way of escaping, and who the hell could blame them? Some of us dealt with it by screwing anything that moved, because we were so desperate to feel something, anything, that would prove to us we were still human."

He got up from the bed and began moving restlessly around the room. "If you managed to survive long enough," he said, "sooner or later they'd send you to Singapore for a few days of R&R. You'd get a hotel room and a whore, and you'd stay drunk the whole time. Then, when you got back, you'd go straight to the medic for a penicillin shot."

He leaned against the dresser and lit a cigarette. "You learned to sleep flat on your back in the mud with your gun in your hands. You learned to watch for the tiniest deviation from the norm: a broken blade of grass, the snapping of a twig. A flock of birds squawking. Or silence." He took a deep drag on the cigarette and slowly exhaled the smoke. "Silence was the worst, because you never knew what it meant. The Cong were born knowing the tactics of guerrilla warfare. They knew how to make themselves invisible, how to hang like monkeys from the trees. We were just a bunch of kids from Boston and Boise who grew up on Lucy and Ricky and Good Humor bars. These guys were out of our league."

He looked around for an ashtray, found one, flicked the ash from his cigarette and tossed the hair back from his face. "So you spent thirteen months in a state of hyper-vigilance, because the piddliest little thing could mean instant death. And then they shipped you stateside and expected you to fit right back into society and play by the rules again. Except that the rules no longer made sense." He drew on the cigarette, exhaled, stared into and through the cloud of smoke. "After consorting with death, twenty-four hours a day for a year, it was impossible to live with the pettiness and the hypocrisy, the canonization of the trivial that was the basis of everyday life back home." He paused, lost in thought. "Sometimes," he said, "it would get so unbearable that you'd want to go back, because at least in Nam things made sense. Life, death, the good guys, the bad guys. Simple, gut-level survival. Some guys kept going back, kept signing up for one tour of duty after another, because they found they couldn't function any longer in the outside world. The rest of us," he said, "learned to pretend."

Cigarette in hand, he began pacing like a caged tiger. "Kenny Bailey and I met in basic. He was a farm kid from Omaha. Red hair, freckles, braces. After basic, we were given the dubious honor of spending the longest year of our lives together in hell. We were part of a ground unit, and we'd broken up into patrols. Usually there were five or six men in each patrol, but on this particular occasion, half the unit was laid low with dysentery, so there were just three of us. Kenny, me, and Chuck Silverstein. We'd walked—Christ, it must have been fifteen or twenty miles that day. It was raining. Not a heavy monsoon rain, the kind that sounded like thunder hitting the ground." He paused in front of the window and looked out, but she knew it wasn't the city of Washington he was seeing. "No," he said, "this was more the type of noxious drizzle that grew fungus between your toes and slowly drove you crazy."

It was a moment before he continued. "Chuck had only been in country for a month or so," he said, "but Kenny and I were two weeks away from shipping out, both of us scared shitless that we'd die before we could escape from that soggy hell. We were razzing each other that night, bragging, seeing who could outdo the other with the biggest line of bull. It was a way of passing the time, a way of laughing in the face of death, a way of trying to fill the silence, because it was too damn quiet.

The jungle's usually alive with sound, but that night, the silence was spooky."

Casey got up from the bed, stood beside him at the window, and lay a hand on his back. Beneath her fingertips, his muscles were rigid and unresponsive. "We'd found what I thought was a relatively safe place to spend the night," he said. "The guy must have been watching us for a while, waiting for the precise moment to strike. The first shot picked Chuck right off his feet. It went in the front and left a hole the size of a watermelon when it came out the back. Kenny and I hit the ground. We knew it was a sniper, but we couldn't figure out where the guy was shooting from. He knew where we were, though, and he was having one hell of a fine time trying to pick us off. I pulled rank on Kenny, ordered him to fall in behind me, and the two of us started crawling through the mud, trying to reach cover. There was no moon because of the cloud cover, and it was dark as the pit of hell out there. One minute, Kenny was right behind me. The next minute, he wasn't. As patrol leader, it was my duty to go back and find him." He paused. "Christ, I'd have gone back anyway. He was my best friend."

He lit another cigarette. "I found Kenny a few yards back. He'd been gut-shot, almost split in two. After I finished puking my guts out, I left him there. I didn't want to, but I had to if I wanted to save my worthless ass. The guy had stopped shooting. He must have thought there were only two of us. I was up to my ass in mud when I reached this clump of cypress, and I really thought I'd made it. I scrambled to my feet, and there he was, standing not five feet away, looking as surprised as I was.

"He was just a kid. Eleven, twelve years old. I looked at him and he looked at me, and for the first time, it dawned on me that this wasn't just some gook, this wasn't just the enemy, this was a real human being like me. Somebody's kid. And he must have felt the same way, because we just stood there, two human beings frozen in hell, and looked at each other."

He was silent for so long that Casey thought he'd forgotten she was in the room. He filled his lungs with smoke, then abruptly crushed out his cigarette. "And then," he said, "I killed him."

***

They headed north out of the District of Columbia the next morning beneath overcast skies. The forecast was dismal: a low pressure system was working its way in from the Midwest, bringing with it rain and sleet and record snowfalls. It had already dumped more than a foot of snow on western Pennsylvania, and it was headed in a meandering northeasterly direction. "A little over 200 miles from DC to New York," Danny said, pressing harder on the accelerator. "From there, we can outrun it."

Casey tightened her seat belt and stared out the windshield at the driving rain they'd encountered just north of Baltimore. It was coming down in torrents, bouncing off the surface of the roadway, awash with reflected light, destroying visibility. "Are you sure you wouldn't rather spend the night somewhere?" she said.

"In some run-down motel room," he said, "with a rock-hard bed? No, thank you. I've spent too many nights in places like that. Tonight, I'm sleeping in my own house, in my own bed." He glanced at her tense face, and his voice softened. "Don't worry, *carissima*. I'll get you there in one piece."

It had been a long time since he'd called her that, and Casey took his hand and threaded fingers with his. "I'm not worried," she said. "I'll just be relieved when we get home."

They ran into the first flakes of snow halfway through Jersey. Danny slowed his speed, but he kept glancing at the dashboard clock and frowning. "Christ," he said in disgust. "Why the hell didn't we buy a house in Palm Beach?"

It was nearly three o'clock when they stopped at a rest area near Newark. While they waited for their meal, Casey sipped coffee and Danny glumly watched the sooty snow outside the restaurant window. "Look at that fool," he said as a beat-up Toyota pulled in a little too fast, fishtailed, and nearly cleaned out the left rear fender of a white Caddy. "It's people like that who make the roads dangerous for the rest of us."

The waitress brought them each a bowl of soup and a sandwich. "You know," Casey said, crumbling oyster crackers into her bowl, "we could just stay in New York tonight."

"And then we won't get home until tomorrow afternoon." He picked up a dinner roll and plucked a packet of butter from the dish in the center of the table. Peeling off the foil, he said, "I thought you weren't worried."

"I wasn't worried then. I am now."

"Let's just see how it goes. If it's really bad, we'll stop somewhere in Connecticut."

It was as good as she was going to get. They finished the meal in silence. By the time they went back out into the storm, the wind had started up, and the snow was blowing in a blinding cloud. They made a run for the BMW, slamming doors against the onslaught. Danny pulled the car out of its parking slot and shifted it into gear. "You're not wearing your seat belt," she said. "And please don't remind me of your 'live hard and fast' philosophy. I'm not in the mood."

Danny cleared his throat. "What I was about to say, before I was so rudely interrupted, was that I'd forgotten. I don't suppose you'd care to fasten it for me?"

She leaned over, reached around him, tugged the belt, snapped it into place. Adjusted the harness until it fit him snugly. "I'm sorry," she said. "This weather's turned me into a basket case."

It took them two hours to get through New York. Bumper-to-bumper traffic moved like a caravan of snails, stopping and starting, splashing and sliding, a sea of tail lights that ebbed and flowed into the night. They sat for a half-hour on the Cross-Bronx Expressway while a wrecker peeled a mangled Ford Granada off the guardrail and towed it away. By the time they reached New Haven, she'd counted seventeen cars off the road, one of them a rollover. "Danny," she said, "I've had enough. I want to stop now."

He glanced at the dashboard clock. "Let's put thirty more miles behind us, and we'll stop. All right?"

Thirty miles loomed like a hundred, but she reluctantly agreed. "Fine," she said. "Thirty more miles, and then we stop at the first motel we see."

"If I'd had any idea it would be like this," he said, "I would have stayed in DC. I really thought we could beat this mess home."

The car lost traction and skidded for a moment, and Casey's heart jumped into her throat. But he quickly brought it back under control, and the adrenaline in her bloodstream slowly receded to a normal level. "Damn it, Danny," she said, "if you kill us, I swear to God I'll never speak to you again."

Gripping the wheel tightly, he said, "I'm not going to kill us."

An eighteen-wheeler sped by them in the passing lane, splattering the windshield with a heavy coating of muddy slush. "Christless idiot," Danny said. "Thinks he's running the Indy 500."

The snow was coming down almost sideways, and they were driving directly into it. He switched his headlights to low beam in a futile attempt to see through the blinding mass. The beam reflected off a road sign advertising food, fuel and accommodations at the next exit. "I guess we'd better stop," he said reluctantly. "How far did it say?"

"Six miles," Casey said, breathing a sigh of relief.

"I'm sorry," he said. "I had no idea it would be this bad. I just didn't want to spend all day tomorrow on the road."

"I don't understand," she said. "What's your hurry? You're not on any deadline. You don't have any commitments. What difference does it make if we spend an extra day or two on the road?"

His knuckles were white on the steering wheel. "I guess I haven't learned to slow down yet."

"If you don't," she said grimly, "you'll die of a coronary before you're fifty."

"I don't think so," he said. "I've changed my mind. I'm not going to crash and burn. I'm going to be right there beside you in your dotage."

For some reason, his words wrought in her an inexplicable sadness. "What about children? What about grandchildren? It's too late for us to start over."

"We'll borrow somebody else's. If Rob would ever settle down, we could use his." The wipers swished across the windshield, and ahead of them, a sign said *Next Exit 2 Miles*. "I hope to Christ there's a restaurant around with a well-stocked bar," he said, "because when I get out of this car, I'm going to want to drink my dinner."

"That makes two of us," she said.

Ahead of them, brake lights flashed, then disappeared. Danny sighed. "Now what?" he said.

"I don't know, but I'd suggest slowing down."

"I'm only doing forty-seven."

"That's too fast for these conditions."

"Look," he said, "if you'd like to drive—" He squinted, leaning over the wheel, and then, in an odd voice, he said, "Christ Almighty."

Casey looked up in alarm. Directly in front of them, blocking the highway, lay the eighteen-wheeler that had passed them earlier, toppled like a turtle, its wheels still spinning in mid-air. She grabbed the dash in terror. "*Danny*," she said.

"Hang on," he said, pumping the brakes like crazy. The car went into a skid and began spinning, slowly at first and then gaining momentum. "Goddamn it," he growled, cramming the shifter into low gear.

At the last possible moment, the wheels caught and they missed the truck. They plowed head-first into the snow bank, sliced through it and came out the other side. *We're all right*, she thought. *We made it*. Then she saw the embankment dropping away in front of them, and she screamed his name. They pitched forward into empty space, and then they were falling, tumbling end over end in the blackness, small objects catapulting like missiles around them as they tumbled and rolled, tumbled and rolled. She reached out for Danny, but she couldn't find him. The car slammed up against a solid object and the windshield burst in her face, and then something struck her in the temple with enough force to snap her head back against the headrest.

And the world went black.

BOOK FOUR

CHAPTER TWENTY-SEVEN

December, 1987
Midland, Connecticut

Dawn was just beginning to lighten the eastern sky when Rob MacKenzie fishtailed his dad's LTD into the parking lot at Midland Hospital. It had taken him four hours of white-knuckle driving to get from Boston to this rinky-dink establishment in this rinky-dink little town. Above the front entrance, *Season's Greetings* was spelled out in plastic holly leaves. Somewhere inside, Casey was waiting for him. Somehow, he had to do this. Somehow, he had to walk into that building and be strong for her when inside he was falling apart.

It had been a rough trip, and not just because he was driving through a blizzard in a rear-wheel-drive gunboat that was as useful in the snow as a surfboard. He had spent most of the four-hour trip trying to make sense of this madness. Danny Fiore wasn't an ordinary man, he was a god. Gods weren't supposed to die. And Rob MacKenzie, a mere mortal, wondered how he would make it through this nightmare without breaking down.

At the main desk, he asked for Father Letourneau. A few minutes later, a white-haired man in a cable knit sweater and a clerical collar greeted him with outstretched hand. "Mr. MacKenzie," he said.

"Father."

The priest held Rob's hand in a strong grip and studied his face. "You and Mr. Fiore were close," he said.

Rob swallowed. "Yeah," he said. "We are. Were."

"I'm sorry." The priest shook his head. "I deal with death every day. It's my job. But sometimes, it really gets to me. This is one of those times."

He cleared his throat. "How is she?"

"As well as can be expected. She's a brave young woman, but the enormity of this hasn't hit her yet. Right now she's quiet and compliant. Some of that's due to the sedation she was given. The rest is nature's anesthesia. Sometimes, when something unbearable happens, nature takes over for a while and we go someplace where the pain can't follow us."

He raked a hand through his tangled hair. "I don't know what to do," he said. "How to help her."

"Allow her to set the pace. Be there for her. Does she have a reliable support system?"

"Lots of family nearby. And me. I'll stay as long as she needs me."

"Good. If she wants to talk, listen. If she doesn't want to, don't push it. If she wants to be alone, respect her wishes, within reason. Try to keep life as normal as possible. But don't expect too much from her at first. She's been through a terrible ordeal. She took quite a bump to the head, then she kicked out a window and went through it, slicing herself up quite prettily in the process. She was in shock when they brought her in."

Rob closed his eyes. "Jesus," he said.

"She'll need time to recover, physically and emotionally." The priest laid a hand on his shoulder. "What about you?" he said. "How's your support system?"

"Don't worry about me."

"It's my job to worry about you. The doctors here take care of the sick and the dying. I take care of the people who love them."

"Thanks, Father, but I'll deal with it my own way, in my own time." His throat clogged up, and he closed his eyes against the sting of tears. "I'm sorry," he said, embarrassed. "I thought I got all my crying out of the way on the trip from Boston."

"It's all right, son. Take a few minutes to pull yourself together."

He drew a long, shuddering breath. "I have to get her out of here before the media gets wind of this."

Father Letourneau nodded somberly. "The hospital hasn't released the name of the deceased yet, but most of the staff knows, and in a small town like this, news spreads like wildfire."

"Has anybody called her father? I don't want her family hearing about it on the radio."

"No. I had enough trouble prying your name out of her. Is there someone you'd like me to call? Mr. Fiore's family, perhaps?"

"Casey and I are the only family Danny has. Had." He hesitated, more rattled than he'd realized. "I'm sorry," he said, rubbing his temple. "I'm not thinking straight."

"It's all right. Take your time."

"I guess I can call her folks from the road." He closed his eyes. "Shit," he whispered. "I can't believe this."

He followed the priest down a maze of corridors, stopping at the door of a small sitting room. Casey was curled in a fetal position on the couch, feet tucked under her, Danny's suede jacket wrapped around her, twelve sizes too big. She was staring blankly at the television, where Lucy and Ethel were up to their usual shenanigans. On the table beside her there was an untouched cup of coffee. In her hand, a wrinkled manila envelope. "Hey," he said softly.

She looked up. There was a bandage over her left eyebrow, and her cheek was peppered with tiny red welts where they'd pulled microscopic glass fragments from tender flesh. There was blood in her hair and all over her clothes, and she had a black eye. She looked like something from *Night of the Living Dead*, and he tried to keep the shock from his face as he entered the room and knelt on the floor in front of her. He wanted desperately to touch her, but didn't dare. Instead, he touched the manila envelope, gingerly, with a single fingertip. "What's in here, sweetheart?"

She let him take it from her, and he opened the flap. Inside were Danny's wallet, his wedding ring, his Rolex. Rob swallowed hard and closed the envelope and gave it back to her, dreadfully sorry he'd asked. He looked to the priest for help, but at some point, Father Letourneau had discreetly left the room. He was on his own.

He cleared his throat. "Did they give you any medication?"

She reached into the pocket of Danny's bloodstained jacket and pulled out a vial of pills and two prescription slips. Valium and Tylenol with codeine. He tucked them back into her pocket. "Are you in a lot of pain?" he asked.

She looked at him, but she wasn't seeing him. "I can't feel anything," she said. "Why can't I feel anything?"

"It's a temporary condition," he said. "Come on, sweetheart, let's go home."

The priest stood in the vestibule and watched them, all the way to the car. The storm was over, the roads cleared, the sun breaking through. Casey burrowed into the seat cushion and Rob drove like a little old lady so he wouldn't frighten her. Out of the corner of his eye, he watched her open the envelope. She took out Danny's Rolex and slipped it on her arm, shoving it all the way to her elbow before it stayed put. And they rode in silence.

He drove about twenty miles before pulling into the parking lot of a rural diner. Casey looked at him blankly. "Breakfast," he said, releasing his seat belt. "If my blood sugar gets any lower, I'll be comatose."

The table was sticky, the menus greasy. The waitress looked at Casey oddly but didn't comment on her appearance. He ordered bacon and eggs, home fries and toast. Casey stared helplessly at the menu. "She'll have the same thing I'm having," he said, and took the menu from her hands and closed it.

The coffee tasted like mud. He loaded it with sugar and drank it to lessen his shakiness. When the food arrived, he dug in, ravenous, but Casey just looked at her plate. "I can't do this," she said woodenly.

"Yes, you can."

"No." She shook her head and looked at him with absolute certainty. "I can't."

He set down his fork and took her hand. "You're strong, babe. You're the strongest person I know. You can do this. You'll get through this."

She looked up at him. "How?"

"You pick up your fork and take a bite. You chew it and swallow it. Then you do it again."

That blank gaze never wavered. "I wasn't talking about eating," she said.

"Neither was I. You have to take life in little bites. If thirty seconds at a time is all you can handle right now, that's how you live life. Thirty seconds at a time, until you're ready to handle more. Then you take it ten minutes at a time, and then a half hour. Nobody's going to ask you to make decisions. Nobody's going to ask you to think. Nobody's going to ask you to do anything you don't feel ready to do. I'll be there to see that they don't."

She set down her fork. "I need to use the bathroom."

"Go ahead," he said, then remembered the pills in her pocket. "But leave the jacket here."

He didn't like the idea of her going alone, but there were some places even he couldn't follow her. While she was in the rest room, he used the pay phone to call her folks and tell them in as few words as possible what had happened. When he returned to the table she was still gone, and he stewed until the door to the bathroom opened and she emerged. He didn't think she was suicidal, but he wasn't about to leave her alone long enough to find out.

When she sat back down, he got his first look at the gash on her arm. "Holy mother of God," he said, and caught her wrist and turned it so he could count the stitches. *Eighteen.* He closed his eyes and dropped her arm, suddenly nauseated. "My turn for the bathroom," he said. "Will you be all right for a few minutes?"

"I'm not an invalid," she said, and took a bite of toast.

The men's room was pretty bad. Not the worst he'd seen, but definitely somewhere in the top ten. He used the facilities, then stared at his face in the mirror and decided he looked worse than she did. He splashed cold water on his face. There were no paper towels, so he dried himself with the tail of his shirt. "MacKenzie," he told his reflection, "you are one class act."

The drive to Jackson Falls took a hundred years. The sand trucks had been out, but the roads still weren't great, and his speedometer never once passed forty-five. It was afternoon when they finally reached her house, and then he discovered that her keys were locked in the house and Danny's were still in the ignition of the wrecked BMW, and he had to break a window so they could get in.

The house was eerily silent. He stood over her and picked a shiny sliver of glass from her hair. "I think you'd feel better," he said, "if you had a hot bath and a shampoo. Will you try? For me?"

She shrugged.

He'd never felt so helpless in his life. She needed somebody to undress her and bathe her and put her to bed. There was only so much he could do. What she needed was another woman. In desperation, he called Trish Bradley.

It was the right thing to do. Trish fussed and clucked and cooed over Casey like she was a small child, and he felt a tremendous relief as the weight of responsibility was temporarily lifted from his shoulders. While Trish was taking care of Casey, he drove back into town and got her prescriptions filled. When he returned, she was sitting at the kitchen table in a flannel nightgown, smelling of soap and eating a bowl of beef stew. He found a roll of plastic in the shed and some masking tape in the kitchen drawer, and he patched up the broken window until he could get the pane replaced.

Then he went upstairs and called his parents. He knew they'd be waiting to hear from him. He filled them in, reassured them that he had everything under control, promised to get the car back to them as soon as possible. Then, while the family took turns fretting over Casey, Rob kept himself busy fielding phone calls. They all called: *People Weekly*, the *Star*, *Rolling Stone*. *Entertainment Tonight*. MTV, CNN, and all three of the major networks. *The New York Times*, the *Chicago Tribune*, the *Los Angeles Sun*. AP and UPI and the various wire services. The goddamn *National Enquirer*. For each caller he had the same brief, canned response. Yes, the reports of Danny Fiore's death were true. No, Mrs. Fiore was not available for comment. While he swallowed gallons of Trish Bradley's potent coffee, the phone rang off the hook, until his voice gave out and he was forced to turn off the ringer and unplug the answering machine.

He folded his arms on the kitchen table and lay his head down and closed his eyes. He'd been up for thirty-six hours, and Trish tried to badger him into resting, but after all that coffee, he was too wired to sleep. Instead, he put on the gray sweats he'd left in the guest room closet the last time he visited, and he went running. It was eight miles from Casey's house to the town line and back, and while he was running, he didn't have to think, didn't have to feel, didn't have to do anything except breathe in and out and will his muscles to keep moving.

When he got back, most of the company had left, but Trish and Bill were still there, drinking coffee at the kitchen table. The way Trish made coffee, none of them would sleep for a month. "Where's Casey?" he said.

"Upstairs, resting," Trish said. "Hey, don't wake her up!"

He squared his jaw. "She's not sleeping," he said.

He knocked softly on her bedroom door and opened it a crack. "It's me," he whispered. "You awake?"

She raised her head. Her shiner was already turning alternating shades of green and yellow. She patted the bed and he sat down on the edge. "You've been running," she said.

"How'd you know?"

"The way you smell."

"Great. I'll go back down and shower."

"No," she said. "I like it. It's the way you always smell when you've been running."

"Sweetheart," he said, "we have to talk about the funeral."

She closed her eyes. "I can't make it go away. I keep trying, but it won't go away."

He swallowed. "I'll do it all, if that's what you want."

She took his hand in hers and stroked the palm with her thumb. "This isn't easy for you, is it?"

"It's easier if I keep busy."

"I trust you, Flash. Absolutely."

"I know. I just didn't want to overstep my boundaries."

"I think we're beyond boundaries," she said. "We have been for a long time." She sat up groggily, got up from the bed and moved stiffly, like an old lady, to the desk. "Will you do something for me?" she said.

"Anything. Anything at all."

She pulled two cards from the Rolodex, moved slowly back to the bed, and handed them to him. "Will you call these people?"

The names meant nothing to him. Anna Montoya and Eddie Carpenter. "Sure," he said. "Who are they?"

She sat down on the edge. "Danny's parents," she said.

"Danny's parents? But I thought—" He stopped abruptly, wondering just how well he'd really known Danny Fiore.

"It's a long story," she said. "Maybe someday I'll tell it to you."

He spent the rest of that day on the telephone. When he finished with the mortician, he made all the necessary calls to reschedule his life, both personal and professional, for the foreseeable future. And then, long into the night, hours after he should have been in bed asleep, he called everybody he could think of who'd known Danny Fiore. He couldn't let Danny go without a proper sendoff.

He finished the last call at two in the morning. Hung up the phone, poured himself a shot of Danny's good bourbon, and sat alone in the dark, brooding. Thinking about his life. His screwed-up past. His uncertain future.

And about Danny's widow.

In despair, he dropped his head onto his folded arms and fell asleep right there at the kitchen table.

***

The funeral parlor was in an old Victorian mansion on a quiet side street in town. Rob helped Casey out of the LTD and took her by the arm, and with slow, measured steps they walked the half block to the entrance. Trish met them at the door, patted him on the arm and spirited Casey away into the next room, where people were gathered in small, hushed clusters. The cloying smells of death and flowers hit him simultaneously, and he panicked. There was no way he could go through with this. He spun around and escaped through the door he'd come in, thundered down the steps to the flagstone walkway, reached into his jacket pocket and pulled out a cigarette.

He drew the smoke in deep, his surprised lungs expanding in welcome. Beside him, Travis Bradley said, "I thought you quit smoking, MacKenzie."

He let the smoke out slowly. "I did."

"Taking it up again, are you?"

He took another long, sweet draw on the cigarette. "I don't think I can do this, Trav. I don't think I can go back in there."

"Get rid of the damn cancer stick. We'll do it together."

Reluctantly, he dropped the first cigarette he'd had in eighteen months and stepped on it, and with Travis by his side, he walked back through the door.

Some of these people he knew. Most of them he didn't. He looked everywhere but at the casket as side by side with Travis he took the longest walk of his life. "Who's the guy hanging over Casey?" he demanded.

"That's my cousin Teddy. He's a pain in the ass. The stevedore over in the corner is his mother, my Aunt Hilda. She's Dad's older sister. The pretty one who looks like Casey is my mother's sister, Elizabeth. And the ravishing blonde beside her is the love of my life. Keepa you hands off."

And then they were standing in front of the casket, and he couldn't avoid it any longer, because this wasn't just death, this wasn't just some abstract concept, this was real, and this was Danny.

Except that it wasn't Danny. It was some wax figure that looked a little like Danny, hands folded in mock reverence, wearing the clothes that Rob himself had picked out of Danny's bedroom closet. They'd combed his hair wrong and they'd put some gunk on his face to make him look like he was in the full flush of vibrant good health, except that he wasn't, he was dead, and nothing they could do would make one iota of difference.

He clutched the edge of the casket. "Fiore," he said, "you goddamn stupid son of a bitch." His voice cracked, and he cleared his throat. "How the hell am I supposed to get through the next fifty years without you?" This wasn't in the script. There were too many words left unsaid, too many songs left unsung. Before his eyes, Danny's face blurred and disappeared. "Jesus, Trav," he said, "get me out of here before I lose it."

Travis hustled him out a side door and onto the verandah. Rob sank onto a wicker chair and buried his head in his arms, and while Travis patted his shoulder awkwardly, he sat there and bawled like a baby.

He felt better afterward. Not great, but better. "Damn," he said, trying to find a discreet place to wipe his runny nose. "Why the hell can't I ever remember to carry a handkerchief?" Danny had always carried a handkerchief. There was one tucked into his breast pocket right now. Maybe he could sneak in and blow his nose on it and then put it back. The thought actually brought a smile to his face because he knew what Danny's response would be.

"What?" Travis said.

"Nothing. Geez, I must look really great." The mental picture of his ugly mug with a drippy nose and swollen eyes was frightening.

"Nobody's looking at you, MacKenzie. Nobody'll even notice. You ready to go back inside?"

"No. But I can handle it now. I guess I needed that."

There were new faces he hadn't seen the first time around. Casey was still sitting in the same corner, and Teddy was still monopolizing her, and he developed an instantaneous, bone-deep dislike for Cousin Teddy. Casey looked up and saw him, and something in his face must have gotten through to her, because she spoke to Teddy and then she got up and threaded her way through the maze of people to him.

He opened his arms and she stepped into them, and they clung to each other in absolute understanding, rocking back and forth in a private world of pain that nobody else could penetrate, only it was all turned around backward, because he was the one who was crying while her eyes were dry, and she was the one who gave comfort although it was her husband who was dead. "I love you," she whispered fiercely. "I hope you realize that."

He tightened his arms around her. "I know, sweetheart. I love you, too."

"God, Rob, what am I going to do?"

He smoothed her hair. "They say it gets easier with time."

"According to who?"

"I don't know," he said. "Some goddamn fool."

"Will you come with me? To see him?"

This time it was easier. He stood guard so she could have privacy, glowering at anybody who came within ten feet of her. "Rob," she said, "do you have a comb?"

He patted empty pockets, shrugged apologetically.

"Of course you wouldn't," she said without censure. "Will you find me one?"

He bummed a comb from Travis and watched while she fixed Danny's hair. "Thank God you did that," he said. "It was driving me crazy."

She stepped back, and he thought he detected a tremor in the hand that held the comb. "I'd like to go home now," she said.

At three-thirty the next morning, he was awakened by a light in the kitchen. He stumbled out of bed and pulled on the gray sweats that were balled up on the floor. He found Casey sitting at the table with tweezers and manicure scissors, trying to remove her own stitches.

"Jesus, Mary and Joseph," he said. "Have you gone around the bend?"

Her eyes were glassy, whether from grief or Valium, he wasn't sure. But the frustration he recognized. She shoved a clump of hair away from her face. "Damn it all, Rob, will you help me? This is making me crazy."

He peered closely at her arm. The wound was still red and angry-looking, and he felt mildly nauseated. "You need a doctor for this kind of thing, Fiore."

"Bullfeathers. You city boys are all alike. Around here, we don't go running off to the doctor for something as simple as having stitches out. We just do it ourselves."

He couldn't believe he was allowing himself to be roped into this. He scrubbed his hands with hot water and antibacterial soap and dried them on a clean paper towel. And scowled. "Did you sterilize those things first?"

"They're clean."

He wasn't convinced, but he knew it would be useless to argue. One way or another, she would get her way. One way or another, she always did. He pulled a chair up at an angle to hers, stretched her arm across the corner of the kitchen table, and picked up the tweezers.

It took him two hours to remove those eighteen stitches. By the time he was done, her face was the color of Philadelphia cream cheese, and he had rivers of sweat pouring down his sides. She never made a sound the whole time, but he knew precisely how many times he had hurt her. He cleared away the mess, then took a wad of cotton and applied peroxide to the jagged gash. He knew damn well it hurt, but she just bit her lip and took the pain. "Never again," he said, capping the bottle and tossing the cotton into the trash. "You hear me, Fiore? Never again." And then he went into the living room and collapsed in a shuddering heap on the couch.

CHAPTER TWENTY-EIGHT

None of this was real.

Not the vast crowd of friends and acquaintances whose stunned silence was occasionally punctuated by weeping. Not the flowers whose cloying odor made Casey retch, so many flowers that the church couldn't hold them all and Rob had ended up sending out a truckload to be distributed to a half-dozen local nursing homes. Not the incessant drone of the minister, who spoke in a language which should have been familiar, but which made no more sense to her than Mandarin Chinese. Not the intricate patterns of stained glass, nor the crimson carpet at her feet, nor the hard wooden bench behind her rigid back.

And certainly not the mahogany casket before the altar.

If she breathed too deeply, if she moved too suddenly, the steely band of control that held her together would loosen and she would shatter into a billion crystalline fragments. She concentrated her attention on Rob's knuckles, bone-white between her clenched hands. In a world turned alien, Rob alone remained familiar. Rob alone could hold her from tumbling headfirst into the black abyss that gaped open at her feet.

The minister finished his sermon. As Bob Dylan sang softly from the overhead speakers, they came forward to speak, one by one, dozens of people Danny had known and worked with over the years. His friends. Her friends. Their friends. They all shared memories of Danny, pieces of the relationships they'd shared, if only for a brief time, with Danny Fiore. She listened woodenly to their stories, knowing she should feel something besides indifference. Her attention wandered, and then Rob was leaning toward her. "Casey," he said, into her ear. "It's over."

She stared at him, uncomprehending, until she realized people were stirring, lining up to file past the casket. She released his hand and watched as the color returned. Row after row, they came forward to pay their last respects to her husband. Each of them stopping to speak to her, to offer their condolences, to give her a widow's due respect. Until the last of them had gone, and she and Rob were the only ones left.

He touched her shoulder. She stood up, and the room seemed to be revolving in slow motion. Each of her legs weighed a thousand pounds. Lifting first one leaden foot and then the other, she followed Rob's lead in a macabre dance. When she reached the casket, she stopped. Rob released her arm and stepped back, and she lay her hands against the polished mahogany. It was hard, cold, smooth as glass, lined with scarlet satin and ornamented with shiny brass handles. She slipped off her wedding ring and worked it onto the pinkie finger of Danny's left hand. It only went as far as the first knuckle. She lay both her hands on his, took a long last look. Bent and kissed those cold lips. "*Ciao*," she whispered, "*caro mio*." And she raised her chin and turned away.

Rob was standing with his back to her, his shoulders squared, his head held stiffly erect. She wet her lips. "Rob?" she said.

He took a long, shuddering breath, but didn't turn around. "Yeah," he said softly.

"I'll be waiting in the foyer."

He nodded, still not looking at her, and she left him there with Danny. In the church's cloak room, she gathered up her coat, her scarf. Shrugged into the maroon cashmere dress coat with its blood-red silk lining. Wrapped her scarf around her neck. She met Rob in the foyer, and without speaking, they walked together out the front door and onto the church steps.

They were waiting outside. Hundreds of them, held back by uniformed security guards and yellow crime scene tape. The curious, the thrill-seekers, the weeping women, the press. At her side, she felt Rob stiffen as flash bulbs went off in their faces. Like a wraith, Travis appeared at her other side and silently offered his arm. "Just fifty feet," Rob said. "That's all you have to do, and then there's a limo waiting."

She nodded her understanding.

A muscle twitched in his cheek. "Ready?" he said.

She concentrated her attention on the rough tweed of his jacket, scratchy against her bare wrist. Took a deep breath of brisk December air, looked at Trav, and nodded. Raising her chin, she said, "Ready."

Faces, twisted with emotion, loomed like Mardi Gras

masks. Arms reached out to her, hands grabbed, patted. Voices called out her name. By touching her, talking to her, in some twisted way they were touching Danny. Fame by association. Some of them used it, like trading cards: *I sat on an airplane once, all the way to Cleveland, next to Mick Jagger's hairdresser's next-door neighbor. Yeah? Well, I touched Danny Fiore's wife the day they buried him.* Another flashbulb went off, another reporter called out. *Mrs. Fiore! Mrs. Fiore, do you have a statement for us?* A young woman plucked at the sleeve of Rob's jacket as he snarled, "No comment!" over his shoulder.

The path before them narrowed, and as though by unspoken signal, Travis and Rob moved in closer as dozens of sticky, anonymous hands pawed and clutched at their clothes, their hair, their bodies. Then, thankfully, the limo was waiting. Massive bodyguards held back the crowd as they stepped inside and the door shut behind them, and Casey closed her eyes and sank into soft leather.

Beside her, Travis loosened his tie. "I never realized," he said, dazed. "Not really. Until now."

She couldn't remember the last time she'd seen her brother so unnerved. "Thank you," she said softly, and turned to Rob. His eyes were closed, his head pressed back against the plush leather seat, his face pale and stony. She took his hand in hers and squeezed it hard. He opened his eyes, and they were damp and feral. "I'm stronger than you think," she said.

Hoarsely, he said, "Are you?"

"Once," she said, "a very wise man told me I didn't always have to be the strong one. That it was okay to accept help once in a while."

He squared his jaw and turned away. "And your point is?"

"It's a two-way street," she said. "We get through this together."

A December burial was unusual in Maine, but since the ground wasn't yet fully frozen, it was what she'd requested. While security guards held the curiosity-seekers at bay, the family and a few friends huddled in a tight little band, high on a hill, shoulders hunched against the wind that shot like darts through their clothing and rattled the bare branches of the elm tree that towered above them. Eyes hidden behind dark glasses, she listened emotionlessly to words that were intended to soothe, as they lay Danny to rest in the family burial plot.

There was no wake. That, too, had been her request. Only stiff hugs at the cemetery, then the brief trip home in the limousine, followed at a discreet distance by the security guards Rob had hired. For days, while her physical scars healed and her black eye made its slow evolution through the color spectrum, the guards worked rotating shifts, one posted in the house, one in his car at the end of the driveway. A precaution, Rob told her. Nothing more than preventive medicine, protection against any potential threat.

Normally, Casey would have balked at the lack of privacy. Instead, she felt only indifference. The security guards knew the short list of people who were allowed in. Everybody else was turned away. One more thing she didn't care a fig about. They could all stay away as far as she was concerned. The only person she cared to see wasn't coming back, and nothing else mattered any more. After six days with only one minor incident involving a fan with a telephoto lens, Rob dismissed the security people and took over the responsibility of keeping the world at bay.

Casey walked through life cocooned in numbness. Friends and family stopped by frequently, offering help and moral support. She thanked each of them politely, served them coffee and pie, and sent them on their way.

Only Rob was allowed to stay. He reminded her daily to change her clothes and comb her hair. He washed her dishes and vacuumed her rugs, he bought the groceries and cooked the meals and badgered her into eating. He kept her functioning with endless games of Monopoly and blackjack. It was Rob who sat up with her at three in the morning when she had to bake pies or go crazy, Rob who ate the pies after she made them. It was Rob who listened during those all-night sessions when she talked incessantly about Danny, Rob who drove her into Farmington and helped her pick out a new car.

Eventually, inevitably, the day came when she knew it was time to send him away. "You've done enough," she told him. "You've gone so far beyond the boundaries of friendship that I don't know how I'll ever repay you."

"We already talked about boundaries," he said. "And I'm

not looking for payment. You know better."

"Rob," she said, "you have a life. You should be living it."

He protested, as she'd known he would, but she thought she detected a thread of relief running through the fabric of his protests. And who could blame him? These days, she could barely stand her own company. She certainly wouldn't wish it on anybody else.

"Come to Boston with me," he said, "for Christmas. Mom and Dad would love to have you."

"And ruin Christmas for everyone? I think not. But thanks for the offer."

"I don't like the idea of leaving you alone."

She braced her palms against the lip of the kitchen sink and watched a chickadee pecking at the tiny black seeds that were scattered across the hard crust of snow beneath the bird feeder. "I have to do this myself," she said.

He squared that stubborn jaw. "Why?" he said.

"Because," she said, "you won't always be here. Because sooner or later, I have to face life on my own. Because it isn't right for me to depend on you for everything."

"You're not ready."

"And if you stay," she said gently, "I never will be."

So he went, and she was left the monumental task of reassembling the pieces of her ravaged life. Christmas came and went, and the family respected her wishes. They didn't try to force her into celebrating. Christmas afternoon, Rob called from Boston and they shared a brief, stilted conversation. He badgered her to visit him in California after the new year. Because it was easier than arguing, and because argument wasn't her strong suit these days, she agreed.

Most nights, she went without sleep. Nights were the worst, because at night there was nothing to fill her mind with, to make her forget. Danny was there, in every corner of that creaky old house, and in the wee hours of darkness, he whispered to her, seduced her with memories of warm, sleek flesh and softly whispered words of passion. As the weeks passed, pain began to eat away at the edges of her numbness. When the longing became too unbearable, she would go to the closet and open the door and bury her face in a great armload of his shirts. His odor clung to his clothing, to the bed linens she still hadn't been able to bring herself to change. On the rare occasions when she actually slept, inevitably she dreamed about him. The dreams were all different, all the same: he was still alive, smiling, arms stretched out to her, but always just beyond her reach. She would awaken and automatically turn to him, and then she would remember, and the pain was like a rock-hard fist in her abdomen.

She wasn't sure exactly when she became aware that the music had died. She only knew that it was gone. Inside her, around her. She locked Danny's piano and put away the key. Meticulously avoided the den where the stereo sat, gathering dust. Never once turned on the radio in the new Mitsubishi sports car she felt such indifference towards. The music had been Danny, and Danny had been the music, the two so interwoven she couldn't separate the strands. Without Danny, there was no music, and the silence was deafening.

Every week, without fail, Rob mailed her what she came to think of as care packages. These innocuous little bonanzas were her only ray of sunshine in an otherwise bleak existence. She never knew quite what would be inside. He always sent a letter, sometimes lengthy, sometimes brief, depending on how busy he'd been that week. He cut out newspaper articles he knew she'd find interesting, and cartoons to make her laugh. He told her all the new dirty jokes he'd heard. Sometimes he would include a cassette of his latest music; a couple of times he tucked in a half-finished song in the hope of enticing her, but she refused to take the bait. He sent a batch of Gary Larsen's *Far Side* paperbacks, and on one occasion, he sent her one of Igor's discarded whiskers scotch-taped to an index card.

Once he sent an old photo of her at nineteen or twenty, mugging for the camera in faded jeans and Danny's old gray B.U. sweatshirt. She had no idea when or where it had been taken, and she studied it at length, stunned by how young she had looked. And how happy.

Sometimes, she wrote back. Sometimes, she actually mailed the letters she wrote. Other times, they were so maudlin that instead of mailing them, she tore them up and burned them.

He called a few days after the photo arrived. "Did you like the picture?" he said.

"I was never that young," she said. "Where on earth did you get it?"

"I've had it forever. Bet you don't remember the occasion."

"Not a thing."

"Boston Common," he said. "A Sunday afternoon in October. Remember the Sunday afternoon football game?"

A bittersweet, piercing pain shot through her chest. "I haven't thought of that in years," she said.

"Every Sunday about half-past one, we'd come by and drag you and the Italian stallion out of bed. You two were always in bed."

"Danny was working two jobs," she said softly, remembering. "Sunday was the only day anything ever happened in bed, and then you bozos had to come by and interrupt. We always tried to ignore you, but you and Trav just kept banging on the door until one of us got up to let you in before the neighbors decided to call the cops."

"We couldn't play without you," he said. "It was Danny's football we used."

"And afterwards," she said, "we'd troop back to the apartment, all muddy and sweaty and grass-stained, and we'd sit around on the floor, eating pizza and drinking beer."

"Glory days," he said softly.

The tightness in her chest had grown nearly unbearable. "He certainly had a way of drawing people to him, didn't he?"

"Oh, Danny had charisma," he said. "But it wasn't Danny who kept us coming back, week after week. It was you."

"Me?" she said, incredulous. "Be serious."

"I am. You were like this earth mother person. You made us feel welcome, kept us warm and fed, made us feel good about ourselves. You have this rare talent, babe. It's the way you relate to people. When somebody talks, you listen. I mean you *really* listen, like that somebody is the most important person on the planet. I've never known anybody else who could do that."

***

The last Saturday in January, it happened again. Rob

picked up the phone to call Danny. He got as far as dialing the number before he remembered, and felt that squeezing pain in his chest as he slowly hung up the phone. Danny had been the linchpin around which his life had revolved for nearly two decades, and even though he'd witnessed death with his own eyes, it was still difficult to believe. It wouldn't sink in for a while. And until it did, he was doomed to flounder, lost in a world of which Danny Fiore was no longer a part.

He called Kitty Callahan instead, and they had dinner at a quiet, out-of-the-way place he knew, in a neighborhood where the rich and the chic never wandered unless they took a wrong turn somewhere. While Gloria Estefan bubbled from the overhead speakers, they had a few drinks and talked about old times. Afterward, he went home with her. They'd been friends for years, casual lovers on occasion, and he knew that whenever he sought comfort, he could find it with Kitty. But tonight, the comfort he'd always found so satisfying failed him. Not that there was anything wrong with the sex. Sex was sex, and Kitty was good at it. But it failed to fill that yawning hole inside him. This time, after they made love, he did something he'd never done before: he climbed out of bed, put his clothes on, and went home.

The Hotel California was too silent, too empty. He changed into his sweats and went running. On silent streets, through the velvet California night, past block after block of single-family bungalows tucked beneath sprawling eucalyptus trees, he ran with a steady rhythm, letting his thoughts run with him. Danny Fiore had always been so certain of precisely where he was headed. For Rob, he'd been a touchstone, a talisman. Without him, Rob wasn't sure where his own life was going. His career was established. He had more money than he would ever know what to do with. But there was an emptiness inside him that threatened to swallow his soul.

He was thirty-three years old, too old to be sleeping in beds all over town. What he needed was some kind of normalcy to his life. Something permanent. Somebody waiting for him when he came home from the road. Danny's death had forced him to face the truth. His life was going down the toilet, and if he didn't make some changes soon, he was in danger of turning into one of those wild-eyed, grizzled hermits who lived among piles of moldering newspapers and spoke to nobody but the cat.

And that was precisely who was waiting for him upon his return. Igor, fresh from a long nap and primed for nocturnal adventure. He let the cat out, stripped off his clothes, and showered. Alone. Toweled off and climbed into his bed, still alone. Turned on the stereo and lay there pondering the mysteries of the universe while Bob Seger crooned a haunting refrain about loneliness, about lost loves and missed chances down on Main Street.

He picked up the telephone. It was 2:30 in the morning on the East Coast, but Casey answered on the first ring. "Hey," he said.

"Hey, yourself."

He shifted the telephone receiver, positioned himself more comfortably in the bed. "You weren't sleeping," he said.

"Bad night. You?"

"Bad night."

"No hot date?" she said.

He thought fleetingly of Kitty Callahan. Not even close. Not tonight. He cleared his throat. "No hot date," he said. "How are you? Really?"

"I won't lie and say it's easy, because it isn't. But I'm surviving, one hour at a time."

"You could come visit me. Hop on a plane and get out of the ice and snow."

"It's too soon. I need to be here right now." She paused. "He's here," she said. "In this house. Everywhere I look."

"I know, sweetheart."

"Right now, that's what I need. It's all I have."

He sighed, but didn't argue. He rolled onto his side and shifted the phone to his other ear. "You'd tell me," he said, "if you were in trouble. Right?"

"I'm not in trouble. I told you, I'm stronger than you think. You're the one I'm worried about."

"Don't be," he said gruffly. "I'm fine."

"Don't lie to me, Flash. You're not handling this well."

He wrapped the coiled telephone wire once around his hand. Twice. "I'm handling it," he said, "the only way I know how."

"And that's the same thing I'm doing."

"I'm one hell of a comfort," he said, disgusted with himself. "I shouldn't have called."

"Rob," she said softly, "what's wrong?"

He took a deep breath. Unwound the cord from his hand. "I went out with Kitty tonight," he said. "Kitty Callahan. I slept with her. It's not the first time."

Softly, she said, "And?"

"I didn't feel a goddamn thing. She's a nice girl, but I didn't feel a goddamn thing. What does that say about me?"

"That you were lonely. It's not something to be ashamed of."

"I'm thirty-three years old," he said. "I'm too old for bed-hopping."

"Yes," she said. "You are."

He plumped the pillow behind his head, propped himself against it. "You never talk about Katie," he said. "Does it bother you? To talk about her?"

"It doesn't bother me. Sometimes it makes other people uncomfortable. Why?"

He toyed with the telephone cord. "I was just wondering what it feels like. To have a kid of your own."

"For me," she said, "it was the most incredible feeling of love I'd ever known. I don't think you can understand the depth of that kind of love until you've experienced it. You'd fight off snarling wolves for that child. You'd give your life gladly. And the feeling you get from knowing that you and the person you love most in the world created that exquisite creature together, that it came from an act of love, is the most profound emotion you'll ever experience."

"One I'll probably never know," he said darkly.

"Yes," she said. "You will. I promise. It'll happen."

"I have to go," he said. "It's the middle of the night. You need your sleep."

"I don't sleep much these days."

"I'm sorry," he said. "The last thing you need right now is me dumping my pathetic little life into your lap."

"Wrong. I'm grateful for the distraction."

"Oh. Well, in that case, I guess it's okay."

"It's always okay. You know that."

"I know. Next time it's your turn to cry on my shoulder."

"I've done more than my share of that lately," she said.
"We have a mile or two to walk before we even up those odds."

"Get some sleep," he told her. "That's an order."

"And you know just how good I am at taking orders."

The corner of his mouth twitched. "G'night," he said.

"Night, lovey."

He hung up the phone and lay there in the darkness,
soothed by the strength of the aura that surrounded her, and fell
asleep thinking about what she'd said.

***

When Trish, trying to be helpful, sent Danny's suede jacket
out to be cleaned, Casey tumbled headfirst into the abyss.

Her sister-in-law was suitably repentant, but the damage
was already done. The coat had held Danny's scent, and had
comforted her through several extremely dark nights. It came
back minus the blood and the broken glass, and smelling of
chemicals. Trish looked so contrite that Casey didn't have the
heart to scream at her. "Just leave, please," she said, and Trish,
not knowing what else to do, got in her car and drove home.

Curled up in a ball on the kitchen floor with the jacket in
her arms, her face crushed against it, the scent of leather
mingling with that of cleaning compound, she wept and ranted
into the dark, empty house, her own voice echoing back to her
because nobody else was there. She smashed dishes, put her foot
through an old door. Broke her favorite crystal pitcher, then
sliced her hand and watched helplessly as the bright red lifeblood
flowed out of her. She cried until there were no more tears left,
and then she fell asleep on the couch, her head cradled on
Danny's jacket.

The next morning, she picked up the broken glass and drew
the shades. There was no sense in leaving them open, for she no
longer had any interest in anything outside her windows. She
stopped answering the telephone, stopped reading the mail,
turned away visitor after visitor until they finally stopped

coming. Sometimes she remembered to eat. Sometimes she didn't. But it didn't matter. Nothing mattered any more, because the light had left her life and the world had gone dark.

After a time, she stopped combing her hair. Sometimes she wore the same clothes for a week. There were days when she didn't bother to get out of bed. It was easier to lie there in her darkened bedroom and pretend she couldn't hear the ringing of the phone. Easier to ignore the messages Rob kept leaving on her machine. Eventually, tired of it all, she unplugged the phone and put the answering machine on a shelf in the closet. That put an end to the aggravation once and for all. And each gray and shapeless day drifted into the next.

Until the day Rob MacKenzie came calling.

CHAPTER TWENTY-NINE

With his untamed mane of blond curls, he looked like an enraged lion, pacing her kitchen. "What the hell is going on here?" he said. "You don't answer my phone calls, you ignore my letters—" He abruptly stopped pacing and stared at her. "And you look," he said, "like bloody fucking hell. Why hasn't anybody done anything about the way you're living?"

She tried to focus on his words, but it was difficult. Grappling with his final sentence, she said, "What's wrong with the way I'm living?"

"For starters, you'd disappear if you turned around sideways. When was the last time you ate something?"

She tried to remember, but couldn't. Shrugging, she said, "Sometime yesterday, I guess."

"What are you trying to do, Fiore? Starve yourself to death? And look at this mausoleum. Doesn't the light ever get in? You're starting to look like Dracula." His mouth thinned into a grim line. "I never thought I'd see the day you'd do this to yourself."

"Damn it, Rob, how long have you had this God complex? It doesn't become you."

He set his jaw at an obstinate angle. "It looks better on me than that crown of thorns does on you."

She narrowed her eyes. "Just what is that supposed to mean?"

"They burned Joan of Arc. Back in those days, martyrdom was in style."

With deadly calm, she said, "Are you through?"

"Through? *Hah!* I've only just begun!"

"By all means, then, MacKenzie, spill it!"

He squared his shoulders. "The man is dead, Fiore. That's spelled D-E-A-D."

"I know how the hell it's spelled!"

"He isn't coming back. No matter what you do, he's *not coming back.* And damn it, woman, you didn't die with him!"

"Maybe I wish I had!"

She spun away from him, but he was quicker. He caught

her by the hand. "Tough," he said. "You didn't." He thrust the hand up in front of her face. "You see this? You cut it, it bleeds." He dropped her hand and stalked to the window and yanked on the shade, and it snapped up with a sharp crack. "I want to see an end to this—" He yanked on another shade. "And this—" He yanked so hard on the third one that it fell with a clatter to the floor. "And this!"

Atremble with fury, she said, "This is my house. You have no right!"

"I have every goddamn right in the world. This is morbid, Casey. The man's been dead for six months. You can't hide forever. You've got brains, you've got looks, you've got more talent in your little finger than I've got in my whole body. You're the best damn friend I've ever had, and by God, I won't let you die up here in the sticks just because nobody else cares enough to help you!"

"Maybe I want to die! Maybe my life ended when that car went over that embankment!"

"Bullshit! Do you still think life is what your Mama taught you? Clean underwear and proper etiquette and 2 point 5 kids and a house in the suburbs? All neat and pretty and ordered, with blooming rosebushes and the lawn trimmed? Well, it isn't. It's a lie. It's all a fucking lie!"

"Get out of here," she said dully. "Leave me alone."

"Not until I've said what I came to say!"

"I don't want to hear it."

"Tough. You're going to hear it anyway." He shoved her into a chair and pinned her hands to the chair arms. "Life isn't pretty or nice," he said, "and you won't go to heaven for being a good girl. Life is flesh and blood, it's tears and sweat and spit. It's being born and dying and all the crap you have to go through in between." His voice thinned to a sharp, hard edge. "It's slow, sweet fucking and it's a saxophone wailing in the night. And you only get one shot at it, baby, so you'd better grab it now before it's too late, because once you're gone, none of it will have meant a damn thing!" He released her abruptly and went to the window and stood there with his forehead pressed against the glass.

For a moment she sat there with her mouth hanging open.

Then her anger caught up with her. "That was very nice," she said. "Have you thought of setting it to music?"

He looked defeated. "You haven't heard a word I've said, have you?"

"Are you finished, MacKenzie?"

"Yeah." He sighed. "I'm finished."

"Fine. You know where the door is. Take it. I don't want to see you, I don't want to hear from you, I don't want to smell you! Get the hell out of my house and my life. *Capisce?*"

"I *capisce*. But when it all falls down around you, don't come crying to me to wet-nurse you, because I just might have something better to do!" He stalked across the room and through the shed, and slammed the door with so much force, the house shook.

She ran to the door and opened it and flung the words at his retreating back. "Insufferable jackass Irishman!"

He paused with the car door open, and the sunset gave his blond curls a reddish glow. "Go to hell," he said.

The rented car spattered rocks and gravel in all directions as he backed it down the driveway and screamed off at breakneck speed. She slammed the door as hard as she could, but she was surprised by the lack of satisfaction the act gave her.

***

The minute Jesse Lindstrom opened his door, Rob blew through it, tracking in mud all over Jesse's clean floors. "What the hell is wrong with you people?" he said. "Are you all stupid, or is it just that you don't give a damn?"

To his credit, Jesse calmly shut the door and leaned against the frame. "Care to clarify that?" he said.

"That woman," he said, pointing in the general direction of Casey's house, "is sitting up there on that hill, and I don't think she's combed her hair in a month." He began pacing, heedless of the mess his size elevens were making on polished oak. "Or eaten anything, for that matter." Scowling, he said, "She's so goddamn thin, it hurts to look at her. She's sitting there in the dark, trying to commit slow suicide, and doing a damn good job of it." He paused just long enough to glare at Jesse. "How the hell can you ignore it? Doesn't anybody in this godforsaken wilderness give a damn about her?"

Jesse folded his arms and casually studied his cuticle. "You finished?" he said.

Rob paused in his pacing. He was breathing hard, like he'd just run the Boston Marathon. He squared his jaw. "Why?" he said.

"Take off the sneakers," Jesse said, "and I might invite you in for a beer."

They drank it in the living room, in front of the hearth. Rob propped his feet on the edge of the coffee table. "Nice fireplace," he said grudgingly.

"You get rebuffed enough times," Jesse said, "after a while, you stop trying."

Rob studied the label on his bottle of Bud. "Couldn't you see what was going on?" he said.

"She's a grown woman," Jesse pointed out. "There's only so much anybody can do."

Rob scowled at him. "Speak for yourself," he said.

"It looks to me," Jesse said, "like what she wants to do is curl up into a ball and die."

"Too bad. It's not on my list of preferred activities for the bereaved."

Jesse took a sip of beer. "You going back over there tonight?"

"Depends." Rob slowly rolled the beer bottle between his palms. Darkly, he said, "I don't suppose you'd happen to know if she owns any firearms?"

Jesse wasn't quite successful at hiding a smile. "I do believe," he said, "that she's a pacifist."

"Damn it," Rob said. "I wasn't supposed to like you. I had myself all pumped up to hate your guts."

"I suppose it would be an odd friendship," Jesse said. "You being you, and me being me."

"And your taste in beer," Rob told him, "is beyond pathetic."

"Really."

"Friends," he said pointedly, "don't allow friends to drink rotgut. I happen to know that the local grocery store here in

Dogpatch carries Heineken. And if we're talking about doing any serious drinking to cement this friendship, then we're damn-well going into town and picking up a couple of six-packs."

Jesse drained his beer and set the bottle on the end table. Stretched out his legs and planted his feet on the floor. "Well, then," he said, "what are we waiting for?"

***

He came hammering at her door the next morning. Casey tied the belt of her ratty old terrycloth robe tighter around her and went to answer the door. He had one shoulder propped against the frame and was wearing that ingenuous little boy look that women of all ages found so irresistible. "Still speaking to me?" he said.

She opened the door farther and stepped back so he could come inside. "Ah, coffee," he said, closing his eyes and inhaling. "You knew I was coming."

"Let's say I had a pretty good idea."

"And I don't imagine you have a meat cleaver hidden anywhere in the folds of that robe. Which, by the way, is a prime candidate for the rag bin."

"I wouldn't talk if I were you," she said. "You look like you slept in your clothes."

"It wasn't the first time, and it probably won't be the last." He followed his nose to the coffee pot and poured himself a cup. Leaned against the counter to drink it. Eyeing her over the rim of the cup, he said, "How much weight have you lost?"

"How should I know? I threw out the bathroom scale months ago."

"You look like shit."

She crossed her arms. "Thank you, Doctor MacKenzie, for that learned diagnosis."

"When was the last time you left the house?"

"Give me a minute," she snapped, "and I'll check my appointment book."

They glared at each other. He uncrossed and recrossed those bony ankles. "You're not half as tough as you think," he said.

"Probably not," she said. "Where'd you spend the night?"

"On Jesse's couch."

They'd been friends for fourteen years, and still he could surprise her. "Really," she said.

"I want you to take a shower and comb your hair," he said, "and try to find something to wear that won't fall off and embarrass me."

"Oh? Are we going somewhere?"

"After I feed you, we are. That is, if you have any food in this joint."

The shower was heavenly. In its warmth, she felt as though she were washing away the remnants of some stranger who had taken over her body. She vigorously toweled her hair, then brushed it back from her face. It had been some time since she'd looked in a mirror. Her face was gaunt and drawn, her cheekbones visibly prominent. Her shirt hung off her shoulders, and her jeans were so loose that she needed a belt to hold them up.

Like an obedient child, she sat demurely at the kitchen table. Rob plunked a bowl of oatmeal down in front of her. "It was all I could find," he said. "What in hell have you been living on?"

"Instant potato. Minute Rice. Canned beans." She spooned sugar on the oatmeal and dug in, astonished by her appetite. "Aren't you eating?"

"I'll pass."

She held out a sticky spoonful of oatmeal. He eyed it suspiciously, then leaned over the table and opened his mouth. Licked the spoon clean. "There," he said, and swallowed. "You eat the rest. That's an order."

She cleaned out her bowl, then looked hopefully around the kitchen. "No toast?" she said.

"I had to throw out the bread. It was green. Where the hell are your shoes?"

"In the shed. You're a really obnoxious human being when you're bossy like this. Have I ever told you that?"

"Once or twice over the years." He went into the shed and rummaged around, came back and tossed her shoes with a thud on the floor at her feet. "Dress your feet."

It was the first week of June, and the world wore the rich, breathtaking green of early summer. Beside the back steps, her lupines pledged allegiance to the sun, and in the velvet pastures that lined the river road, dandelions grew in wild profusion.

They were there before she realized where he was taking her. He drove through the open cemetery gate and up the hill, stopping beneath the giant elm at the top. When he turned off the car, the whine of a distant lawnmower cut the silence. She inhaled the pungent scent of fresh-mown grass. "What in hell are we doing here?" she asked.

"Don't you think it's time?"

Wild daisies grew between the gravestones, and from somewhere, on the breeze, came a wispy scent of roses. Rob held out his hand. She gripped it hard, and together they stood over a simple granite headstone that read *Daniel Fiore 1951-1987.* Softly, he said, "I never realized how big a part of my life he was. Not until he was gone."

"This is the first time I've been here," she said. "I couldn't make myself do it."

"I brought something. Be right back." He released her hand and walked off across the grass. She knelt by the headstone, touched the polished granite with a fingertip. He returned carrying a gardening trowel and a flat of yellow and purple pansies. Kneeling beside her, he said, "I thought the place could use a little jazzing up."

She bit her lip as her eyes filled and overflowed. He dropped the trowel and took her hand. "I made you cry," he said. "I'm sorry."

"I hate to have to admit this, Flash, but you're a very nice man."

"Yeah? You think so?" He cocked his head and smiled crookedly from behind wispy blond curls, showing her a glimpse of the man who'd stolen so many feminine hearts over the years. He reached out his thumb and wiped a tear from her cheek. "You're not so bad yourself, pudding. Are you with me on this?"

"I'm with you, hot stuff. You dig, I'll plant."

She took out each plant separately, carefully untangled the roots, tucked them into the holes he made and then filled in around them with rich, black potting soil. When they were done, she tamped down the soil and he watered the tender young plants from a plastic container he took from the trunk. They stood back to survey their handiwork and he draped an arm loosely around her shoulder. "Feel better?" he said.

"Yes," she said, surprised to discover that it was the truth. "Thank you."

"So where would you like to go, pudding?"

"I can't go anywhere," she said. "I'm not ready."

"You're going. It's not optional. But it's your call, sweetcakes. Anyplace at all. London, Paris, Newark—"

"The beach," she said with sudden and absolute certainty. "I want to go to the beach." And experienced an exhilaration she hadn't felt in half a year.

School wouldn't be out of session for another week, so the summer hordes hadn't yet hit the North Atlantic beaches. They shared the mile-long strip of sand with a bevy of gulls and a handful of young mothers with pre-schoolers. The sand seared the bare soles of her feet, and when they reached the water's edge, he made her close her eyes. "This is silly," she said.

"Shut up and do what I say. Take a deep breath. Good. Now let it out and take another one. And tell me what you smell."

Eyes still closed, she breathed in again, deeply. "Salt water," she said. "Seaweed." She sifted and categorized the sensations that accosted her from every angle. "Roses," she said in surprise. "I smell roses."

"We passed them coming in."

"And you," she said. "I smell you."

"Me?" he said.

She opened her eyes and smiled. "You just smell like...you."

He chucked her under the chin. "Okay, kiddo," he said, "close those eyes again. This time I want you to tell me what you hear."

She bit her lip in concentration. "The roaring of the surf," she said. "I hear it breaking, behind me, before it hits the shore." Still concentrating, she added, "and I hear the hiss it makes as it rolls back into the sea."

"Good," he said. "What else?"

"Gulls. And children, laughing."

"And what do you feel?"

"Hot sand. Hot sun. Sticky ocean spray. And your hands on my shoulders."

He was silent for a single heartbeat. And then he removed his hands. "You can open your eyes now," he said.

She blinked at the sun's brightness. "Do you understand why we just did this little exercise?" he said.

Her throat tightened, and she swallowed. "Yes," she said.

"I meant every word I said yesterday, Fiore. You're thirty-one years old. You're not ready for the boneyard yet. And I'm not ready to let go of you. I don't know what I'd do without you."

"You'd do what you always do," she said. "You're like a red rubber ball. You just bounce back, no matter what."

"Yeah, well, I haven't been doing such a great job of bouncing these last six months."

Side by side, they walked barefoot along the narrow strip of wet sand at the water's edge. Rob shoved his hands into his pockets. "Why didn't you tell me?" he said. "You promised you'd tell me if you got into trouble."

Casey folded her arms across her chest. "I couldn't," she said.

He gave her a look that spoke volumes. "All right," she conceded, "I chose not to."

"Why?"

"I didn't think you'd understand. If you haven't experienced it, you can't begin to comprehend."

"What about the music? I saw you flinch when I turned on the car radio."

"I couldn't do it any more." Ahead of them, a pair of laughing children ran into the surf. It rushed in and caught them, and they squealed in delight. "My whole life with Danny was set to a soundtrack," she said. "I can't untangle the music and the memories. Everything that happened to us for thirteen years has a song attached." They passed the two kids, who were rolling in the sand like overgrown pups. "I can tell you exactly what was playing on the radio the first time we made love. And the last time." She stopped abruptly, bit her lip. "I couldn't deal with it any longer. When Danny died, so did the music."

"It's not over," he said. "You have years and years ahead of you. Good ones."

"I'm not sure I care any more."

"Too damn bad. I care."

She slipped her hands into the pockets of her jeans. "What do I have to look forward to, anyway?"

"Jesus, Casey, it's not like you're some dried-up old prune. You're young and gorgeous and sexy—"

She snorted, loudly and inelegantly. "You can cut the bull, MacKenzie. I looked in the mirror this morning. I could be a poster child for Auschwitz."

"You just need to put a little weight back on. You'll get it all back."

"What makes you so sure?"

"Because if you don't start eating, I'll put my foot up your ass."

"How touching."

"I'm telling you, Fiore, you'll have men swarming around you thicker than a flock of gulls circling a tuna sandwich."

In her pockets, she clenched her fists. "Clever analogy," she said, "but I don't want men swarming around me."

"I'm just warning you what's going to happen."

Suddenly furious, she wheeled around to confront him. "Listen to me," she said, "and listen good. There will be no men. There's only been one man, ever. *Only one.* As far as I'm concerned, there *are* no other men. And there aren't going to be. That part of my life is over. Kaput. *Finis.* Do you understand?"

He opened his mouth to speak, then clamped it abruptly shut. Squared his jaw. "I get it," he said.

"Good. See that you don't forget it."

CHAPTER THIRTY

Three days after Rob left, she called Jesse and he came over with Dad's old John Deere and plowed her garden. The next day, she started planting. She knew she was getting a late start, but the garden was more symbolism than practicality anyway, and even if nothing grew, working in the rich, moist soil was good for her soul. She started running again, slowly at first as she built up her endurance, and then she couldn't be stopped. She ran eight miles a day, began eating like a lumberjack, making up for lost time, and watched as the pounds reappeared and she grew strong and lean and muscular again. She joined the garden club, renewed her library card, began volunteering at the hospital.

As the weeks went by, she talked to Rob often on the phone, but he was tied up with his new album and was anticipating another lengthy road tour, so he didn't have time to visit. He was uncharacteristically mute regarding his love life, and she wondered what had ever become of Christine Hamilton. For all she knew, they were still seeing each other. The idea left a strange sensation in the pit of her stomach, so she avoided thinking about it.

Summer eased into fall, and fall into winter. Jesse kept her driveway plowed, and she reciprocated by baking him bread and having him over to the house for dinner once or twice a week. Sometimes they went to the movies together. She'd known Jesse all her life, and he was easy to be with. They went ice fishing together, snowmobiling, to the high school's winter carnival. She even accompanied him to a couple of school board meetings.

Somehow, she survived that long, dreary winter. In March, seemingly overnight, winter gave way to the first flush of spring, and she had to wear rubber boots just to get to the mailbox. She got her car stuck in the quagmire at the end of her driveway and had to call AAA to come and pull it out. Danny had been gone for more than a year, and the pain was gradually losing its fierce edge.

Spring gave way to the hottest summer in ten years. The Fourth of July dawned blistering and muggy. At noon, the entire clan gathered in Trish and Bill's back yard to feast on lobsters and steamed clams, hot dogs and hamburgers. While Bill alternated between manning the grill and showing off his vegetable garden, Casey and Trish and Millie waded through dogs and cats and kids, boyfriends and girlfriends and assorted playmates to set the picnic table with gargantuan bowls of potato and macaroni salad, cole slaw, home-canned pickles, five dozen freshly baked yeast rolls, an enormous plastic keg of lemonade, and the biggest strawberry shortcake in three counties.

When Billy and Alison arrived with their new baby, all the women took turns making a fuss over him, but it was Casey who got final custody. "You just go enjoy yourself," she told Alison. "I'll take care of this little guy."

She didn't have to offer twice. Alison gave her a grateful smile before going off hand-in-hand with Billy to inspect his father's garden. Casey buried her face in the baby's belly. "Oh, you sweet thing," she said. "I can hardly wait to spoil you."

"Sorry," Trish told her, "but Grampa Bill already bought the franchise."

"You and Bill," Casey said, "grandparents. It's hard to believe. You're too young."

"You're telling me. I thought I'd have a stroke when we found out Alison was pregnant. Babies having babies. But it seems to be working out. Ali's a nice girl, and Billy's crazy about her and the baby."

Casey found a shady spot and settled down to feed little Willie his bottle. He fell asleep in her arms, and she balanced him on one arm while she picked halfheartedly at the plate of food that Jesse brought her. She was studying the miniature curled fists, transfixed, when Trish sat down on the grass beside her. "You know," her sister-in-law said, "it's not too late for you."

"Too late for what?"

"To have another baby."

She snorted. "Be serious. I'm thirty-two years old."

"And we both know that age doesn't mean doodly-poop. Women are having babies in their forties and loving it. Compared to them, you're practically a teenager."

"Besides," Casey said, "I happen to be lacking one

essential ingredient: a husband."

"So? Get married."

"I suppose you have someone picked out? Like maybe your brother?"

"You could do worse."

"Jesse and I are just friends."

"Being friends is a place to start. Look, hon, I'm really not trying to push. But the two of you seem to get along so well, and there has to be some attraction there. After all, you were engaged once."

"Fifteen years ago! We were children!"

"And God knows, that boy needs a mother."

Appalled, she said, "You think I should marry the man because his son needs a mother?"

"There are worse reasons for getting married."

"What about love?"

"I hate to be the one to break it to you, sweetie, but you can get pretty lonely sitting in your ivory tower, waiting for love to come along."

"I'm not waiting for anything," she said, "and I am most certainly not marrying your brother."

"Well," Trish said, patting her arm with maternal concern, "you think about it."

She had no intention of thinking about it. She couldn't believe Trish could suggest such a thing, as though Danny were no more than a worn-out winter coat she could simply replace with next year's model.

The kids began a rousing game of volleyball, and as she watched their young, strong limbs, so tanned and muscular, nineteen seemed a lifetime ago. She wondered if it was normal to feel this old, this tired, this used-up at thirty-two. "Good lord, woman," she said aloud, "you're morbid. Snap out of it." She kicked off her shoes, handed the baby over to Trish, and joined the volleyball game. The physical activity was invigorating, the company stimulating. Swept up in the excitement, she forgot to feel sorry for herself.

At dusk, she and Jesse loaded a half-dozen teenagers into the bed of his pickup and drove into town to watch the fireworks. The kids disappeared into the crowd before Casey could finish spreading a blanket on the grassy riverbank. She looked at Jesse, and he shrugged. "Old-timer's disease," he said. "They wouldn't want to be seen in public with us. It might rub off."

She sat on the blanket with Jesse in the gathering darkness, watching people and fighting off mosquitoes. There was something about hometowns that made a fireworks display special. The ear-splitting booms, the collective *ahhhs* from the crowd, the children dancing joyously as they waved sparklers above their heads. It had something to do with tradition, something to do with the sense of community that was such an important part of small-town life.

It was over too soon. She and Jesse were folding the blanket when Mikey came running with a friend in tow. "Can I stay tonight at Troy's house?" he asked. "He just got the new Space Blasters game I was telling you about."

"Did you ask his parents?"

"My mom said it was okay," Troy said. "She's right over there."

Jesse looked and waved. "Okay," he said, "as long as Troy's parents don't care. But—"

He never got to finish his sentence. The boys were already gone. Casey hugged the blanket to her chest and grinned. "Parental influence," she said. "Gives you a real feeling of power, doesn't it?"

Her nieces, Jenny and Kristin, were sitting on the tailgate of the truck, waiting for them. The other kids had all dispersed in various directions, so the four of them squeezed into the cab. Casey listened as her nieces rattled on about the fireworks and about who was dating whom. When they dropped the girls off, Trish came out on the doorstep to wave, and Jesse said dryly, "My sister's been pushing me at you, hasn't she?"

"How did you know?"

"She's been doing the same thing with me. I told her I'm thirty-four years old and my sex life is my own business."

"Do you think she took the hint?"

He smiled wryly. "Probably not. With Trish, you need a sledgehammer to make a point."

Not wanting to go into that big, empty house alone, she invited him to stay. They killed an hour drinking lemonade and making easy conversation on the porch swing. After he left, she loaded their glasses into the dishwasher and tried to read. But it was unbearably hot, the night sounds of the old house were distracting, and the emptiness gnawed at her insides. She decided to take a cool shower. The water felt glorious, but the moment she stepped out from beneath the spray, the heat and the emptiness closed in on her again.

She tied her robe around her and went into the bedroom and sat on the edge of the bed, looking at the phone. She picked it up, listened to the dial tone, then hung up. It was one in the morning, ten o'clock California time, and Rob probably wasn't home. Most likely, he was at some wild July Fourth celebration that would go on for three days. And if he was home, he was probably partying in private with someone slender, blond, and very young.

At one forty-five, she gave up on sleeping. At two-ten, she turned on the bedside lamp and dialed Rob's number. Three thousand miles away, he picked up the phone. "Hey," she said.

"Hey, light of my life."

"Happy Fourth of July. Am I interrupting anything?"

"Yeah. I'm sitting here sharing a can of cold ravioli with Igor."

"That's revolting. How can you eat that slop?"

"I happen to like that slop. And so does Igor. So how'd you celebrate the Fourth?"

"I went to a barbecue at Bill's house, and then I watched the fireworks with Jesse."

"The two of you are getting pretty cozy lately. Started picking out china patterns yet?"

"Jackass," she said.

"I've told you this before," he said, "and I'll tell you again. It is legally and ethically impossible to be unfaithful to a dead man."

"Thanks," she said. "Whatever would I do if I didn't have you around to tell me how to run my life?"

"You'd probably learn to do it yourself."

"Why do I feel as though I've heard this lecture before?"

"You have. But last time, I was on the receiving end." He paused. "You know," he said thoughtfully, "maybe it's time we weaned ourselves."

Her fingers tightened on the telephone receiver. "What's that supposed to mean?"

"Has it ever occurred to you that our relationship might be unhealthy? We use each other as a crutch. Maybe it's time we cut the umbilical cord and got on with our lives."

The silence between them was awkward and profound. Aghast, she told him, "I can't believe you said that."

"Don't go to pieces on me, Fiore. It was just a suggestion."

"Oh, really? So you think you can dump a bombshell like that in my lap and expect me to just forget about it?"

"All I said was that we seem to have an unhealthy dependence on each other. From now on, I'll keep my opinions to myself."

"Fine with me, MacKenzie. As far as I'm concerned, that's exactly where they belong!" She slammed down the receiver and then, to her utter amazement, burst into tears.

The telephone rang. It shrilled five times, six, while she sat with folded arms, rocking back and forth, tears streaming down her cheeks. On the twenty-third ring, she picked it up. "I'm sorry," Rob said. "I really don't mean to be an asshole. I think it's some kind of genetic defect."

With a shuddering breath, she wiped her wet cheek on the back of her hand. "Why is it," she said, "that I can never stay mad at you?"

"In spite of your best efforts, Fiore, you love me."

"You must be right. I can't think of any other reason I'd continue to put up with the misery you bring into my life."

"Listen, babe, I have this enormous steak in my freezer that has your name written all over it. Why don't you come spend a few days with me? I promise to keep my mouth shut."

She needed some time away, some time to come to terms with herself, to think about where she was going with her life. She reached for a tissue and swiped at her nose. "Yes," she said, "I'll come. And you don't have to keep your mouth shut. I love you just the way you are."

***

Lost and ignored in the crush of people at LAX, Casey worked her way toward the baggage claim. A skycap wheeling a mountain of luggage nearly ran her over, and she ducked to avoid a collision. Rob had promised to meet her, but in this swarm she'd never find him. She clutched her carry-on more tightly, and then she saw him through an opening in the crowd. Hands tucked loosely in his pockets, wearing dark glasses and the godawful felt hat she'd wanted to burn for a decade, he looked cool and untouched by the mayhem that surrounded him. Rob MacKenzie was a conundrum, a law unto himself, wearing $250 Nikes with a pair of scruffy jeans he'd owned since high school. And he looked good enough to eat.

When he saw her, he held out both hands, palms up, as if to indicate he was unarmed, then gave her a smile that contained enough wattage to light the entire city of Los Angeles. She set down her carry-on and opened her arms. "Hey," she said.

"Hey, sweetheart."

They embraced warmly, and then she stepped back and he planted a kiss on the top of her head. "You look spectacular," he said.

She was wearing her traveling clothes, jeans and a tee shirt, and she looked down at herself in surprise. "Me?" she said. "Spectacular?"

"You've got a tan that any one of my sisters would kill for."

"Believe me," she said, "I earned it. This comes from weeding the garden and mowing the lawn, not from lying under any sun lamp."

"I wouldn't expect anything less from you."

It was a sunny, smogless day, and as he drove, he kept up a steady stream of conversation, brought her up to date on the local music scene, told her who was new and who was working and who was washed up. She let him run down before she attempted conversation. "So," she said at last, "what's on the agenda for tonight?"

"You hungry?"

"Famished."

"You're in luck. I've been taking this Oriental cooking class, and I thought tonight I'd make *moo goo gai pan*. It'll knock your socks off."

He was right. The *moo goo gai pan* was out of this world. After dinner, they retired to the living room with two jelly glasses and a bottle of Chablis. "MacKenzie," she said, stretching her legs and leaning back against the couch, "you certainly do know the way to a woman's heart."

"Aha! The truth comes out. It's my cooking that keeps luring you back to my den of iniquity."

"I thought you knew," she said. "It's your record collection. You just happen to have the most extensive collection of Jimmy Buffett recordings on the planet."

"Laugh. Someday they'll be worth a fortune."

"But you'd never sell them," she said. "You're more the type to will them to the archeology department of some prestigious university. Of course, they'd reward you handsomely by naming a wing after you. The R.K. MacKenzie Clinic for the Terminally Free-Thinking, or something of that ilk."

"Are you calling me unconventional, Fiore?"

"Nobody in their right mind would call you unconventional. Eccentric, maybe, but certainly not unconventional."

"That's a relief. For a minute there, you had me worried." He stretched out his lanky legs and crossed them at the ankles. Took a sip of Chablis and studied the contents of his glass. "So," he said, "what's going on between you and Jesse?"

"Nothing's going on," she said in exasperation. "Why does everybody keep asking me that?"

"Well, for starters," he said, "you're dating him."

"Oh, for the love of God. I am not dating him. We're friends. We spend time together because we're both alone and we enjoy each other's company. But I'd hardly call it dating. I'm not in the market for another husband. I'm never getting married again."

"Never," he said thoughtfully. "I don't know, babe. Never's a long time."

"Danny would always be there between us. Nobody could ever measure up."

"I suppose it would be hard," he said, his voice gone suddenly flat, "competing with a ghost."

She looked at him in surprise. "Are you mad at me?" she said.

He squared his jaw. "I don't know," he said. "Should I be?"

"I can't imagine why."

"Look around you, Casey. Don't you ever wake up in the middle of the night and wonder why nobody's there?"

She thought of the emptiness of her king-size bed, of the black void she faced nightly. "More times than you'd care to know," she said. "But you see, I have you."

"Oh, yeah, I forgot. Damn cozy, those three thousand miles of telephone line." He folded his arms across his belly and studied his toes. Quietly, he said, "I do, you know."

"You do what?"

"Wake up in the middle of the night and wonder why nobody's there."

Inside her chest, she felt the tug of an emotion she couldn't identify. "Flash," she said, "why don't you find yourself some nice girl and get married?"

"You sound like my mother. It's not like I haven't been looking. Is it my fault that Miss Right hasn't shown up?"

"Ms. And in the immortal words of Johnny Lee, you're looking for love in all the wrong places."

"That's what my mom says. She wants me to come home to Southie and marry Mary Frances O'Reilly."

"Ah, yes," she said. "The infamous Mary Frances. Still single, is she?"

"And getting more desperate by the hour. Her biological clock is ticking like crazy."

Glenn Frey, in an earlier incarnation, was singing in full, lush stereo about taking it easy. In the flickering light of a single candle, Rob held up his Flintstones jelly glass and stared morosely into its depths. "All I know," he said, "is that something's wrong with my life, and I don't know how to fix it."

Casey rested her glass on her knee. Toying with a strand of his hair, she said, "You could do something really radical."

He leaned his head back and studied her. "Yeah? Like what?"

She wrapped one golden curl around a slender forefinger.

"Maybe move to the East Coast."

"And give up all this?"

She looked around the room. "Maybe you could buy the Hotel California and have it dismantled and moved, piece by piece."

They shared a wry grin. "I think," he said, suddenly serious, "that you're the only person in my life who's ever loved me unconditionally." He drew a pattern on his glass with a fingernail.

It was a curious thing for him to say. Still toying with his hair, she said, "How's that?"

"You accept me for what I am. You don't have any preconceived expectations. No matter what damn-fool thing I do, you love me anyway." He turned his jelly glass in his hand. "Do you realize how old this thing is? They had these when I was a kid. It's probably an antique by now."

***

They spent the next few days in the studio, re-recording and remixing portions of his new album, drinking murky coffee and eating stale doughnuts and cold pizza. She'd been away from all this long enough to have forgotten the exhilaration she felt surrounded by the lively chaos of a recording studio. This was a world she understood, a world a million miles away from the one she'd been living in since Danny died.

A little after nine on Saturday night, exhausted but pleased with the way the session had gone, they wound things to a close. As Casey was boxing up the remains of the pizza, Niall, one of the sound engineers, swung his jacket over his shoulder and said, "A bunch of us are stopping by the Blue Onion for a while. You two want to come with us?"

"What's the Blue Onion?" she said.

"It's a blues club," Rob said around the pencil clenched between his teeth. He tucked a cluster of sheet music into a leather portfolio, dropped in the pencil, and zipped it up. "They opened up about three months ago."

"Very hot," Niall added.

"This isn't one of those see-and-be-seen places, is it?"

Pizza box in hand, Casey looked down at her jeans and flannel shirt. "I'm not exactly dressed for going out."

"It's very low-key," Niall said. "Ultra casual."

"Everybody's there for the same reason," Rob said. "To drink, to dance, and to hear some of the best blues on the West Coast."

"Sounds like my kind of place," she said. "Let's go."

The Blue Onion was a musician's hangout, liberally sprinkled with familiar faces, people Casey had known and worked with over the years. There were a few well-knowns scattered among the crowd, but the majority were the backbone of the music industry, the studio musicians, the songwriters, the backup singers who made the stars of the industry sound good on vinyl, tape, or CD. As usual, she was the lone woman at the table, and as usual, the guys talked shop. It was inevitable. Get a bunch of musicians together, and you could almost guarantee that they'd be either listening to music, making music, or talking about making music. Frequently, it was a combination of the three. Over the years, the talk had changed; new words like *MIDI* and *download* showed up with regularity. Computers had taken over the recording industry—to its detriment, some believed. Certainly the new technology had put a number of sessions musicians out on the street. Electronic technology was cheaper and easier in the long run than live musicians, so competition for available jobs was fierce, and only the strongest and the best survived.

Other things had changed over the years, too. Looking around the table, Casey realized that their group was aging. Receding hairlines and graying ponytails weren't uncommon, and most of the guys here tonight would have a drink or two and then go home to their wives and kids. Only Niall and Rob remained single. Casey took a sip of beer, closed her eyes and let the music take her.

Ah, the music. It was rich and earthy, cool and jazzy, hot and steamy, with a disturbing, primitive sexual rhythm that moved her in a way she'd never been able to translate into words. Her response to the blues was overwhelmingly physical, visceral and erotic, bringing to mind something she'd heard Rob say years ago: *Good blues is like good sex; you can feel it from your toenails to the roots of your hair.* She opened her eyes and caught him watching her, and she flushed red-hot. He casually rested his elbow on the back of her chair while he continued his conversation with Mike Andreason. Crowded together as they were, six of them sitting around a table designed for no more than three, she was crammed tight against him, hip to hip, thigh to thigh, knee to knee. He gave off so much heat, she could feel dampness forming under her arms and beneath the collar of her shirt. She discreetly peeled the damp fabric away from her chest, wondering why on earth she'd worn flannel, in California, in July.

Rob shifted position, rested his hand on the back of her neck. She shot him a quick, speculative glance, but he was still deep in conversation, slumped on his tailbone with those long legs spread wide before him, seemingly oblivious to her. Casey took another sip of beer, relaxed into his warmth, and made a halfhearted attempt to follow the conversation. But it was impossible; she was too distracted by the thumb that was lazily stroking the tender flesh just behind her left ear. Had he been any other man on the planet, she would have thought he was coming on to her. But Rob was an extremely physical person, eminently comfortable inside his body and free with his affection, and she doubted he even realized what he was doing.

She, on the other hand, was excruciatingly aware of what he was doing. And if he didn't stop doing it, she was going to experience nuclear meltdown, right here at the table. She reached up and removed his hand, then patted his shoulder. "Bathroom run," she said. "Be right back."

She stood in front of the mirror in the powder room beside a leggy twenty-year-old blonde who was applying eyeliner. Feeling like the frumpy country mouse, Casey splashed cool water on her face and the back of her neck. The window was open, a soft breeze drifting in, and she undid the top button of her flannel shirt for ventilation. The blonde eyed her distastefully before pulling out lipstick and pursing pouty lips that would have given Jagger a run for his money. Ignoring her, Casey took out her brush and tried to tame her hair into some semblance of order. But it was useless; the humidity inevitably removed what little body it had and left it limp and straight as a stick. She gave up, crammed the brush back into her purse and left the blonde to her toilette.

A friend of Niall's had shanghaied Casey's chair, so she stood behind Rob with her hands resting lightly on his shoulders, her body swaying restlessly to the rhythm of the music. He reached up, caught her hands in his and leaned his head back. "Wanna dance, sweet stuff?" he said.

He didn't have to ask twice. When the music moved her, Casey wanted to move to the music. They found an empty spot on the dance floor and she stepped into his arms with an ease born of years of familiarity. He was warm and damp, slender and solid, and she had forgotten how wonderful it felt to be held in a man's arms, engulfed in his searing heat, pressed against a hard body from knee to shoulder. It was true what they said about people having their own unique scents; blindfolded, in a room full of people, she could still have picked Rob out by smell alone.

She wound her arms around his neck and did her best to follow his lead. Rob MacKenzie danced the way he did everything in life: full speed ahead, with rhythm and panache. He wasn't a flashy dancer, but had an innate, organic understanding of music that went light years beyond any scattered pieces of theory he'd picked up in a college classroom. He was a natural, born to make music, born to translate it into a language that other, less fortunate creatures could comprehend.

She lost all sense of time as they swayed together, bluesy ballad segueing into bluesy ballad. The humidity ceased to have meaning as they melted together like a pair of Crayolas left out too long in the sun. Her dampness was now his dampness, and his hers. She could no longer distinguish up from down, Casey from Rob, and she wondered how she could possibly be this drunk when she'd only had one beer. It had to be the music, that damned erotic music. Nothing else could explain the hollow ache inside her. Nothing else could explain why his body crushed against hers was sending sparks shooting off into the stratosphere.

She needed to get away, to get some air. To step out of his arms and walk away. But she had been overcome by an inexplicable lethargy, and a soft, insistent voice inside her was telling her that it was, after all, just dancing. Could it possibly hurt, just this once, to relax and allow herself to enjoy what she was feeling?

"Ah, Flash," she whispered, adjusting the fit of her head against his shoulder. "You feel so good."

With the tips of his fingers, he brushed the hair back from her face. "So do you, sweetheart."

"Forgive me for making a fool of myself," she said. "It's just been so long since anybody held me like this."

His cheek touched hers, the rasp of his whisker stubble sending heat through her body in a fluid rush. Gruffly, he said, "You were born to be held."

Suddenly the heat, the stuffy closeness of the room, *his* closeness, became too much for her. "I need air," she said, and like a coward she fled, leaving him standing alone in the middle of the dance floor.

Outside, she leaned up against the building and took great, gasping gulps of fresh air. Eyes squeezed shut, she bent forward from the waist, hands on her spread knees. The door opened, then closed, and beside her, in the darkness, Rob said, "Are you okay?"

"I'm fine," she said, straightening up. "I just felt a little queasy."

His hand was cool and damp against her cheek. "You don't feel feverish," he said.

Beyond his shoulder, a dying star burned out and plummeted in a streak of fire across the velvet blackness of the sky. She reached up and removed his hand. He was standing far too close. "I told you," she said. "I'm fine."

Still he didn't retreat. He ran the tip of his finger along her jaw, and her breath caught in her throat at the curious combination of pain and pleasure that was scrambling around inside her. Then the door swung open wide and a half-dozen boisterous voices broke the silence. Music and loud male laughter spilled out into the night, and Casey drew in a huge gulp of air. "I'm tired," she said. "Can we go home now?"

Rob was uncharacteristically silent as he maneuvered the sleek, black Porsche through the darkened streets of Los Angeles. He drove with the top down, and she closed her eyes and reveled in the cool air kissing her face and threading fingers through her hair as Percy Sledge crooned into the darkness about a man loving a woman.

The Hotel California was dark, and somewhere in the shrubbery beneath his landlady's parlor window, a cicada chirped his solitary song. They went up the stairs together and Rob unlocked the apartment door. He dropped his leather portfolio on the kitchen table, and Casey put the pizza box into the refrigerator. He cleared his throat. "Want a nightcap?" he said.

She closed the refrigerator door and leaned against it. "I'm tired," she said. "I think I'm just going to bed."

He didn't say anything, just propped those lanky hips against the kitchen counter and folded his arms. After a minute, she said, "Good night," and turned to walk away.

Softly, he said, "Babe?"

She paused, turned slowly to look at him. "What?" she said.

He crossed his ankles. Squared his shoulders. His jaw. "Never mind," he said. "G'night."

The bedroom was hot and sticky. She hated taking his bed away from him, but he'd insisted, the night she arrived, that she was a guest and that he would be the one sleeping on the couch. It was too hot to wear pajamas, so she peeled off her damp clothes and stood naked at the window, letting the night breeze cool her heated skin.

She cast aside the heavy bedding and lay between cool percale sheets, but sleep was elusive. The bed linens smelled of Rob, and she floundered, sleepless, wondering what on earth had gotten into her. It must have been the dancing that had made her so jangly inside that she couldn't lie still. Her breasts ached at the memory of being crushed up hard against him, and she finally fell into a restless and troubled sleep filled with erotic dreams in which a shadowy, faceless man subjected her to electrifying and unspeakable pleasures.

She woke grainy-eyed and hung over. Rob was still asleep on the couch, and she showered and put on cut-offs and her *Sexy Senior Citizen* tee shirt and went outside. In the deep shadows of morning, the grass was cool and damp between her bare toes, and

Mrs. Sullivan was on her knees, pruning the peony bush that grew at the corner of the house.

"Good morning," she said as she approached. "Your peonies are spectacular."

At eighty, Rob's landlady had blue eyes as sharp and clear as those of a young girl. "Your Mr. MacKenzie planted them for me," she said. "Three summers ago."

Casey didn't bother to clarify that he wasn't precisely *her* Mr. MacKenzie. She knelt and began picking off dead leaves. "He does a lot for you, does he?"

"I don't know what I'd do without him," Mrs. Sullivan said. "Why, just last week he fixed a leaky faucet in my kitchen. Imagine if I'd had to pay a plumber to do it." She moved on to intently examine the rosebush that climbed up the trellis beside the bay window. "Damn aphids," she said.

Casey couldn't help it; she laughed aloud. It was so unexpected, the profanity coming from that sweet, grandmotherly lady. "They're eating up my garden," the old woman explained. She picked up a sprayer and began pumping some noxious chemical onto the leaves of the rosebush. "You know," she said, "I've seen a lot of women in and out of that apartment over the years."

Casey picked up a waxy peony leaf and smoothed it against her bare thigh. "No doubt," she said.

Mrs. Sullivan glanced at her, then back at her lethal task. "But it all stopped a while back." *Squirt.* "You're the only woman he's had up there—" *Squirt, squirt.* "—in nearly two years."

She glanced up at the old woman in surprise, but before she could say anything, Rob clomped down the front steps and loped across the lawn toward them. "Hey," he said.

Casey sat back and smiled. "Hey," she said, wondering how any man could look so appealing in wrinkled gray sweats.

"Ready to run?"

"Just give me a second to run upstairs and get my sneakers."

Rob's neighborhood was flat as the proverbial pancake, so the biggest challenge to running there was finding her way back home. The streets were a maze of trees and houses that all looked alike. Every time they ran there, she was dependent on his homing instinct to keep her from getting hopelessly lost.

They skirted a parked Oldsmobile and gave a wide berth to a barking Rottweiler. "I'm going on tour next month," he said. "Want to come with me?"

"Not hardly," she said. "Not in this lifetime."

A dark-haired, dark-eyed child on a tricycle solemnly watched them pass. "Sing with me," he coaxed, "and I'll give you equal billing."

"Hah! I'd rather have my toenails yanked out, one by one."

"Where's your sense of adventure, Fiore?"

"I can tell you where it's not: crammed inside a bus, cruising America's scenic interstate highways."

"You've grown hard in your old age, woman."

"Wrong. What I've grown is smart."

They returned home aching, sweaty, and energized. He showered first, then made breakfast while she washed away the stickiness. Whatever demons she'd been chasing the night before had disappeared in the light of day. The shower revitalized her, and she sat down to breakfast with a gargantuan appetite.

Rob stirred sugar into his coffee and said, "I thought since it's your last day here, we might do something touristy."

She spread jelly on her raisin toast. "Touristy? As in Disneyland touristy?"

"We could do Disneyland. Or," he said, "we could just go down to the beach and hang out."

"I vote for hanging out," she said.

So they drove down to Venice and strolled the boardwalk. Ate greasy French fries and cotton candy, watched the surfers, the skaters, the jugglers and the kids leaping and squealing in the swirling Pacific surf. The women were all tall and blond and gorgeous, spilling out of minuscule thong bikinis that made the one she'd worn in Nassau look like a nun's habit. "Poor thing," she said, as one particularly ripe specimen skated by. "I hope she doesn't catch cold."

"It's a hardship," he said, his eyes following the skater with obvious appreciation, "living here in California. But somehow, we all muddle through."

"It must be a terrible tribulation," she said, and remembered Mrs. Sullivan's words. *You're the only woman he's had up there in nearly two years.*

He grunted and gazed out over the Pacific. Beside him, she said, "Do you ever miss the East Coast?"

"Every day of my life. Even more since you moved back east."

A cloud skittered across the face of the sun, stealing some of the day's brilliance. "I know," she said softly. "I miss you, too."

He tucked his hands into his pockets. "Did you really mean what you said, about never getting married again?"

She looked out at the ocean, now a dark, tempestuous blue. A multicolored sail appeared as a speck on the horizon. "I don't see any benefit to it," she said.

"Aside from not drying up," he said, "and dying old and alone."

"We all die alone," she said.

"You know what I meant."

"I've been in the business too long to marry a civilian. What would we talk about at the supper table? And if I married someone in the business, it would be a disaster. Two of us spending all our time on planes headed in opposite directions."

"Aren't we just Little Miss Sunshine today," he said.

"You asked. I'm answering."

"What about sex?"

She glanced sideways, but he was watching a volleyball game on the beach. "What about it?" she said.

"Do you plan to go the rest of your life without that, too?"

"I hadn't really given it much thought." *Liar!* a tiny voice inside her accused. *You've thought about it. Last night, on the dance floor. And afterward. Especially afterward.*

"You told me once that celibacy was an unnatural condition," he said. "Or did you forget?"

"Being married," she said, "isn't a prerequisite for sex. But I don't have to tell you that, do I? After all, you are the world's expert on recreational sex."

He eyed her coolly. "Are you trying to start a fight?"

"You started it," she said. "Not me."

"Damn it, Casey, this is your last day here. I don't want to fight."

Ashamed, she plucked at the sleeve of his shirt. Smoothed out a wrinkle. "Neither do I," she said.

"Then why the hell are we fighting?"

She shrugged. "I don't know," she said miserably.

He lifted his arm and she ducked her head beneath it, and he looped it around her shoulders. "Let's try to be civil," he said. "I know it goes against your nature, but we could at least try."

"Insufferable ass," she said, but without enthusiasm.

"Look," he said. "Look at the sailboat." It was racing toward them, sails billowing with a strong tailwind, veering and tacking, tilting and twisting in a riot of red and orange and yellow against a background of blue.

"It's wonderful," she said wistfully. "I've never been sailing."

"Me either." He folded both arms around her from behind and tucked her head beneath his chin. It was a perfect fit. "Maybe we could rent one sometime and try our hand at it."

Just for curiosity's sake, she allowed her fingers to explore his slender, bony wrist. The hair on his arms was soft and springy. "We'd probably drown ourselves," she said.

"There you go again," he said, "Little Miss Sunshine."

That night, they stayed up late watching an old Cary Grant movie. They overslept the next morning, and had to rush to make her flight. The line at the check-in counter was a hundred miles long, and Rob held her carry-on while she maneuvered in and out between people to check her suitcase just minutes before the flight. "Better hurry," the ticket agent said. "They just started boarding."

It was going to be close. Boarding pass in hand, she sprinted through the terminal with Rob at her side, past weary businessmen in rumpled suits, past a statuesque blonde walking a black poodle, past a family of four wearing white shorts and matching Mickey Mouse shirts. They reached the gate just as a nasal voice said over the intercom, *"This is the final boarding call for Delta Flight 1300 to Boston."*

Rob slung Casey's carry-on over her shoulder and spent a minute fiddling with the strap. His hand lingered, warm against her bare arm, as he said, "All set. Got your boarding pass?"

"Right here." She held it up for him to see.

"Call me when you get in."

She nodded, suddenly unable to speak. For the first time ever, she was having difficulty saying good-bye to him. She took his hand and threaded fingers with his, and they gripped each other tightly. They stood there looking at each other, neither of them wanting to break the physical contact.

"Oh, hell," he said, and yanked her to him and kissed her.

It was the element of surprise that brought her into his arms. It was something else that kept her there. Excitement shot through her, spiraling upward from a core of longing deep in the pit of her stomach, the same longing she'd felt on a moonlit beach in Nassau. He plunged his tongue inside her mouth, hot and wet and silken smooth, and the world tumbled and rolled around her in a mad search for equilibrium. She gasped, lungs bursting from the need to breathe, and then he placed his hands on her shoulders and slowly, reluctantly, pushed her away. "Go," he said raggedly. "You'll miss your plane."

It took her a moment or two to come back, and then reality seeped in. *Airport. Home. DC-10.* "Shit," she said, possibly the first time in her life that she had ever uttered the word. She hesitated, one hand absently toying with the collar of his shirt.

"Go on," he said again. "It's a long walk to Boston."

"Damn you," she said. "Damn you to hell!" And she turned and raced toward the door that was already swinging shut. "Wait!" she gasped, and the uniformed attendant pulled it open again. She flashed her boarding pass and took a quick backward glance. Rob was standing there with his hands in his pockets, his expression unreadable behind dark glasses. "I'll call," she shouted, and hustled down the corridor toward the waiting plane.

The flight to Boston was endless, the drive home monotonous and nerve-wracking. She had a killer headache by the time she pulled into her driveway and parked the Mitsubishi in the shade of the elm tree that dominated the front yard. Inside the house, it was cool, with that silence peculiar to empty houses. Her mail was stacked neatly on the kitchen table next to a plastic freezer bag of snapped beans and a half-dozen ripe tomatoes. Beside them was a note in Jesse's precise handwriting. *Gave some beans to Millie. Had to use the ripest tomatoes. These should last a few more days. Might want to check on the cukes, they're about ready.* Brief, businesslike, and to the point. That was Jesse. He was as dependable as the change of seasons, as steady as a rock, civilized right to the marrow in his bones. Half the women on the planet would consider him a prize catch. Only she seemed to prefer cave men.

She took aspirin for the headache and went upstairs to unpack. Her bedroom was hot and stuffy, and she threw open a window to let in some air. Hoping the headache would slow down to a dull roar, she left her suitcase on the floor and lay down on the bed.

Instead, the scene at the airport returned to haunt her, and to her chagrin, she went hot all over. Groaning, she covered her face with her hands. The man had no decency at all. He'd never learned one iota of civilized behavior. He was a barbarian, and she had every intention of telling him so the next time she talked to him. How could he have kissed her like that? How could she have kissed him back?

Because you liked it, that little voice inside her said. *Because you wanted it as much as he did.*

She knew what she needed, and the need for it was turning her inside out. But it was out of the question. Most certainly out of the question, for God's sake, with Rob. What she needed was a discreet, civilized little affair. A few quick tumbles between the sheets. No commitments, no expectations, no impossible-to-keep promises. Plain, simple, recreational sex. Maybe she could post a notice on the bulletin board down at the Wash-n-Dry. *Hot-blooded widow seeks stud muffin for mutual pleasure. For a good time, call....*

Or maybe she simply needed to acquaint herself with the concept of cold showers.

She looked at the phone in distaste as she lay on her king-size bed in her too stuffy, overly prissy bedroom. How was she going to face him after the little scene at the airport? How was she going to talk in any sort of civilized manner when all she really wanted to do was slug him?

Dread turning the inside of her mouth to cotton, Casey picked up the phone and dialed his number. It rang four times, each time making her heart beat a little faster, and then, to her relief, his machine picked up. She released the breath she hadn't realized she was holding. "Hi," she said. "It's me." She took a breath. "I'm on the ground, I'm exhausted, and I'm going to take a nap. Give me a call when—"

There was a click, and then he said, "Hi."

She wet her lips. "Hi," she said.

Silence. On the road in front of the house, a car went by, too fast. For the first time in fifteen years, she didn't know what to say to him.

He cleared his throat. "How was your flight?" he said.

"Terrible."

Again, silence. "Did they feed you?" he said at last.

"Yes. I think it might have been chicken, but it was hard to tell."

"I've been thinking," he said.

"Marvelous. Should I applaud, or just run up the flag?"

"Maybe you're right," he continued, ignoring her. "Maybe I should move east."

She ignored the adrenaline that shot through her veins. "Suit yourself," she said.

"Maybe Boston," he said. "We could spend weekends together. We could rent one of those little sailboats and go out on the Charles."

Inexplicably, her eyes watered, and a single tear spilled and rolled down her cheek. "I told you already," she said. "We'd end up drowning ourselves."

"Are you crying?" he said.

"No," she lied.

"Fiore," he said, "you're the lousiest liar I've ever known. What's wrong?"

She drew in a ragged, shuddery breath. Pulled a tissue from the box on the dresser and dabbed at the corner of her eye. "It's nothing. I'll be fine."

He let out a huge sigh. "Look," he said, "we hit the road in two weeks, and I'll be in pretty heavy rehearsal until then." He paused. "You know how it goes."

She knew. "Yes," she said, and swiped her nose with the tissue.

"Sure you won't change your mind and come with me?"

That she found the offer tempting told her just how far around the bend she'd gone. She squared her shoulders. "Bad idea," she said. "But thanks for the offer, just the same."

"Yeah," he said. "I guess you're right. Look, I gotta run."

They were both silent, but neither of them hung up. "Flash?" she said.

"Yeah, babe?"

"Call me from the road. Anytime. I'll be here."

CHAPTER THIRTY-ONE

Life on the road took its toll on everyone, and you did whatever it took to get through the night. In his years of touring, Rob had seen it all: the drinking, the drugging, the backstage whoring. He'd never been much into partying. He drank a little, but then so did everyone. In his younger days, he'd smoked a joint or two, but he'd never touched hard drugs. He'd seen too many road musicians so strung out on bennies and ludes that they couldn't function without them. Too many others so deep into the white powder that they'd have sold their own grandmothers for a single snort. Everybody had something that kept them sane, but he was getting too old, too tired, for the party scene. It was his phone calls to Casey that helped him maintain his tenuous hold on sanity.

He lived for precious stolen moments like this one, leaning against a dirty cinder block wall with a telephone receiver pressed to his ear, while around him, the crew broke down and packed up the equipment so they could move on to the next stop. As he waited for Casey to answer the phone, somebody walked by with an open box of pizza, and he reached out and snagged a slice. He couldn't remember the last time he'd eaten.

She picked up the phone, and he swallowed the bite of pizza. "Hey, pudding," he said.

"Hey," she said groggily. It was astonishing that she could pack so much warmth into a single syllable. Even half-asleep, she managed to sound as though she'd been waiting all day for his call.

"I woke you," he said. "I'm sorry."

"I can sleep anytime." She must have shifted position, because he could hear the rustling of the bedclothes. "I'd rather talk to you."

It was difficult to find anything meaningful to say in five minutes, once or twice a week. Instead, they dwelt on mundane details of their lives, concrete topics that were easy to talk about. Her nephew's new baby. The drummer he'd fired in Buffalo after the guy went on stage stoned one too many times. The proposed sewage treatment plant that had all of Jackson Falls in an uproar. The teenage groupie who'd somehow managed to sneak onto one of the buses and hide in the bathroom, and hadn't been discovered until they'd driven nearly a hundred miles. He'd made the girl call her parents, and then he'd put her on a bus for home. "At your own expense, of course," Casey said dryly.

"What was I supposed to do? The kid was fourteen years old, and she had six bucks to her name."

"You're too soft, MacKenzie. People take advantage of softies like you."

"You know me," he said. "Always a sucker for a pretty face."

"Oh?" she said coolly, primly. "And was she pretty?"

"Very pretty. Jealous, pudding?"

"Certainly not."

A pair of roadies rolled a heavy amplifier past him, nearly running over his toes. He tucked himself in closer to the wall. At the other end of the hall, Jerry Nelson, his road manager, held up an arm and pointed to the watch on his wrist. Rob glared at him, then sighed. "Sweetheart," he said, "I gotta go. Jerry's giving me the evil eye. Did you get the tickets I sent for Portland?"

"I got the tickets. I'll be there."

"Next Friday," he said, in case there could be any mistake about the date.

"Next Friday," she agreed. "Listen, try to keep sane."

"I'm trying." He paused, itching to say more, knowing he couldn't.

"You'd better go," she said, after a minute. "You wouldn't want to screw up your itinerary."

"Hell, no," he agreed. "Wouldn't want the world to come to an end."

"You need an attitude adjustment, MacKenzie. Get with the program, for God's sake. You know the routine."

"Yeah. Money for nothing, and chicks for free."

"Exactly. Quit your sniveling, wipe your nose, and get your carcass on that bus."

In spite of his misery, he felt the corner of his mouth

twitch. "Thanks, Sarge," he said.

"You're welcome. See you next Friday."

And she hung up, leaving him holding a dead telephone receiver.

***

When Casey and Jess stepped from the hotel elevator, the din shook them. People cluttered the hallway, standing in clots and leaning against the frames of open doors. "Take a deep breath," she warned him, "and just plough through."

From somewhere, in booming stereo, Jon Bon Jovi was singing about being shot through the heart. As the bass line thundered in a vibrating rhythm around them, she and Jesse squeezed between bodies flying under the influence of various substances, both legal and illicit. She knew many of these people, and those who still hovered somewhere in the vicinity of planet earth nodded or raised bottles in greeting as she passed. The air was thick with cigarette smoke and the stench of burning marijuana. They passed a scantily-clad young couple who were drunkenly groping each other with total disregard for their audience. Casey glanced back at Jess. With his customary aplomb, he was taking it all in stride. "Class," she said to him over the music. "These people have such class." And Jesse shook his head in good-natured disbelief.

It took them twenty minutes to locate Rob. In the midst of the mayhem, they found him sprawled across the foot of a king-size bed, nursing a Heineken and staring glumly at the moving pictures on a silent television screen. "At last," he said, "the cavalry! I thought you guys would never get here." He offered a hand to Jesse. "Jess," he said. "Thanks for coming."

"I didn't know what to expect," Jesse said. "But I have to admit I was impressed. It was a great concert."

"Coming from you," Rob said, "I consider that a real compliment."

They chatted for a few minutes before Rob said, "Listen, can I talk to Casey in private for a minute?"

"Sure thing," Jesse said. "I'll be waiting outside."

Ever the diplomat, he discreetly shut the door behind him,

leaving her to face Rob alone. "Hey," he said.

She shoved her fists into her pockets. "Hey," she said.

"Look," he said, "I want to apologize for what happened at the airport. I was way out of line."

"Damn right, you were. Why the hell did you kiss me like that?"

He looked down at his Reeboks, shuffled them around a bit. Shrugged. "Damned if I know. It was completely spontaneous." He looked at her speculatively. "Why'd you kiss me back?"

Because every time you touch me, I start to quiver and shake. "I don't know," she lied.

"I think we need to have a long talk."

"You have lousy timing, MacKenzie. This isn't the time or the place."

He squared his jaw. "And just when will the time or the place get here, Fiore? When we're both ninety years old?"

"I don't even know what it is we're supposed to be talking about!"

"Jesus, Mary and Joseph!" He slammed a flattened palm down on the top of the television. "You're lying!" he said. "You're lying to me, and you're lying to yourself!"

"Damn it, Rob, this wasn't supposed to happen! Sex wasn't supposed to rear its ugly head! It wasn't part of the deal!"

"Well, here it is, baby! And like it or not, we have to deal with it, or it'll blow us right out of the water!"

Casey stared at CNN's silent pictures of gaunt and pathetic children in some third world country. She cleared her throat. "When do you leave?" she said.

"Six-thirty tomorrow morning." He looked at his watch, and grimaced. "This morning," he amended.

"Until when?"

He walked over to the window and looked out. "A week before Christmas."

Christmas was three months away, three months in which he would be crisscrossing the country, playing one-night stands, consorting with women with names like Kiki and Diedre and Sunshine. Something hard and unpleasant settled itself into the pit of her stomach. "Where do you go next?" she said.

He rested one hip on the radiator in front of the window.

"Springfield. Albany. Providence. Hell, I'm not sure. I just get on and off the bus when they tell me to." He drummed his fingers on the radiator. "I'm so tired of it. It gets to the point where the music doesn't matter any more. It's just a way of getting what you really want. The only thing that matters is how soon you can get to your next fix." He crammed his fists into his pockets and squared his shoulders. "And it doesn't matter," he continued, "what you're hooked on. Drugs, booze, sex, money, power—it's all the same."

"Since when did you become a cynic?"

He shrugged and rubbed his temple. "I'm just tired. I won't get any sleep tonight in this zoo, and I'm coming down with the cold from hell."

She crossed the room, took his hand in hers. His fingers were icy, and she held them until they warmed. "You need a break," she said.

"Right." He crossed one bony ankle over the other. "I'll get a break at Christmas."

She squeezed his hand. "We'll talk then."

"Yeah. Sure we will." He withdrew his hand. "Look, why don't you and Jesse just go home? I'm not very good company tonight."

"Damn it, Rob, don't be this way."

He squared his jaw. "What way is that?"

"You're being a brat. I hate it when you're a brat."

"In the words of that great philosopher Popeye, I am what I am."

"You make me crazy!" she said. "Why do you have to make me so crazy?"

"I don't know!" he said. "You make me crazy, too! Maybe this should tell us something!"

She wheeled around to leave, but he caught her by the arm and spun her back around, yanking her up hard against him, imprisoning her in his arms. Heart hammering, legs trembling, she pushed ineffectually against his shoulders. "Let me go," she said. "This isn't going to solve anything!"

"For once in your goddamn life," he said hoarsely, "will you please not analyze what's happening and just let it happen?"

She opened her mouth, but no sound came out.

"Just let it happen," he whispered.

It was a spectacular kiss, loaded with heat and fury and breathless anticipation. They broke apart, green eyes probing green eyes, before coming back together with a heated, liquid fusion that rendered her incapable of rational thought. He tore his mouth away from hers and buried his face in her hair. Her heart was beating so hard she was sure it would jump out of her chest. She raked both hands through his hair, marveling at its texture. "Don't go," she said. "Stay here with me."

He rubbed the collar of her shirt between his thumb and forefinger. "Oh, baby," he whispered, "you don't know how much I wish I could do that." He nuzzled her neck, kissed the sensitive spot just behind her left ear. "Come with me," he said.

She actually considered it. Considered the implications, thought about what it would mean if she went with him. Did she really want to live with him on a bus or in an endless series of cheap, anonymous hotel rooms? "I can't," she said, surprised by how much it hurt.

He sighed. "You're right," he said. "It's not what I want, either."

In despair, she said, "This isn't working. It just isn't working."

He caught her earlobe between his teeth, drew it into his mouth, released it. "What isn't working?" he said.

"You living on one coast, me on the other."

He raised an eyebrow. "And this," he said, "is news to you?"

"Yes," she said. "I guess it is."

"Good. It'll give you something to think about while I'm gone. You'd better get on out of here now. Your date's waiting outside in the hall."

"Why does it seem like we've spent half our lives saying good-bye?"

His mouth thinned into a grim line. "Because we have."

***

For eight days, she paced her ten lonely rooms like a cat in heat. She should have known that a civilized little affair would never satisfy her. Somewhere inside her, hidden behind that tight-assed, oh-so-proper exterior, lived a woman who had never been willing to settle for anything less than passion. She'd been sure that passion had died with Danny, until Rob MacKenzie's kiss had taught her that what she really wanted was heat so hot she melted, and a man who would give her not only his body, but his soul along with it. She wanted an affair of the heart, not just one of the body. Messy, bloody, maddening passion.

And there was only one man she wanted it with.

He called around one-thirty on a blue and gold Indian summer afternoon, just as she was making a salad from the last of summer's bounty. With that peculiar clairvoyance they'd always shared, she knew it was Rob before she picked up the phone. Softly she said, "Hey, Flash."

"Hey, darlin'."

"Where are you at?"

"Providence." He went into a spasm of coughing that lasted for half a minute before he regained control. "Sorry," he said.

"Rob," she said, alarmed, "you sound terrible."

"I can't throw this damn cold." He sniffed. "It's really got me down. Along with about a hundred other things."

"What's wrong?"

"I'm tired of living out of a suitcase. Half the time, I wake up in the morning and I don't even know what state I'm in. It's all falling apart, and I don't know what to do about it."

"Hey," she said, trying to keep her voice light. "Are you okay?"

"I'm not aging gracefully, babe." He stopped to cough again. "It's like yesterday I was in high school, and today I'm thirty-five, and I don't know how or when it happened. How the hell did I get to be thirty-five years old?"

Gently, she said, "It happens."

"I'm beginning to wonder if I'm doing it all wrong. I mean, is this what I really want to do with my life? Jesus, Casey, there has to be more."

"Come on, Rob, get serious. Music is your life."

"Yeah, well, maybe it's time I took up some other line of work. Maybe I should be painting pictures." He went into another spasm of coughing. "Or houses," he added darkly.

"Cancel the tour."

"Are you nuts? You don't cancel in the middle of a tour."

"Why not?"

"You just don't. It must be written in stone somewhere."

"You have to take care of your health." Pointedly she added, "And that includes your mental health."

"Right. And what kind of excuse do I use?"

"Call it burnout, call it exhaustion. I don't care what you call it. You shouldn't need an excuse. This is your life you're talking about, not some two-bit concert tour."

He coughed again, a dry, tight cough that frightened her. "Have you seen a doctor?" she said.

"I don't need a doctor. I can take care of myself."

"Of course. I forgot you had your medical degree. And what have you prescribed for yourself, Doctor MacKenzie?"

"Aspirin. Nyquil. Some twelve-hour crap that's supposed to help me breathe, only I've been taking it every six hours and it does really funky things to my head. I'm supposed to go on stage in seven hours, but there's no way it's going to happen." He paused before letting loose with a magnificent sneeze. "No way in hell," he added darkly.

"Rob, you're scaring me. Won't you please see a doctor?"

"Damn it, woman," he snapped, "I don't want a doctor! I want you!"

There was a moment of silence as, somewhere in the vicinity of her heart, she felt the fluid rush of an emotion she didn't dare to name. "Where are you?" she said.

He sneezed again. "Providence," he croaked.

She felt it again, that heady, terrifying rush of emotion. "I know that, lovey," she said. "You already told me that. But where in Providence?"

"I'm sorry. It's this damn Nyquil. It's fogged my brain."

"Rob," she said, "where the hell are you?"

"The Worcester Hotel."

"What room?"

"Damned if I know."

"Never mind, I'll find you. Start packing. I'm coming to get you."

"What about the tour?" His voice had gone thin and reedy.

"Let me worry about that. You just get some sleep. *Capisce?*"

"Yeah." He managed, somehow, to inject immense relief into that one syllable.

***

His eyes were bloodshot, the pupils dilated, his face ashen beneath a three-day growth of reddish beard. He looked as though he had barely enough strength to stand as he held open the door of his hotel room. "Only for you, MacKenzie," she said as she breezed past, "would I brave Route 128 at rush hour. All those yuppies in their Volvos, changing lanes at ninety miles an hour. Not to mention the vultures at the front desk downstairs. They wouldn't even admit you were here, let alone tell me what room you were in, until I told them I was your wife and if they didn't let me in, I'd knock on every damn door in the place until I found you."

He gave her a weak grin. "What a woman," he croaked.

"You look like roadkill," she said, and touched his forehead. "Rob, you're burning up! You need to see a doctor."

He scowled. "I don't need any doctor."

"Listen, you jackass, I'm not about to let you die on me."

"I'm not dying," he said. "What about the tour?"

"It's all taken care of. I'm surprised you didn't hear the screaming."

"Holy shit. Canceled?"

"The whole ball of wax."

"Jesus, woman, get me out of town before they lynch me."

"Let them try. They'll have to go through me first." She touched his cheek and was frightened by the feel of his skin, dry and brittle, like onionskin paper. "You're too thin," she said, smoothing his hair. "Have you eaten anything lately?"

"Not unless you count big red and yellow pills."

"Oh, that's really healthy, MacKenzie. I don't suppose this joint has room service?"

"Are you kidding, Fiore? I'm lucky to have soap and toilet paper."

"We'll have to stop somewhere, then. I left my lunch sitting on the kitchen table when you called."

He was asleep before they crossed the state line. As she drove north through eastern Massachusetts, she darted brief, worried glances at him. He was much too pale, and his raspy, uneven breathing frightened her. He slept fitfully. When she stopped for food and fuel, he washed down a fistful of pills with a swig of her Coke, then reclined his seat and drifted back into an uneasy sleep.

Somewhere north of Portsmouth he began having cold chills. Casey pulled the car into a rest area and got a blanket from the trunk and wrapped him in it. He was afire with fever, soaked with sweat, trembling uncontrollably. It was nearly midnight when they reached Jackson Falls, and he was too weak to protest when she turned into the parking lot at County General. She steered him in the direction of the emergency entrance and left him slumped on a chair in the waiting area while she spoke with the charge nurse. And then she bit her lower lip in determination and followed him into the examining room.

The doctor was quick but thorough. "Viral pneumonia," he pronounced as he tucked his stethoscope back into his pocket.

Casey stepped forward in alarm. "Shouldn't he be hospitalized?" she said.

"It looks a lot worse than it really is." The young intern gave her what was supposed to be a reassuring smile. "His temp's nearly 105. That's why he feels so rotten."

Her pulse began a slow hammering. "Isn't that dangerous?"

"Let's say we wouldn't like to see it go much higher. Fever's a perfectly normal reaction, the body's way of fighting the infection. We'll give him aspirin to bring down the fever and an antibiotic to prevent complications. Keep him off his feet, make sure he gets plenty of liquids, and he should start feeling better in a few days."

Rob grumbled when the nurse gave him an antibiotic injection, but he fell asleep again once they were in the moving car, and she had to wake him when they reached the house. With the blanket wrapped around his shuddering body, he stood up, took a step, and faltered. She caught him by the arm and supported his weight all the way to the house, silently thanking God that she had a guest bedroom on the first floor. She could never have gotten him up the stairs.

When she came back with his luggage, he was slumped on the edge of the bed, head cradled in his arms. She rubbed his shoulder. "You get into your jammies," she said, "and I'll heat you some soup."

His pupils were dilated, and he had a drifty look about him that frightened her. But his grin was sassy, if weak. "I don't own any jammies," he said.

"Then get into your birthday suit," she said briskly. "I'll be right back."

When she returned with the soup, he had discarded his clothes and was nestled beneath the covers. Like an obedient child, he allowed her to feed him, and it was his docility that frightened her more than anything. He ate half a cup of Campbell's chicken noodle before burrowing back under the covers and falling asleep.

Casey tossed another blanket over him and pondered her dilemma. Her bedroom was upstairs, and she was terrified to leave him alone. She would have to sleep here. On the shelf in the closet, she found a spare pillow and a comforter. Overwhelmed with fatigue, she curled up beside him on the bed, expecting sleep to overtake her immediately. Instead, after eight hours behind the wheel, she saw a continuously moving expanse of gray asphalt passing behind her closed eyelids.

Fighting back nausea, she cautiously shifted position and rearranged her blanket. She couldn't allow herself to get sick. Rob needed her. Three years ago, she'd slept by her daughter's bedside like this. If she could do it then, she could do it now. But those three years seemed half a lifetime ago. She'd been younger then. So much younger, and not nearly as tired.

His thrashing woke her near daybreak. He was tossing restlessly, mumbling disjointed words in his sleep, the bedding askew and tangled around his lanky limbs. His side of the bed was saturated with sweat. She touched his bare shoulder, and he mumbled something and twisted away from her. "Wake up, Flash," she said. "Time for your medicine."

"Lemme sleep," he mumbled. "Do th' damn sound check tomorrow."

His skin was hot as smoldering coals. "Rob," she said again, "you have to wake up."

"I am. I'm awake."

"Then open your eyes for me, sweetheart. Look at me."

"Jus' wanna sleep."

"Rob," she said, more forcefully this time. "Open your eyes."

"No," he said. "Lemme sleep."

"I can't," she said. "If you won't wake up and take your medicine, I'm going to have to go call the doctor again."

"Don' leave me...need you."

It struck her again, that nameless emotion that kept worming its way into her heart uninvited. She brushed a single curl away from his face. "I won't leave you," she whispered. "I'm right here beside you."

"So tired," he said. "Jus' wanna sleep."

"All right," she said, and patted his shoulder. "You sleep."

When he had quieted down again, she went to the kitchen phone and called the hospital. "Look," she told the doctor, "he's still running a raging fever, he's delirious, and I can't get any medicine into him. I don't know what to do."

"He'll continue to run a fever until the virus works its way out of his system. What you need to do at this point is bring the fever down."

"Marvelous. And how do I do that?"

"Cold water. As cold as you can get it. Throw in a few ice cubes if you have any. And call me back if it doesn't work."

She went to the kitchen and grabbed an armful of dish towels, filled her biggest Tupperware bowl with cold water, and dumped in a tray of ice cubes. She'd probably never earn any humanitarian awards for her nursing skills, but at this point, she was so desperate that she would have scattered the entrails of small animals around the bed if the doctor had told her to.

She set the bowl on the night stand, dipped a towel into the frigid water and wrung it out, then hesitated, belatedly aware of the intimacy of what she was about to do. She stood momentarily paralyzed, looking at the man in the bed.

Don't be ridiculous, Fiore. You're thirty-three years old. It's not like you've never seen a naked man before. This is no time for modesty.

But I can't—

Of course you can. You have to. There isn't anybody else.

"Oh, for the love of God," she said aloud. She flung back the covers, wrung out the towel a last time, and resolutely applied it to his heated flesh.

He let out a string of curses and fought her like an enraged grizzly. She fought back with all her strength, dodging his flailing arms and ignoring his disjointed words of rage as she soaked towel after towel in ice water and pressed them to his fevered flesh, dipping, wringing, pressing, clenching her teeth and rolling with him when he tried to avoid her, murmuring gentle words to soothe his agony.

Outside the window, the sun rose, but she was too intent on her struggle to be aware of the passage of time. He outweighed her by a good sixty pounds, and if the pneumonia hadn't weakened him, she could never have held him down. Her shoulder muscles felt as though they were being ripped from her body, and just when she knew she couldn't possibly fight him any longer, the fever broke, sweat beading up on his damp skin and pouring off him in tiny rivers. She pulled the covers back up over his shoulders and collapsed in exhaustion next to the pile of discarded towels on the floor. Drenched to the skin, sore and bruised and shivering, she buried her head in her arms and rocked, too drained to cry.

After a while, she pulled herself to her feet and staggered to the bathroom to stand beneath a hot shower until her shuddering stopped. She put on a flannel nightgown and Danny's faded terrycloth robe and went back to check on Rob. He was lying on his stomach, his breathing raspy, but he seemed to be sleeping comfortably. She adjusted the covers, touched the back of her hand to his forehead. To her relief, his temperature felt normal.

For three days and three nights, she stayed with him, reading in the rocking chair by day, catnapping on the bed beside him at night. Attuned to his every breath, she woke him every eight hours for his medication, force-fed him liquids, monitored his temperature fanatically. He was passive, agreeing to whatever she said.

Sometime during the fourth night, she awoke to find his side of the bed empty. She bolted upright in panic, and then he padded barefoot into the room, wearing wrinkled jeans and a towel around his shoulders. His hair was wet, and he'd shaved. Scowling, he said, "You look like hell, Fiore."

"Where were you? You scared me half to death."

"I took a shower. I was so ripe I could smell myself." He sat on the edge of the bed and looked at her with eyes that were still glassy. "I mean it, Casey. You're ready to drop. You need some sleep."

"I've been sleeping," she protested.

"Yeah, right. Two or three hours a night."

"Do you have any idea how sick you've been?"

"Yeah," he said softly. "I know." He buried his face in his hands, rubbed his temples. "What day is it?" he said.

"Tuesday."

"How long have I been here?"

"Since Friday."

"Jesus," he said.

"Park your carcass in the chair," she said, "and I'll change the bedding while you're up."

"You're wiped out. I'll do it."

"Shut up," she told him. "I'm in charge here, and you don't get a vote."

She stripped the bed and remade it with fresh linens, then carried the dirty bedding to the bathroom and stuffed it all in the hamper. When she returned, he was back in bed, jeans tossed carelessly on the floor, one hand rubbing his forehead. "I think I overdid it," he said. "My head's spinning."

She bent over and picked up his jeans, folded them. "Will you please stay in bed? I'm too weak to pick you up if you fall flat on your face."

"At least I remember my own name now." He drew back the covers and patted the mattress, and she didn't even consider turning down his invitation. After all they'd been through together, propriety was no longer even a consideration. She crawled in between crisp, cool sheets and he turned out the bedside lamp and drew her into his arms, and tangled together like lovers, they slept.

She woke up alone, disoriented because the sunlight was slanting into the room at the wrong angle. She stretched and glanced at the clock on the bureau and was astonished to discover that it was nearly three o'clock in the afternoon and she'd been sleeping deeply and dreamlessly for twelve hours.

She found Rob slouched on the porch swing, a cup of tea in his hand, his bare feet propped on the wooden railing beneath her pink hanging geranium. "Hey," he said, his face lighting up, "she lives. My very own sleeping beauty."

His color was vastly improved, and the glassy look had left his eyes. "You look almost human," she said, sitting beside him and resting her bare feet on the railing next to his. "How long have you been up?"

"Since about nine-thirty."

"Why didn't you wake me?"

"I figured if you didn't get some sleep, I'd the be one taking care of you."

"And just what have we been up to all day?" She took the teacup from his hand and helped herself to a sip of Earl Grey.

"Absolutely nothing. I forgot how great it feels." With one foot, he set the rocker into languid motion. "You shouldn't be drinking after me," he said. "I might still be contagious."

"We've been sleeping in the same bed for four days," she reminded him. "I've already been exposed to any germ you might be carrying."

"True," he said. "You're the first woman I ever slept with that I never slept with."

She wiggled her toes in the warm afternoon sunshine. "Clever," she said.

"I thought so. Of course, we could remedy the situation pretty quickly if we wanted to." He rubbed his foot suggestively against hers.

"You'll live," she pronounced. "If you're feeling randy, you must be better."

He left his foot where it was, resting lightly atop hers. "This place is so peaceful," he said, leaning his head back and closing his eyes. "I could get real used to being here."

"I could get real used to having you here," she said. "You

have no idea how scared I've been. I thought I was going to lose you."

He threaded his fingers in the hair at the back of her neck and began aimlessly stroking the skin beneath. Gruffly, he said, "Don't you know I'm too ornery to die?"

Thinking of Danny, she said, "Nobody's too ornery to die."

He hesitated just long enough to tell her he'd followed her train of thought. "Well, I'm better," he said. "Tired and weak, but better."

"Thank God. What would I do without you?"

His fingers continued to play restlessly in her hair. "It probably wouldn't be a pretty picture," he said.

"It would be a very ugly picture," she said, turning to look at him. His eyes were still closed, and his fingers were working their magic on her, and something warm and tenacious worked itself into the crevices around her heart and squeezed tightly. She cleared her throat. "Did you find something to eat?" she said.

"Tuna fish sandwich. There's more in the fridge if you want one."

"I think I'll take a shower first. I'm beginning to understand what you meant by ripe."

She took a long, hot shower and dressed in real clothes for the first time since Friday, and then she made a much-needed trip to the grocery store. Rob insisted on coming along, even though she thought he needed more time to recuperate before he ventured too far from home. "I hope," she told him as they strolled the snack food aisle, "you're going to give yourself some real down time before you get back to work. You need it desperately."

"Don't worry," he said, selecting a package of fig bars and tossing it into the shopping cart. "I might just hide out here for the next six months."

"You hide out here," she said, "for as long as you need to."

"I have to reschedule the tour sooner or later, or they'll sue me."

"After the tongue lashing I gave them," she said, debating whether to buy onion or cheese crackers, "your cash flow could be a little funky for a while."

"What'd you do to me, woman?"

"I saved your scrawny ass, that's what."

"Yeah," he said. "I guess you did." He tossed another package of cookies into the cart. "Hey, Fiore? Thanks."

He bounced back quickly. Each day, he grew stronger and more robust, and the house seemed so much less empty than it had before. They puttered around the house and the yard, comfortable with each other's presence but neither of them craving constant companionship. He lounged on the porch swing with his guitar while she dug up tulip bulbs to be stored in the cellar until spring. He washed windows while she made applesauce, the scent of cinnamon mingling with that of ammonia. He went through her dusty album collection and played records she hadn't listened to in years.

Just past six on Saturday morning, she crawled out of bed and into her running clothes, and tiptoed down the creaky stairs so she wouldn't wake him. But he was already up, dressed in his gray sweats, one foot propped on a kitchen chair as he tied the lace to his sneaker. "What do you think you're doing?" she said.

"What's it look like, Fiore? I'm running with you."

"You're just getting over pneumonia. You're not up to running."

With a flourish, he finished tying the knot. "Shut up and put on a sweatshirt. It's cold this morning."

She purposely kept her pace slower than usual. He was too obstinate to admit it, but she could tell he was having trouble keeping up with her after the first couple of miles. When they reached the bridge over the inlet between the river and Spencer's Pond, he veered off the road. "I need a break," he gasped, and sank onto the guardrail, elbows braced on his knees, hands tangled in his hair, chest heaving as though he'd just finished the Boston Marathon in record time.

Casey knelt in the gravel between his knees and checked his forehead for fever. "Did I not tell you," she said, "that you weren't up to this?"

"When I want your opinion," he wheezed, "I'll ask for it."

Green eyes gazed boldly into green eyes. A car passed, so close its sweep blew dust around her ankles and tore at her hair. "Get out of the road," he growled, yanking her in close until she was wedged between his thighs. He was warm and damp, and he smelled of Ivory soap and clean sweat. Deep inside the pit of her stomach, something awakened, something hot and yearning that had lain too long dormant. He had pale freckles scattered across the bridge of his nose, and his eyes were a deep green, warm and vibrant, and she was trembling like a willow in a high wind.

His hands took a leisurely stroll beneath her sweatshirt and his fingers played up and down her bare back. She closed her eyes as he rubbed his cheek against hers, morning whiskers stiff against her skin. He nibbled at her neck, his teeth just touching her skin as he took gentle love bites that turned her insides to molten lava. She slid her hands beneath his sweatshirt and buried her fingers in the triangle of silky hair that covered his chest. Breast to breast and pelvis to pelvis, they touched each other, his hands exploring the soft hollow of her belly, hers skimming hard ribs and sleek muscled biceps. He ran his fingers up her ribcage to just beneath her breasts and back down, teasing her, until she was half crazy with desire. Then he stilled against her. "Babe," he murmured. "We have company."

She came back from a great distance to realize she'd been hearing the soft metallic tinkling for some time. She sprang to her feet, mortified, as Greg Weisman, her new neighbor from down the road, jogged past with his beagle on a leash. "Morning," he said.

Rob saluted. "Morning."

She glared at him, furious with him, more furious with herself. What on earth had she been thinking of, necking with him by the side of the road like a pair of hormone-driven teenagers? She called herself a few choice names, maddened by the realization that, had they not been interrupted, in another minute she would have been rolling with him on the grass, right there by the side of the road. In broad daylight, less than a mile from her father's front door. That would certainly have given Greg Weisman and the rest of Jackson Falls something to talk about.

The thought should have shamed her. The fact that it excited her increased her fury. "I think we'd better go home now," she said.

He leaned back on the guardrail, lanky legs sprawled out

before him, wearing that ingenuous, lost puppy dog look that had stolen the hearts of women from Tijuana to Tokyo. "I was hoping," he said, "that we might take up where we left off."

He was the most infuriating man she'd ever known. He had bony shoulders and knobby knees, and when she touched him, she'd been able to count every one of his ribs. He ran around most of the time looking like a sheep dog in need of a trim, he had trouble picking out socks and a shirt that matched, and he was addicted to junk food. He always left his wet towel on the floor after a shower, and he'd been a charter member of the girl-of-the-month club for years. No woman in her right mind would want him. No woman in her right mind would fall in love with a man like that.

The truth struck her like a blow to the stomach, and all the air left her lungs. Stunned, she opened her mouth. Snapped it abruptly shut. And in sheer terror, she wheeled around blindly to flee.

His voice followed her. "Go ahead, Fiore! Run away! But it won't go away with you!"

She turned to look at him. The puppy dog was gone, replaced by six feet of quivering, furious testosterone. His legs were braced apart, his jaw set at that familiar angle that meant trouble was brewing. His blond curls were in their usual glorious disarray, his clothes wrinkled. And in those green eyes was something she'd never seen there before. "What?" she said. "What won't go away with me?"

He took a single step toward her. "The way we feel," he said, "when we're together."

This couldn't be happening. She was thirty-three years old. Too old to feel like a giddy teenager in the throes of adolescent passion. Too old to feel as though she would burst if he didn't touch her soon. Too old for the erotic fantasies that played in her head like home movies. She'd already been in love once, the kind of love that addled her brain and tore out her heart and turned the world upside-down. It wasn't supposed to happen again. Not like this. Not at thirty-three. Not with Rob.

"Ever since Nassau," he said, "we've been dancing around each other in circles. We could keep it up for another ten years, but to tell you the truth, I'm not getting any younger and neither are you. Don't you think it's time we stopped running away from this and did something about it instead?"

"What if we're wrong?" she demanded. "What if we're making some monumental mistake?"

He stepped closer, so close she could feel the heat from his body. When he took her hand, he was trembling as hard as she was. "We're not making a mistake," he said.

Green eyes probed green eyes and searched deep, both of them thinking about fifteen years of friendship, both of them pondering the uncharted territory that lay between them. Hoarsely, she said, "What the hell are we doing, MacKenzie?"

With his free hand, he tucked an errant lock of hair behind her ear. "We're going home, Fiore, and we're making breakfast. After that—well, we'll take it from there."

In her upstairs bathroom, Casey stripped off her sweat-soaked clothes and threw them down the laundry chute, then stepped beneath a stinging hot spray. She soaped and scrubbed until she was nearly raw, but it didn't help. The water felt like warm fingers on her skin, deepening the yearning she couldn't seem to squelch. In desperation, she turned off the hot water and stood there stoically as it turned frigid, so cold it hurt, like hard little cubes slamming into her body.

The result was immediate and effective. The icy water cooled her ardor with a vengeance, briefly rendering her incapable of movement or thought. She emerged from the shower covered in goose bumps, teeth chattering, her limbs stiff from the brutal cold.

And smelled breakfast.

She followed her nose to the coffee pot. Poured a cup and stood there watching him. He was making some kind of omelet that he'd thrown together from the contents of her refrigerator. He was barefoot, wearing jeans and a crisp hunter green shirt, and he smelled of shampoo and bacon. It was a heady combination. "Want to check the toast?" he said, as if nothing remotely extraordinary had transpired between them only minutes earlier.

Casey popped the toast and buttered it. "It's a beautiful day," he said, still busy at the stove. "I thought we might go for a ride."

She turned to look at him. "A ride?"

"Yeah, Fiore, a ride. Bask in the sunshine, gawk at the scenery, travel to distant and exotic places." He turned off the burner and shot her a glance. "Maybe spend the night somewhere along the coast."

Her heart began to thud. The significance of his suggestion was clear. If she accepted his offer, tonight they would be sharing a bed. And whatever transpired between them, it would happen in a neutral location, instead of here, in the house where she'd lived with Danny. There would be no old memories to overcome, only new ones to create. Nothing to remind her of anyone else, only the heady, terrifying experience of being with this man for the first time.

CHAPTER THIRTY-TWO

It was a sunny autumn day, near seventy degrees as they cut across country toward the coast and Acadia National Park. They stopped for lunch at a McDonald's drive-thru. When Casey offered to pay her share of the bill, he just stared at her through dark glasses, and she put her money away. "I give up," she said. "You win."

He handed a twenty to the cashier. "When I take a woman out on a date, Fiore, I pay her way."

"Oh," she said. "Are we on a date?"

He took his change from the cashier and pocketed it. "Yeah," he said, handing her their drinks. "Try to act like it."

"It's been so long," she said, "I'm not sure I remember proper dating etiquette. Should I sit on your lap or something?"

"Tacky, Fiore. Real tacky." He handed her the bag of food. "You don't sit on my lap until *after* we eat."

He parked in the shade of a maple tree that was turning a brilliant orange, and they ate at the picnic table beneath it, tossing scraps to the seagulls who hovered just out of reach. When he finished his Big Mac, he slid across the bench and wrapped an ankle around hers. "Now," he said, "it's time for you to sit on my lap."

She bit into a French fry. "I thought you knew," she said. "I'm not that kind of girl."

"You mean I spent all this money on you, babycakes, and I don't get anything in return?"

"That's how it lays out, MacKenzie."

"Doesn't seem quite fair."

She crumpled up her sandwich wrapper. "You get what you pay for," she said. "If you'd sprung for a nice little sirloin instead of a fish filet, I might have been able to demonstrate a little more gratitude."

When he smiled, she felt as though she were emerging from darkness into the light of a thousand suns. "The day is young, sweetheart," he said. "Anything could happen."

The view from the Cadillac summit was worth the trip.

Inland, splashes of blue alternated with patches of glorious reds and yellows and oranges for as far as the eye could see. In the opposite direction, the spiky backs of the Porcupine Islands dotted the iridescent blue of Frenchmen's Bay. Hand in hand, they climbed over rocks and wandered among the scrub pines and juniper that lived here at the top of the highest peak on the Eastern seaboard.

When they tired of exploring the mountain top, they drove back down and followed Ocean Drive around the perimeter of the park. At Thunder Hole, they parked next to a Buick with New Jersey plates, and together with a retired couple from East Orange, they listened to the ocean's roar. The surf slammed in against the rocks and shot skyward, and Rob wrapped an arm loosely around her and pulled her back out of the path of the churning water. Casey leaned into him, and together they stood mesmerized by the relentless power of the surf that had pummeled these rocks for a billion years.

Farther down the road, they discovered a rocky beach where they sifted through the seaweed, gathered unusual rocks, explored the tidal pools. "Look," she said, lifting something from crystal-clear water. "A starfish!"

Like two kids who'd made some momentous discovery, they examined it, studied its shape and form, marveled at the texture of this living creature before Casey returned it to the water from which she'd plucked it.

He was watching her with a bemused expression. "What?" she said.

"You look about twelve years old, Fiore, playing in the water with the fishies."

"Me?" she said. "What about you? Jeans rolled up, sunburned nose—"

"At least I don't have seaweed in my hair," he said, plucking out the offending object and tossing it away. "You're starting to look like the Wicked Witch of the West. Good thing I know what you're supposed to look like. Otherwise, I'd probably run away in fright."

"One more crack like that," she said, "and you'll be hoofing it home."

"That's what you think, darlin'. I'm the one with the car

keys."

She leveled a long, steady look at him. And smiled wickedly. "I can find them," she said.

He grinned and edged closer. "Maybe I was wrong earlier," he said.

For no discernible reason, her heart began to hammer. "About what?" she said.

"Maybe this is the part where you're supposed to sit on my lap."

"And search for car keys?"

He toyed with a strand of her hair. "And search for anything your little heart desires," he said, and lowered his head toward hers.

Behind her, a car door slammed, and the high-pitched voices of children floated over the nodding beach grass. Slowly, her eyes opened and looked directly into his, just inches away. "Jesus, Mary and Joseph," he said. "I can't take this any more. Let's go find a room somewhere."

They walked back to the car in silence. He popped open the trunk and she dropped in her bounty of rocks and shells. He unlocked the driver's door and got in, unlocked her door, and without speaking, they busied themselves adjusting seats and fastening seat belts. He started the engine, released the emergency brake, stepped on the accelerator, and popped the clutch.

The car came to a sudden, jerky halt, and he flushed. "Goddamn Japanese cars," he muttered, and started the engine again.

This time, he managed to keep it running. She lay her hand atop his on the gearshift knob. "Where are we going?" she said.

"How the hell am I supposed to know? I've never been on this frigging island in my life!"

So she wasn't the only one who was a basket case. She wondered if his stomach felt the way hers did, all hollow and jumpy and queasy. "Just up the road," she said with a calm she was far from feeling, "there's a turnoff that'll take you back to Bar Harbor."

He found the intersection, made the turn, and followed the twisting road back through the wilderness, past beaver dams and rusted trailers and road signs with bullet holes in them. Through Bar Harbor, with its crumbling mansions, and out onto the main route that led back to Ellsworth. There, perched on a sprawling hillside that looked out over Frenchmen's Bay, they found a motel that hadn't yet closed for the season.

He left her waiting in the car, her insides knotted in terror. It had been too long since she'd been with a man. She wouldn't know how or where to begin. She wanted to be perfect for him, but she wasn't. Her neck was too long, her breasts too small, and she had the tiny beginnings of crow's feet around her eyes. What if he found her lacking? What if she found him lacking? What if they ended up destroying fifteen years of friendship?

The car door opened, and he got back in. "I rented a cabin," he said. "I hope that's okay with you."

A cabin was less impersonal than a motel room. More private. "A cabin's fine," she said.

"Look," he said, his gaze focused on the narrow road he was navigating through the back forty, "there's something I have to say before this goes any further. I'm thirty-five years old. I've been married and divorced twice, I've had some really lousy relationships, and in between, I haven't exactly lived like a monk."

"You don't have to apologize for your checkered past," she said softly. "I know all about it, and it doesn't matter."

"I just want you to understand where I'm coming from. For a long time now, there's been nobody. Not for lack of opportunity, but because I haven't wanted anybody but you."

The cabin was immaculate, with knotty pine walls, a fieldstone fireplace, and a magnificent mahogany four-poster bed. Casey looked at her face in the mirror over the bathroom sink and was horrified by her windblown appearance. Rob brought in her overnight bag, and she shut herself in the bathroom and tried to repair the day's damage. She washed her face with cool water, brushed her teeth, her hair, and thought about hiding in the bathroom until tomorrow. Was she afraid they wouldn't be good together? Or was she afraid they'd be too good together? She knew him better than anyone else in the world. Why did she feel as if she were about to face a stranger?

While he took his turn behind the bathroom door, she stood

gazing out at the ocean that was so close she could hear its muffled roar through the closed window. On Frenchmen's Bay, a lobsterman was hauling traps. The afternoon sun caught on some shiny object on the deck of his boat, exploding with blinding brilliance. In the bathroom, Rob was running water into the sink. Casey adjusted the window blinds to allow the sun in while still ensuring privacy, and sat in the wicker rocker to wait.

In the bathroom, she heard the *screek* of the ancient faucet, and the water stopped running. Then silence, and she wondered if he was gathering his thoughts, and his courage, the way she'd done. The door opened, and he came out, crossed the room slowly and sat on the floor in front of her, his lanky body folded like a pretzel.

"Hey," he said softly.

"Hey."

He wrapped a hand around her ankle, snagged the strap to her sandal with a finger and peeled it off. Deep inside her, something began to pulse with a slow, measured thudding. He tossed the sandal aside, peeled off its mate, and rested her bare feet on his raised knees. She wiggled her toes against soft denim as he drew her feet slowly along the length of his thighs and planted them flat on the floor on either side of him. Hands bracing her ankles, he said softly, "C'mere, woman."

There was only one direction she could go, down the length of those lanky legs and into the valley between his knees and his shoulders, her hips riding his, her knees flanking his ribcage. Even through all the layers of clothing that separated them, she could feel that this was the way they were meant to fit, man and woman, and in spite of her fear, already he had her so excited she thought she would explode. "Told you," he said lazily, "that I'd get you on my lap before the day was out."

In a voice like raw silk, she said, "Is this any way to treat a lady?"

"Who the hell wants a lady?" he said. "I'd rather have a woman."

She took his hand in hers and placed it on the upper slope of her breast, just above her racing heart. "Well," she said, "here I am."

"Your heart," he said. "It's thudding like a jackhammer."

"That's how much I want you," she said. "Just in case you had any doubts."

His hand lingered, warm against the curve of her breast, while they studied each other, their rapid, shallow breaths mingling as green eyes probed green eyes. Her fingers played up and down his arms, felt the quivering tension in his muscles. Then his warm hand slid up to the back of her neck and tangled in her hair, and all the breath left her lungs as he closed the gap between them.

She knotted her fists in his hair and lost herself in him as he kissed her until she was fluid and boneless, breathless and gasping and senseless and giddy. She'd waited so long for him. *So long.* A muffled moan broke from her throat as he worked his way from the corner of her mouth to the soft underside of her jaw.

"This time," he said hoarsely, "we're not stopping." She tipped her head back and he ran his tongue along the spot where the pulse beat at the base of her throat. "This time," he said, "I'm taking you all the way. All the way to heaven."

"Yes," she said, excitement billowing and swirling inside her. "*Oh, yes.*"

He ran his thumbs up the inside of her thighs to the heated place where they joined, and she gasped as he stroked her boldly, with no hesitation or shyness because that was how it would be with them, they would love each other openly and fiercely and in the broad light of day. His hands continued their plunder, up over her hip bones and past her navel, and she was shuddering with excitement when at last he touched her breasts. She closed her eyes and forgot to breathe as he made slow, erotic circles around the sensitive peaks. "Ohmigod," she said.

"Feel good?" he whispered.

"Oh, yes."

"Wait. It gets better." He tugged at her shirt, bunched it up in his hands as he pulled the wrinkled fabric from the waistband of her jeans. Clutching soft white cotton, he popped open a single button. "I'm gonna get you so hot—" Her heart lurched as he opened the next button. "—that you'll be jumping out of your skin." The third button popped open, and he stripped the shirt from her shoulders, worked it down her arms and off over her wrists. Her heart thundered when he pressed his face to the damp hollow between her breasts. "And then," he said hoarsely, his mouth soft and wet against her skin, "I'm gonna give you the ride of your life."

She cupped his face in her hands and kissed his brow, the faint webbing of laugh lines at the corner of his eye, the indistinct prickle of whiskers on his jaw. He fumbled awkwardly with the front clasp to her brassiere. Impatient, she helped him with it, and his laughter came out on a warm gusty breath against her cheek. "I'm not nervous," he said.

Her cheek pressed to his, her nose buried in his blond curls, she laughed. First one side and then the other, he peeled back ice blue silk, damp and warm and still molded into the shape of her breasts. "You are so damn beautiful," he said raggedly.

With the tip of his tongue, he traced a moist trail from her chin down the column of her throat, followed the outline of her collar bone, the slope of her breast. Just when she was sure she would die from the agony of anticipation, he reached the swollen tip of her breast and took it in his mouth.

She gasped. He drew on her deeply, suckling like an infant, melting her, destroying her. She cradled his head in her arms, guided him as he pleasured first one breast and then the other, robbing her of breath, of sanity.

He stopped too soon, left her still hungry. With shuddering fingers, she struggled with the buttons to his shirt. They refused to give, and in exasperation, she yanked hard, sending several buttons skittering off across the wooden floor. He shrugged off the shirt and they met breast to breast, skin to skin, hands tangled in each other's hair as they tasted cheeks and ears and necks and shoulders, his tongue dipping into the soft hollow at the base of her throat, hers exploring the prominence of his Adam's apple.

He took her over backward to the floor, pelvis to pelvis, belly to belly, heat to heat. Breathless, they paused to study each other, hot flesh sticky against hot flesh. "This is all I've been able to think about all day," he said hoarsely. "You and me, together, like this."

With a fingertip, she traced the narrow white scar that angled downward from his ribcage to disappear beneath the waistband of his jeans. "When did you have your appendix out?" she said.

"When I was twelve."

"So many things," she said with genuine sorrow. "So many things I don't know about you. The name of your first-grade teacher. What you were like at twelve."

"Sister Mary Elizabeth. And tall and skinny, with feet like Bozo the Clown." He closed his eyes. "Ah, baby," he whispered, "you've got me so damn hot."

"I know," she said. "I can tell."

He opened his eyes again. "Yeah?" he said with interest. "How can you tell?"

"I thought recreational sex was your area of expertise, MacKenzie. Am I going to have to teach you *everything*?"

"I hate to burst your bubble, pudding, but this is not recreational sex. This is love."

"Oh," she said, inordinately pleased by the sentiment.

"And you know what else?"

She drew his lower lip into her mouth, slicked her tongue over it, released it. "What?" she said.

"No boundaries. Anything you want, just ask, and it's yours."

Although it was a joint effort, it still took them some time to get her out of the rest of her clothes, since every so often they had to stop to kiss or fondle, to taste or tickle, some heretofore unreachable portion of anatomy. She scooted up onto the bed and sank deep into the goose down mattress, watching in admiration as he peeled off the rest of his clothes in the dying light of an October afternoon. He was beautiful, all lines and angles, a splendid combination of hardness and softness, a work of art haloed by the setting sun's glow.

Finally, she thought. *Finally.* And then he was in her arms and they were rolling naked on soft goose down, on sheets that smelled faintly of lavender sachet, and he was all hers to touch and taste and explore, this man she knew better than anyone, this stranger she had never met before.

They studied each other solemnly, both of them contemplating the gravity of what they were about to do. "Swear to me," she said, "that this won't change anything."

"Ah, baby, you know I can't do that. Ask for something

easy. Ask me to tell you I've loved you since the first time I laid eyes on you. Ask me to tell you I'll keep on loving you till the day I die. That I can do."

She kissed him tenderly, and they rolled across the bed, limbs tangled, breathing labored, his breath hot against her neck as he whispered ragged endearments, both tender and obscene. "I've waited years for you," she said breathlessly. "Don't make me wait any longer."

Gnawing gently at the taut cord that ran from her collarbone to her ear, he whispered, "Tell me what you want."

In response, she ran her fingers down his chest, past his flat, hard stomach, and he made a soft, strangled sound in the back of his throat when she boldly took him, hot and thick and rock hard, in both hands. "This," she said. "Inside me. Now."

He let out a hard breath and rolled her onto her back, and while they watched each other's eyes, he filled her slowly, exquisitely. "Better?" he said.

"Oh. My. God. *Yes.*"

"Feel good, babydoll?"

"Oh, yes."

She arched her back, eliciting a sharp gasp from him, and they rocked together in sweet, fluid delight. It had been so long since she'd known the liquid pleasure of fusing with a man. She didn't remember it being this good. She didn't remember anything, ever in thirty-three years, being this good.

She rolled beneath him, and he groaned. "Take it slow, baby. *Slow.*"

"I can't. Oh, God, Flash, I can't. You feel so good."

"Ah, baby," he said warmly, "so do you. Touch me again, right there. It hurts so damn good."

She laughed. Had she ever before laughed in the middle of making love? "Here?" she said, touching him experimentally.

"Just like that," he breathed. "Jesus, woman, I love you so much."

"I love you, too. Oh, baby, please. *Harder.*"

"Any harder and it'll be all over."

"I don't care."

"Are you ready? Already?"

"Yes!"

"But sweetheart, we just got started."

"We can do it again."

And he laughed. "Listen," he said, "I've waited thirty-five years for you. I don't want a ninety-second quickie."

"I'll try. I'll try to slow down. But I'm not promising anything."

Fingers tangled in his hair, she held his face between her hands and they watched each other's eyes as they moved together, hot and slick and sweet, and this was love *oh god* like she'd never felt it before, the pungent scent of lavender rising as they crushed the sheets beneath them, gasps and soft, breathy moans as they rolled together, *oh baby yes do that again* sweet, languid thrusting, disjointed words of love evolving into wordless sounds more eloquent than words, throaty sounds half uttered but fully understood *oh stop please I can't take it any more you feel so good don't stop* as they breathed in each other's air, gasped and shuddered, sound and movement quickening *oh yes baby hurry now hurry* until they exploded in a violent, shattering climax and collapsed in a shuddering heap, slick and sated, dazed and sticky and utterly, wildly, unabashedly happy.

They lay there in a chaotic tangle of arms and legs and bedding for a very long time before the capacity for speech returned to either of them. Finally he regained his breath. Nibbled at her earlobe. "I think we just broke some kind of land speed record," he said.

Against his damp chest, she laughed. "I'm sorry. I tried. I really tried to take it slow."

"It's okay," he said. "I'm just a little embarrassed, that's all."

She ran her hands down his back. "Why?" she said.

"The last time I came that fast was in the back seat of my dad's '68 Galaxie, with Mavis Kirkpatrick, and I was seventeen years old."

She raised an eyebrow. "Mavis?" she said.

He propped an elbow on the mattress and rested his chin on his hand. "She was one hot ticket, and I'd been chasing around her like a lovesick puppy for weeks. She finally said yes, but I was so worked up that the minute I got inside her, I went off like skyrockets. She wasn't impressed. It was the first and last time she ever went out with me."

"Poor baby." She wrapped a single golden curl around her index finger, released it, and watched it spring back into place. "But you've polished your technique since then. You certainly didn't leave me behind. I was with you every step of the way."

"I think you have it backwards, Fiore. I was the one in danger of being left behind."

"It's your fault," she said, "for getting me so hot."

He grinned wickedly. "And I'm planning on doing it again in the very near future. But this time, we're going to do it long and slow and sweet. Think you can handle that?"

"I don't know," she said. "Keep talking like that, and we could be in trouble."

"I'll try to keep my mouth shut."

She kissed him tenderly. "You couldn't keep your mouth shut if you tried, MacKenzie. I believe you came out of the womb already talking."

"Then you'll just have to get used to it. Starting right now."

In mock astonishment, she said, "You're ready again?"

"Sweet stuff," he said, "I was born ready."

***

The emptiness was gone.

The fading light of afternoon had been gradually replaced by the shadows of an October dusk. The restlessness was gone, the urgent voices inside her silenced. Casey couldn't remember the last time she'd felt this content. Everything she'd ever wanted, everything she'd ever needed, was right here, packaged inside the heart of this man whose warm body was pressed snug against her backside. His love had taken her to heaven, and she still hadn't come floating back down to earth.

From the shadowy twilight, his voice said softly, "You awake?"

She nestled closer to his warmth. "Mmn."

He kissed her shoulder, his mouth lingering at the ridge of her collarbone. "So, dollface," he said, "now that we've had carnal knowledge of each other, are we still okay?"

She turned in his arms, ran a hand along the line of his jaw, delighting in the rasp of whisker stubble. "Oh, yeah," she said. "We are *so* okay."

He played idly with a strand of her hair. "You hungry?" he said.

She ran her fingers in an exploratory course down his rib cage, investigating every ridge, every indentation. "It's always food with you," she said, "isn't it, MacKenzie?"

"I'm a growing boy."

"We could just stay here forever," she said. "And live on love."

"Sooner or later, they'd probably throw us out. Or find us, two skeletons, dead of malnutrition but still grinning."

She smiled into the darkness. In the distance, a fog horn sounded its eerie echo. "Tell me your stories," she said.

After a moment, he said, "What stories?"

"There's a part of you," she said, "that I don't really know. I know who you are now. But I don't know how you got to where you are. What it was like growing up in your family. What your dreams were as a child."

He wrapped his lanky thigh around hers and settled her more closely against him. "I wanted to play for the Red Sox. I was going to be the world's greatest first baseman until I found out it meant I had to practice every day."

"Ah," she said. "You discovered that play meant work."

"Yep. And then, when I was nine, my brother Pat came home one day with a secondhand Gibson he'd picked up somewhere. Somebody put the idea in his head that it would attract girls." He shifted his hand on her breast. "The only problem was that Pat didn't have a musical bone in his body."

She lay her cheek against his shoulder. "But you did," she said.

"But I did. One day when he was at work, I snuck into his room and wiped the dust off the Gibson and just started playing. Jesus, was he pissed. Here he'd been working at it for months, and in his hands it sounded like a cat in heat. Then I waltzed in, this skinny little snot-nosed nine-year-old kid, and played it like I'd been born with the damn thing in my hand."

"And the world's greatest first baseman," she said softly,

"died that day, unrecognized and unmourned."

He tasted the skin of her shoulder and adjusted the bedding around them. "Pretty much," he said. "I was hooked. I did Pat's chores for the rest of that summer to pay for the guitar."

"Sounds like he got the best of that deal," she said.

"Oh, I don't know. How can you put a price on what he gave me that day?"

"You have a unique way of looking at life, my love."

"Well," he said, "the way I see it, there are two kinds of people in the world. Pragmatists and dreamers. The pragmatists keep the world running smoothly. But the dreamers," he said, "they're the ones who feed our souls."

"And you're a dreamer."

"So are you, pudding."

"Me? A dreamer? I'd say I'm more of a pragmatist."

"Only on the surface. Scratch that surface and underneath the pragmatist you'll find a genuine, hundred-proof dreamer."

"Ah, Flash," she said, "where were you when I was eighteen?"

"I was right there. You, on the other hand, were a little preoccupied."

"Ironic, isn't it? All my life, I've needed someone like you. And there you were, standing right in front of me all along."

He took her face in his hands and kissed her. "Imagine that," he said.

CHAPTER THIRTY-THREE

It was a Saturday in early November, and Rob was leaning against her bathroom door frame, watching as she pulled a towel from her head and shook her hair free. In one hand, he held a pint of Ben & Jerry's. "Trish is downstairs," he said, scooping up a spoonful of Cherry Garcia. "She just waltzed in, plastic in hand, ready to singlehandedly slay the dragons of a depressed economy." He held out the spoonful of ice cream, and Casey took a bite. "She uttered the word mall," he added, "and I ran for cover."

She ran brisk fingers through her wet hair. "It's been ages since I've been shopping. Want to go?"

"No, thanks." He scooped up another spoonful of ice cream. "This is one of those female bonding things, isn't it? I know about this stuff. I have five sisters."

She lowered her eyelids. "I'd rather bond with you," she said.

He licked the spoon clean. "If we do any more bonding, Fiore, neither one of us will be walking upright for a week."

"That's a shame," she said, "because I was thinking of stopping by Victoria's Secret."

"Of course, I've been known to be wrong. By the way, purple just happens to get me hot. In case you're interested."

"Everything gets you hot, MacKenzie."

"Only if you're in it, sweetheart. Or out of it, depending on the circumstances."

"Aha," she said. "Brownie points."

He flashed her a grin. "How'm I doing?"

"Pretty good so far."

"So there's a little leeway," he said, "in case I feel some urgent need to be bad?"

She stepped closer to him and rested a hand on his sleeve. "When you're bad," she said, looking wistfully into his carton of ice cream, "your score goes up."

"That's not all that goes up." He offered her another spoonful of ice cream.

"Ah, Flash," she said, "I love it when you talk dirty."

They exchanged a damp kiss that tasted of chocolate and cherries. "Go ahead," he said, "go shopping. Have fun."

"What will you do all day?"

"I'll probably sit around watching soap operas and drinking beer and imagining you in something purple from Victoria's Secret."

She found Trish standing at the kitchen sink, finishing the breakfast dishes that she and Rob had renounced in favor of more pleasurable pastimes. "Hi, hon," Trish said. "I was starting to think you were dead. I haven't seen you in ages."

"I'm sorry," she said. "I've been intending to stop by. I've just been busy."

Trish dried her hands on a dish towel. "Doing what?"

Casey looked to Rob for help, but he was leaning those lanky hips against the kitchen counter and had apparently discovered something riveting inside his carton of Cherry Garcia. "This and that," she told her sister-in-law. Trish gave her a long, hard look, but didn't ask any more questions.

The mall was crowded. They wandered through the shops, looking at everything, buying little. "This place is exhausting," Trish said. "Why do I even come here?"

"Female bonding," she said. "That's Rob's theory."

"To hell with bonding," Trish said. "Just give me a tub of ice for my feet."

"Just one more stop," she said. "There's one place I still have to visit."

She'd always loved Victoria's Secret. The smell of the place was so exotic, the atmosphere so feminine, the clothes so beautiful. While Trish looked at lounging pajamas, Casey fingered her way through a rack of silk teddies, pausing to examine the white lace one with the satin ribbons and the spaghetti straps. At her shoulder, Trish sighed. "Sweetie," she said, "if I had a body like yours, I'd buy the whole rack. What's his favorite color?"

"Purple," she said softly, still stroking the lace with her fingertips. Then flushed, realizing what she'd admitted.

"Buy the orchid one with the black ribbons," Trish said. "It'll drive him crazy."

Casey sighed. "I can never keep anything from you," she said. "How did you know?"

"Honey, I've never known any man to take that much interest in the inside of an ice cream carton. Are you going to tell me about it? Or did you plan to keep it a secret forever?"

"I'm not sure I can. It's like—" She tried to find words, realized she couldn't. "I've never felt this way in my life. Never. Not even—" She paused to tamp down the seed of guilt that had sprung to life inside her. "Not even with Danny."

"Oh, honey. This is serious, isn't it?"

"I'm thirty-three years old. Am I supposed to feel this way at thirty-three?"

"I don't know. How do you feel?"

"Like a teenager, high on hormones."

"Well, hon, it isn't over till it's over." Trish shoved aside a couple of teddies, pulled out a peach-colored one and examined it. "So how's the sex?"

"*Oh. My. God.* White-hot. Steamy. Incredible. Trish, he makes me laugh. In bed. Right in the middle of making love. And it's not just the sex. He's bright, he's funny, he's kind and gentle and talented—"

"Sounds like a regular Lochinvar," Trish said dryly.

"He's also jackass stubborn, colorblind, and prone to occasional tantrums when things don't go his way."

"He's been in love with you for years." Trish fingered a black satin ribbon. "I knew it when Danny died. I saw the way he hovered over you, like a mama bear protecting her cub, ready to maul anybody who came within twenty paces. At one point, I thought he was going to haul off and boot your precious cousin Teddy out the back door. Not that I would have objected." Trish's eyebrows rose. "Why are you looking at me that way? Don't tell me you didn't know."

"I guess," Casey said, "maybe I didn't want to know."

"Not everybody gets a second chance. If I were you, I'd latch onto him and hang on for dear life."

***

He was in the process of becoming intimately acquainted

with Casey's laundry equipment when he decided to do something about Danny's car. He'd found it in the barn a couple of days ago when he'd been looking for the storm windows, and it had been eating at him, the image of that exquisite machine lying dormant beneath a shroud of dust. Danny had passionately loved that car, and he would break down and cry if he knew what had become of it. So while a load of whites tumbled in the clothes dryer, Rob took the spare set of keys from the hook in the kitchen, flung the barn door open wide, and climbed in behind the wheel of the Ferrari.

He fitted the key into the ignition. After a moment's hesitation, the engine roared to life. He could feel the power in the vibration of the steering wheel beneath his hand, could hear it in the engine's aggressive purr. He caressed the shifter, then eased it into reverse and backed the car out of the barn.

Car washes be damned; he'd always felt that a man didn't truly know a car until he'd washed it by hand. There was a communion between man and car, something to do with the laying on of hands, something that few women seemed to understand. He hosed off the top layer of dust, then soaped the car lovingly, rinsed it and wiped it dry with a chamois so it wouldn't water spot. On a shelf in the barn, he found a half-empty can of car wax, and he waxed and buffed and polished until the finish was sleek as butter beneath his fingers. And he left it there, glistening in the sun.

He whistled as he folded towels and underwear, not in the least fazed by the intimacy of handling a woman's lingerie. He wanted everything to be perfect, the house spotless when she came home, for tonight he wanted no distractions. Tonight, to the tune of dim lights and soft jazz, over a dinner accompanied by flickering candlelight and Dom Perignon, he was going to ask Casey Fiore to be his wife.

He distributed the towels evenly, half in the downstairs bath, half upstairs. Laundry basket in hand, he swung through the door to Casey's bedroom. On the night stand was a framed photo of her with Danny, his arms folded around her, both of them smiling into the camera. It must have been taken shortly before he died. Even though that damned baby face had kept Danny looking a decade younger than his thirty-six years, it was evident in his eyes, in both their eyes, the hell they'd been through.

Feeling as though he'd accidentally stumbled into some private moment where he didn't belong, Rob set the laundry basket on the foot of the king-size bed, realizing too late that it was a blatant reminder that the woman he loved had slept here with another man. His mouth dry and acrid, he went to the bureau and flung open the top drawer, prepared to cram in Casey's lingerie and scurry back downstairs where he belonged. But it wasn't lace and silk that stared back at him from the open drawer. It was Fruit of the Loom. Danny's underwear.

She still had Danny's underwear in the bureau drawer?

In the second drawer he found Danny's socks, neatly paired up. In the third, his tee shirts, precisely folded. By the time he reached a drawer that held feminine apparel, his hands were shaking so hard he didn't care if it was the right drawer or not. He just dumped in her bras and panties and slammed it shut.

The laundry basket was empty now. He had no reason to linger. But of their own volition, his legs carried him to the closet. He opened one of the bifold doors slowly, breathing a sigh of relief as he saw dresses and skirts, blouses and slacks and a single lacy peignoir. Then he flung open the second door, and his body went numb. The left side of the closet was crammed with Danny Fiore's clothes: pants and shirts and jackets and a black tux in a dry cleaner's bag, ties and leather belts draped neatly from an elaborate contraption that hung from the back wall of the closet.

It didn't have to mean anything. She simply hadn't gotten around to getting rid of Danny's things yet. But a nagging little voice reminded him that it had been nearly two years. Why would she keep a dead man's clothes where she would have to look at them every time she opened the closet door?

She wouldn't. Unless she hadn't yet accepted his death.

Rob slammed the door shut and took a look around the room. It was all still here. Cufflinks on the dresser, Danny's silver-handled hairbrush, his electric shaver still plugged in, just in case.

It was the shoes that did him in, those goddamn size twelves sitting there beside the dresser where their owner had left them, patiently waiting for his return. Just like his loving widow.

Jesus, Mary and Joseph. How the hell could he fill a dead man's shoes?

Retrieving the empty laundry basket, he fled down the stairs and flung the basket through the door to the laundry room. Two years should have been time enough for any woman. And he would have sworn on a stack of Bibles that what they'd shared had been genuine. But the evidence was all there. She still hadn't accepted Danny's death. She was still waiting for him to come home.

And he, Robert Kevin MacKenzie, had made a fool of himself.

***

When she pulled into the driveway, the Ferrari was the first thing she saw. It gleamed blood-red in the afternoon sun, and the pain hit her like a fist. She yanked on the emergency brake and sat there, staring in silence while Trish gathered up her bags. *Keep your cool*, she told herself. *Take a deep breath and try not to lose it.*

"Hey," Trish said, "are you okay? All of a sudden, you're white as a ghost."

"I'm just tired," she said, struggling to keep the tremor from her voice. "Shopping wore me out."

Trish looked at her oddly, but accepted her explanation at face value. "Get some rest," she said. "You look like death warmed over."

On the pretense of rounding up her packages, Casey stayed behind the steering wheel, forcing herself to take deep, relaxing breaths, until Trish had backed her Jeep around and driven away. It was only then that she trusted herself to get out of the car. She skirted the Ferrari, quietly let herself into the house, and dropped her bags on the kitchen table.

She found Rob in his favorite spot, on the porch swing, his feet up, a Heineken in his hand, his jaw set at that familiar angle that told her he was spoiling for a fight. "What the hell do you think you're doing?" she said. "Why did you take Danny's car out of the barn?"

He looked at her blankly. And then something in his eyes sparked and caught fire. "I washed it," he said brusquely. "It was filthy."

She took a deep breath, but it failed to stop her trembling. "You should have asked me first."

Color flushed his face, and he slammed down his beer bottle. "Forgive me," he snarled, "for defacing a priceless exhibit from the permanent collection of the Daniel Fiore Memorial Museum."

She took a step backward. "What are you talking about?" she said.

"I've been in your bedroom, sweetheart. You've turned it into a fucking shrine to His Eminence. Jesus Christ, Casey, his goddamn *shoes* are still sitting there where he left them!"

"We're not talking about shoes," she said. "We're talking about Danny's car!"

"We damn well are talking about shoes! And about underwear, and about cuff links, and about his goddamn razor that's still sitting there, plugged in and waiting!"

Her throat constricted so tightly she had trouble breathing. "None of that," she said quietly, "is any of your business—"

"*Nothing* is any of my business! I'm no more than a house guest, am I? Good enough to fuck, as long as I don't forget my place. MacKenzie's stud service. You should pass the word around to all your friends. Maybe they'd like to take advantage of my special offer. Two for the price of—"

She slapped him, hard, and they glared at each other. "You just don't get it, do you?" he said bitterly. "You just can't see me. You never could. All you could ever see was Danny. The man's been dead for two years, and he's still all you can see! No matter what I do, I always come in a poor second!"

"Is that what you think?" she said. "Is that what you really think? Because if you're that stupid—"

"At least I'm smart enough to get the hell out of here!" He got up from the swing and slammed into the house, stalked to the guest room. Flinging his suitcase on the bed, he began opening drawers and dumping their contents into the open suitcase. "I thought two years was time enough," he said. "But you know what? No matter how long I wait, it'll never be time enough.

They should've put you in the ground right along with him!"

She clutched the door frame. "Where are you going?" she demanded.

"Home." He closed the suitcase and snapped the locks. "Where I belong."

In the vicinity of her heart, she felt a dull ache. "Fine, then!" she said. "Go! Get the hell out, because if you're that stupid, I don't want you! I don't love you, and I don't want you! Go back to your bimbos, and good riddance!"

He glared at her. "Yeah? Well, guess what, dollface? I don't love you, either. I say that to all the women I fuck. You're just one of many."

She picked up a ceramic figurine from the dresser and heaved it at him. He ducked, and it shattered against the wall. "Get out," she said through clenched teeth. "Get out of my life and don't come back!"

Rob yanked on his leather bomber jacket and picked up his suitcase. "Send me a bill for services rendered," he said. "You know my address."

And he shouldered her aside and slammed out the door.

CHAPTER THIRTY-FOUR

When Danny had died, she'd gone blessedly numb, and the numbness had held the pain at bay. This time, there was no numbness. When Rob MacKenzie amputated himself from her life, she felt every slice of the scalpel. For fifteen years, the one constant in her life had been Rob. He'd shared her moments of triumph and supported her through her moments of anguish. Danny Fiore had been her love, her heart, her obsession, but Rob had been everything else: friend, mentor, pillar of strength. Sounding board, collaborator, keeper of secrets. And, ultimately, lover. The emptiness he left behind was too vast to be filled. Casey would have welcomed some of that soothing numbness, for she felt as though she'd been scoured with sandpaper and then rolled in salt. It was difficult to remember what her life had been like before Rob. It was impossible to imagine her future without him.

Sleeping was impossible; when at last sleep did come, she would inevitably awaken with her body clenched tight around a hard core of yearning deep in her belly. She tormented herself by reliving every moment of their lovemaking. A part of her had died with Danny, and after two years of a sterile, barren existence, Rob had brought her back to life. He'd unleashed a tide of raging hormones that had lain dormant through two years of sexual starvation, and she hungered after him with a yearning so carnal it astonished her.

He had resumed his tour. One dreary November day as she listlessly thumbed through the newest issue of *Variety*, she found an ad listing the dates and the cities. Now she had a new method of torturing herself. She knew that he was in Denver on November twenty-seventh, and in Dallas on the thirtieth. He'd picked up twelve extra cities this time around, and a part of her hated him for continuing on with his life, as if the time they'd spent as lovers had never happened.

She spent Thanksgiving with Bill and Trish because she had to eat somewhere or risk undergoing the Spanish Inquisition. That night, Casey went to bed early and lay alone in the darkness, thinking about the man who'd always been her Gibraltar, who'd always known the right words to say and had seemed to carry the solutions to all her problems in the palm of his hand. How could he have been so wrong? Had he really expected her to erase the years she'd spent as Danny's wife, to just wipe the slate clean and pretend those years had never happened? She'd loved Danny passionately. He would always retain his rightful place in her heart. Rob should have understood that. He should have understood that her love for Danny in no way negated her love for him. She'd loved Rob since the beginning of time. That love had simply ripened into something neither of them had expected, something tender and lusty and beautiful.

On Christmas morning, she exchanged gifts with her father and Millie. That afternoon, she called Travis in Boston and talked to him for a half-hour. Leslie was pregnant with their second child, and they'd just bought a ranch house in Chestnut Hill. It was on a dead-end street in an upper-middle-class neighborhood, and there was a big back yard for the kids to play in. The schools were wonderful. And Casey couldn't help smiling just a bit at the irony of her rebellious brother's defection to the suburban bourgeoisie.

It was the first Christmas in fifteen years that she hadn't talked to Rob, and the significance wasn't lost on her. She thought about tracking him down, but what would she say once she had him on the phone? They'd both said things that couldn't be taken back. *I don't love you. I don't want you.* Lies. Every word a lie. They'd deliberately hurt each other, and she wasn't sure they could ever recover from that. It would be best for both of them if she held onto the shredded remains of her pride and left him alone.

***

It was always the same. Night after night, town after town, until it all blended together into a single, continuous nightmare. He played until his fingers were raw, gave them what they'd come for, but his heart was no longer in it. Onstage, it was possible to maintain a certain detachment, to hide behind his instrument and the physical separation from the audience. Offstage, where life was a perpetual party, it was more difficult. In real life, he was expected to interact with people. So he complied indifferently with their expectations, and if anybody noticed the change in him, nobody had the nerve to say anything.

Then, in Denver, Kitty Callahan fell off the stage during rehearsal and broke her ankle. Rob paid her hospital bill and had her flown home, and then he had to do some serious scrambling to locate a replacement backup singer on such short notice. One of the roadies knew a local girl, a leggy blonde named Kimberly, who had a beautiful voice and didn't mind giving up her day job to play twelve cities in twenty days. She spent most of her off-duty time making cow eyes at him. After a few days of that, he decided one night in Memphis to exercise his *droit du seigneur* and take her up on her implicit offer. It might not cure what was wrong with him, but it couldn't hurt. Through the smoky haze of an overcrowded hotel room, he made eye contact with her. He lifted a shoulder and tilted his head toward the door, and she nodded. He almost laughed at how easy it was. He might be thirty-five years old, but he hadn't lost his touch yet.

On his way out the door he grabbed a bottle of coffee brandy before guiding Kimberly down the shabby hallway to his room. He set the brandy down on the vanity and got two Dixie cups from the bathroom. He poured a cup of brandy for her, then filled his own, wondering how many he'd have to drink before he could convince himself that this stunning blonde was really a green-eyed brunette.

She had the bluest eyes he'd ever seen, and right now they were looking at him as though he were the big, bad wolf. For the first time, he wondered if she were underage. She looked about sixteen. "How old are you?" he asked, the first words he'd spoken to her, probably ever.

"Twenty," she said.

He drained his cup of brandy. "You'll do."

She came to him willingly, and he relaxed. He might not be much good at polite conversation these days, but getting laid he could handle. It didn't require polite conversation. It didn't require any conversation at all. He crumpled his empty cup and dropped it on the floor, drew her into his arms and kissed her.

Easy, he thought, as that sumptuous body became pliant in his arms. He'd done this a hundred times before, with a hundred different women. This time wouldn't be any different.

They fell across the bed, and he peeled her shirt up and off over her head. Her breasts were firm and round and unfettered, and he sampled them, forcing his attentions on first one breast and then the other, wondering as he did so why her ample mammary glands had failed to arouse him. Where was the excitement, the anticipation, the pleasure? If he was going to the trouble of getting laid, he ought to at least enjoy it. He drew back his head and looked at her, and she opened those incredible blue eyes in puzzlement. "Rob?" she said.

And he realized, with utter astonishment, that he didn't want her.

"Jesus, Mary and Joseph," he said, rolling away from her to lie staring at the ceiling.

"What is it?" she said. "What's wrong?"

"I can't," he said. "I can't do it."

"I don't understand."

He looked at her. "I don't even know your last name," he said.

"Is it something I did? Something I said?"

"Look at me," he said. "I'm thirty-five years old. I'm old enough to be your goddamn father." Those bare breasts staring him in the face embarrassed him. They looked so vulnerable. He bent and picked her shirt up off the floor and tossed it to her. "Put this back on," he said.

She plunged her arms into the shirt and yanked it down over her head. "What did I do wrong?" she asked in bewilderment.

He would have liked to offer consolation to this young girl who thought she'd been rejected, but he realized with tired resignation that he, who had always been so adept at giving, had nothing left to offer her. Somewhere between Jackson Falls and Memphis, the well had gone dry. "Nothing," he said. "Just leave. Please."

When she was gone, the bedside clock ticked in the silence. Rob got up and walked to the vanity where he'd left the bottle of brandy. He stared at his reflection in the mirror, and then he picked up the bottle and uncapped it.

"Well, kiddo," he said, "looks like it's just you and me."

***

The call came from Drew Lawrence at the end of January. "We found something the other day," he said, "sitting on a back shelf, covered with dust. Masters of some tracks that Danny laid down about three years ago. Do you know anything about them?"

"No," Casey said, surprised. "Danny never said anything to me about unreleased material."

"It was an album he'd been working on while you were separated. When the two of you got back together, he shelved the project." Drew paused. "Casey, we'd like to release it."

"As an album? Posthumously?"

"It's not unheard of—"

"No."

He continued as though he hadn't heard her. "Danny wasn't under contract to us at the time these recordings were made. Legally, they belong to you. We want to buy them from you."

"They're not for sale."

"Why not?"

"The man is dead, Drew. But you're still trying to drain blood from him. What's wrong? Is your supply of Armani suits running low?"

"That's unfair. This stuff is dynamite. We owe it to his fans to make it public."

"Come on, Drew. We both know that for ten years, Danny Fiore was your meal ticket."

"Casey," he said, "if we don't release this material, it'll die with him. Is that what you want?"

She hesitated. He had her, and he knew it. "No," she said at last, "I suppose it's not. Let me hear it. Then we'll see."

"Great! I'll have a copy made and in your hands by tomorrow morning. Call me as soon as you've heard it, and we'll talk."

The package arrived by Fed Ex around ten the next

morning, an anonymous-looking CD in a paper wrapper with *Fiore Master, Copy 2* printed on it in pencil. She popped the disc into the CD player, then went to the kitchen to pour herself a shot of bourbon. For this, she was going to need fortification. Shot glass in hand, she returned to the living room and sat in the Boston rocker to listen.

His voice still tore her to pieces. It always had, and it always would. Nobody else could do with a song what Danny Fiore could. That voice was liquid velvet, wrapping itself around the notes, seeping into all the crevices, evoking memory and emotion, light and darkness, heaven and hell and everything in between. For a moment, she was back in that dark cellar in Boston, hearing him sing for the very first time, and her response was the same now as it had been then, the same as it had been every time she'd heard him sing. He'd had the gift of magic, and it broke her heart to know that extraordinary voice had been silenced forever.

Most of the songs she'd written herself, with Rob, and that was a whole different heartache. Memories came back to her in bits and pieces, scraps of conversation, rough spots where they'd had to go back and rewrite, jubilant moments when it had come so quickly they couldn't write fast enough to get it all down. Some of the material was new to her, but it was impossible to mistake a Rob MacKenzie composition. Like a fine wine or a Monet, Rob's music bore a signature all its own. She would have recognized his work if she'd encountered it on a mountaintop in Tibet.

She poured another bourbon and ran the whole thing through a second time. This time, she froze her emotions and listened with a professional ear. Drew had been right. This was the best work Danny had ever done. She sat in the rocker with the shot glass, thinking about the words he'd said to her so many years ago: *I want them to kiss my ass. I want to prove I'm more than just some bastard wop kid from Boston's Little Italy.* She'd always known he was more, much more than that. But had he ever really believed it himself?

A half-hour later, she called Drew. "Casey!" he said, sounding jovial and paternal. "I didn't expect to hear from you so soon."

"Really? I have fifty bucks that says you're eating a pastrami sandwich at your desk because you were afraid you'd miss my call if you went out to lunch."

At the other end of the line, he chuckled. "You win the bet," he said. "Only it's liverwurst."

"I'm ready to deal," she said.

"I knew you'd see it my way. We're prepared to make a generous offer—"

"I've already decided on my price."

When she named it, there was silence at his end, a silence that stretched out between them. He cleared his throat. The joviality was gone. "You can't possibly be serious," he said.

"That's my asking price, Drew. You can't have him for a penny less."

"That's absurd. Totally out of the question. We're running a small operation—"

"You and I both know that we're sitting on a gold mine here. You'll get your money back threefold."

"But that kind of up-front money—"

"Listen to me," she said, "and listen good. When you signed Danny, you were a bit player with a temporary secretary and a crummy office on 42nd Street. Look around you, Drew. Who do you think paid for the custom-made Italian suits and the diamond pinkie rings and the *Moet et Chandon*? Who paid for the Jaguar and the Madison Avenue office suite and the high-maintenance women? Danny did, that's who. You owe him."

"Casey, you're killing me here. My neck is in the noose. I can't agree to a deal like that."

"Fine. There are plenty of other record companies out there. I'm sure one of them would be more than happy to pay my price."

"Jesus, Casey—"

"Maybe I'll just keep the damn songs." She paused for emphasis. "Or torch them."

"I have the originals."

"And I have a lawyer whose suits make yours look like they came from Wal-Mart."

"Wait!" he said. "Wait. Maybe I can work something out."

She smiled, picturing the perpetually elegant Drew Lawrence sitting in his equally elegant office, squirming. "I thought maybe you could," she said.

"That much money. Jesus."

"And when will you ever again get your hands on anything this big? Don't you understand, Drew? This is Danny's swan song. I'm not doing this for me. I don't need the money." She paused, thinking of the frightened boy who had left his innocence behind in the jungles of Southeast Asia, and of the broken man who'd returned in his place. More softly, she said, "I'm doing this for him."

"He'd be impressed. You strike a hard bargain. Whatever happened to that sweet girl I remember?"

"She grew up."

"With a vengeance."

"For the first time in my life, I'm holding all the cards. I'm the one calling the shots. Power, Drew. I never before realized how good it feels."

Forty minutes later, he called her back. "Mrs. Fiore," he said, "you've got your deal. Congratulations."

"Thanks," she said, "but it wasn't me who made this deal. It was Danny. Think of him when you open that next bottle of *Moet*."

She hung up the phone and sat in the rocker for a long time, looking at his picture on the fireplace mantel. She would set aside a reasonable portion of the money for Anna Montoya. No matter what the future brought, Danny's mother would never want for anything, ever again. The rest would go, in Danny's name, to some organization that provided support services for Vietnam vets. Somewhere out there in the great beyond, Danny was watching, with understanding and approval. She raised her glass to his picture. "*Ciao*," she said softly. "*Caro mio*." And drained her glass.

She was ready now to let go.

***

With trepidation, Rob called his mom. "I'm moving back east," he said cautiously. "Can I stay with you and Dad for a while? Just until I can find a place of my own?"

After he'd missed Christmas with the family, he wasn't sure she was still speaking to him. But he should have known better. They probably heard her gleeful whoop in Seattle. "Patrick," she shouted, "turn down that blasted TV and listen to me. Robbie's coming home!"

He spent a couple of weeks tying up loose ends, then packed all his belongings and sent them east in a moving van. He took Igor, his Gibson, and a single suitcase with him in the Porsche. It took him four days to cross the country, four days of sleeping in cheap motels and subsisting on fast food and FM radio. When the Boston skyline appeared before him, he felt a sense of homecoming unlike any he'd ever known. He might be deluding himself, painting brilliant illusions and dreaming impossible dreams, but no matter what the outcome, one truth couldn't be denied: Casey was just three hours north.

His sister Rose took him apartment hunting, but nothing they saw suited him. Over lunch at Top of the Hub, she let him have it with both barrels. "Listen, Robbie," she said, "we've been looking at apartments for two weeks now, and so far, you haven't liked a thing we've seen. They're all either too big or too small, too new or too old. You don't like the neighborhood or you don't like the kitchen or you don't like the color of the goddamn living room carpet! You're my baby brother, and I love you to pieces, but my universe doesn't revolve around finding you an apartment. Believe it or not, I have a life I could be living."

She looked so indignant, his red-haired dynamo of a sister, that he felt ashamed. "Rosie," he said, "I'm sorry."

"You ought to be. What's the matter with you? Mom hardly dares to say more than three words to you for fear of getting her head ripped off. Michael spent ten minutes in your company and told me that as far as he's concerned, you should have stayed in California. You actually started a fight with Dad—"

"I offered to buy him a new car. His old one's being held together with Juicy Fruit and Band-Aids!"

"That's not the point. You've only been here for three weeks, but already you've managed to disrupt the whole family.

You've got everybody walking around on eggshells. Nobody dares to say boo to you. I don't know what's going on, but I miss my little brother. He was a real sweet guy who always used to have a smile for everyone and something funny to say. Where the hell is he? It's like aliens have moved in and taken over your body."

The Charles River was white and frozen. In the distance, the red line train crawled across the Longfellow Bridge toward Cambridge on the other side. He looked at his sister. "What do you want me to say?"

"I want to know what could possibly have turned my baby brother into Godzilla on wheels." She placed a hand on his. "You're not sick, are you?"

He snorted. "Where the hell did you get an idea like that?"

"You know Mom. She always imagines the worst."

"Tell her to stop worrying. I don't have AIDS."

When she frowned, the freckles on her forehead drew together. "Are you having a sexual identity crisis?"

"Care to try that again in English?"

She looked around furtively and leaned over the table. "Are you gay?" she whispered.

He gaped at her in astonishment, and then he laughed, a deep, rich belly laugh, his first in ages. He laughed so hard it hurt. "Jesus, Rose," he said, wiping tears from his eyes, "you gotta stop watching *Geraldo*."

"Then there's only one thing it could be. It has to be a woman."

"You know what? You remind me of a woman I know. Her name's Trish. Do you suppose every family has one?" And he was off again on a gale of laughter. "You two should get together," he said, holding onto his belly. "You'd make one hell of—" He had to stop because he was laughing so hard. "—one hell of an investigative team." He covered his mouth with both hands, but the laughter escaped anyway. At the next table, a woman peered discreetly at them from behind her menu.

"Rob!" his sister hissed. "You're making a scene!"

He took a couple of deep breaths and waited for the laughter to subside. "I'm sorry," he said. "It's just been so long since I've laughed. It felt so good."

"You didn't answer my question."

"You didn't ask one."

"I did, too. I asked you if it was a woman."

"No, you didn't. You said it had to be a woman. You didn't ask if you were right."

Beneath the freckles, her face was turning an interesting shade of pink. "Damn it, Robbie, is it or isn't it a woman?"

"Yes!" he shouted. "Yes, it is a woman! Are you satisfied?"

For a moment, there was dead silence as everyone within hearing distance stopped eating to stare at them. Rose closed her eyes and sank lower in her seat, her face so pale the freckles stood out in stark relief. "More like mortified," she said. "But satisfied will probably catch up to me. I just won ten bucks."

For the second time in as many minutes, he regarded her with astonishment. "You *what*?"

Her recovery from mortification was amazingly rapid. "I bet Michael ten bucks it was a woman." She gave him an impish smile. "And I was right."

"Gee, thanks. I love hearing that my life's providing entertainment for the whole family."

"What do you expect, Rob? You've been a monster ever since you came home."

"Yeah? Well, maybe I should just stay in my room and hide!"

"Maybe you should!"

They glared at each other until the glares dissolved into sheepish grins. Rose shook her head. "Now that you've ruined my reputation to the point where I'll never dare to show my face in this joint again, little brother," she said, "I figure you owe me one."

He squared his jaw. "Yeah?"

She matched his expression. "Yeah. You're rolling in dough, and I'm in the mood to go shopping."

"I get it," he said. "Hit me where it hurts."

She grinned. "And if you behave yourself, I might even tell you a few things you don't know about women."

CHAPTER THIRTY-FIVE

In February, she sold the Ferrari.

She didn't expect it to go so quickly. She placed an ad in the Portland newspaper and promptly forgot about it until she got a call from a Westbrook attorney who wanted to know if she'd sold it yet. When she told him it was still available, he asked if he could drive up that afternoon and see it.

She sent him out to the barn alone. This was a huge step, one she wasn't sure she was ready for. The sandy-haired attorney returned, his enthusiasm obvious. And then he asked it, the question she'd been dreading. "Why are you selling it?"

"It belonged to my late husband," she said, amazed that the words came so easily, so naturally. "It's been sitting for two years, and it should belong to somebody who'll love it as much as he did."

He thought her asking price was fair, and while his L.L. Bean boots dripped melted snow on her kitchen floor, he wrote her a check and she gave him a bill of sale, and it was done. She'd taken the first huge step with frightening ease.

The closet was more difficult.

Every item she handled had memories attached, and she removed them one at a time, letting herself feel the bittersweet emotions as she meticulously folded each shirt, each pair of pants, before placing them in a big green Hefty bag. She emptied the bureau drawers, added his ties and his belts and his shoes and his electric razor, then cleared the last of his toiletries from the bathroom medicine cabinet. She filled two huge bags, knotted them tightly, and carried them downstairs and out to the trash barrel beside the barn.

The next morning, at dawn, she burned them.

She wasn't sure what she'd expected to feel, but certainly not this relief. She probed her emotions cautiously, searching for the guilt that should have been there. But it wasn't there, only the relief and the sense that an overwhelming burden had been lifted from her shoulders.

After that, it got easier. She emptied her closet and her

drawers and moved her belongings to the downstairs guest room, then gave her bedroom set to Billy and Alison. She stripped the wallpaper from the bedroom walls, painted the woodwork a warm antique white and repapered the room in dusky rose. In an antique shop she found a rose-colored brocade love seat and matching wing chairs. An oriental rug and Tiffany lamp completed the ensemble, and her former bedroom became a sitting room. And then she tackled the room across the hall.

It had windows on two sides and a strong southern exposure, but the closet was abysmally inadequate. She called Jesse and asked for the name of a good carpenter, and to her surprise, he came over and built it himself, a beautiful walk-in closet twelve feet long, with shelves for shoes and sweaters and linens. When he was done, she painted the woodwork the same antique white as the sitting room, then papered the walls in an aqua floral print and hung curtains of teal and blue.

She thought of Rob often as the weeks went by, especially on the day the new bedroom set was delivered and set up and she covered the mahogany four-poster bed with the new spread. She hadn't relied on memory; she'd actually driven back to Bar Harbor, to the cabin where she and Rob had become lovers on a golden October afternoon, and then she had shopped around until she found a bed identical to the one where they'd first made love. She supposed that most men wouldn't notice. But Rob would. He would notice, and he would understand.

The month of March slipped by, and one April evening as she sat on her back porch, she heard the first spring peepers. The next day she cut a half-dozen of the bright yellow daffodils that grew next to the old stone foundation of the house, put them in a jar of water, and drove to the cemetery.

Katie was here, and Mama, and Grandma and Grandpa Bradley, but it was Danny she'd come to see. She knelt in the damp grass by his gravestone and arranged the flowers in front of it. "See what I brought you, darling?" she said. "Daffodils, because I know they're your favorite." She sat quietly, drinking in the peacefulness of this place where he rested. Tugging at a tuft of grass near his headstone, she said, "There are some things I need to talk to you about."

The sky was vivid blue, the air clean and clear. Toying

with a blade of grass, she said, "I imagine you know about the deal I made with Drew. And why. You always needed so much to be somebody. I had to prove to you that you were. Not too shabby a deal for a bastard wop kid from Little Italy."

She gazed up into the towering elm that had somehow escaped the fatal blight that had attacked so many of its fellows. "I suppose," she said, "you know about Rob, too. I took my marriage vows very seriously, Danny. I loved you desperately, and I was always faithful to you, even when I knew that my feelings for Rob had gone miles beyond platonic." Her voice softened. "Not a day goes by that I don't miss you."

She plucked at a blade of grass, caught it and rolled it between her fingers. "But I have to move on now," she said, tearing at the slender green stalk. "You're gone, but Rob's here, and I love him, Danny, I love him so much it hurts. I've always loved both of you. My feelings for him simply deepened into something neither of us expected." She dropped the blade of grass, shoved up the sleeves of her sweater, and leaned back to better see the brilliant blue of the April sky. "He's a good man," she said. "And if it's not too late, I'm going to marry him."

Still gazing at the sky, she said, "I know you loved us both. I'd feel better if we had your blessing."

She stayed there for a long time in the spring sunshine, waiting patiently for his answer. When it came, she stood up slowly, her knees wet from the squishy ground. She bent and removed a single daffodil from the jar and lay it across her daughter's grave.

And held her head high as she walked back to her car.

$$***$$

When she dialed Rob's number, a woman answered. Stricken, Casey broke the connection. *What did you expect?* she chastised herself. *Did you think a man like Rob MacKenzie would stay celibate forever? Did you expect him to sit around waiting for you?*

But of course, that was exactly what she'd thought. She had obviously been mistaken. Six months had gone by, six months in which he hadn't even attempted to contact her. That should have told her something.

She agonized for hours before she worked up the courage to try again. This time, when the young woman answered, she took a deep breath and asked for Rob. "Sorry," the woman said. "Wrong number." And hung up.

Casey stared in disbelief at the bleating receiver. Again, slowly and meticulously this time, she dialed Rob's number. Again, the woman answered, and this time she sounded irritated. "Look, lady," she said, "I told you before there's no Rob here."

"Wait!" Casey said. "Please don't hang up. I'm calling long distance."

Something of her desperation must have gotten through, because the woman's voice softened. "I've only had this number for a couple of weeks," she said. "Looks like your friend moved and forgot to tell you. Men!"

It didn't make sense. Rob wouldn't have moved. He loved the Hotel California. Maybe, for some reason, he'd had his number changed. To avoid overzealous fans.

Or to avoid her.

Directory Assistance was no help at all. Nor was Rob's answering service. "Mr. MacKenzie stopped using us in January," Judy Rossiter told her. "He paid his bill in full and we haven't heard from him since."

She pondered the meaning of all this. Was this Rob's idea of retaliation, forcing her to track him down? Or was his disappearing act a message to her that they really had nothing more to say to each other? Maybe, just maybe, she'd pushed him too far this time.

She tried Marty Bonner next. Marty had been Rob's agent for five years. He would certainly know where Rob was.

Except that Marty didn't. Coolly, he said, "Mr. MacKenzie and I are no longer associated."

"Marty? What on earth are you talking about?"

"He fired me, Casey, three months ago. Just like that. Said it had been great working with me, but he needed to make some changes in his life, and he couldn't do it in L.A. Very unprofessional behavior, if you ask me. He said he was leaving town, but he didn't say where he was going, and I didn't ask." Marty paused. "Hell, I figured if anyone knew where he was, it would be you."

She'd hit a dead end. If Rob had really left Los Angeles, he could be anywhere between Tijuana and Bangkok. If he didn't want to be found, finding him would be next to impossible.

Unless...

It was a long shot, but if he'd made some kind of permanent move, he must have gotten around to telling his mother by now. And if he hadn't, Rob mailed money home to his parents on a regular basis. Those envelopes had to be postmarked.

Mary was overjoyed to hear from her. "Casey Fiore, it's been too long!" she said. "I thought you'd up and forgotten us!"

"Of course not. I don't mean to neglect old friends. But life just gets so godawful messed up at times."

"Troubles, darlin'?"

Casey hesitated. She would have liked to lay her head on Mary's ample bosom and cry. But how could she spill her troubles to the older woman when it was Mary's own son who was the cause? "It's nothing," she said. "I called because I'm trying to find Rob. I thought by some wild chance you might know where he is."

"I know where he is, all right," Mary said darkly. "And driving us crazy, he is."

Adrenaline shot through her veins. "He's there?" she said. "In Boston?"

"He's been here for going on two months, moping about the house with this long face, and mean as an old tomcat. He got into a fight with his dad, tried to talk poor Patrick into buying a new car. Said the old one was no good, and you know how much stock Patrick takes in that car. Wanted him to buy a Lincoln Continental, of all things. Can you imagine?"

Casey made a small, strangled sound. "He won't talk about it to me," Mary continued, "but it's woman trouble. He admitted it to Rose. I've prayed to the good Lord above that the boy will settle down, find himself a decent wife, but—" She paused, then heaved a mighty sigh. "I don't know what to do with him. He's been puttering around this old house, playing with the plumbing, caulking the windows, complaining that the place'll fall into the cellar one of these days."

"Mary," she said, "I'm so sorry. It's all my fault."

On the other end of the telephone, there was a measured pause. "Now, darlin'," Mary said carefully, "how could it possibly be your fault?"

"Trust me, you don't want to know. Look, I'm coming to Boston."

"Good girl. Maybe you can talk some sense into him. Should I set another place for dinner?"

"I'd like that. But, Mary—"

"What, child?"

"It's really important that I talk to him. Sit on him if you have to."

There was another pause. "For you, sweetheart," Mary said, "I'll rope him and tie him to a chair if I have to."

***

The kite was bright red, a Chinese dragon, and the kid was having trouble with it. It took a nose dive and plummeted toward the sea, recovering at the eleventh hour and swooping back upward with a crisp snap that he heard clearly from three hundred yards away. Except for the two of them, Rob and the kid with the kite, Revere Beach was deserted. Over the past few weeks, he'd come out here often enough so the residents of the massive, ugly condos that lined the beach were probably familiar by now with the black Porsche with the vanity plates that said *WIZARD*. Seldom given to introspection, Rob MacKenzie had found in his thirty-fifth year that he had a great deal to think about. And Revere was the ideal place to do it, close enough to the city so he could watch the silver birds at Logan, people coming and going and living their busy lives, yet isolated enough so he could watch without having to be a part of that busyness.

Mostly he thought about the three of them, and about the complexities of their interrelationships over the span of fifteen years. He remembered vividly the first night he'd met Casey, and how they'd clicked, right then and there. He might have even let himself fall in love with her then, if it hadn't been so obvious that she and Danny were blind to everything but each other. He could never compete with Danny. Who could?

Danny had something that drew people to him, men and women alike. He had dazzled, and Rob had never begrudged him that. Dazzling involved certain responsibilities that Rob wouldn't have welcomed. He was too much his own man to covet the opportunity to live his life to please other people. He lived his life for Rob MacKenzie, and he wouldn't want it any other way. It wasn't Danny's charisma he coveted; it was Danny's wife. Or, more precisely, Danny's widow.

And that, he reluctantly admitted, was the real reason he'd turned tail and run. The plain truth was that Danny Fiore was a hard act to follow. He didn't have Danny's looks or his charm or his goddamn sense of style. Danny was silk and *Dom Perignon*. Rob was denim and Heineken. Danny was filet mignon, he was Big Mac. Danny was a god, while he was just a mortal man, trying his best to survive in this mixed-up world.

He'd said some terrible things to her. He'd accused her of not being ready, but the truth was that he wasn't any more ready than she was. He'd run away because he was so afraid that some day—maybe not next week or next month, but somewhere down the road—he would see it in her eyes, the disappointment she was too much of a lady to voice. And he couldn't face that.

The kid with the kite was way down the beach now, and somehow he'd finally got the thing to fly. It dipped and swooped, then climbed steadily into the blue brilliance of the spring sky. Rob got up from his seat in the pavilion and shoved his hands in his pockets as the wind that was left over from March whipped his shirt against his lanky frame. Maybe it didn't matter that he was something less than a god. Maybe being with her was more important than worrying about the future. Maybe loving her would be worth taking the chance.

He found his mother in the kitchen, mixing a cake, those sturdy arms whipping the wooden spoon in a rapid motion perfected by decades of cooking for a small army. Her hair was a mess, reddish-gray strands poking out in every direction, and for the first time, Rob realized how old she looked. He crossed the room and wrapped his arms around her and gave her a bone-crunching hug.

"And what in blue blazes might this be about?" she said.

"Women may come and women may go," he said, "but a

man's mom is always his first and best girl."

She snorted. "A mother continues to love her child," she said, stirring the cake batter with a vengeance, "even when he acts like an abominable ass."

"Is that how I've been acting?"

"I sugarcoated it so I wouldn't hurt your precious feelings."

"I'm sorry. I don't mean to be a shithead."

"Watch your mouth. I don't know whether to hug you," she added, wiping the spoon on the lip of the bowl, "or take you over my knee. Exactly what kind of foolishness have you been perpetrating?"

He felt the same way he'd felt at twelve, when she caught him smoking out back of Billy Neely's store. "What?" he said with exaggerated innocence, and stuck a finger into the cake batter.

"I talked to Casey today."

He froze, the batter halfway to his mouth. His mother's lips were pursed and she looked as though she knew every rotten thing he'd done in his entire thirty-five years. "I don't know why I didn't figure it out sooner," she said. "The way you've been pissing and moaning about the house. I knew three years ago that she was sweet on you."

"What?" he said. "What in hell are you talking about?"

"Lick that damnable batter off your finger before it drips all over my clean kitchen floor. When Casey came to visit me, the summer she and Danny, God rest his soul, were renovating that money pit they bought up in the wilderness, all she could talk about was you. It was Rob this, and Rob that. Rob, Rob, Rob. Some way or another, we ended up looking through the family photo albums. Pictures of you kids when you were little. She swallowed up those pictures of you like they were sugar candy. I thought, *Lord have mercy, there's heartbreak ahead here.*"

His stomach did a hard somersault. "Jesus, Ma, why didn't you tell me then?"

"She was a married woman. You weren't brought up that way. And much as I loved her, I couldn't see any good ever coming of it."

"What did she say? Today?"

"Not nearly enough. That's what tipped me off. Suddenly,

everything fell into place. What in God's name did you do to that sweet girl?"

Blood rushed to his face as he remembered precisely what he'd done to that sweet girl, but it wasn't exactly the kind of thing a man discussed with his mother. He squared his jaw, and she rolled her eyes. "For the love of Mike," she said, "you're blushing like a seventeen-year-old virgin bride. I've been married for forty-three years and I've raised nine babies. I think I should know by now what it is that men and women do together. That's not what I was talking about, although it does clarify things a bit."

"What do you mean?"

"What I mean, my hardheaded son, is that although you may be an alley cat, Casey's not the kind of woman who'd sleep with a man she doesn't love. And if sleeping together is what you've been doing, you'd best make things right with her."

"After the fight we had," he said grimly, "she'd probably shoot first and ask questions later."

"Hmph." She poured the batter from the mixing bowl into a greased cake pan. "And what was it you fought about?"

He crammed his hands into his pockets and began to pace around the kitchen. "It was stupid," he said.

"It usually is. What happened?"

"I found out she still had all Danny's stuff. His clothes in the closet, his shoes still under the bed. His goddamn underwear still in the drawers."

"Mmn hmn. And?"

"I freaked."

"And she told you what a flaming ass you were being."

"Jesus, Ma, whose side are you on, anyway?"

"I'm not taking sides. I'm just trying to figure out what manner of stupidity the two of you have been embroiled in. Did you think she'd stop loving Danny just because he was dead?"

"No!" he said. And sighed. "Yes. Oh, hell, I don't know."

"God help us. He was her husband for what—thirteen years? They had a child together. The man was her whole life. Did you really think you could take his place?"

Bleakly, he said, "Pretty stupid of me, wasn't it?"

"Ah, Robbie, inside that tall, good-looking man, you're still just a little boy. Of course you can't take his place. It's already taken. You have to take your own place."

"My own place?" he said.

"There'll always be a place in her heart that belongs to Danny. But that doesn't mean there's no room for you. That girl loves you. But she doesn't love you more than Danny, or less than Danny. It's not a contest. Do you think I love any one of your brothers or sisters more or less than I love you? Do you think the fact that there are nine of you dilutes my love for any of you? Love is a gift, Robbie. Don't question it. Don't spoil it by being jealous of a dead man."

"I can't help it," he said. "I love her so damn much, it's killing me."

"And you're afraid of losing her. But your jealousy is what'll drive her away. You don't always have to be in control. Let her love you in her own way. It'll be well worth whatever you have to give up. You've been a long time looking for the right woman. Don't lose her on account of stupidity."

"What should I do?" He couldn't remember the last time he'd asked his mother for advice. Probably when he was ten or eleven. By the time he was twelve, he'd already been too much of a jackass to listen.

She glanced at the kitchen clock. "Well, if I was you, I'd go comb my hair, because she'll probably be here any minute."

His heart nearly jumped out of his chest. "What?" he said. "She's coming here?"

"For dinner. And to talk to you. Let me give you one more word of advice, and then I'll shut my mouth. I suspect she's coming here to tell you what a blooming idiot you've been. If you have half the brains God gave a dandelion, you'll just smile and agree with whatever she says, and be grateful that while you were being such an ass, she didn't go out and find someone a little smarter."

***

Red Sox fever had taken over the city, and traffic was backed up from Fenway to East Boston. After forty minutes of fighting traffic, she parked her car in a garage near Quincy

Market and ploughed her way through wall-to-wall tourists, heading directly for the open air florist. She had to pay an exorbitant price for it, but she found exactly what she sought: a single, perfect, long-stemmed rose. Red, the color of love. As the florist wrapped the stem in green tissue paper, she wondered once again if it was too late. But she refused to dwell on the possibility. She was going into this with her eyes wide open, and nothing would stop her.

Rob's mother was a familiar, warm presence, ruddy-cheeked and exuberant. They embraced, then Mary held her at arm's length while with shrewd blue eyes she studied Casey's pallid face. "He's around the back," she said, then added, "Don't look so frightened, child. It'll all work out."

Casey's eyes widened in surprise, and Mary shook her head. "I'm not blind," she said. "It's about time the two of you stopped being so pigheaded and admitted you belong together."

She found Rob on his knees in the garden, digging ferociously with a spade, wearing a pair of worn gardening gloves and his leather bomber jacket. He looked up and saw her, and she watched the play of emotions across his face: pleasure, pain, uncertainty. It was the uncertainty that remained. "Hey," he said.

"Hey," she said, and stepped over a clump of moist soil. "What are you doing?"

"Planting tulip bulbs." He dropped the spade, rose and dusted his knees, removed the gloves and stuffed them in his pocket. For a long time, they just looked at each other. Then he reached out a tentative fingertip to touch a scarlet rose petal. "What's with the flower, Fiore? Somebody die or something?"

"It's for you, MacKenzie. It's a peace offering."

When he took it from her, his knuckles brushed hers, warm and rough against her skin, and she felt his touch like a blow to her solar plexus. They lingered that way, barely touching, neither of them willing to break the contact. "I'm only going to say this once," she said, "so please hear me out. You have to understand the powerful hold that Danny had over me. He'd walk into a room and I'd melt. It wasn't something I could control, and no matter how bad things got between us, we couldn't seem to stay away from each other."

"I know," he said. "I was there."

"So you were," she said. "But you don't know all of it. That weekend you and I spent in Nassau, you unleashed something inside of me that I hadn't known was there. And I was so confused. I still loved Danny, but suddenly I was having feelings for you that a married woman doesn't have for a man who's not her husband. I tried to believe it was like you said, some heady combination of celibacy and proximity. Maybe I could have handled it better, but I did what I thought was best for everyone involved. I took my husband back. Not because I didn't care about you, but because I did. Am I making any sense at all?"

"Yeah," he said softly. "You are."

"Danny was really trying to be a husband, putting everything he had into it. But I felt like I had this gaping hole inside me that was clamoring to be filled, and I couldn't figure out what was missing. I tried to fill up the emptiness with activity, but it didn't help. And then you walked into my kitchen one hot August afternoon and you took me in your arms, and all the voices inside me quieted."

She took a deep breath. "Part of me wanted you to stay away," she said, "and part of me just plain wanted you. I told myself it was some kind of thirty-something midlife crisis. At one point, I just about had myself convinced that if I went to bed with you, just once, I'd get it out of my system. Of course, it was out of the question, because I would never have cheated on Danny. Not in a million years."

"I know," he said hoarsely.

She took a deep breath. "When he died, I would have lost myself if it hadn't been for you. You brought me back. And all those feelings I'd tried so hard to deny came rushing back. All that incredible heat, all that passion. I'd never had any idea it would be like that between us."

He toyed with a strand of her hair. "I could've told you."

She traced the line of his jaw with her thumb. "Of course," she said. "I keep forgetting you're a wizard."

"I didn't need any crystal ball," he said, glancing down at his dirt-encrusted Reeboks. "Just my heart."

"Oh, Rob, I'm so sorry. The closer I got to you, the more I

saw Danny slipping away from me. So I clung desperately to
what I had left of him, because I was afraid if I let go, I'd lose
him completely. Instead, I lost you." She took his face between
her hands, and his skin was smooth and warm. "Will you forgive
me?" she said.

"Ah, baby," he said, "there's nothing to forgive. It took
two of us to screw things up this bad." He caught her hands in
his, kissed the palms, then threaded his fingers through hers.
"When Danny died," he said, "it was the worst thing that'd ever
happened to me. I didn't handle it well. In every way that
mattered, he was my brother. Sometimes I hated him for the way
he treated you, but I loved him just the same."

Softly, she said, "I know."

"After Nassau," he said, "I was so much in love with you
that it was eating me alive. But you were Danny's wife, and I
had no right to feel that way about you. So I forced myself to
keep my distance, for the sake of my sanity. Then he died, and
the whole world came tumbling down on my head. I know there
are people who'll say that it was damn convenient for me, to
finally have him out of the picture. But it wasn't like that. His
dying didn't make things easier. It made things so much worse.
Because as long as Danny was upright and breathing, I could go
on deluding myself into believing that sooner or later, you'd
wake up and realize it wasn't worth all the pain he kept putting
you through. And then, by some miracle, you'd turn around and
see me standing there, and realize—" He broke off abruptly,
then shrugged. "Like I said, I was delusional. Then, suddenly,
he was gone, and you were in so much pain. We both were.
That was when I realized it was hopeless. He was the love of
your life, and there was no way I could ever compete with his
ghost. And the bitter truth is, I was jealous of him. I was more
jealous of him as a dead man than I ever was while he was alive.
The legend was dead, bigger than he'd ever been in life, and I
couldn't imagine how you could love me after having him."

"Oh, Rob. How could I possibly not love you?"

"Danny was a god," he said. "Don't you see? I'm just an
ordinary guy."

"No," she said. "What you are is the air that I breathe."

He let out a sharp explosion of breath. "I've thought about

calling," he said, "but my stubborn Irish blood wouldn't let me. I wanted you to make the first move. I'm too proud to beg."

She brushed a single golden curl away from his face. "I'm not."

Hoarsely, he said, "I was afraid you wouldn't come."

"I was afraid you wouldn't want me to."

Solemn green eyes met equally solemn green eyes, and then, ever so slightly, she saw the hint of a smile beginning. "What in hell took you so long?" he said.

"I had to work up my courage."

"Courage?" he said. "Courage for what?"

"To ask you to marry me."

He examined her fingers, one by one, studying them in minute detail, as though he'd never before seen a human hand. "Marry?" he said.

"Yes, MacKenzie, marry. As in two gold rings and people throwing rice."

"I'm familiar with the custom, Fiore. Think you can live with my bad habits?"

"You don't have any bad habits."

"Oh, yeah? Tell that to my mother. She's about ready to throw me out on my ass."

"She doesn't know you," Casey said, "like I do."

He stepped closer, so close she could feel his breath on her face. "That's for sure," he said.

She smoothed the collar of his shirt. "Just to be safe," she said, her hand still lingering, "maybe you should outline those bad habits. I wouldn't want to think I'd missed anything."

"Number one," he said, "I'm a slob."

"We'll hire a maid."

"Shut up until I'm finished. Number two, I snore—"

"We'll sleep in separate bedrooms."

"Like hell we will. Didn't I tell you to shut up? Number three, I always have to be right."

"That one could pose a problem," she said, "because I always have to be right, too."

Suddenly serious, he placed a hand on the nape of her neck and drew her to him, burying his face in her hair. "Maybe we could learn to compromise," he said.

Casey wrapped her arms around him. "Oh, Flash," she said, "I have missed you so much."

"Good. I'd hate to think I was miserable alone."

"Insufferable jackass Irishman." She wondered why the words came out sounding like an endearment.

"Shut up, Fiore, and kiss me."

Her pulse began a slow thrumming. "Rob," she said, "your mother's watching. I can feel her eyes on us."

"Good. I want to make sure she knows Mary Frances O'Reilly's out of luck."

They kissed fiercely, a heated kiss filled with passion and promise, a kiss that left her shuddering and dissolved her very bones. Pressing her face to his chest, she listened to the steady beating of his heart. This was where she belonged. She had finally come home to this man's arms. If anything at all in this crazy world made sense, it was that she and Rob MacKenzie belonged together. They were coming together as two flawed individuals, but together they would forge a new and perfect whole.

The kitchen window whooshed open. "If you two could possibly find time," Mary said cheerfully, "dinner's ready." And she closed the window with a bang.

He rubbed his cheek against hers. "If we don't go in," he said, "she'll have us tarred and feathered."

"I can't possibly eat," she said. "My stomach's all tied up in knots. It isn't every day you ask the man you love to marry you."

He tilted her chin upward, kissed the slender column of her throat. "Fake it," he whispered.

She tightened her arms around him. "They'll see right through me."

He worked his mouth deep into the vee at the collar of her shirt. "Is Mom still watching?"

"Are you kidding? She's probably already addressing the wedding invitations."

He looped an arm around her shoulders, and together they began walking toward the house. "After we eat," he said, "we can sit down together and look at my baby pictures."

"I can't think of a more romantic way to celebrate an

engagement," she said. "Is there some special reason why I'd want to look at your baby pictures?"

His smile illuminated the world as he held open the kitchen door for her. "I just thought you'd like some idea," he said, "of what our kids will look like."

THE END

www.lauriebreton.com
lauriebreton@gmail.com

Now that you've finished this book, I'd love to get feedback from you. Feel free to stop by Amazon and give the book a brief review. Your feedback will help with future books!

**FREE PREVIEW OF BOOK 2 IN THE JACKSON FALLS
SERIES!**

SLEEPING WITH THE ENEMY
**IS NOW AVAILABLE
FOR KINDLE OR IN PAPERBACK!**

Summer, 1990
Jackson Falls, Maine

Damn, but she hated weddings.

Rose MacKenzie Kenneally edged closer to the buffet table
and plucked a cocktail shrimp from a heaping platter. Nibbling
at it, she leaned against the table and critically surveyed the
circus that was her brother's wedding. The ambiance
surrounding this little shing-ding had improved dramatically
since Uncle Seamus had spiked the punch, effectively lubricating
the starch out of this dour band of Down East Yankees her new
sister-in-law called relatives.

Casey and Rob should have known better than to think they
were going to have a quiet, tasteful little wedding. Rob had
spent thirty-six years as a MacKenzie, long enough to know that,
wedding or wake, if the MacKenzies had an excuse to party, they
were determined to do it up right.

Not that either of the principals in this little domestic drama
had even noticed that their carefully planned wedding had
deteriorated into a free-for-all. The bride and groom were in
their own little world, oblivious to everything but each other as
they danced cheek to cheek on the makeshift dance floor that had
been built on the back lawn of Casey's New England farmhouse.

Somebody nudged her elbow, and Rose looked up to find
her older brother Pat standing beside her. At forty, his sandy hair
was beginning to recede, but beneath that high forehead sat the
twinkling green eyes that were the MacKenzie family trademark.
In a lilting Irish brogue, he said, "Such a fine institution,
marriage," raised his bottle of Sam Adams to his mouth, and

upended it.

Irritated, Rose folded her arms across her chest. "Fine it may be," she said, "but who the hell wants to live in an institution?"

He cupped his hand over his mouth to hold back a small belch. "A little jealous, are we, Rose?"

"Dream on. This broad has seen more than enough of marriage for one lifetime, thank you. I burned my bra the day I gave Eddie Kenneally the boot, and it didn't take me more than five minutes to figure out that the ratio of frogs to princes is radically skewed in favor of the frogs. End of story."

Pat slung a heavy arm around her shoulder. Watching the bride and groom, he said philosophically, "Don't use Eddie as a yardstick. Not all guys are determined to test drive every female from here to Baltimore."

"And what doesn't kill us makes us stronger. Spare me. I've already heard it."

"Your bitterness is showing, Rose. Be happy for Rob. He deserves it."

She opened her mouth to protest, but he was already gone. She *was* happy for her brother. But truth was truth: some people were cut out for marriage, while others weren't. And Rose had been taught by a superb teacher that she belonged in the latter category.

Across the lawn, Uncle Seamus was pontificating, no doubt on some obscure point, with his arms gesticulating wildly as he waved his flask of Irish whiskey for emphasis. His victim stood listening politely, his weight thrown on one leg, his hands tucked into his pockets, but even from this distance, Rose could see the glassy glaze in his eyes. Tall and lean, with chiseled cheekbones above dark hollows that rendered his face a study in light and shadow, he was immaculately dressed in a dove-gray suit. Neatly trimmed hair the color of moonbeams touched the starched white collar of his shirt.

She uttered a small snort of derision. *Moonbeams, for the love of Mike. Time to have your head examined.* But she could think of no other word that fit, no other word to describe hair so blond it was silver.

He looked up and met her gaze, and something went hot

inside her. *Celibacy*, she told herself as she tried to slow the sudden hammering of her pulse. *Too damn much celibacy.* It made a woman crazy after a while. In a split-second decision, she began marching resolutely across the grass to rescue him from the clutches of her uncle.

He watched her coming, his dark eyes openly following the sway of her body in the green jersey dress. With hair that color, his eyes should have been the blue of his Norse ancestors, but as she drew nearer, she realized with a sudden shock that they were a deep, liquid black. And right now, they were warm with a combination of humor and masculine appreciation.

"Excuse me," she said to him, and tapped her uncle on the shoulder. "Uncle Seamus, I think maybe you've had a little too much joy juice."

Her uncle wheeled and flung his arms wide in delight. "Rosie, darlin' of me heart, when d'ye think we'll be dancing at *your* wedding?"

The lilt of the emerald isle always grew thicker in his voice when he was in his cups. Rose reached for the flask before he could dump it on her, turned her face away from the breath that could knock a longshoreman on his keister, and flashed a quick grin of apology to the stud muffin. "Better make a run for it while you can." She capped the flask, tucked it into her uncle's pocket, and steered the old man in the direction of the coffee urn.

But Seamus had other ideas. "Since we can't dance at your wedding, me dear, we'll dance at Robbie's instead."

As she tried to keep the heels of her dyed-to-match shoes from sinking into the sod and sending her tumbling, he hauled her toward the dance floor. And with the grace of a man half his age and nowhere near as drunk, he whirled her around in an elegant two-step that had her laughing aloud in delight.

Together they spun around and around, until she was breathless and giddy. The band slowed to a waltz, and the old gentleman wheezed in her ear, "Ah, Rosie, happy it makes me to see the bloom back in your cheeks. Now this old man needs a rest, and you, me girl, need to find a more suitable partner."

With a steady gait that belied his inebriated condition, he trotted off affably to whisper some naughtiness in the ear of the bride, most likely sage advice regarding the wedding night. Rose watched him go with a smile on her face. She turned to exit the dance floor, and suddenly forgot to breathe as she saw the Viking god striding steadily, determinedly, in her direction.

For an instant, she was accosted by the bewildering sensation that this moment was somehow of utmost significance. But that was absurd. She was thirty-six years old, and hard experience had taught her that if something appeared too good to be true, it probably was. She didn't even know his name. Didn't know if he was married or single. He could be an ax murderer, for all she knew.

Breathe, idiot! she commanded herself. *Breathe, or you'll pass out at his feet and make a complete fool of yourself!* But her stubborn lungs refused to function.

Then he was standing in front of her, and even with the three-inch heels, she still had to lean halfway to China to meet those bottomless dark eyes.

"Would you like to dance?" he said.

She must have answered him. She had no memory of speaking, but she must have answered him because a moment later she was in his arms, and the musky scent of his aftershave, released by the heat of their bodies pressed so close together, hit her with almost physical force. Rose slowly, tentatively, rested her cheek against his crisp white shirt. Beneath her cheek, his heart beat strong and steady, and she prayed he couldn't hear the erratic racing of hers.

He danced divinely, his steps simple and easy to follow. Rose closed her eyes and forgot to tuck in the tummy that wasn't as flat as it used to be, forgot that the humidity was frizzing her tangled red mane, forgot everything but the feel of this man and the delirious pleasure of following his lead as they swayed together in time to the music.

She would have been content to go on dancing forever, but as usual, the gods declined to smile upon her. When the waltz gave way to a Bob Seger baby boomer classic, she realized she was still standing there in his arms. Reality washed over her, bringing her common sense rushing back. *Jesus, Mary and Joseph.* Here she was, thirty-six years old and hyperventilating over some man she didn't even know. Uncle Seamus obviously wasn't the only one who'd overdone the sauce. What she needed was a cup of black coffee. A big one. Or maybe a cold shower. Something, anything, to whip her overheated hormones back into submission.

She stepped out of his arms. Discreetly peeled her dress away from her sticky body. And gave him a quirky grin. With forced lightness, she said, "Thanks for the dance."

And without another word, she walked away from the best thing she'd seen in thirty-six years.

Made in the USA
Charleston, SC
31 October 2012